THE PAIN OF WINNING
The Hardrow Chronicles
Volume IV

David Fraser, author of The Hardrow Chronicles, of which The Pain of Winning is the fourth volume, is also a biographer and a military historian. He has previously published eight novels, including the Treason In Arms series which spans two world wars. He was once one of Britain's most senior generals, is married, has five children and lives in Hampshire.

Further Titles by David Fraser from Severn House

The Hardrow Chronicles

ADAM HARDROW
CODENAME MERCURY
ADAM IN THE BREACH
THE PAIN OF WINNING

THE PAIN OF WINNING

Volume 4 of
The Hardrow Chronicles

David Fraser

0516532

This first world edition published in Great Britain 1994 by
SEVERN HOUSE PUBLISHERS LTD of
9–15 High Street, Sutton, Surrey SM1 1DF.
This title first published in the USA 1994 by
SEVERN HOUSE PUBLISHERS INC., of
425 Park Avenue, New York, NY 10022.

Copyright © 1994 by David Fraser

All rights reserved.
The moral rights of the author have been asserted.

British Library Cataloguing in Publication Data
Fraser, Sir David
 Pain of Winning. – (Hardrow Chronicles; No. 4)
 I. Title
 823.914 [F]

ISBN 0-7278-4573-X

All situations in this publication are fictitious and
any resemblance to living persons is purely coincidental.

Typeset by Hewer Text Composition Services, Edinburgh.
Printed and bound in Great Britain by
Redwood Books, Trowbridge, Wiltshire.

CHAPTER I

"The instant imposition of the death penalty," Klaus Mosten had said harshly. That had been yesterday morning. Since then, during the hours of darkness, the tanks, the assault guns, and the half-tracked vehicles carrying Panzer Grenadiers had been clanking the final few miles towards their assembly positions. The last weeks had witnessed several moves, all conducted under conditions of extraordinary secrecy even for wartime. Most movement had been in darkness, over limited distances, not too exhausting for the drivers, admirably coordinated. And the secrecy which had shrouded actual movement had been more than echoed in the orders. For the orders – anyway in the case of this particular Battalion, Klaus Mosten reflected – had been non-existent.

They had been told, all of them, that because of excellent intelligence about a forthcoming American offensive certain concentrations of troops had been ordered by the High Command. There was no need whatsoever for them to know for what purpose or when or where. Their only necessity was to be informed of the route and destination of the next march. In carefully cultivated ignorance, therefore, the Battalion – Panzer Grenadiers, motorised infantry carried for the most part in lightly armoured half-tracked vehicles – had moved to an assembly area in the Eifel mountains, worked on their vehicles, done a certain amount of low-level training, repaired equipment and been restored to full establishment in men and kit. Then movement again, westward, in the darkness. And then again. Three days ago snow had come, and special clothing designed for the Eastern front had been issued. And total radio silence had been imposed.

Although the whole operation was conducted under conditions of absolute secrecy nobody, of course, could prevent men guessing. *Sturmfuhrer* Klaus Mosten had his own guesses but kept them to himself, and when a subordinate started shooting his mouth, only yesterday, he had snapped at him bleakly. The man, a section commander, had stood rigidly to attention.

"Naturally, I know nothing, *Sturmfuhrer*. I was only wondering."

"If you were wondering and happened to be heard wondering correctly, even if only correctly by accident, I suppose you are clear what could happen to you?"

"Yes, *Sturmfuhrer*."

"As was made clear to all Battalion Commanders by the *Standartenfuhrer*, penalty for indiscretion about the forthcoming operations is court martial and the instant imposition of the death penalty. It was also made clear – and I made clear to you – that even the Army Commanders were warned to the same effect. Any breach of security, whatsoever the rank of the offender, would be treated without mercy."

"Yes, *Sturmfuhrer*."

Mosten had given him a hard stare and turned away. That had been yesterday and the man had avoided his eye earlier this afternoon when orders and objectives and forming-up places had at last been given out. For the fool had guessed well, and had some other nosey parker heard him speculating it might easily have been supposed that Sturmfuhrer Klaus Mosten himself had both learned and imparted more than was permitted. And then sentence

2

and a rattle of musketry in some Belgian quarry. And disgrace.

Now, however, they at last knew what they were to do and spirits were high. Klaus Mosten recognised that the very fact of going forward, of being ordered to advance and attack and achieve a major operational object after so many withdrawals, so much tragedy – that, of itself, was tonic. The Battalion had been transferred from the Eastern Front in July and the Eastern Front had already witnessed appalling disasters, with the Red Army about to smash its way into Rumania, and the Ukraine already lost or so it had seemed. They had reeled back from one inadequately manned position to another, as tank and vehicle strengths had seeped away, like the blood of the Waffen SS, into the cornlands of southern Russia.

Then they had moved west, troop trains limping over the dislocated railway system of the Reich, a system which seemed to get more and more dislocated the further west they went. They had moved, peering – for the first time in the case of some of them – at the tortured cities of Germany where the tracks ran near; tortured cities, whole areas of buildings showing nothing but piles of rubble, citizens with pale, hopeless faces; only the occasional wave. Then, with relief, they had reached the comparatively clean area of the Eifel, and been nurtured and restored. And now they were to attack – attack and take at least a measure of revenge for the frightful destruction being visited daily and nightly on families and Fatherland – a Fatherland on whose actual soil, in some places, the enemy had now set his foot. There had been bad times but now, again, they were ready.

And now they had had, last night, their orders. Today was "the day".

Klaus Mosten thought that everything had been done which could be done. Conditions would be harsh, it was a cold winter, but nothing compared with last winter in Russia. Or the one before that. Here, as often as not, there were barns, buildings, shelter. The men were used to operating in snow and ice. What they were not used to – and here the God that cared for Germany had surely been active – was operating under the ever-present eye of an enemy air force; and the weather was so poor that it should, they had been told by the meteorological people, absolutely prevent major Anglo-American air activity for some time. And in that time the first objectives must be gained.

Yes, the men were in good shape on the whole. Mosten considered them. He was very proud of them. There was no doubt that quality had been slightly diluted by the policy of drafting men from the ranks of the Wehrmacht into the *Waffen SS* to make up numbers – you couldn't expect some of these fellows to act and behave or, for that matter, look as if they were the genuine SS article, brought up in the most demanding, the toughest, recruit training system in the world, moulded and indoctrinated to be the elite such undoubtedly were. You couldn't expect that – there was nothing to compare with initial training, nothing to replace it. But these newcomers to the *Waffen SS*, young conscripts (some of them only fifteen or sixteen though they might be) soon took on its colouration, were soon knocked into some sort of shape, soon seemed to accept its ethos, might even have acquired something of its skill. Soon learned, a point sometimes emphasised with a fist or a boot, that "*Waffen SS*" meant the finest fighting men in the world, fighting men who had only a remote, constitutional linkage with the various other divisions of the *Schutz Staffel*, the home-based, black-uniformed variety in particular. The *Waffen SS* set the standard, newcomers were told grimly, for the entire Wehrmacht, and don't forget it. And there were, praise God, still quite a few veterans around. The

Battalion, Mosten reckoned, would do well if given a fair chance. They'd need to – there was a lot of ground to cover, and although the Americans were known to be in no great strength it would be essential to knock them out of the way extremely quickly so that the Panzer columns could grind forward and slither with minimum delay down the icy roads, over frozen slopes, to the Meuse.

Defensible country, Klaus reflected, very defensible country, narrow roads, defiles, steep gradients; but they'd done it before, exactly here. He had not, personally, taken part in the great adventure of 1940 when the Wehrmacht had rushed the so-called impenetrable Ardennes and settled the French for good, but he'd talked to many an old hand who'd been there. If you kept up the momentum, the old hands had said confidently, you can do it – throw everything at them, fire, fire, fire with everything you've got directly you meet them, and get the boys out and working round their flanks as an instant reaction, without delay. And when you've punched a hole go flat out. The Fuhrer has assembled over 1,200 tanks and assault guns in this sector and the Yankees are known to be in little strength here and probably half asleep. And our tanks, certainly our Panther Mark Vs, even our Mark IVs, are superior to the Yankees' tanks. Don't fuss about flanks, or getting cut off, or losing touch with the comrades behind you. Just go flat out! It should suit the *Waffen SS* admirably.

Klaus Mosten looked at his watch. Despite himself he shivered. Dawn was still some hours distant. The new rockets, in multiple salvoes, were already streaming over towards Belgian towns and cities which would soon once again fall to the Wehrmacht. It was very dark and very cold; and in five minutes' time, Klaus knew, almost every piece of artillery the High Command had been able to assemble on the Western front, over 2,000 guns as well as each Division's artillery, would open up. Thereafter *"Marsch!"*

Adam Hardrow gazed at the posting order. There was something almost reassuring about the way the Army, no matter what drama of blood and fire was or was not engulfing the men in it, ground out ordinary-seeming, routine pieces of paper. It reminded all that although death or wounding might be just round the corner there were certain forms to complete meanwhile, certain Army Council Instructions which applied and to ignore which carried a penalty, certain paragraphs of King's Regulations which governed conduct and disposal whether one's body was living or dead. This particular bit of paper said that Lieutenant (war substantive Captain) (temporary Major) A. Hardrow would be posted from 5th Battalion Westmorland Regiment to 2nd Battalion Westmorland Regiment in January 1945, taken off strength 5th Battalion at the date of movement, to be promulgated through Command channels. Movement to 2nd Battalion would be via the United Kingdom, where Major Hardrow would be taken on ration strength by Depot Westmorland Regiment who would issue railway warrants and ration cards as appropriate for seven days' leave before onward movement. Major Hardrow would report date of arrival in the United Kingdom to OC Depot, Westmorland Regiment who would arrange to publish the necessary casualty. And so forth.

The 2nd Battalion! the old 2nd Battalion! His first home in the Regiment! The 2nd Battalion with which, as a starry-eyed innocent, he had first gone to war and first discovered that whether in the Westmorland Regiment or any other, not all men are heroes; but a few are. Discovered that in the British Army not all battles are intelligently and efficiently planned or conducted; but a few may be. Since then, Adam thought, there's been so much, so many very different experiences, none of them lasting very long except that bloody, wasted year of my life spent in an Italian prison camp. Wasted? Adam recognised his own ingratitude. Had he not been a prisoner he wouldn't have escaped, and if he hadn't escaped he would never have met Anni.

So in January, next month, it would be farewell to this 5th Battalion which he had learned to love, this Territorial battalion with its own enthusiasms, ways of looking at life, distinctive approach to soldiering. This 5th Battalion in which, since joining it after escape and repatriation, he had served with some of the finest men he'd known, including its commander, the inimitable Wainwright, whom they'd buried in Holland so recently. Including many others since the D-Day landings. It's always the best who go, Adam thought more than once – a banal and not necessarily accurate or provable reflection he supposed, but one which always struck with repetitive force whenever a friend fell. A friend of whatever rank.

And now, the 2nd Battalion. And he, Adam Hardrow, only twenty-six years old, to be second-in-command of the 2nd Battalion, and especially sent there to earn a firm recommendation for Battalion command. There were, Adam knew, Battalion commanders of twenty-six in this war, just as there had been in the last, but it seemed incredible nevertheless. And the 2nd Battalion was in Italy – part of the British Army in Italy, glimpsed by Adam during that extraordinary, unreal interlude between reaching British lines and repatriation. Italy, where the fighting seemed very different from this cold, damp, dispiriting slogging match on the Dutch–German border. Italy, scene for Adam of past horror and past ecstasy. Italy, a week or two from Britain by troopship. Italy and the 2nd Battalion.

The posting order came as no surprise. He'd been

warned that it was in the offing, warned by beloved old Whisky Wainwright, after giving him the rocket of his life for making a real balls-up of a company battle just before they crossed from Belgium into Holland in September; and warned again by the Divisional commander, no less, when giving him yet another memorable rocket for conduct which should, the General had made clear, have led to a Court Martial. But they'd both said in their own fashion that he, Adam Hardrow, whatever his faults and errors, had been recommended for battalion command and would probably be appointed Battalion second-in-command in another theatre first. To see how he did.

Adam wondered how much flexibility there might be about dates. "In January" was the order, and of course exact dates and timings depended on movement resources. You could find yourself kicking your heels in some transit camp for weeks on end. The great thing was to have friends in high places, pull strings, beat the system. Adam had no friends in high places (rather the reverse, he reflected) and he was pessimistic about his chances of beating the system. He would, he supposed, be sent back to England like a parcel when somebody sent a signal, take his week's leave, see his mother, the very Russian Natasha Hardrow, affectionate and impulsive and, if her letters were anything to go by, as indiscreet as ever; and then go to the Depot at Kendal and wait for further movement instructions. It might, of course, be possible to wangle more leave out of the Depot Commander, even to stay in London and avoid the journey north altogether; but Adam had his own reasons for wanting to pay at least a short visit to Kendal.

He would, he knew, be sad to leave the 5th. They had become his home in a way a battalion in wartime so memorably did. His own A-Company – surely they were as good now as any company he'd known? Of course the stars had gone, the stars like Sergeant-Major Cowan; Adam told himself not to be morbid. There were good men left, officers too. There were friends he'd feel bereft without, at least for a bit. Perhaps, he reflected not without pleasure, they'd feel a little bereft as well. And it would have been sad not to spend Christmas with them, although his first, selfish reaction on reading the posting order was that if he were going back to England in January for onward movement to Italy it would have been even nicer to go in December and share Christmas with his mother, Natasha, for the first time in many years. She'd have loved that. The posting order was clear, however. January.

So December would run its cold and somewhat boring course. The Battalion had been withdrawn to Belgium from an exceptionally dreary sector of the so-called front – sitting some way from the Germans in conditions of rain and mud, on the frontier between Holland and the German Reich, waiting for developments in other parts of the Allied front, waiting for the next great battle, which had to be the elimination of the Wehrmacht west of the Rhine, the crossing of the Rhine itself and the invasion of Germany. That, however, couldn't now be until 1945. Time for Adam Hardrow to move to the Mediterranean. Time, even, for him to fight a battle there before the war ended unless, which God forbid, it dragged on through the following year.

Adam yawned. One couldn't take more than the shortest of views in wartime. Here he was, dry and reasonably warm, sitting in the small house of a Belgian garage proprietor who had been induced, without too much difficulty, to make it available as A-Company Officers' Mess. A-Company were billeted in various halls and outhouses in the large "village" – really adjoining suburban sprawls – which housed 5th Westmorlands in this peaceful area of Brabant. They had been told they would have Christmas here, a blessed thought, and arrangements were under way. Thereafter, they knew, there would be movement eastward, fresh orders, mustering for another phase of the campaign. And thereafter, Adam thought with mixed feelings, I'll be away. Meanwhile there's a surprising amount of paperwork which we'll all be badgered to catch up with. And meanwhile we must use our ingenuity to the maximum to work the men, train the men in certain essentials where they're rusting, find ways of improving the feeding of the men and the conditions of the men. Above all, scratch our heads how to warm the men when in quarters – the weather's turned icy. Today's Sunday, a day of rest, a few ill-attended church services. It feels like snow.

In the village which housed A-Company, 5th Westmorlands, snow indeed started to fall on that afternoon of 17th December with a week still to go to Christmas Eve. Then rapid footsteps outside. And through the snow there crunched to the door of A-Company Mess the figure of Lieutenant Bill Travers, 2-Platoon Commander. The inimitable Travers, Travers who, as Corporal Travers, had commanded a section in Adam's own platoon in the 2nd Battalion in 1940 – and splendidly. Travers who, as a sergeant-major, had once recognised the limping figure of escaping prisoner Hardrow as it regained British lines. Travers, fellow volunteer for Chisforce, the desert-raiding force from which Adam, wounded, had been plucked into captivity. Travers, now commissioned, mountain of common sense, invaluable old friend. Adam looked up from the table where he had been pretending to write but in reality daydreaming. It was already almost dark.

"Hullo Bill."

"Heard the news?" Bill said.

"I haven't listened to the wireless if that's what you mean. What news, anyway?"

"The Jerries," said Bill Travers. "The Jerries have started an offensive." He looked as if he had been running – excited and out of breath. Adam looked at him with astonishment.

"Steady, Bill, they've hardly got it in them. They're just about hanging on to where they are. An offensive? A real offensive? Where?"

"Here! I saw Barney in the street and he'd just come from Divisional Headquarters." Barney Brown was Battalion Intelligence officer.

"Barney Brown had the whole picture. CO's giving out orders at seven. Jerries are advancing towards us through the Ardennes! Started this morning. About thirty divisions, at least ten Panzer divisions, Barney said! Marching west, just like bloody 1940! Through the Ardennes!"

Aylwyn Kentish gazed at his company commanders in his usual mild, genial and unemphatic manner. Aylwyn had assumed command of 5th Westmorlands when their last and revered commanding officer, the late Whisky Wainwright, had most unfortunately fallen to a stray shell when on a reconnaissance. As Second-in-Command Major Kentish had, inevitably, gathered up the reins of command but it had been understood that this would be temporary only and Aylwyn, modesty incarnate, had been the last person to dispute or resent this understanding.

Then, however, there had been hitches. Another officer, from another regiment, had been nominated. There had been a delay – his present battalion had been engaged on a particularly tricky operation (he was already commanding and was being "moved sideways") and since 5th Westmorlands were scheduled for a fairly quiet few weeks the appointment had been postponed. Nobody had minded – newcomers and outsiders were always suspect and Aylwyn, although regarded with affection as a pretty unmilitary figure, was a Territorial of long service, well-rooted in the northern counties, an unfashionably amateur officer for these times but well-liked. Aylwyn had an agreeable way with soldiers. He was vague, scholarly, amiable and devoted to the Westmorland Regiment. He was extremely rich. He was popular, although his subordinates were by no means sure how he would cope with the tests of command in battle. Nobody doubted Aylwyn Kentish's courage, but some certainly doubted his rapidity of mind and his military skill. Adam Hardrow was among the doubters.

Aylwyn Kentish knew all this and inwardly accepted it without serious anxiety although he knew – and being a sensible man also accepted – that in battle, if it came to battle, he would be more in the hands of his company commanders than might be altogether for the battalion's good. He would, he knew, be privately relieved when his successor arrived, a man younger than Aylwyn but with a considerable reputation.

Then the blow had fallen. Aylwyn Kentish's successor – due to join the battalion, his present labours triumphantly concluded, on 10th December – had become seriously ill on 7th December. The posting stood, the authorities decreed, but there would be a delay. A further delay. Meanwhile Major Kentish would continue in command.

The Brigade Commander had said, "Rather tough on you, Aylwyn, I wish they'd confirm you in command but you know what the Military Secretary people are like, even in wartime. And the Territorial thing complicates it."

"Yes, sir," Aylwyn had responded, smiling pleasantly. He knew that the Brigadier was being weak and false, that he had earlier told his own superiors that Kentish was "up to minding the shop during a quiet patch but not much more". Aylwyn Kentish was no fool and had a wide acquaintance.

"Yes, sir. Thank you, sir. I'm perfectly happy."

Now Aylwyn looked at his assembled company commanders and said, "There's rather a flap on. I'm sorry to have got you all in at such short notice but I'm afraid our little period of peace and quiet has been somewhat rudely interrupted. Barney will explain what's happened, as far as anybody knows, and then I'll tell you what I think we're going to have to do."

They had moved in darkness and taken over at dawn.

The drill for blowing the Meuse bridges was very exact. It was specifically laid down which officer, holding what appointment, could authorise the bridge to be blown, and it was equally clearly laid down what was to be done, and by whom, if the bridge was at risk of capture before an order to blow had been given or received. At the bridge itself was the demolition party, Royal Engineers, dug into a slit trench to protect from blast and debris. The demolition party had laid the explosive charges and the cable to the plunger whose brisk downward thrust would send a massive stone structure, a pride of Brabant, into the air in a thousand blasted fragments of stone and chip.

Protecting the demolition party and the demolitions themselves was the close bridge garrison. The close bridge garrison commander was responsible for defending the bridge against capture intact by the enemy; for defending the demolitions against interference by some enemy *coup-de-main* party; and, when ordered, for blowing the bridge. In certain circumstances the courage, coolness of head, speed of reaction, and judgement of a particular close bridge garrison commander was what lay between an army and disaster.

5th Westmorlands had been ordered to take over responsibility for three of the Meuse bridges and Aylwyn Kentish was visiting them. He had deployed a rifle company at each of the three and he was philosophically aware that having done so the course of the battle was in the hands of his subordinates. The Battalion had been ordered to "find" three companies for the task, and each of the companies was now under direct command of another brigade – 5th Westmorlands, out of the battle for the time being, was simply "helping out" with the provision of small and, it was hoped, combat-worthy packets to take part in somebody else's show. 5th Westmorlands CO and Headquarters and reserve had simply the task of seeing everybody was fed and watered, Aylwyn reflected. No question of "commanding" the battalion, none at all. There were three close bridge garrisons to find, and found they had been, by A-, B- and C-companies. Now it was a matter of "administering" them, and wishing them luck. Forward of each bridge garrison some British armour was deployed, armour which would defend the approaches to the bridge and then, on orders, withdraw across it as the final "friendly" force before the crash and roar of the bridge's destruction. Aylwyn, feeling something of a fraud, was doing the rounds. He started with the left-hand bridge for which he'd furnished troops. A-Company's close-bridge garrison. Adam Hardrow.

Aylwyn had wondered whether, in fact, to send Adam Hardrow with his company at all. Percy Prinn, Company Second Captain, remarkably equable and reliable despite his own matrimonial problems, was going to take over A-Company on Adam's departure, and Aylwyn had meditated ordering Percy to take A-Company to the bridge. Adam Hardrow, he would have announced, is due to leave the battalion on posting, soon after Christmas; this job as long-stop to the Allied Armies defending in the Ardennes may go on some time and we don't want more changes in responsibilities than necessary. It would have been defensible to make Adam "LOB" – "left out of battle"; the more so since Aylwyn, due to the unexpected vicissitudes of his own position, had no Battalion Second-in-Command. Adam's presence at Battalion Headquarters, thought Aylwyn, would be remarkably heartening; even though there might not be much to do.

But Aylwyn had decided that it would be wrong to adopt this device; and as he drove up to the bridge where A-Company were deployed and swung his legs out of his jeep he knew he had been right. Adam would have chafed angrily at being away from his company in what might, Heaven knew, turn out to be the most critical battle of the whole damned campaign. Adam might be – was – due to go off to England en route to Italy, might be "called forward" by the movement people, as the military jargon had it, any time after the turn of the year and have to move at the drop of a hat; but he could be extricated from his close-bridge garrison as easily as dammit and until the moment came – and Aylwyn devoutly hoped it would be later rather than earlier, January was still some weeks away – the more time Adam Hardrow spent looking after A-Company the better his commanding officer was likely to be pleased.

"Morning, Adam."

Adam Hardrow saluted. The CO was no Napoleon but he was a decent, honest man who'd never shuffle off responsibility on to juniors, who'd take the decisions when he had to – perhaps not very quickly, perhaps not very brilliantly but take them nevertheless – and take the blame as well. He was also, Adam reflected with some gratitude, an exceptionally nice man. Not everything but something.

"Morning, sir."

Aylwyn smiled his rather whimsical smile, which seemed to say, "what odd things we do find ourselves doing in this peculiar world". He started, at Adam's invitation, to walk round the Company positions, sparing a friendly and often a joking word with every man he passed. Very much including the Royal Engineer detachment. Adam ran through the communications set-up.

"Its obviously the key to everything."

"Quite, quite."

"I rather think," Adam said – with a touch of diffidence because he'd not directly experienced it and because he was anxious not to show off, not to emphasise that he, unlike Aylwyn Kentish, had known the grim days of 1940, those days when the Germans had also been rushing towards the Meuse – "I rather think that when this happened last time and the Jerries were coming through the Ardennes, there were quite a few unblown bridges. Often because our own people were on the far side and I suppose chaps turned up and pleaded and so forth and the orders didn't get down or weren't obeyed. In fact I – I rather think we had something not unlike that happen. In the 2nd Battalion."

"Ah!"

"How's the battle going, sir?"

Aylwyn smiled. He said, "Remarkable, quite remarkable. Everyone thought the old Huns were absolutely on the ropes and suddenly they come back with something like this. Americans haven't known what's hit them! Not surprising, they weren't thick on the ground, everybody's been thinking about our own next big offensive to clear the country up to the Rhine, all that. And suddenly bang! And the old Panzers on the march again. Remarkable! And getting it lined up without giving anything away— "

"How far have they got, sir?"

"It doesn't seem entirely clear. Do you know where Malmedy is?"

Adam shook his head and Aylwyn said, "Well, have a look at this," and produced a smaller scale map, pointing.

"There's Malmedy. They're past it."

Adam nodded thoughtfully. He said, "They've come quite a long way. Presumably they're pretty well confined to the roads in that country? They were before."

Again that note of spurious, old-hand, knowingness Adam thought, regretting it. But Aylwyn said, seriously, "That's right. And the various road junctions are what the Americans are concentrating on holding."

"Of course."

"But they've lost some of them."

Was this, despite every likelihood, going to be a repetition of those extraordinary days of May 1940, when the Wehrmacht had moved with what had seemed at the time almost supernatural speed, had arrived in the Meuse Valley while all the world was watching a front-line miles to the east of it, had crossed the great river and started their amazing advance? One thing, at least, was completely different.

As if reading Adam's thoughts Aylwyn said, conversationally, "Of course it's been rotten flying weather. When that improves I imagine the old Huns won't find it so enjoyable. But of course they may be here by then!"

He chuckled and Adam liked him. Aylwyn reminded him of the warning which had been circulated throughout the Anglo-American forces – the Germans were reputed to have deployed a number of armed parties in Allied uniforms, to travel thus disguised and commit sabotage ("or grab bridges, of course") behind the Allied lines. In the short term this was probably the principal threat to the bridges, and a rapidly produced guidance pamphlet had been issued on the best method of proving a German saboteur in American uniform was a German saboteur in American uniform and not a well-meaning Texan with an incomprehensibly transatlantic turn of speech. Aylwyn chuckled.

"Don't want to make any unfortunate mistakes!"

Adam smiled rather thinly. He said, "It's against all the rules, isn't it?"

"Of course. No mercy on them if we catch them."

"I think," said Adam, "you can rely on that."

"One last and very important thing, Adam. Percy will take over the Company from you from tomorrow for two days. He's on his way up this afternoon." Percy Prinn had been left in reserve with the Battalion Transport Echelon.

"How do you mean, take over for two days, sir? What do you want me to do?"

"There's a visit planned to the Americans. We may have to operate under their command – and since not many of us have had direct experience of them the General has got approval to send one Brigade commander, two battalion commanders and six company commanders on a sort of liaison trip. Idea is to see how it all works and spread the word, make cooperation easier thereafter, that sort of thing."

Adam stared at him.

"Six company commanders from the whole division doesn't seem much, sir."

"It was all the General could get the Yanks to agree. Better than nothing."

"I don't blame them. They're fighting a battle. If the wireless news is anything to go by rather a hard one."

"Well, you'll soon have the chance to see for yourself, Adam. The General and the Brigadier have agreed you're to be one of the company commanders."

Adam had seen this coming and felt his pulse quicken. He nodded and said, "It should be interesting. And then I report back and disseminate some news, some latest battle technique reports, that sort of thing?"

"That sort of thing. If there's time I expect there'll be a coordinated report, widely circulated. I suppose that will be up to the Brigadier – as I said there's to be one representative Brigadier in charge of you, in charge of the visitors."

"Our own Brigadier? From this Brigade?"

"No, no. It's to be Brigadier Chisholm."

Adam smiled and said, "My brother-in-law!" And Aylwyn said yes, of course, he'd forgotten. Orders would come through during the course of the day about where the visitors were to rendez-vous for their journey to the American front under Brigadier Chisholm's orders. Where, Adam asked, were they going, did the CO have any idea? And Aylwyn Kentish said yes, as a matter of fact he had, he gathered they were due to visit the Yanks at a place called St Vith.

CHAPTER II

There had been, they were told, "one or two hiccups" before their liaison visit was confirmed as acceptable to the American authorities and it was not until ten o'clock on the morning of 20th December that Adam, having handed over responsibility for one of the smaller Meuse bridges to Percy Prinn, left A-Company and joined the other nominated officers at a rendez-vous in the northern suburbs of Liege. He climbed out of his jeep and saluted Brigadier Ian Chisholm with a broad smile. The smile was returned and Ian said, quietly, "You'd better ride with me. Put your driver in with mine to follow on."

Adam nodded. A talk with his brother-in-law as they sped through the icy morning in an open jeep would be a rare treat. One of the greatest joys war afforded was the occasional and unexpected encounter with somebody dear to one and Ian Chisholm, not only Adam's sister's husband but once his own admired leader in the African raiding force, "Chisforce", was dear indeed.

Ian told them briefly what they were to do. When the plan for this visit had been put forward two or three days previously the German operation had only just begun and it had been generally supposed that it was simply designed as a "spoiling" attack, a flourish intended to disrupt and delay an American offensive further north. It had taken almost until now for the Allied High Command to appreciate that this, in fact, was the real thing. Incredible though it might appear, said Ian, Intelligence was now certain that the Germans were not only trying to reach the Meuse but aiming to cross it, advance deep, seek a major strategic victory. And they had assembled from somewhere a great mass of divisions, including a lot of Panzer divisions, assault guns and artillery.

"In those circumstances," Ian said, "very good of the Americans to agree some of us can come and see them. They've been fighting very, very hard for three days."

From the rim of the little circle standing round Ian's jeep a voice said, "And moving pretty rapidly, from all one hears, Brigadier, isn't that so?" Somebody else gave a snigger.

Ian Chisholm looked very directly towards whoever had spoken. He said, "I don't, I'm sure, need to tell you that we are guests. We are scheduled to spend twenty-four hours in the area of the American First Army, who have, I repeat, been fighting extremely hard and if reports are anything to go by extremely bravely since the balloon went up last Saturday."

It was Wednesday, and silence followed Ian's remark. He continued, "I need hardly say that if I get the slightest, the very slightest, hint of any patronising attitude being adopted by any British officer in this party while we are visiting I shall send him back to the Divisional Commander forthwith, carrying a note of explanation from myself. I'm sure that is unnecessary to say but we'd better be clear that we are here to listen and to learn. The Americans have had, are having, one hell of a fight."

Ian told them that they would be assigned to different units at the Headquarters of the First Army, whither they would now go. It's not far, Ian said, it's in the eastern outskirts of Liege. It won't take half an hour.

"The original idea," Ian said conversationally, "was that

we should all go to St Vith, but the battle seems to have moved a bit and we certainly mustn't get in the way, we must go, each of us, exactly where we're told."

A knowing voice, one of the commanding officers, Adam didn't recognise him.

"I thought their First Army was in Spa, Brigadier?"

"They've moved," said Ian briefly. They glanced at each other. Moved back from Spa! Spa was a long way from the frontier and the frontier, roughly speaking, had constituted the front line. Jerry was certainly making distance!

"So you're off any minute, Adam?"

"January." The air was freezing as the open jeep ran down to the main Meuse bridge into Liege. Adam felt extraordinarily happy.

"Rather bad luck getting caught up in this business. You might have had Christmas at home."

Adam said that the same thought had occurred to him, but it was hardly the moment to run for home!

"What do you think will happen, Ian? Were we all caught by surprise? Is it really serious?"

"Yes, I think people have been totally surprised. They didn't think the Germans had got enough for a really major operation. Enough to make a demonstration, yes, but a real breakthrough, no."

Ian drove on for a minute and said, "Nor do I think they have."

"Not enough for a real breakthrough?"

"Exactly. Its inevitable that if they mount a first-class attack with concentrated strength against an unexpected bit of the front, held by weak forces – it's inevitable they'll give us some shocks at first. And then you'll get a certain amount of panic here and there, exaggerations, distortion, you know—"

Adam nodded. His mind went back to France in 1940. He said, "I do indeed know."

"My impression," said Ian, "but it's only based on reports so far, not observation, is that the Americans have recovered their balance in most places with remarkable speed. Remarkable speed. And although it all looks pretty dangerous in terms of arrows on the map the Jerries haven't really got all that far."

He sounded strong and confident and Adam wondered whether even to him, Adam, his friend and brother-in-law, Ian Chisholm wasn't speaking slightly more for effect than from the truth in his heart. Then for a little they talked of family, of home, of Adam's loved sister Saskia and her baby, of Adam's mother, Natasha, and her life in a London now, it seemed, at last free of the fear of air raids. They talked a little of Adam's immediate future – Italy, the 2nd Westmorlands, a very different campaign. For a few minutes uniform disappeared, war receded, as they talked of places and people they shared and loved.

The Headquarters of the United States First Army was in an hotel in the village of Chaudfontaine, almost, as Ian had said, in the outskirts of Liege, and Adam marvelled that in what must be a situation certainly of stress and perhaps of confusion anybody had the time or inclination to pay any attention to the British party. An officer whom Adam identified as a lieutenant-colonel met Ian Chisholm and led him to a large room, the rest of them following, the British colonel who had supposed First Army Headquarters to be in Spa making knowing comments as they trailed along. The large room was filled with American officers and soldiers, some talking in groups, one or two speaking into radio microphones. Maps were spread on walls and multiple briefings appeared in progress. They came to rest standing in front of a map of the entire Ardennes, and the American lieutenant-colonel told them in a matter-of-fact sort of way that in the southern part of the Army front the road junction of Bastogne was under attack from three sides, and there had been "considerable penetrations". In the northern part of the front the Germans were attacking St Vith, had reached Stavelot ("An advance of twenty miles, as the crow flies" Adam's neighbour breathed in his ear, "and only about twelve miles from here!") but were still having a tough fight east of Malmedy, where the flank of the German penetration was holding. It was, the Lieutenant-Colonel said, a pretty wide penetration from north to south, pretty wide. Two Panzer Armies abreast, G2 said. And pretty deep, although slowing quite a bit.

"Reckon the Krauts aimed to bounce the Meuse crossings at least by now." The Lieutenant-Colonel smiled. He didn't, Adam thought, seem in the least panicky. He started giving them their "attachments", looking at a piece of paper.

"Major Adam Hardrow?"

"That's me," said Adam and was conscious of a very fair-haired rather small American captain standing at his right side.

"Major Hardrow, I'm Captain Lewis Parney. I'm assigned to look after you, sir."

"That's very kind of you – "

"Major Hardrow?" The Lieutenant-Colonel's voice could be heard.

Adam turned and said again, "That's me."

"Major Hardrow, may we have one word?" The Lieutenant-Colonel, whose name Adam never discovered, drew him a little way from the group which was now splitting into three or four sub-groups with various bearleaders. God knows how they've found people to make the time available, Adam thought, they really are marvellous hosts! The Lieutenant-Colonel was speaking low and rather urgently.

"Major Hardrow, you are assigned to Captain Lewis Parney. Just by yourself. I want to explain something. Captain Parney is a very fine young officer."

Adam nodded and the Lieutenant-Colonel said, "He has had a very tough few days, very tough. There are several officers whom the General would like to send back for a rest after certain experiences but has retained here at Army Headquarters the while, for any special assignments. Your visit is such an assignment and Captain Parney is one such officer."

"I see."

"He was captured when his unit was overrun. He is just about the only survivor."

"He escaped?"

"He escaped. There is a report that some of his companions were shot. By the Germans. After capture."

Adam was silent and the Lieutenant-Colonel said, "I am just telling you this to explain that Captain Parney really needs a change. I hope you will be forbearing."

"Good Heavens, Colonel," said Adam with a smile, "it's the other way round. I don't see why he should have to put up with me!"

"He will be happy with the assignment, Major Hardrow. But he may appear slightly— " the Lieutenant-Colonel paused.

Adam thought it best simply to say, "I understand. Perfectly."

A moment later Lewis Parney managed to lead Adam out of the building and to a jeep. It had been agreed that the British vehicles and drivers were to remain at First Army Headquarters until the visit ended on the following day. Lewis Parney was clearly going to drive and when they'd climbed in Adam said, "Where are we going?"

After one silent minute, during which he drove the jeep down the cobbled centre of ChaudFontaine faster than Adam had ever experienced anybody drive a jeep before, Captain Lewis Parney said, "Well, Major, I've been told I have discretion but I'm not to get you into any sort of trouble. So it's maybe for you to say where we go. I've just been told to show you around."

"Showing me around presumably means something more than the rear areas, doesn't it?"

"If you say so, Major."

"Where is your own unit now?" Adam cursed himself; the Lieutenant-Colonel had said that Lewis Parney was about the only survivor. But in a very natural voice, driving at speed the while in what Adam thought was an easterly direction, the direction of Spa, Lewis said that the outfit he belonged to was holding some high ground beyond Malmedy.

"Can't we go to see them?"

Lewis shot a look at him and grinned. He said, "Kind of a hot spot, Major."

"Can we get there?"

"Reckon so. But they're in contact, Major. Have been ever since things started. I was dumb – I and the unit I was with got overrun but the rest's still there. Its a good position too."

"Will you get into trouble if you take me there?"

"Well," said Lewis, "who's to know, Major? And if the trouble gets real bad it'll be all the same anyway!" He swerved his way past one, two, three heavy trucks, missing them by inches and Adam wondered whether his companion's balance had been more than a little upset by his experiences. He also, however, found himself liking him very much indeed.

Lewis's spontaneous comments on the vehicles, the people, the Belgian landscape or snowscape were apt, original and often extremely funny. Adam heard himself laughing aloud more than he had for some time. Lewis turned and smiled as Adam laughed. He had a charming, rather quizzical smile.

Adam said suddenly, "I'm enjoying this drive!"

"That's good, Major."

A moment later Lewis swore. "Aw, hell!" He slammed on the jeep brakes. Two columns of vehicles, passing each other with difficulty, were blocking the road for miles ahead. Stopping and starting, making only a few yards at a time, Adam and Lewis Parney resigned themselves. The cold became a little more bearable as wind speed reduced. And Lewis Parney, encouraged by a word or two from Adam now and then, began to talk.

"Their artillery," said Lewis, "that was quite something. That sure was quite something. The German artillery. No preliminaries. They started up, their guns started up, at the same time as the Heinies took off, started to come over. And did they start up! None of us had ever heard the like!

"Trouble was, we were in pretty small parties, just a tank or a car or maybe two and a squad of infantry, you know. Based on a farm or one of these small villages, there'd be one or two guys looking out, sentries, but there wasn't anything to look at and we'd been there since end-October mostly. The Ardennes was a quiet sector, that was what they told us, nothing likely to happen, can't happen. We've got a big attack starting soon south of Aachen in the north, they told us. Just keep a watch here, that's all, in case the Heinies try an upset of some kind. So all along our sector we were doing just that, keeping a watch, more or less. And mostly trying to keep warm, but we knew we were lucky, we had houses and everyone had a roof overhead. We got pretty comfortable. In small parties, like I say."

Adam watched him. He enjoyed the way Lewis expressed himself. It vividly conveyed impression.

Lewis continued, driving forward a short distance to the next blockage. It was clear to Adam that they might spend the day in a traffic jam, freezing to death out of contact with the Wehrmacht, but Lewis's company was agreeable and informative so what the hell?

Lewis said that the trouble was they were so widely spread in their small parties that it didn't seem many American guns could be brought to bear on any one point. And later, when he'd learned more of what had happened, he'd been told that a good many American artillery positions had actually been overrun by the advancing Germans.

"What time did it all start, Lewis?"

"Early morning. Dark. They turned searchlights on the clouds, gave some illumination."

"So I've heard."

Cut both ways, Lewis said, they'd seen something of the Heinies as well, they'd come on real packed, shouting, making a Helluva noise. But too many. Far too many. And every post had been overrun, or surrounded and cut off.

"If we stopped 'em and in a lot of places we *did* stop 'em, they'd just switch off and move round some place else. Then they'd be behind us. They sure had something. They were good."

"Yes," said Adam, "I bet they were. They are."

"White uniforms, some of them had, kind of snow camouflage. Didn't make much difference really. And then their tanks came. We'd stopped the infantry, in our sector. They'd gone round, like I say."

"That must have taken some doing, Lewis."

"Yeah." Adam watched his profile as they jolted along, stop, start, stop, start. The Colonel at First Army Headquarters had implied that Captain Lewis

Parney was in bad shape, needed a rest, had been kept in the rear areas, at Army Headquarters, pending some sort of more permanent recuperation. He didn't seem like that. He seemed, in his jerky way, to be full of vitality, not exhausted at all. Adam supposed it was good for Lewis to talk about the battle – he seemed to want it. He'd not come to the point of his own capture and escape, not come to the horrors. He probably wouldn't.

"Yeah, they came on again and we beat 'em off and they went back and round again. Went on all day, that did. Till dark. We could hear tanks and tracks south of us, all the time, moving west."

"And you were still in your original positions?"

"Yeah. Then the tanks came," Lewis said, "with more infantry in vehicles, tumbling out of vehicles. We'd lost one helluva lot of men by then and we'd not been able to get all the wounded back, there was some in pretty bad shape. They caught us in this village, we'd been in position on the outskirts, we were back, some of us were back getting something to eat, a bit of rest. I had the roads stopped and watched but this tank and some squads of Heinie infantry got past without any alarm given, my guys were real tired, it can happen. Next thing, there was a tank outside the house we were in, me and my best radio man and a top sergeant. Kraut tank. Outside the house, traversed the turret, pushed the tank gun through the door and fired into the room."

Adam opened his eyes wide, his mouth grim. He could imagine the scene but only just.

"Fired two rounds into the room. Smashed everything to pieces, fire started, my top sergeant was pretty well blown to bits. A bit of wall came down on me. Next thing I was dragged out into the street, house on fire of course. Found I could stand, I wasn't hit bad at all, just a bit shaken I guess. And Heinies everywhere. Major, the traffic's easing up in front and I have to ask if you want to go left or right at this next place. Right towards Stavelot, left round north of it."

"Go wherever you want. And Lewis do you mind calling me 'Adam' and not 'Major'. I'd appreciate it. I'm only a captain really." And may be a lieutenant-colonel soon, Adam thought to himself, embarrassed. He wondered if he'd upset Lewis by any suggestion that his military protocol had been faulty, but to his relief Lewis chuckled and said, "OK. Adam."

He took the road towards Stavelot but after a mile, driven in silence, a whitehelmeted military policeman stopped them. He peered curiously at Adam and addressed Lewis. The morning light was still misty grey, as if darkness would never be completely dissolved and ice never thaw.

"No traffic down this road, Captain. Where are you going?"

"British observer officer," said Lewis smartly, "Stavelot."

"Heinies are in Stavelot, Captain."

"Is that so? Since when?"

"Since now, Captain. I've gotta stop all traffic beyond this point, right here."

Lewis looked at Adam and leant over to look at the map on Adam's knee.

"We'll turn round, Major. Adam. Turn round and go back and north-east, OK?"

"OK."

"We'll go round north of Malmedy. There look to be some small roads. North-east of Malmedy, that's where my Regiment are still holding. That's what the map at Army said. The Heinies broke in here and there, but the position's still holding." He swung the jeep round and bumped off back down the frozen pavé.

"Lewis," said Adam, "I think you're bloody marvellous!"

"Why so?"

"You hung on to a position against one hell of a lot of Germans, quite obviously all day, and half the night— "

"Only four hours of the night."

"Four hours of the night and then a tank gun blasts you at point-blank range, inside a building and most of it comes down on you— "

Lewis grinned.

"Part of it comes down on me!"

"And you're alive and laughing!" If he wants to talk about the next bit, thought Adam, now's probably the time. They had driven back a short distance and were now slithering along a very small road which Adam tracked on the map as running towards the high ground north of Malmedy. We'll need to go north again soon, Lewis had said, to get round north of Malmedy and east of it. "The Heinies are round Malmedy but north of that we're holding them. That's where I was until they got me."

Klaus Mosten knew that even his proud Waffen SS men had had enough. To Mosten loyalty was a virtue beyond all others and unquestioning obedience the first military quality but when, as had just happened, he received an order that "the ridge ahead of us must be taken at all costs" he wondered whether he and the man from whom the order emanated were inhabiting the same planet. "At all costs" – those words, so easy to enunciate or scribble, might be common currency in all armies. Klaus didn't know. All he knew was that this ridge had been defying attempts to clear it of Yankees for a long time. They'd made ground, been driven out, made ground again, been driven out again. They'd initially advanced as planned and predicted – bypassed strong points, opened up minor routes forward for the operational advance when major routes were contested, taken advantage of the considerable gaps between Yankee positions, taken advantage of the surprise and shock which a hurricane bombardment had clearly inflicted. For the first miles, the first hours, it had gone well. South of them routes had been opened, albeit with some difficulty, for a "*schwerpunkt*" and the word passed that there it had gone exceptionally well.

But here! Here the Yankees, after being knocked off balance at the start and caught – very literally in many cases – in their underpants, here the whole thing had hardened. The Yankees – the German *Landsers* tended to refer to them as the "*Amis*", but Klaus, with a certain sophistication, used the word "Yankee" in his own mind – the Yankees had recovered some strength, and a good deal of spirit. They'd collected a good many tanks, and although this high-built Sherman tank of theirs wasn't a match for the Mark IV or the Panther in open country – the long-barrelled high-velocity 75 mm could beat any Yankee gun for range and penetration and the Sherman armour wasn't up to much – nevertheless the enemy had been using Shermans at close quarters in the villages and behind farm buildings and doing deadly damage by shooting German tanks in the sides and rear where any tank, even the Panther, was vulnerable. And the Yankee bazookas! They were as effective as our own Panzerfaust, and the numbers! There seemed to be one bazooka per American soldier and even the tanks of the Waffen SS were hesitating before going into built-up areas. Result? Very large numbers of German tanks burnt out on the approaches to this *verdammte* ridge. And on top of it.

And the American guns! Time and again Klaus had been ordered to form the battalion, or groups from it, up for another attempt on one or other of the enemy positions which swept the ridge with fire and which blocked any attempt to open westward routes past it. And time and again, once formed up or once moving forward, they'd been virtually blown to pieces by the weight of American artillery fire! Klaus hadn't taken an up-to-date tally of casualties in the last two hours but he knew, with bitterness in his heart, that of the eager young men he'd exhorted four days ago, had inspired with the grandeur of the task ahead – of these nearly half lay in the Belgian snow or were on their way to the field hospitals. And many wouldn't reach them alive.

And now it was early afternoon and Klaus had been ordered to attack once again "as soon as possible". That was another phrase used without much thought or calculation by higher authority, "as soon as possible". It would be better to wait until nightfall, of course it would. It would be better to give the men a few more hours rest. But no, "as soon as possible"; and "at all costs".

Klaus Mosten spoke sharply to his three subordinates, summoned and standing in the snow by his own half-tracked vehicle, with the cross of the Wehrmacht painted on its side and the lightning flashes of the Waffen SS not entirely concealed by the caked mud and snow. Klaus's arm was in a sling – his shoulder had been dislocated, or so it seemed, by the burst of an American shell which had blown him several yards and smacked him into one of his own vehicles, miraculously breaking neither bones nor skin but leaving him with unremitting pain. He told them the plan, speaking briefly, in a matter of fact voice, feigning a confidence he very certainly didn't feel. They would be going for the same objectives, the villages here and here – he tapped the map; they knew it backwards. Moving north-west and then turning and going at the villages from the north this time. Grenadiers riding on the tanks, tank destroyers and assault guns thus and thus.

They nodded. When he gave them the timings they raised their arms – "Heil Hitler" – and moved off through the snow. Klaus watched their backs and knew that he was looking at beaten and dejected men.

"I only had about seventeen men left by then," Lewis said, "and nine of them were out in the street with me, all hit or bleeding or bandaged in some way or other, you know. I don't yet know about the others, whether they were all taken or killed or what – maybe one or two got back, trickled back. The Heinies were all round us by now.

"We were pushed along to the end of the village and down a kind of track beside a house, there was a garden at the back, I suppose it was a garden, there was snow of course but a fence round it, small place. The Heinies with us, who'd been prodding us along, they were screaming at us. My head was bleeding quite bad, it was nothing really but it felt like I was bleeding to death! And then they yelled at us to lie down."

Adam said, conversationally, "There's a lot of shelling going on to the south. And ahead."

It was true. There was a constant rumble of shell bursts south of their road and an equally continuous rumble ahead. At greater distance they could hear the almost continuous thunder of the guns. Lewis nodded and said "ours". He drove expertly past a small column of tanks and self-propelled guns stationary beside their small road, helmeted American soldiers standing by them looking cold and disconsolate.

"If you look at that map, Major— "

"Adam."

"Adam. If you look at that map there's a village where the road forks, maybe two miles ahead."

"You know the country well, Lewis."

"We came in this way. I know it. And at that village we'll go left again."

"Up onto a ridge."

"The road runs behind the ridge, west of the ridge. Out of sight of the Heinies, unless they've made the ridge."

"I see it. About a mile west of the crest."

"That's right. You'll find our Regimental Command post there, I checked. If you want to. They've had a tough night. And they may be having a tough day."

"We mustn't – I mustn't – be a nuisance, Lewis."

"They're friends of mine," Lewis said easily, "you'll be welcome. Well, like I said, these Heinies yelled at us to lie down and I lay down in the snow, we all lay down, maybe nine of us like I said, maybe less. Then I just heard a shot, and a kind of a groan and then another, very quick. From my left. There were two guys on my left. The others on my right. They'd shot 'em."

"God!"

"You'll not believe this bit. Several shots from my right as well, same thing. All happened quickly. I told you I was bleeding some. I dug my head, blood and all into the snow, stretched out an arm and lay like dead. I heard the Heinie shoot the guy on my right, a decent kid called Granger from Ohio.

"Then I reckon he thought I'd been fixed already, wasn't sure maybe, hesitated.

"Then, a second or two, seemed like an hour, there was a lot of shouting. An officer, someone senior to those ones with us anyway. A lot of shouting and noise and '*Jahwohl*, Herr whatever-it-was'. And then they went off."

"Left the village?"

"Left the village. I reckon the Colonel back at Army told you I was taken prisoner. Well, I wasn't taken prisoner, or only for a few minutes. When I could get up I got up. The Heinies had gone. The other guys were dead. The village, or some of it, was burning. I had to make my way somewhere and dodge the Heinies – they were behind us by then, of course, and more were coming on through. But I made it. Jesus, was I tired!"

"Your head was OK?"

"It was nothing. I was still bleeding like a stuck pig but it was nothing. And if we go a mile along this track, Adam, we'll come to a Regimental Command Post. That's what they thought at Army but they may be kind of out of date."

"Lewis," said Adam, "I suppose you've made out a report about all this?"

"You bet I have! Adam."

Adam remained astonished that in the midst of a battle the Americans were prepared to accept a stranger among them, and one with absolutely no contribution to make to their task. It was so, however, and for the next two hours he was able to watch work at the Regimental Command Post which had once been the superior authority of Lewis Parney's shattered and murdered little command and where Lewis himself was now welcomed like a prodigal son.

"Hi, Captain!"

His story, it was clear, was by now familiar to them. The Command post was in the capacious cellar of a farmhouse well below the ridge to which Lewis – rather proudly – had referred. It was, Adam thought from studying their situation map as unobtrusively as he could, a plateau rather than a ridge and it clearly dominated the surrounding country. It was obvious why the Germans needed it and equally obvious why the Americans had reinforced it and allocated as much artillery as they could manage to support its defence.

Every officer or soldier in the cellar seemed, Adam noted, to keep his helmet on at all times. It was probably sensible, he reflected, although it looked curiously – what?

"Intense" perhaps? But, again, why not? And then Adam, keeping as much out of the way as he could, listened to the battle as it was relayed over the Regimental command net. For a battle it was, and it had already started. Less than two miles away.

"Comin' in from the north! Fifteen, no twenty of them comin' in from the north!"

"OK, OK!"

Radio procedure was easy, conversational. Several conversations seemed to be going on simultaneously in the Command post. Adam had been shown a radio diagram to identify outstations but he couldn't make a great deal of it.

"It's twenty, maybe more. Panzers. And assault guns. Heinie infantry jumping off them. Just right for Lambskin. On Prairie."

Control, a saturnine major, grinned.

"Lambskin, OK, you said it!"

"What's Lambskin?" Adam muttered to Lewis, who was sitting on the floor next to him and looked as if he were positively enjoying himself.

"Lambskin's the Divisional Artillery. May be more, if the target's right."

"So he – the battalion – was calling for artillery fire?"

"That's right. On Prairie. Prairie's one of the preplanned target areas." They heard, louder than hitherto, a rumble of distant artillery and some seconds later, very much nearer, the crash of shell bursts. The shell bursts seemed, in fact, to be remarkably near to the Command Post. Adam squinted carefully at a map above Lewis's head with some names scrawled on it, one of several so marked in the cellar. He identified "Prairie". On the ridge. So the Germans were on the ridge itself and trying to fight their way south, down it.

Prairie appeared to be only about a thousand yards

from where they were squatting. Simultaneously Adam heard the same voice as previously on the radio. The voice was saying, excitedly, "Boy, oh boy! Was Lambskin beautiful!"

"You want more?"

"Do I want more!"

"OK."

Unnecessarily, almost pedantically, as if fearing that a British visitor might be gaining an inward impression of frivolity in battle, Lewis said, "He's asked for a repeat of fire."

"So I gathered."

"Are you OK, Major? Adam?"

"Lewis," Adam said truthfully, although he couldn't say why, "I'm loving it!" At that moment everyone in the cellar heard the familiar sound of a *Nebelwerfer* salvo, "moaning minnies" as the multiple German rockets were known to the troops of both the United States and Britain. There was, there could be, a very distinctive note sounded when the particular rockets were coming close to oneself and that note sounded now. The same saturnine Major who had been running the command net, yelled, "Down everybody!" And bodies flattened.

The roar of the explosions sounded all round the little farmhouse and there was a crash and tinkle as a window on the first floor, by the main door, shattered, a window whose survival so long was a source of some wonder. Down the cellar steps, from the tiny hall inside the main door, there drifted the familiar acrid smell and dust of high explosive. Several shouts from outside sounded. The Major said "Jesus!" There were heavy footsteps on the stair and there burst into the crowded cellar a perfectly enormous man, with a very red face covered with dust.

He yelled, "The Goddamn bastards are learning their job! They've got the range of my CP!" Then he gave a huge shout of laughter, saw Adam sitting on the floor, and said, "Jesus Christ, an English major! What in hell are you doing here?"

Sotto voce, and once again entirely unnecessarily, Lewis muttered to Adam, "The Regimental Commander."

Adam stood up, saluted and started to explain. When he'd got out a few sentences the Regimental Commander cut in.

"We've just seen 'em off again! I was up there, it was beautiful, just beautiful!"

Knowing that he was pushing his luck, Adam said, "Colonel— "

"Yeah?"

"Would it be possible for me to go up to a forward battalion? We've been told, on this visit, to learn as much of your methods as possible." He knew that Lewis Parney had been told to keep him out of trouble. He also knew that Lewis, himself, needed a rest. But it was a chance, fascinating. The Regimental Commander looked at him.

"You know what? Your General Montgomery, sorry, your Field Marshal Montgomery, has been given command over half the US First Army? Of all of us north of this penetration the Germans have made south of here?"

"No, Colonel. I didn't know."

"So I suppose— "

The Regimental Commander seemed to think better of what he'd started saying. His face was rather grim. He said, quietly now, "I don't mind Captain Parney taking you to a forward battalion, but the battle's over. They won't come again. Not for this ridge. We licked 'em. You can look at our positions, but the battle's over."

The Regimental Commander's name was Colonel William B. Clare. He looked at Adam speculatively and said, "OK. If that's what you want. You can go up to Major Marassi's battalion. Hank Marassi. He and his boys have done a good job. Best go up in one of the ambulances."

Five minutes later Adam, accompanied by a perfectly happy-looking Lewis Parney was moving up towards the ridge and the headquarters of Major Hank Marassi's battalion. Lewis was aware that this Major Adam Hardrow was going further forward than would have been blessed at First Army Headquarters, where Lewis had been originally briefed on his mission, but what the hell? Colonel Clare had given permission. And why were visiting Britishers so precious, anyway?

Major Hank Marassi was sitting on an iron bedstead in the corner of the farmhouse kitchen, his steel helmet beside him, a cigar jutting from between his teeth. He acknowledged Adam's salute and held out his hand, inspecting his visitor. Colonel Clare's Regimental Command Post had passed the word. Pretty funny idea, entertaining sightseers at a time like this but Hank Marassi was a large, equable man and since he was quietly proud of his Battalion's performance during the last forty-eight hours he didn't mind how many Britishers came to call. He gave a tired smile, without much humour or friendliness in it, and his eyes, bloodshot from lack of sleep, were penetrating.

"Hi!"

Adam said that he appreciated being permitted to pay this visit. He, Adam, was a Company Commander and a few of them were on this brief liaison trip in order to look and learn. He'd keep out of the way.

"Sure, sure."

Adam had felt, rather uneasily, that his request to visit a forward battalion might have appeared a piece of bravado – ostentatious, inexperienced; might have, in truth, had a touch of bravado in it. With part of himself he knew perfectly well that he had no particular desire to suffer more German shot and shell than strictly necessary. Italy beckoned, and before Italy, England. What irony if he were shot up, wholly unnecessarily, on this inquisitive little expedition! But Adam also knew that it would be a job only half-done if he were to return from this visit to the United States forces without a single contact with men who'd actually been fighting the Germans, on the ground. Lewis had been fighting, of course, but Lewis was already simply recalling recent events. That might have been done in a café in Liège.

To Major Hank Marassi, therefore, Adam said, persevering, "Could I look round outside, Major?" It had been made clear to them when they'd arrived in the armoured ambulance that, just for now, the headquarter farmhouse, the Marassi Command Post, wasn't under direct fire. Men had been moving around outside the farmhouse door.

"Sure." Marassi put on his helmet and said, "C'mon, Major. You are a major?"

"That's right."

Privately, Hank Marassi thought he looked mighty young to be a major but you could never tell with the British. He, himself – face lined with exhaustion, two days' stubble on beard, the black mark of one very adjacent German mortar bomb blast discolouring his forehead – he, Hank Marassi, was aware that he looked about sixty, and he felt it.

They emerged into the icy grey light of early afternoon. Cloud was low, fog had been drifting over the ridge, settling, dissolving, drifting in again. No colour showed in any quarter. The ground seemed to fall sharply to the eastward, less sharply north of them where the ridge appeared to be a large, flat plateau, running away on a gentle downward slope. Adam knew from his map that there were forests to both east and south but visibility was limited and one could see nothing but this featureless expanse, whitened by a light coating of snow.

Marassi pointed.

"Last lot came from north."

Adam saw four shapes of German tanks, burnt out. The nearest was about two hundred yards away. They were already covered by a powdering of snow although no snow was falling at that moment. He also saw, not yet snow-covered, what must at a quick count be about thirty bodies. Some of the attacking German troops, Lewis had said, wore white snow-camouflage but these still shapes were, it appeared, in the grey, woollen overcoats of the Wehrmacht.

Hank Marassi nodded. "We caught 'em good, this time. And our artillery caught 'em real good, further out, you can't see. Caught another six, maybe seven Panzers. They got to hell out of it."

"This was the latest attack?"

"Yeah. Second today. Four attacks yesterday, same thing. You can't see the Panzers we knocked out then without taking a walk east, over the ridge. I wouldn't advise it."

"How many?"

"Maybe fifteen. Hell, they may have recovered two or three, towed 'em out, but I'd say fifteen. And the Heinie infantry – did we hit 'em!"

Marassi gave more details, pointed out ground, walked round to the other side of the building and a short distance from it, talked more, described earlier German attacks, gave Adam a pull of Bourbon whisky from a bottle, yawned, grinned, lit another cigar. He pointed, east and south-east, to what Adam counted as nine Sherman hulls, fire-blackened.

"That was yesterday. Kraut '88s."

Adam asked, carefully, about the American battalion's

own casualties and Hank Marassi said that on this position, in the six German attacks to date, they'd lost 55 men evacuated.

"Can't say how many dead. Can't say. But we made 'em pay!"

"You certainly did," Adam said softly. He looked over the stark landscape, photographing it on to memory. It was bleaker than anything he had seen in Holland – or anywhere else for that matter. A gust of wind carried a tiny drift of snow across his vision. He remembered a poem – something about "through the twilight filled with flakes, the white earth joins the sky".

"Thank you for allowing this visit. Its been instructive."

"I'm glad, Major." Marassi chuckled. "Come again!"

A little later a young lieutenant called over to him. They had returned to the farmhouse and were standing just inside its door. Lewis Parney, who had been shadowing Adam unobtrusively, was looking at his watch. He had established at the Marassi command post that another armoured ambulance was due to go west with one or two lightly wounded men to a rear echelon dressing station and he reckoned that he and Adam should hitch a lift.

The young lieutenant was standing in front of a large situation map on which he had been scrawling with grease colour pencils, recording a wider situation, it seemed.

"Krauts are round St Vith, Major."

"Round it," asked Marassi, "or in it?"

"Both, I guess, Major. But our guys are still in it as well. And the Krauts are right round Bastogne."

"St Vith," nodded Hank Marassi, eyes on the map which he knew by heart, "St Vith! And Bastogne! Well, dip me in piss and call me mother! Have a good trip back, Major!"

The jeep drive back towards Liège was even colder than

the morning's westward journey. During it Lewis talked and talked, by now as if to an old friend – Adam felt flattered and privileged.

"What are you doing when you go back to your unit? Adam?"

"I'm commanding a company looking after a bridge over the Meuse. And from what I've seen and heard it's perfectly obvious the Germans won't reach it."

Lewis chuckled. He said, "They're round Bastogne and St Vith."

"Even so."

Lewis chuckled again. "He's quite a guy, Colonel Clare."

"Obviously."

Lewis was silent for a moment and Adam knew what a barrier had been breached and what an honour was being done him when Lewis said, looking straight ahead in the gloaming, "Mighty different from some. When you're back like I am, sent all the way back to Army Headquarters because they thought I'd maybe crack up, you meet people, you hear things. In some sectors, some units, the fighting wasn't like with us. There was some surrendering after no casualties at all. Guys just gave up. Bugged out without orders or packed it in. And there was some senior officers – and junior, I guess – who broke, couldn't take it."

Adam said, "I expect so." He knew that this, above all, was the moment when friendship could either be cemented or ruptured. It had cost Lewis Parney a lot to say what he'd said to a foreigner, a Britisher, a major. Adam wondered whether he could convince with his reply? He wanted to tell the exact truth but he dreaded sounding even the slightest quaver of condescension.

"Lewis, I was in France in 1940. When we retreated to Dunkirk. I saw a lot."

"I guess so."

"You've talked of people bugging out without orders, of officers cracking up."

"I didn't mean there was a lot of it. But it happened."

"I can only tell you that it happened with us too, my God it happened with us. Again I don't mean a lot. But it happened. It does happen. And when one sees it it's pretty upsetting."

"I was lucky," said Lewis, and Adam felt with a spasm of relief, that the tone of his voice was friendly and devoid of embarrassment or reservation. It's all right, Adam thought, it's worked, it was the right way to handle it.

"I was lucky. I didn't see it but I heard of it. And the word's gotten around."

"I think that always happens. And I'm ready to bet that there was mighty little of it among frontline units. And even when the rear echelons start moving faster and earlier than intended – because rumours spread quicker in rear – they often give an impression that isn't true. If you're going, after all, why the hell hang about?"

Lewis grinned and Adam said, "I think the truth is both the heroics and the disgraces get exaggerated."

Lewis considered this. Then he grinned again and said, "I reckon that's good. Heroics and disgraces both exaggerated. Yes, that's good. Adam."

"Thank you."

"And you experienced all that sort of thing in 1940?"

"I did indeed."

"Still, that was a bit different, wasn't it? The Krauts had everything then and you didn't have much. They had an air force and from what I've heard you didn't have much of that either. Whereas here everyone reckoned we'd got such a superiority over them they couldn't do a darn thing. But they did."

"Yes," said Adam, "they did. They certainly did."

CHAPTER III

"Apparently," said Aylwyn Kentish, "your little report made quite a stir." After return, each of Ian Chisholm's party had been required to write "in confidence submitted through commanding officers", an account of impressions received during attachment to the Americans. They had all taken leave of their hosts at First Army Headquarters, expressing appreciation in fulsome terms and Ian Chisholm had had a brief interview with the Army Commander himself. Ian had told them, to the surprise of some, that he had received a clear impression that the German offensive was already running out of steam.

"Not the way it seemed in the bit I visited," one of Adam's colleague company commanders had muttered to him as they dispersed. "I reckon the Brigadier's being optimistic!" He was unaware of Adam's relationship to Chisholm and Adam had just shrugged and said, "Maybe. Maybe." Ian had certainly looked firm and robust.

"Why did my report make a stir, sir?" Aylwyn was in his last few days of command. The "outsider" was due to arrive on 10th January. Nobody could remember his name. 5th Westmorlands had given up responsibility for the Meuse bridges and was concentrated in a village called Lateppes, five miles north of the river, in the open, rolling plain of Brabant.

"It seems," said Aylwyn, smiling easily, "that you were pretty well the only one who found and said that the Yanks are doing rather well. The rest of the chaps who went with you were critical."

"Including Brigadier Chisholm?"

"I've no idea about that. Our own Brigadier mentioned it to me. About you, I mean. He was rather amused. Apparently the reports went in verbatim and were read at some very exalted level. Yours, it seems, didn't tally with what they wanted to believe."

"I suppose they wanted to believe that the Americans were so disorganised and useless everywhere that only our own assistance and advice could turn the tide!"

"Something like that, I daresay!"

Adam chuckled. "We've not given much assistance so far, have we? Unless you mean my guarding a bridge the Germans never got within miles of. Because of successful American action."

Aylwyn raised his eyebrows. "We're going to join in this counter-attack, as you know. Under American Army command. We've not had the details yet but its firm. Wednesday."

Wednesday would be 3rd January.

Adam said, "About time too!" He knew that he had neither the knowledge nor the right to offer a critical opinion on 21st Army Group operational policy but dear old Aylwyn didn't in the least mind his subordinates being as irreverent about higher authority as they liked.

Aylwyn grinned and said, "Adam! Bolshy as ever! And you obviously thought the Yanks were good!"

"In a lot of places I expect they were useless, just as we've been useless in similar circumstances. When you're taken by surprise and you don't know what the hell's happening and your flanks are giving way and rumours are flying around and panic's in the air and you're frightened and confused and without orders – well, then, in any army, discipline goes and self-respect goes and people go to pieces and some of them run away. Of course. Heaven knows we've had our own experiences of that."

Aylwyn nodded. He had been training at home in 1940 and he knew it was to 1940 that Adam Hardrow chiefly referred. He knew, also, Adam Hardrow's reputation at that time. There were stories, some of them rather grim.

Adam was continuing, "But I can tell you that the Americans I, personally, visited – admittedly only for a very short time – had had one hell of a fight and had, quite obviously, done magnificently. They'd held their ground, they'd taken a lot of punishment, they were cold and hungry and tired and they'd faced and beaten off six powerful German attacks by tanks and infantry in two days and nights. And killed a lot of Jerries and knocked out a lot of Jerry tanks. And were still full of fight."

"Good. Good. Not quite the impression given to the British people by some of our Press."

Adam disregarded this. He said, "And the enemy were Waffen SS, as I said in my report."

"You did indeed, Adam. Well, the Yanks certainly fought on when they were completely surrounded, when they were having to be supplied by air if at all. As at Bastogne."

Bastogne had now been relieved. The tide had, beyond question, turned although here and there German attacks were still reported. Adam smiled and said, "Exactly. Exactly so. And, again, after what sounds like one hell of a fight."

Aylwyn Kentish had no mind to argue, didn't, indeed, have any particular opinion about American prowess one way or another. He said, amiably, "Well, anyway, thank Heaven the weather's allowing some flying once again."

"It's allowing both sides some flying once again!" Adam said, "From what one gathers the Germans haven't much left with which to profit from that." And Aylwyn Kentish, who was fond of Adam but was, like most of them, occasionally nettled by the Hardrow propensity of being right, couldn't resist reminding him on the following evening, a Monday, that the Luftwaffe had just mounted one of their heaviest low-level raids of the campaign and that over a thousand aircraft (or so Divisional Headquarters asserted) had written off between 150 and 200 Allied planes on the ground. The beast might be turned and cornered, they all thought in their own particular and private ways, but God! he still had fangs!

It was not the remaining fangs of the Luftwaffe, however, but once again the low cloud and fog which prevented a single Allied fighter-bomber from supporting their attack, and on 5th January 5th Westmorlands were once again struggling forward supported by an impressive weight of artillery on call, by a squadron of tanks – new to the Battalion; the "Cleveland Horse" now riding in Shermans – and by assurances that the Germans were only fighting a delaying action and would pull out when pushed hard or plastered with a sufficient weight of fire.

It didn't appear, Adam observed to Aylwyn Kentish at the latter's order group, that there was any idea now of surrounding and destroying the German Panzer Armies which had made the incursion. It was to be a matter of pushing, taking position after position at minimum cost. Aylwyn agreed. That, certainly, was to be 5th Westmorlands' task. No question, Aylwyn said comfortably, of sticking our necks out. But Aylwyn, perfectly well briefed in the Brigadier's own orders, demurred at Adam's comment of "no idea of surrounding and destroying them".

"I don't think that's right. It's very much hoped that the Americans, from both north and south, will have the effect of trapping the Jerries. They're in a sack and the Americans will pull the cords tight. Or that's as I understand it. Our job is to hit them at the tip of their thrust so to speak."

"I can't really see why," Adam said, but only to himself. It wasn't his business. He retained a strong impression, or hunch, that the British could have done more and done it earlier, but how could a mere company commander possibly have an opinion? He was, he supposed, unduly swayed by having witnessed for a few brief hours other soldiers, fighting for their lives and doing so well. He was also, he knew, adversely influenced by a rather smug tide of chauvinistic complacency which had run through the British command. It had irritated Adam and he had, he thought, probably over-reacted.

A-Company's task was now to push up a minor road running eastward towards a large village south-west of the considerable town of Marche. The village, whose name was Matogne, appeared from the map to be a long straggle of houses along a shallow valley. This part of the Ardennes was not particularly steep, but it was thickly afforested, with occasional clearings only, and snow lay everywhere. The roads were icy and off the roads the banks were slithery and treacherous. Snow drifts abounded. Men on their feet could only move slowly and laboriously, while tanks could too easily belly in snow or slither, out of control, down a slope or bank on which the Sherman's track treads could fail to grip. Men's hands froze quickly, and the working parts of rifles and machine guns were constantly sticking.

3-Platoon was leading A-Company. 3-Platoon was commanded by Sergeant Paul, a lugubrious man with the ability which some lugubrious men possess of making others laugh. Paul had a turn of phrase which often turned the most frightful situations into occasions for mirth, his sallies always delivered from a face like a stage undertaker's. Adam appreciated him. Men felt secure with Paul, and he kept their spirits up.

Moving with 3-Platoon, along the road, was one troop of Shermans, a troop from C-Squadron of the Cleveland Horse. They'd not had much practice with each other and the Westmorlands decided to reserve judgement on the Cleveland Horse. Adam had liked the troop commander, a young officer named Ewen Traill, but thought him over-confident. But, Adam said to himself, that's maybe because we, in this battalion, and I in particular, are getting too cautious. I criticise, within my heart, our own command for being slow in rushing to the aid of the Americans but isn't the truth that none of us wants to take risks any more?

Montgomery sees the war going towards inevitable victory, just needing a little pushing here and there; and I want to get home and then, if the war's still going on, to Italy and promotion and a warmer clime. When this freezing, bloody walk is over, any time now, I might hear I've been called forward to move. So who wants to stick his neck out? And I don't want to get any more men killed in A-Company, not one. Perhaps, he suddenly thought, Montgomery feels like that too.

Adam moved along behind Ewen Traill's troop of tanks, with Sergeant Paul's men plodding on each side of the road parallel to them. Adam had his jeep and jeep-mounted radio move from bound to bound with him but most of the way he tramped along on foot, trying to keep circulation going. Moving as second platoon in the company was No. 2, with Bill Travers; and Bill Travers moved with instinctive skill, he needed little telling. If Sergeant Paul's command came under fire, got into trouble, Bill Travers would have his men in hand, ready to react but not involved in the preliminary shoot-out. And on Adam's orders Ewen Traill, too, was moving his tanks cautiously, from bound to bound, covering each other, ready to react.

It was, therefore, the lead tank of the Cleveland Horse and the lead section of Sergeant Paul's platoon which simultaneously came under fire, not from Matogne but from the edge of a fir wood several hundred metres on the near side of the village, a fir wood running up from the road and curving back at an angle of about 45 degrees. One, two, perhaps three Spandaus and the echoing crack of a German antitank gun. Sergeant Paul's men were down in the snow before the echoes had even reverberated and, as Adam quickly discovered, not one was hit. The leading Sherman, however, was ablaze – but there had been a slight, a very slight delay between explosion and fire and during that delay the Cleveland Horse crew had managed to abandon tank with an alacrity which was almost supernatural. As they, too, dived towards the snow-filled ditches a Spandau crackled again and one man dropped.

Ewen Traill's second tank, two hundred yards to the rear, was jockeying into a fire position. The road had been climbing and Adam could see that by a rapid reverse of not more than ten or twenty yards the Sherman could probably get hull down to the enemy woodline. This, Adam knew, was Ewen's own tank and he prayed that his own assessment of the ground wasn't over-optimistic. With Adam was the Artillery Forward Observation Officer of their affiliated Battery of close-support artillery. He had his own vehicle and his own radio; and Gunner radios always worked. His name was Joe Pringle, a cheerful young man.

"Come on Joe."

Adam leapt into his jeep and raced up the frozen road to the point where he reckoned Ewen Traill's tank would be backing rapidly towards cover. His instinct was entirely sound and one minute later he had climbed on to the engine covers of the Sherman, Ewen having turned a head to see him and welcomed him aboard. They were, Adam noted with some relief, what was called "turret down" from the enemy and with luck and good judgement could evade German attention.

Joe Pringle had also scrambled up. The top of a Sherman wasn't a perch on which to settle for long, he thought, when German mortars were adjacent but with luck this conversation wouldn't go on for long anyway. Adam was talking urgently to Ewen Traill. From the vantage point of the tank he had seen where A-Company could be got into position, Cleveland tanks supporting them, to spray with fire the Wehrmacht-held wood line. That had to be the instant thing to do. There was little hope of getting round the defenders by any close encircling move – the snow was too thick, the slopes too steep, and the vulnerability of Westmorland infantrymen grinding through it would be self-evident; nor was there anything like a decent tank approach to Matogne except down the road. He nodded a command and a farewell to Ewen Traill and jumped from the tank. Rejoining his jeep he spoke very clearly to Bill Travers and to Sergeant Dove, 1-Platoon's commander, on his infantry company radio net.

So far so good. Adam, however, had identified further possibilities, and he grabbed his Battalion command net radio microphone to talk urgently to Aylwyn Kentish. The Jerries couldn't, from all they'd heard, be on a wide front. They'd be holding roads and road junctions but determined and wider movements round a flank, or both flanks, should lever them out. It was even possible that a strong return of fire from the front would boot them out! That would depend on how determined they were to stay.

Adam knew from the map that tracks ran, roughly

parallel to the Battalion centre line, on either side of Matogne, a little way up the northern and southern slopes from their own east-running valley. A company group on each of those, he thought, moving steadily, taking on anything they find, ready to pour everything they've got in the general direction of Matogne – that ought to get the Jerries jumping. And if they're sufficiently strong and on a sufficiently wide front to hold up such a movement it means that Matogne is held by at least a battalion, a battalion supported by tanks, by assault guns; and to dislodge it will need a brigade attack.

Adam got Aylwyn Kentish to the set and suggested what they should do next. He was content when he heard Aylwyn's agreement. B- and C-companies would move astride of Matogne, by tracks north and south of the place, respectively. Each would be supported by a troop of tanks. A-Company would meanwhile take up fire positions, roughly on present ground on and astride the road, ready to work their way forward any and everywhere if circumstances looked like making it possible; and D-Company would remain round a small farm one mile west of Adam's present position, in reserve. It'll all take time, Adam thought, but what the hell? British 25 pounder shells were already falling on the edge of the wood from which the Germans had first opened up. Aylwyn Kentish, having started companies moving towards their allotted routes with commendable alacrity, was coming forward to join Adam and discuss.

Klaus Mosten was angry and his anger made his exhaustion the harder to bear. He had not immediately believed the report received from his *Oberfeldwebel*.

"True, *Herr Sturmfuhrer*. Their hands were bound. Shot in the head."

Two Waffen SS men, prisoners as they must have been,

wounded as they undoubtedly had been, tied and shot! Could it have been the Yankees? It might have been – such incidents had already been reported, and rumours had been running through the dispirited ranks of the battalion ever since the second or third day of the advance. Now, in this place, Matogne, there was clear evidence. Mosten's mouth set grimly. He would report, very exactly, to his superiors.

There was, however, a query.

"Might it have been Belgian terrorists? Civilian *francs-tireurs*?"

The *Oberfeldwebel* shrugged. "We've found no Belgians with arms so far, *Sturmfuhrer*. And they're lying very low." "They've undoubtedly been concealing terrorists – and Yankee soldiers for that matter – in some places. The reports have been circulated."

That had been yesterday, when they'd first entered Matogne. And now there were new orders, inevitable but miserable to receive and deeply depressing to execute. They were to go back. To give the place up, go back.

And yesterday evening had come the incident of the wounded Yankee and the terrorist attack. Klaus had been standing in the main street of the village as the dusk gathered when he'd suddenly heard an explosion which seemed to come from just outside one of the small houses standing a little back from the roadway near the end of the place, next to a bakery. He'd moved sharply towards the detonation. Positions had been taken up over a kilometre to the west and Matogne itself was readied for defence in so far as it could be. Men were by now agonisingly few.

A knot of soldiers were bustling about in and round the doorway of the house in question. One SS man, however, was sitting on the ground his face very pale. Klaus strode over to him. A grenade had gone off very near him and fragments looked as if they'd punctured his stomach. A medical orderly was already running towards them. It didn't look good. A junior NCO saluted and spoke.

"Grenade, *Sturmfuhrer*."

"Of course it was a grenade."

"They were in there."

At that moment Klaus saw more SS men emerging from the house, pushing, dragging and in one case carrying various bits of humanity. The one being carried was in American uniform. Klaus walked over and looked at him. An American soldier! Without doubt an American soldier! An American soldier with both legs smashed. In a bad way.

"The *Ami* was being hidden by the Belgians in the cellar, *Sturmfuhrer*. And one of them threw the grenade."

Yankee soldiers were hung with grenades as often as not. It made sense. A terrorist attack. And because the Wehrmacht was now rumoured everywhere to be pulling back the brutes thought they'd get away with it. Klaus addressed the American soldier. He spoke some English.

"You will be taken back with our own wounded and treated correctly, according to the regulations. Which is more than happened to some of my own men."

The American looked up at him without expression. He's lost a lot of blood, Klaus thought, he's probably dying. If these Belgian fools hadn't hidden him he might have received decent attention. From us. Typical. And now they try to kill young Franz Rutter here. Idiots! He glared at the little knot of Belgians. There were three middle-aged men, five women ranging in age from what might well be seventy to a skimpy, pale little creature of perhaps fifteen; and a boy of maybe ten. One of the men spoke. In German.

"It was an accident. Herr, Herr . . ."

"*Accident?*" Klaus Mosten's voice rose to a scream. "*Accident?* You murdering pig— " He stepped towards the man and brought the back of his gloved hand across the Belgian's face with great violence. Klaus was breathing deeply. His emotions were fuelled not only by the treachery and criminality of the Belgians but by the entire, wretched situation. They had entered Matogne, put it into a state of defence, suffered these miserable indignities and would very soon, he knew well, suffer the further and indescribable indignity of being ordered to retreat once again. The *Standartenfuhrer* had made that abundantly clear on a fleeting visit this very afternoon. The next orders would be about going not forward but back. The *Standartenfuhrer* was a devotee of the Cause but he was also a realist.

"*Accident!*" Klaus glowered at the man, hatred in his eyes.

"The boy was playing with it Herr, Herr . . . he meant no harm. It wasn't deliberate."

A medical orderly was pumping morphine into Franz Rutter. Klaus Mosten flicked his fingers towards the group of Belgians.

"They are all guilty of hiding a combatant and engaging in an attack on the forces of the Reich. They will be punished accordingly. Keep them in a cellar under guard. I will deal with them tomorrow."

Why not now, one or two SS men muttered to each other, eyeing the group of Belgians like wolves round a sheep-pen. But *Sturmfuhrer* Mosten was a man whose orders were not for disputing. He knew his mind. The Belgian captives were locked in a small cellar, all nine of them, age and sex regardless.

And now it was the following day, midday. And orders to give the place up, withdraw. And there'd already been British or American tanks and troops reported tapping down the valley on the outskirts of Matogne. Enemy artillery fire had already fallen round the forward positions near the forest edge. Klaus reckoned he could hold Matogne for a long time – the weather was foul again and there wouldn't be many aircraft up, thank God. But the orders were crisp, brief and clear. Back.

They weren't under pressure. Klaus snapped out his own orders. He didn't foresee difficulty in extricating the forward troops.

"*Herr Sturmfuhrer—*"

"Yes?"

"The Belgian terrorist group?"

"Take them," said Klaus, "to the mill at the end of the village." He had noted a disused millwheel and mill race, with a snow-covered patch of ground beside it and a steep drop to the main river bed.

"*Jawohl, Herr Sturmfuhrer.*"

It was an hour later, with the withdrawal well under way, and apparently undisturbed, that Klaus walked back through Matogne, one of the last to leave the place, and spoke curtly to the two SS men guarding the little huddle of Belgians. Line them up, Klaus said, along the edge of the river and kneel them down.

They did so, the Belgians appearing confused and submissive, the SS men almost solicitous in the way they pressed a shoulder here or there, as if regretting that the order was not as clear as it might be, a language problem, no more. One woman let out a cry "*Non, non!*" as if at last seeing something obscure until this moment but now plain and terrible. Klaus, without a word, stepped back and pointed to the Schmeiser machine carbines in the hands of each of the Waffen SS men. Still without a word, he nodded towards the back of the Belgians and ten seconds later what sounded like a surprisingly loud and echoing burst of fire rang through the eastern end of Matogne.

As Klaus had intended, the bodies all pitched forward and down a little way into the snow-edged river. The young boy's body, lighter than the others, lighter than the fifteen-year-old girl's, stuck on a tussock and remained suspended above the stream. Not, Klaus thought, that it mattered. He spoke a word to the two SS men and regained the road. He heard what sounded like an enemy tank gun firing from unpleasantly close to the west end of the village but Gruppe Mosten was now pretty well clear and Klaus caught them up.

Matogne had been abandoned by the Waffen SS, and when Adam Hardrow and A-Company of 5th Westmorlands pushed cautiously into it they found it apparently devoid of life. As we hoped, Adam thought, the Jerries realised we were getting round on either side and they baled out. And we've been able to push straight ahead and through the place without so much as a Panzerfaust bark or a Spandau crackle! The Belgians seem to be lying pretty low, but they'll soon come to life.

"Adam," said Aylwyn Kentish, "you've been called forward."

"What, immediately?"

"Tomorrow. You'll be in England by about 12th January with luck. Might be earlier – you can never tell with Movements. And then a week's leave, and then Italy. God, I envy you! I'm sure Italy's very demanding but anything would be better than this bloody place!" But Aylwyn smiled. One of his most endearing characteristics was the genuine pleasure he took in the good fortune of others. "And a week's leave!" he said.

"It'll be good."

"While we're off north again! To bloody Holland." The Battalion had just received orders to withdraw back across the Meuse and move northward, to the same area they had occupied before the recent excitements. Their new Commanding Officer was to meet them and take over in the next location. Adam's mind went to the Dutch frontier and the autumn battles in the mud. He could envisage what was to come. He felt a swine to be abandoning his friends but he couldn't pretend he envied them. He grinned at Aylwyn.

"I'll give your regards to the Depot! I bet Kendal's almost as cold as the Ardennes!"

"Adam," said Aylwyn seriously, "in spite of what your orders say I don't expect you need go to Kendal."

"After leave I'm due to report there. There'll probably be a hold-up before onward movement, one can imagine."

"I know. But ring them up. Suggest you stay south and keep in touch by telephone. I imagine you'll want to be in London." Aylwyn knew that Adam's mother lived in London. There were no doubt girlfriends too, that sort of thing. And Adam Hardrow deserved it if anybody did. Aylwyn again, encouragingly.

"Give them a ring when you're on leave. They're perfectly reasonable unless things have greatly changed for the worse. Unless some awful little bureaucrat insists on it you don't need to go to Kendal at all. Waste of energy. Waste of time."

"As a matter of fact," Adam said, "and perhaps surprisingly, I do. Need to go to Kendal. I've got business there. Very important business indeed."

CHAPTER IV

Whenever officers in the Westmorland Regiment spoke of him, which certainly wasn't often in wartime, it was as of an extraordinary, ancient, distinguished old buffer whose soldiering days had been crowded into a period as remote as the Crusades. Lieutenant-General Sir Mason Vine had joined the Regiment in 1898, the year before the second and most serious South African War broke out, that war which had produced distant legends, shadowy places and figures from history – Mafeking, Colenso, Roberts, Buller, De Wet. Vine had been a Westmorland subaltern in that war, and some of his usages of speech still seemed to derive from it. He apparently kept himself well-informed of the doings of modern armies, the ebb and flow of the North African campaign, the slow, gruelling business in Italy, the Normandy invasion, but his comprehension of such matters was assumed to be minimal by those of his brother officers who ever gave the matter a thought.

A few – the Regimental seniors, the commanding officers, men now in their late thirties or early forties, as well as those who had themselves now achieved higher rank – knew better. Especially if, like Adam Hardrow, they possessed what was called a "Regimental background" – family connections, inherited acquaintance with Westmorland legend – they often knew much better. They knew, they had been told, that Mason Vine had been a particularly well-respected young divisional commander in France in the Great War – a divisional commander at forty, appointed just after the muddy bloodbath of Third Ypres in 1917, and still revered by members of his old Division at periodic pre-1939 bemedalled get-togethers. They knew that his reputation had made him a model of a Westmorland soldier in men's eyes. They also knew that after 1918 Mason Vine – "Grapeskin" to most of his contemporaries – had been shunted sideways as well as demoted like most others in the small peacetime Army. He had ended as Governor of a remote African colony, acquired from German protection as one of the pickings of the Versailles Treaty, had ultimately retired from the King's service with the customary knighthood and had, somewhere along the way, become a Lieutenant-General.

Now General Vine lived in a small house in a village in the dales, liked, above all things, news of his old Regiment, and treasured beyond most else his position as its Colonel, a position held since 1938. Few of the traditional duties or privileges associated with the Colonelcy could be exercised in this present perplexing war, with battalions of the Regiment strewn over the map of the world; but General Vine carried out an assiduous correspondence and he knew that battalion commanders – boys whose fathers or grandfathers he had in some cases known – wrote a line to him when they could. When battalions had been in England he had visited them as often as possible and rather more often than the instructions of the Army Council encouraged.

It was not practicable in the hurly-burly of wartime – and the confusion of a mass army in which Regimental system and protocol had been largely set aside for the duration – to interview young officers on joining, or commanding officers on appointment. All that had finished in 1939. Mason Vine kept in touch, however, as well as he could.

He suspected that to the military bureaucrats in the War Office positions such as his were often regarded as tedious anachronisms, and he didn't waste much ink or paper on pestering the authorities to little effect about the doings or sufferings or inadequate treatment accorded to his beloved Regiment: but he kept in touch.

Mason Vine was a widower. He had loved his wife dearly and had missed her every day since her tragic death in a car smash at the age of only fifty-one, fourteen years ago. They had had no children and this small, grey, agreeable village house – long ago a school-house but discarded when the village had grown and received a graceless new building surrounded by concrete and railings – had been exactly what they had both desired as a retirement home. Since 1931 it had been lonely, but Mason Vine undertook a large number of local activities; he was busy, popular, active, a keen sportsman and not one to mope. With the coming of this war and the rationing of petrol, social activity was undoubtedly more difficult, often the evenings were long and Mason Vine was aware of the sixty-seven years which he carried. Most of the time, however, he simply felt lucky – lucky to be comparatively fit, comparatively well-fed, to see a comparatively large number of old associates and to have as many interests as he did.

He was a lonely, uncomplaining, friendly man who read a good deal and enjoyed his wireless set for the excellent concerts and the indispensable news bulletins. His housekeeper was Mrs Braithwaite – as was highly fitting, the widow of a colour-sergeant in the Westmorland Regiment. She saw to the General's needs, was a shrewd manager of wartime rations, and bickered in animated but unresentful style with Bill Cargill, a pensioner who worked two days a week in the General's small garden. Mrs Braithwaite was fond of the General but believed that men were the better for straight talk.

At three o'clock in the afternoon of 18th January 1945 Mrs Braithwaite put her head round the door of the General's study. The small drawing room was seldom used now.

"Will this young man that's coming to see you want tea? There's next to nothing in the house."

"I think we ought to give him some tea, Mrs Braithwaite, don't you? He hopes to be here about four. The Appleby bus."

"These lads think its like the Army, where there's rations and waste galore. They've little understanding of what it's been like at home."

"I'm sure there's plenty of bread, Mrs Braithwaite. And we've always done rather well for butter. Please do what you can, we'll have it in here."

Mrs Braithwaite said, grudgingly, that there was one pot left of the blackberry jelly she'd been saving and General Vine said that there was no need whatever to save it any longer. He could have added that he didn't like it anyway, but that would have been cruel. Mrs Braithwaite said that she'd see what she could do but she knew these lads' appetites, and General Vine said, not for the first time, that Major Hardrow wasn't a boy, although he might have an enormous appetite for all the General knew. Anyway he wasn't coming for a meal, he was coming at his own suggestion, because he was spending a few days at the Depot between postings and had asked to see the Colonel of the Regiment "for a few minutes, if you can spare the time".

Spare the time! The note had rejoiced Mason Vine's heart. He knew about young Hardrow, he'd known his father, and he'd been told great things of this one – a DSO in Normandy, added to two MCs, one of them won in France in 1940 and one in Africa. It was a great record. And the boy had certainly seen some variety in this war. He'd been taken prisoner and escaped as well!

General Vine had been looking forward to the Hardrow visit ever since he'd written a postcard of welcome back to the Depot and hurried with it to the post box. Old Beatrice Hardrow, over at Stonehead, must be a cousin, too, although this young fellow didn't necessarily know her.

"Very good of you to come over to see me, Hardrow. Very good. Long way."

Mason Vine had said this before, said it when Adam Hardrow had first arrived. Then he'd had the great pleasure of listening to Adam's account of some of the recent fighting of 5th Westmorlands in Holland, and their even more recent actions in the Ardennes. He had interjected a few questions and Adam had been mildly surprised at their shrewdness – the old boy understood all right. Mrs Braithwaite's noisy interruption with a tea-tray had been handled with praiseworthy tact by Adam, expressing his gratitude with a smile and in a voice which Mason Vine knew was still warming Mrs B's middle-aged heart no end.

"And now," General Vine said, "you're off to Italy once again, I gather."

"I should leave the day after tomorrow, sir."

"Battalion Second-in-Command for a bit, but probably getting command pretty soon. Or so they tell me. I had a letter from Ben Jameson last week." Ben Jameson commanded 2nd Westmorlands, and General Vine remarked that of course he'd not been able to be very precise about the Battalion's whereabouts, but it sounded as if they were still in the mountains.

"So I believe," Adam said. The German Army was still desperately hanging on to a line in the northern-most part of the Appenines. Once the Allies burst out of the mountains into the flat lands of the Po valley the end could surely not be far away. Similarly, in western Europe, once the British and Americans crossed the Rhine.

General Vine puffed at a pipe and nodded. They must be approaching the core of this interview, for he was sure it was designed by young Hardrow as an interview. They were quiet for a little.

"I wanted to speak to you, sir, about one personal matter."

"Then please do." Tea was over. There was, they both knew, fifty minutes before the Appleby bus, connecting with one to Kendal, was due to leave.

"It's a bit hard to explain convincingly, sir, but when I was in Italy I met somebody whom I very much want to marry. Whom I'm determined to marry."

"I thought you were in a prisoner-of-war camp when you were in Italy."

"I was. For a long time. But when the Italians made peace there was a chance to escape and I got away. A few months later I reached British lines. In a sector held by our 2nd Battalion as it happens. Astonishingly. But I was three months on the run."

"And met a lady."

"Yes. She hid me and she saved me."

"An Italian."

"A widow, whose husband was an Italian officer. She's German by birth."

General Vine said nothing to this but stared at Adam, his expression puzzled and rather stern. What an exceptionally handsome boy he is, he thought. Like his father, but even better-looking – Adam Hardrow senior had been severely wounded in 1918 and died a few years after that war's end. Mason Vine remembered him well – he'd never, he thought, met the mother, come to think of it he fancied she was a foreigner too. Russian? Something like that.

"The reason I'm troubling you with my private affairs, sir, is that when it becomes possible, as I'm sure it will if I survive myself, I'm determined to find this – this lady. And marry her."

"An enemy alien."

"No, sir. The Italians are on our side now and she has Italian nationality. I'm sure of it."

"But German by birth."

"Certainly. And very anti-Nazi. Her family are the same."

"I expect you'll find all this somewhat difficult, Adam. I can't imagine what Italy is like at the moment but I doubt if what you've set your heart on will be easy."

"Probably not, sir."

"And is it wise? You've not come to me for personal advice of that kind, but as you've told me what's in your mind I suppose I'd better be frank. Is it wise? I don't imagine you and this – this lady can really know each other very well."

"Well enough to know what I feel."

"And what she feels?"

"I think so, yes."

"I take it that she isn't in the part of Italy already liberated, if that's the word, by us? Or you'd have somehow made contact, wouldn't you? Perhaps you have?"

"Her home's south of Rome, sir. That's where I was hidden – south of Rome, north of Cassino. Posts aren't functioning at all of course. I've written to a friend in the 1st and another in the 2nd Battalion, in case somebody got local leave to Rome, I believe it happens. No real luck. One chap – a company commander in the 1st Battalion – wrote to tell me that he'd actually managed to speak to an American officer who was going to drive through those parts, and that he'd got in touch with him later. The American had been through the village in question and asked some questions and identified the house."

"Well?"

"The house had been taken over by the Army – the American Army – and people in the village seemed to shrug their shoulders and look vague when he asked about Signora Carlucci. That's her name. Of course the American didn't know what to ask or how to press it, and anyway why should he? I expect that she . . . Anni – the person I'm going to marry – had had the house requisitioned and had moved to friends or relations. Something like that."

Mason Vine was watching Adam's face, noting the whiteness of an old scar on the brown forehead, studying with pleasure the wide, mobile mouth, the very blue eyes, the alertness of the expression. He said again, "Well?"

"I can't fool myself, sir, that the authorities will necessarily take a good view of my intention to marry this lady. They may. They may not. You yourself used the expression 'enemy alien'. It's not so, but there may be a bit of that reaction. Red tape, regulations and so forth."

"There may indeed. Quite apart from the fact that you are off to Italy to fight the Germans, not to pursue private marriage plans. Or not primarily."

"Of course, sir."

"And if you really intend what you've said you would be well-advised to talk to your commanding officer before you do anything precipitate."

"Quite, sir."

"Or to your Brigade Commander if you, yourself, are by then a commanding officer. Which I understand is not unlikely."

There was a short silence. Adam looked very directly at General Vine. "In peacetime, sir, it would be the correct thing to notify you, as Colonel of the Regiment, of my intention to become engaged to be married. To seek your permission, in fact."

"As a courtesy, yes. Such things are impossible, in wartime. They belonged to the tribal customs," Mason Vine smiled pleasantly as he said it, "of a small Regular Army. With inherited social taboos." He added, "and I never remember refusal – unthinkable unless an officer were really planning to marry someone so notorious that it would make the Regiment a laughing-stock. We are a family, after all. But wartime conditions are totally different. I've not had an application formally addressed to me in years – just notifications by Regulars, after the event and only in some cases, as a matter of politeness to the old boy. That sort of thing."

"This is one, sir."

"One what?"

"An application. I want to be able to say that the Colonel of my Regiment approves my intentions."

"I certainly wouldn't approve them if they ran counter to Army Orders or policy at the time."

"Would you not, sir?"

They stared at each other, Mason Vine taken with this hard, slender, quiet young man whose fighting reputation was so considerable, whose name for independence of thought and action had even reached the ageing Colonel of his Regiment, and whose charm when he smiled was so extraordinary.

Again Adam said, "Would you not, sir? Not approve, if I could explain to you why I know it's the right thing to do, whatever the rules, whatever the circumstances?" And Mason Vine looked away and then looked at his young visitor again.

"Explain," he said, "if you could explain, you said— "

"Yes, sir. May I try?"

Anni Carlucci had grown accustomed to the uncertainty, the confusion and the fear. The uncertainty meant that every day might bring new horrors, or, for that matter death; the confusion lay in the sense of muddle which surrounded her and those who had for some months been her companions in captivity, shuffled from one camp or train to another, ordered to "prepare for a move" which never happened, lied to, screamed at, abused, but above all victims of confusion; and the fear, of course, never voiced, was of reaching some even worse place of imprisonment, some place designed purely for extermination where she – they – would vanish, anonymous, destroyed by the inhuman processes of the Third Reich.

Kurt had told her, what seemed long ago, that such places existed. It was a capital offence to talk of such things and even Kurt had spoken obliquely. Why should she and the curious little company of people thrown together during these last months presume that one of those unimaginable places was not their own natural and ultimate destination? They were clearly a nuisance, of little value. And, like the others, Anni had given up any simplistic idea that she might actually be charged with an identifiable offence, straightforwardly, in a courtroom; with a fighting chance of establishing a credible defence. Although, of course, she was in fact guilty.

But Anni had grown used to all these emotions, just as she had grown used to the hunger. She couldn't remember what it was like not to be hungry. There were only two things which custom couldn't soften. One was dirt. She was and she felt filthy, all the time. Washing facilities had varied between the wholly inadequate and the non-existent. Soap – difficult everywhere in Europe – had been unknown for the last three months, since reaching what they all reckoned was Bohemia in the

Czech protectorate. And in this new camp, where they had arrived last night, there was every indication that conditions would be, if anything, worse.

The "camp" appeared, in fact, to be a small requisitioned warehouse, large, bare, bitterly cold and unpartitioned. They had seen wire fencing outside it, but without the appearance of sophistication or permanence, and everything about the place seemed grubby and improvised. They had been pushed through a wide doorway, wide enough to receive a vehicle (or a small rail-car: there were shallow rails let into the floor) and the door had clanked into place behind them. There was one darkened bulb in one corner – the interior was about thirty metres square – a high window, small and barred, in each of the four walls, and in one wall a tap.

Carefully, Dr Wemmer had approached the tap. No luck. Of course no luck. He had turned with his gentle, courteous smile, shaking his head. Nobody had expected better. Two guards brought in four buckets of cold water when they'd been there an hour, and after another half-hour there had been a container of the usual unidentifiable and nauseating soup, shared out with meticulous equity and consumed with silent relish. Things were certainly not going to be better here.

But surely this couldn't be for long? It had the appearance of a place of transit. Inevitably two buckets were the sole sanitary provision: the prisoners had become adept at using these and improvising some sort of privacy with ingenious rules applied by themselves to themselves, solicitous, unspoken. This sort of thing is meant to degrade, Anni sometimes thought, but I suspect we have actually become somewhat better rather than worse people. To dirt, however, she was irreconcilable.

The other intolerable circumstance was her ignorance of the fate of Guido. Five-year-old Guido, last seen when they had arrested her in early May in Italy. They had been very polite. The Signora was requested to accompany them for further questioning. For how long? It was impossible to say. I must make arrangements about my son – Clara, my maid, will need—

And they had intimated that the "authorities" (which meant the German authorities) would assume responsibility for Guido should Signora Carlucci be detained long. Meanwhile, of course, the boy could remain at the Villa Avoria.

Anni had told Clara that she would return soon, very soon, it was all some sort of muddle. Clara was howling in an uninhibited and unhelpful way and thereby upsetting Guido even more than had the sudden appearance of two Germans in civilian clothes who were, as had been instantly announced and in his hearing, going to take his mother away. And thereafter, at every "interrogation", Anni had managed to end with a firm and dignified request. May I be informed of where and how my son is? Surely it can not be the policy of the Reich Government to keep a mother in unnecessary anxiety?

Anni, despite her misery and her hatred of the system in whose power she was, reckoned that she handled this with a certain ingenuity, making her enquiries support her "innocence" in their phrasing. From the first she had recognised that since she was known as a German by birth there was no point in striking attitudes about her legal Italian nationality. The Italians had thrown in their lot with the Anglo-Americans, had changed sides, were causing considerable trouble to the Wehrmacht with their partisan groups, and were, in German eyes, lowest of the low. Italians caught helping the Western Allies or individual members of the Allied forces could expect instant execution. To be Italian in law was no help whatsoever. And to be the widow of an Italian officer who had died fighting against the British alongside the Germans in North Africa was, equally, no help whatsoever. Anni had been canny in her language.

"My son, Herr— " she was never sure of what rank she was addressing and generally gave a military rather than SS title. It never seemed to grate. "Herr Hauptmann, my son may now be in territory occupied by the enemy. You will recognise a mother's anxiety for news."

And news of the war, she thought. The prisoners, eternally on the move, got rumour but little substantial. Initially she had been fobbed off about Guido – smooth words, nods.

"The boy is at your home, he is well, Frau Carlucci."

It was almost as if she really were shortly to be released. Or a little later came shrugs.

"We will enquire."

"Is he still at my house?"

More shrugs. Of course, she thought, the Villa Avoria is probably in American or British occupation by now. It was a curious sensation. And was Guido there? She prayed so. Harm was unlikely to come to him. But he might, he so easily might have been evacuated. Northward.

She had again pressed her enquiry about Guido at the end of July, in a temporary camp in the Emilia, a ghastly place where the intense heat of the Po Valley intensified their other miseries. Rumour had it that the Americans had recently entered Rome and that they and the British were racing northward. One didn't, Dr Wemmer had said with a sigh, race through the Appenines: Dr Wemmer was a professor at Bologna university, a native of Sud Tirol, an Austro-Italian of mild appearance. God knew why he was a captive. Anni had once, delicately, probed and Dr Wemmer had understood her and said, "No Signora Carlucci, I am not, as it happens, a Jew." Nobody was in earshot and he had added, very softly, "If I were a

Jew I should, I think, have been separated from you and gone somewhere worse. Perhaps never to return. That is what was rumoured in Bologna when they" ("they", as always, being the Germans) "took over, as they did, last autumn."

Dr Wemmer was a courteous, intelligent, uncomplaining man with beautiful hands. The captives looked to him for advice and even information. The group had been largely unchanged since July, that temporary camp near Forli where Anni had again managed to face one of her interrogators with a direct question about Guido. Recently questions had been dealt with roughly – "Later, later" or, more infuriatingly, "You will be informed tomorrow." Tomorrow never came.

"Herr Hauptmann, I surely have a right to know whether my son, five years old, is in enemy territory."

Anni knew with every instinct that this group of prisoners was privileged. Hungry, dirty, pushed around like cattle and told nothing; denied all contact with others than themselves except for the ever-recurring, futile interrogations; but privileged. Privileged because there were no beatings, no physical violence beyond a periodic shove to board a truck or train with more alacrity. Privileged to wear their own clothes, verminous though these now were. Privileged because Anni could say, "I surely have a right," without the certain response of a whip across the face and a shriek asking what she meant, that she had no rights – Anni guessed with awful accuracy that a less privileged captive than she would probably have a broken spirit by now. As it was they had been treated with callousness, with a sort of official shrug of the shoulders, but without actual brutality. They sensed that nobody in authority was entirely clear as to why they were wherever they were.

"Herr Hauptmann, my son— "

He looked at her without expression. This one was a good-looking, brown-faced man, in what looked like his middle thirties. He had an athlete's figure, but a stump and hook showed a missing left hand. He had, at that time, been with them a week. His voice showed him to be Austrian.

"Frau Carlucci, you speak of enemy territory. You are an Italian national. What does an Italian national regard as enemy territory? Or enemy-occupied territory? The Italian so-called government made peace with the Americans and the British last year, 1943. And declared its hostility to the Reich."

"Herr Hauptmann, I am a German born."

"That I know perfectly well."

"When I speak of enemy territory I mean Italian regions occupied by the British or Americans. My son is a German's son. His father was an Italian officer. I have no idea how he would be treated or regarded."

"Nor have I, Frau Carlucci."

"So as far as is known, he was left at home?"

A shrug. The war situation was certainly not for discussion with prisoners. Anni, on that occasion, had said, "But you would know, would you not – or could discover – whether he had been evacuated northward, taken away to safety?"

Please God not, she prayed; but I must look as if my chief worry is that he should now be behind Allied lines! What irony!

Hauptmann Felder said that he knew nothing. There would be enquiries. Anni knew perfectly well that there would be no enquiries. Felder, his superiors, the authorities in general, were bored with her, bored with Guido, bored with her case.

The interrogations were by now monotonous rather than alarming. In September Felder had himself conducted one, uninterested except in Anni as a woman. He's thinking, she knew with loathing, that if I were fed up a bit, cleaned up, got into decent condition I'd be quite a bedworthy little creature.

"Frau Carlucci, the old woman, the old nurse who lived in a cottage on the hill near your home, whom you used to visit – she has confessed. She was arrested again soon after you were taken into custody and she has confessed."

"To what?"

"To hiding a fugitive from justice, a criminal. On your instructions."

"Absolutely impossible. I gave no such instructions." This was almost true. Anni had handled old Maria cautiously, had mentioned "a friend in difficulties, hiding for a few days", had undertaken all arrangements herself. All old Maria had had to do had been to keep her old nose out of the disused mill house at the back of her cottage. To keep her old nose out of Adam Hardrow's temporary abode, knowledge of which would mean a firing squad for old Maria and for Anni Carlucci too before you could say *"Entrinnende Kriegsgefangen"*.

"If Maria has said that, it can only be because she was frightened and confused. I told your Feldpolizei everything on the very first evening they visited me. A young Italian stranger, making his way north, had used that hut for shelter, helped my son when he had a slight accident, and then disappeared. That is the truth."

Felder had looked at her. Familiar with the file he didn't believe a word of it, but for some reason the instructions were to handle her "correctly", and she'd certainly stuck to her story. Like his predecessors at the game of interrogating Anni he had changed tack. The real reason she and most of them were here, after all, was not the criminal matter, the capital matter, the unproven matter of helping an enemy of the Reich. The real reason was the very certain matter of being closely related to a traitor. To one of those involved in the appalling events of July, the attempt on the Fuhrer's life. This little Carlucci baggage had been arrested in May on suspicion of the first charge which might never be proved, but was now held on the second count, kinship with one of the treacherous bastards who'd tried to destroy Germany from within.

"We will now, Frau Carlucci, talk for a little about the visits to you at your house in Italy of your brother, Kurt Karlsheim."

"I have, countless times, told all that I can about that. My brother is in the German Foreign Service— "

"Was in the German Foreign Service, Frau Carlucci."

"Is my brother dead?"

"I have no idea. Continue about his visits to you."

It was always hard at this point. Anni loved Kurt dearly. She had realised since July, since some time before this interview with Felder at which she'd pressed about Guido, that Kurt must be in trouble, must have been arrested. He'd never concealed his determined association with others of like mind who wanted to get rid of Hitler and his entire gang. He'd often talked with what she recalled with a shudder was terrifying indiscretion. She, thank God, knew no details, nothing. But when the prisoners' group heard of the attempt on HItler's life – one of the only pieces of news from the outer world which had instantly penetrated – she had guessed that Kurt must be involved. And the persistence of questions about Kurt implied that it was as Kurt Karlsheim's sister rather than as Adam Hardrow's deliverer that she was a prisoner of the Reich.

Felder's questions, that scorching, airless September day had followed a familiar pattern. Frau Carlucci's brother must surely have talked of mutual friends in Germany, at these meetings. What friends? Anni couldn't remember. No particular friends – acquaintances from home in Bavaria came up in conversation, of course they did. And what about Herr Karlsheim's work – did he never talk of it, of how it was going, of how the war was going, of how the general situation appeared? This much-travelled, experienced diplomat with some sort of roving commission from the *Auswartiges Amt*, did he never talk of such matters, matters of such compelling public interest? To a sister? Come, come, Frau Carlucci! Yes, of course we talked, as people talk in wartime – of how things are going, of the latest bulletins. Of course we did. But more generally we spoke of the small things – of my son Guido's character, education, of the privations of wartime—

Privations?

The shortages, the inevitable shortages, that sort of thing.

And had Frau Carlucci's brother discussed, in critical terms, or in any terms whatsoever, the policies of the Reich Government?

Certainly not. My brother, Anni said fiercely and sincerely, was the most loyal German alive. It's true, she thought, and they can make of it what they will.

Interrogations, interviews, travels. Exhaustion, interrogations, interviews. Always she had pressed about Guido.

"There is no information on that, Frau Carlucci."

Anni had for some time decided that she must believe Guido was still at home, in the Villa Avoria – or had been taken by Clara to friends or confided to the aged care of Maria in her hut on the hill if Maria was still there. Her principal terror – that he himself had been "arrested", taken to some refuge for the children of suspects – was something she firmly suppressed. She reasoned. If Guido was some sort of hostage, in the custody of the Reich, he would surely have been used by now as a lever of pressure in her own interrogations? This hadn't happened.

"There is no information about the child, Frau Carlucci."

About Kurt she also enquired, but less insistently. Something deep within her said that Kurt must be dead. It was known – another rare piece of information – that there had been trials and executions, starting on the very night of the attempt on the Fuhrer. The interrogations about Kurt continued.

"We are not convinced that you have been entirely frank with us, Frau Carlucci, about your brother's conversations. Did he, for instance, ever discuss a visit he made to Madrid?"

"Probably. I don't remember anything in particular."

"You are playing the fool, Frau Carlucci. It has been established that your brother was treacherously hostile to the Reich Government. That he actually believed contact should and could be made by dissident groups in Germany with the Reich's enemies."

"You astonish me."

"And you say that you had no inkling of this in his conversation?"

"None whatever. We never discussed politics."

"Brother and sister. Very close. And you never discussed politics."

"Precisely so, Herr Hauptmann. Is my brother alive?"

"Why should he not be?"

"I don't know. It is wartime. People die."

"They do, Frau Carlucci. They do indeed."

And now it was February – February 1945. A cold, bare, grimy, requisitioned warehouse. Another temporary halt, this time, as far as could be gathered and as far as the admirable Dr Wemmer could calculate, still in Bohemia, somewhere north-west of Vienna.

The Battalion had been temporarily re-organised on a three-company basis. Ben Jameson disliked it but recognised its inevitability until more drafts – and more officers – arrived. The drip-drip of casualties as they had pushed northward through the Appenine mountains had been undramatic, incessant and demoralising. The Westmorlands' progress since the previous summer, since the heady days of June and July when they had advanced north of Rome and indulged for a little the sensation of a pursuit, of driving rapidly down the highroad to victory – this progress had been bought dear.

At first the Germans had, undoubtedly, been going back fast and the battalion's few battles had been small-scale affairs against rearguards, comparatively inexpensive in casualties. There had been a few German counter-attacks, company engagements, fierce, brief, disconcerting – which had shown the Westmorlands very clearly that it didn't yet pay to take chances with the Wehrmacht – but there seemed no doubt about the general trend. The Allies were going forward and the Jerries were going back. After the pasting they'd taken in the great battles of Cassino and the breakout to Rome, how not?

But then in September they had reached what everybody, including the newspapers, knew the Germans called the Gothic Line, and thereafter things had gone hard and gone slow. At first it had seemed Jerry wasn't holding to his last gasp, and here and there the Westmorlands heard of significant Allied advances to their left or their right. These advances never seemed to change the general situation, which was that the Germans were perfectly content to go back from mountain ridge to mountain ridge, from one hairpin bend in a steep road to another hairpin bend, from one fast-running mountain stream with mined banks to another fast-running mountain stream with mined banks.

"We now know," the Brigadier had told the Battalion

officers on a visit in which he'd thought it right to give them something of the larger, strategic, picture, "that the Huns prepared the Gothic Line in very great depth. Very great depth." You could have fooled us, the cynical expressions of some of his audience implied. There were an awful lot of Appenines, every crest sequence defensible; and Jerry was thorough.

October, Ben Jameson recognised, had been their worst month. The Battalion had been in high mountain, with company positions only reachable by narrow and precipitous paths, generally under German observation. Enemy mortaring and sniper fire had exacted a nasty toll, taking up food and ammunition to the forward platoons had been a nightmare and getting casualties back had been worse. The weather had broken and the conditions of life in the forward slit-trenches had made it imperative to relieve the lead companies with reserves after a dangerously short period. And the reliefs themselves had been hazardous, as men slithered up or back in the darkness, ever vulnerable to the flash, crump or clatter of a German flare, a German shell, a German machine gun firing on a fixed line.

The men's exhaustion was palpable. Even the mules, indispensable creatures for supply, hardy, sure-footed, had on occasion dropped dead from sheer fatigue. There had been two Battalion attacks in October – both successful and neither particularly difficult – and there had been two long periods of holding positions against incessant counter-attack. The holding had been much the worst, Ben reckoned. An attack worked or it didn't and if it didn't it was hell; but when it was over somebody else had to come to the front of the queue and stir themselves. Whereas these defensive positions in the mountains . . .

In early November the first snow had fallen. And by then the Battalion was almost within sight of the end, the last mountain ridges before the Po Valley, back-stop of the Gothic Line. But Ben Jameson, although he did his best to generate some sort of enthusiasm, some sense of approaching triumph, of hard-won achievement, was sceptical. The Jerries would hang on to a hill-line to the very last. Once the Jerries were back in the valley they would be at the mercy of the Allies' mobile troops, rich in that fuel the Jerries lacked totally.

Once the Jerries were back in the valley they would be dependent on whatever defence they could construct on the river lines of the Emilia, but they would have little chance – either of halting the Allied advance or of getting away to the Alpine passes beyond which lay the Reich. And it would be spring. The Jerries, Ben knew, would postpone that moment as long as humanly possible. Whatever the occasional euphoria of higher authority, the last Jerry positions in the Appenines might well be the hardest to crack.

Snow and frost had come as friends. Mud had been the unrelenting enemy – mud and rain. Winter conditions were harder and cleaner. Spirits revived somewhat. But Ben Jameson somehow doubted whether the Allies would tread the Po Valley before spring. Then, in mid-December, the Battalion had been relieved – not simply for a short break such as had recently alternated with periods in the line, but for what they were assured would be a long rest, almost certainly over Christmas and the New Year, in fresh and comparatively unsullied country far to the south-east, country apparently touched only peripherally by the war, last August. Country where the Battalion would be made up to strength, train, refresh itself, even enjoy itself. Because it was now accepted that the great and, it was presumed, final battles of Italy would not take place before 1945; and in those the Westmorlands, restored, strong, must surely have a part to play.

As Ben looked round his subordinates in December,

therefore, he recognised their sense of pleasant anticipation, so different from the resigned, hard-bitten stoicism with which they had generally come to receive orders. He was, he knew, incredibly lucky. Of the four rifle company commanders with which the Battalion had pushed northward from Salerno sixteen months ago, two – Harry Venables with B and Bill Andrews with D – were still with the Battalion. Both held the Military Cross. Were they stale? In those two cases Ben thought not – he had taken trouble with them, sent them off on some pretext when he thought they needed a break, but each, in his very different way, had shown considerable resilience. Bill Andrews, as ever, was meticulous, somewhat self-righteous, know-all; but reliable and trusted by his men without much warmth. Harry continued light in touch, easy-going, a natural leader, idle if allowed to be idle but never idle when it mattered, and with an excellent tactical eye, and flair. These two were stalwarts.

Geoffrey Purvis, once Ben's own Company Second-in-Command and more recently A-Company commander, had left them – some peculiar sounding job at Caserta. Temporarily – because Ben planned to expand the Battalion to four companies again, when human resources permitted – there was only one other company commander. Simon Entwether had taken over C-Company from the old and true Bobby Forrest in November.

Simon Entwether, Ben had decided, would need watching. He was careful in the judgement because he recognised his own prejudices. First, Entwether was from a different regiment – nothing curious about that in this war but it meant that he didn't begin with the built-in advantage of being one of the family. He was an insurance broker in civilian life, a man of thirty-one or two, who had got a commission in the first year of war, had served with the Pembroke Fencibles – a fancily named Territorial battalion of the Pembrokeshire Regiment, with a long pedigree – in North Africa and Sicily, had done well, achieved company command and won a Military Cross at Salerno. Nothing whatever wrong with the record and when the Brigadier had told Ben that Simon Entwether was joining them and that Ben was lucky, he'd nodded neutrally and reserved his opinion.

It was still reserved. Entwether was a black-haired, tall, strong, apparently robust man who clearly knew his job. He had spent most of the last three years commanding Welshmen, but he'd soon learn that Westmorland soldiers were different, and he was obviously intelligent. The other company commanders – unsparing judges – seemed to accept him. The Regimental Sergeant Major showed no instant antipathy. Ben liked the way, as he could observe, Simon Entwether quietly taught things to his platoon commanders.

He was, indeed, a great teacher, something of a lecturer, and Ben supposed that one of his unspoken reservations came from the sense that Entwether knew and knew that he knew more than most people. In this he resembled Bill Andrews, but Bill was so well-known for his wise-acre, extrovert cockiness that people laughed at him, and he had come to smile at his own words or reactions now and then, and thus, as happens, people had come to laugh with him. Besides, Bill had grown up in the Regiment. He'd been a private soldier, a lance-corporal in this Battalion before being commissioned and joining the 1st. Bill was family.

Simon Entwether wasn't family, not at all. He had an impeccable record and there was no reason to take exception to the frequency with which he cleared his throat and prefaced a faintly dogmatic observation with "In my last Regiment, actually . . .". Ben's irritation was less with the observations themselves (often sensible, by no means bombastic or self-glorifying) than with the insensitivity he reckoned underlay their frequency. Doesn't he realise, Ben thought, that he grates on people unnecessarily? I don't want company commanders grating on each other – he's got a skin like a rhinoceros. But then Ben would tell himself that they were all tired and tetchy, including himself. Entwether did his work well and the Battalion were lucky to have him. Ben knew from discussion with other commanding officers in the brigade how weak many battalions were in subordinate commanders.

There was, however, another reason why the Entwether personality irritated Ben, and Ben was honest enough to recognise his reaction as humbug, and mentally castigate himself for it, to no avail. Simony Entwether fancied himself as a ladies' man. His conversation was laced with accounts of conquests, whether at home, in various adventures in Tunis and Sicily or on occasional forays in Italy itself. The Mediterranean campaign, as far as Entwether was concerned and according to Entwether, had been a merry business except where fear and killing periodically intervened, a progress of Mars and Venus hand in hand. Ben – himself exceptionally active in that direction albeit discreetly so – found this aspect of the Entwether character tedious. He supposed it was sexual jealousy disguising itself as good taste, but whatever it was it nagged him and when he found himself on the rim of some circle regaled by Entwether he as often as not caught himself frowning – or, more characteristically, smiling his very cool somewhat contemptuous and wholly unamused smile. Particularly infuriating – but impossible to isolate and define, let alone do anything about – was Ben's sense that Simon Entwether, aware of his Commanding Officer's own reputation with women, hoped to attract the admiration of a kindred spirit, a fellow-hunter. Ben disliked this impression of his very much indeed, although once again he recognised, very frankly, that there was a fair measure of humbug in the dislike.

The whole Battalion stood somewhat in awe of Colonel Jameson, cool, quick, decisive, apparently at leisure, totally unimpressed by higher authority unless he thought its decrees sensible, unerring in his own military judgement, never raising his voice. The whole Battalion stood in awe of him, and most feared him somewhat. So should Entwether, Ben decided, worthily or not. It would be a good thing if Entwether were left a shade uneasy in the Jameson presence, if Entwether's pulse should quicken slightly when his ears heard the Jameson voice. Running a team with the right mix of whip and affection was a tiring business, Ben reflected – one can seldom be purely natural in human relationships in this game, one would be failing if one were. To an extent everything has to be calculated, every remark or gesture has an effect and one must consider the effect beforehand. It becomes subconscious, of course, but a commanding officer certainly has to wear a mask, and at times its lonely. A second-in-command should help, Ben thought, and I've not had one for three months. Adam will make a difference – Adam arrives in January. Adam, absurdly junior in the Regiment, actually junior by several years to Harry Venables, but so well recommended that they've pushed him out here to succeed me – and more power to them. Adam, years younger than me but with whom I share many perplexing memories, some splendid, some disturbing, none of them dull – Adam will make a difference to us all here, although God knows exactly what form that difference will take.

CHAPTER V

"It doesn't look a bad place," said Simon Entwether, smiling his easy confident smile, "not unlike Corvano if you know what I mean."

"No, I don't know what you mean."

"Sorry, I was forgetting." Toffee-nosed young bastard, Simon Entwether said to himself, referring privately to the new Battalion second-in-command who was visiting his Company. Toffee-nosed young bastard, thinks he's been everywhere and done everything. Hung with medals, never stayed anywhere for long, put in a few months with the ruddy BLA (the British Liberation Army in North-West Europe under Montgomery's command was by no means believed by everyone in Italy to have undergone superior trials to Alexander's men in the Appenines), come out here to lord it over officers who've been crawling up this bloody peninsula since Salerno. And some of them, like Harry Venables, senior to him on the Regular list of these snooty-faced Westmorlands anyway. Not that Harry could go any higher, he's too idle. Still, Hardrow arrives and walks about as if he owns the place; and the Colonel's off to Rome for three days, lucky bugger, and Hardrow's minding the shop. *And* the buzz is that he'll actually get command of us next month or the next. At twenty-six!

They strolled on down the narrow, picturesque central

street of Sotovilla which was not unlike Corvano, whatever that implied, and Adam found himself disliking his companion without justification or cause.

Ben Jameson had been scrupulous. He had said, "Simon Entwether's perfectly efficient. Gives the impression of being a bit pleased with himself but he's all right." There had, Adam recognised, been a reservation in the Jameson voice but it wasn't articulated further.

Adam asked what sort of reception Simon's Company had found in Sotovilla and Simon said, non-committally, that the people had been friendly but quiet. Astonishingly, Sotovilla appeared to have been pretty well left out of the war until C-Company 2nd Westmorlands had moved in for what, with luck, would be several weeks' resting and training; in reserve. It had been different in some places entered by the advancing Allies, Simon said reminiscing. In some places there'd been a Fascist mayor lording it over a cowed population almost until the last moment, and still putting up a bombastic show of being in charge – a Fascist mayor who might still, the population clearly reckoned, have power of punishment. Then there had been other places where the local "partisans" had been active, inflicting, in some cases, their own sort of terror against those they suspected of hostility. If the partisans were Communists – as the most active and effective were – they were determined to frighten into subjection anybody opposed to them on political grounds. A cry would be raised of such a citizen's having "helped the Germans" and no questions would be asked about a summary execution. The British troops had, on the whole, shrugged their shoulders at such alien manifestations. Bloody wops, they said without animosity, often indeed with affection, bloody wops scrapping between themselves, they understand what it's all about and who cares? Roll on the end!

Meanwhile relations with the inhabitants had been jovial

and enjoyable in these last comparatively relaxed weeks. There had been football matches, improvised concerts, plenty of generous if simple hospitality and a good deal of more or less surreptitious courtship. Sotovilla. Not unlike Corvina. Not a bad place at all.

Then there had, Simon said with a curious smile, been other places, where the inhabitants had already experienced the arrival of Allied troops and the experience had been alarming.

"We got into one place where the French colonials had been before us. Goums, they were called, Algerians. The place was deserted. And the Goums had certainly taken it apart."

"Looted it, you mean."

"I do indeed. But that wasn't the main thing which put the wind up the locals!" Simon grinned and said, "And not only the wind! The Goums raped, or had the reputation of raping, everyone in sight – girls, boys, old women, you name it. Everything that moved. They reckon human flesh is one of the spoils of war. It's their way."

Adam digested this. Such barbarity, if stories running like wildfire through Europe were true, was the norm on the eastern front, the usual behaviour of the advancing Russian armies. Something better was expected by the public opinion of the world from the troops under General Alexander's supreme command, but Simon's cynical little sentence, delivered with an "as everybody knows except newcomers like you" note in the voice, held a ring of only slightly exaggerated truth. Adam disliked it and, unreasonably, found that it endeared Simon Entwether to him even less than hitherto. He also noticed Simon's eyes go to two girls who passed up the village street carrying heavy loads, but with bright expectant eyes in their heads. Frowzy black dresses, bare slender legs; Simon's head turned back to the Battalion Second-in-Command. He shot Adam a speculative half-smile, opened his mouth and appeared to think better of it. Adam started asking some quiet, pointed questions about C-Company.

Colonel Ben Jameson, as ever, had been cool and uneffusive when Adam had first arrived. Adam recognised that slightly twisted smile, that somewhat ironic expression in the eyes. Inevitably it would always bring to his mind Felicity Jameson, Ben's wife, bring to his mind Felicity's smooth, firm body which had once, twice, lain in Adam's enthusiastic arms without a shred of profound emotion felt on either side. Did Ben guess? Perhaps. He and Felicity had never pretended to faithfulness as Adam knew well and Ben, long ago, had looked at Adam with a particularly speculative look. Long ago, long, long ago, Lieutenant Hardrow a platoon commander on leave from Captain Ben Jameson's company in France. And now Major Hardrow DSO, MC, was Second-in-Command to Lieutenant-Colonel Jameson DSO, commanding officer of the same Second Battalion.

"Glad to see you, Adam. You certainly get around."
"I'm glad to be here."
"Have they told you that you're likely to take over the Battalion from me at the next General Post of COs?"
"Not officially. I find it altogether incredible."
"Quite. Still, it may happen. I think *will* happen."
"And you? Sir?"
"Brigade command," said Ben with a chuckle. "Brigade command! While this absurd war lasts! That's what the General's told me! Remarkable."
"Not remarkable at all. Absolutely right."
"Thanks, Adam. Meanwhile I'm going to Rome for three days' rest which is the last thing I need. We've been doing damn all for weeks and are likely to continue doing damn all for the forthcoming few weeks. Until the next

big battle, in fact, and there's a chance it will be the last."

And then Ben Jameson talked about the Battalion.

"You're very junior, of course, Adam, but it doesn't matter a damn. Harry Venables is several years your senior, but you've been specifically posted in as Second-in-Command, here it is in writing, and that's that."

"I feel a fraud."

"Probably. I'd simply enjoy it if I were you."

They'd had, in the next few days before Ben departed for Rome, two other and very different conversations which mattered a great deal to Adam. One had taken place far to the north of the Battalion's area, an area with companies scattered among three villages near the Adriatic coast some miles behind the front. Ben had said that there was an excellent viewpoint on a particular mountain village, perched on a spur of the Appenines which ran northward towards the town of Forli. They drove there by jeep, Ben driving himself most of the way. Then they climbed for twenty minutes and Ben brought up his binoculars,

"There!"

Adam followed suit. Ben pointed to certain features – an early February day, the light was clear and beautiful with visibility excellent. Ben indicated where in the far distance lay the ancient city of Ravenna, nearly twenty miles to the northward.

"We got Ravenna before Christmas. But to the west of us the Jerries are still hanging on to a line in the mountains."

Ben pointed. There was the historic Via Emilia, the great straight road linking Rimini to Bologna. It had acted as the indispensable lateral line of communication behind the German Appenine front. Now its eastern, Adriatic, end was in Allied hands, and with the Allies in Ravenna they were astride that same Via Emilia and facing north-west. One more push and Alexander's Armies would be ranging wherever they wanted in the flat lands of the Po Valley. Adam gazed through his binoculars, fascinated. Far to the north were mountains.

"Ben, it looks like Holland! I'd not envisaged this."

Ben nodded. He said, "So much water!"

"So much water. Flat. Water wherever one looks."

"You're looking towards Lake Comacchio."

"It's huge. An inland sea."

"It's certainly big, but the Jerries have enlarged it no end. They've flooded the country west of it, made an enormous water barrier on their left flank. Their present line is along the Senio river which is nothing. Over there. But with a small sea on their left and the mountains on their right they've made it something."

Adam could see dykes, banked-up river banks, what looked like tiled farmhouses. He could imagine their roofs speckled with shell holes, their structures sagging here and there. It certainly was like Holland, astonishingly like. Ben was saying something about having wanted Adam to have a picture of the country, it would now make more sense when they talked about the next Battalion operation, a talk Ben was not yet at liberty to have, even with Adam.

"Some way away, as you'll have gathered."

"When?"

"Depends a bit on weather, inevitably. Not before end of next month. April, even. By which time," Ben added cheerfully, "you'll probably be doing my job. And how delighted I'll be. Meanwhile, however, there are certain things I'm not allowed to discuss."

Then they had driven back to 2nd Westmorlands, a freezing two and a half hour February drive in an open jeep, and when they had arrived and drunk some whisky and thawed out in the dry of the Battalion headquarters Mess in a large Umbrian farmhouse, Adam broached another subject.

"I hope you have a grand time in Rome." Ben was leaving the following morning.

"Thanks. Anything I can do for you?"

"Yes," Adam had said, "there is." And he had explained, jerkily and with embarrassment, that he hoped Ben would find it possible to go to the Vatican City and discover the whereabouts of a certain Father Flynn: would, if possible, actually make contact with Father Flynn in person.

"He rescued me. Hid me when I was on the run. I was in a bad way. I'd just jumped a train and watched Bob Darwin and Tony Perry being murdered."

"We heard all about it."

"Yes. Father Flynn is a wonderful man. He hid me in the Church of St John Lateran and then set me on my way, gave me the addresses of country people who wouldn't give me away, all that. Until I reached your lines, this Battalion's lines, astonishingly!"

All that had been in 1943, Christmas just over a year ago. Since then the Allies had fought their way up the leg of Italy, while in France, with Adam Hardrow landing on D-Day, they had invaded North-West Europe, smashed the Germans in Normandy and advanced to the Rhine.

Ben Jameson said, "I remember all right! Well, what do you want me to do? Find your Mick priest and reassure him that you got away and are still grateful?"

"No, there's more to it than that. I want to find out whether he knows what's happened to a friend of mine. A friend who also hid me and saved me. He knows her, he put me in touch with her."

"Her?"

"Her name," said Adam, "is Anni Carlucci. She was born a German, name Karlsheim." Meeting Ben's amused look and raised eyebrow, he added, "If I may I'd like to tell you about her."

Very quietly he did so. At the end of it Ben said, "You ought to be going to Rome instead of me. Clearly. Equally clearly you're not going to. All right, Adam. I'll do what I can."

Lieutenant-Colonel Wolf von Pletsch gazed through his binoculars at a low, wooded ridge ten miles to the north, one of a succession of ridges which lay between the Drava river immediately behind him, and the ancient Hungarian city of Pecz. The country was not unlike parts of his native Westphalia. There had been snow earlier but by March most of it had melted and the land was green. The next attack was due tomorrow, 10th March 1945.

Wolf von Pletsch recognised that he did his duty on sufferance, working like many of his friends under the suspicious eyes of members of the "Nationalist Socialist Leadership organization", an odious network of Party enthusiasts with representatives, these days, right down to Battalion level. Since the previous July a wave of mistrust had swamped the Army. Generals, Colonels, senior Staff Officers had disappeared. Some had actually and publicly been tried for "attempting to betray the State", and had been executed. The fate of others was unknown. Close friendship, let alone blood relationship, with any of these unfortunates could lead to denunciation, interrogation and the gallows. The gallows, no doubt, after torture.

Von Pletsch was one of a small group of staff officers at the Headquarters of Army Group E, based, if one could call it that, in northern Yugoslavia. Transferred to Germany in 1943 after the Tunisian debacle from which he had been evacuated just in time with a minor leg wound, he had found himself posted to Greece a year later. At first von Pletsch had welcomed the move, and in particular welcomed the fact that a considerable distance lay between himself and the capital of the Reich in the summer of

1944, welcomed, too, the idea of Greece, the image of the Aegean, relief from the incessant pounding inflicted on Germany by Allied air raids – he had been serving in Army Headquarters in Berlin.

Wolf von Pletsch was a good soldier, an efficient Staff Officer, a patriotic German. He had, however, some time previously lost his belief that Germany's future could be anything but disastrous. The war would end in defeat and defeat would be attended by every circumstance of humiliation and atrocity – his intellect had told him that since early 1944. And both his intellect and his conscience told him that the evil he saw coming had been provoked by Germany herself. The cause was flawed. The sacred cause of defence of the Fatherland had been indelibly tainted by the aggressive adventures and the unprincipled character of the Nazi regime.

Wolf von Pletsch had heard in August about his brother, Heinrich. Heinrich, a member of the Foreign Service, had been serving in the German Embassy in Madrid. Wolf's first intimation of tragedy had come in a carefully worded letter from his mother.

Heinrich had been assassinated by brigands of some kind in Spain. The Spanish authorities had not succeeded in discovering the culprits. The Reich authorities had written a nice letter to her – it was terrible, terrible: two Germans, Heinrich and another, had been murdered at the same time. Yet Wolf was somehow certain that his mother was deeply suspicious; had, deep in her heart, felt that behind the "brigands" might be yet darker and bloodier hands.

Wolf had not seen Heinrich since autumn 1942, on leave from North Africa just before the Allied invasion of Tunisia. Wolf realised – it was impossible to be unaware – that Heinrich even then was profoundly sceptical about the government of Germany. This was before Wolf, himself, had lost all faith. They had spoken of the Russian campaign

– the German Sixth Army had reached Stalingrad, the Germans were deep into the Caucasus.

"I suppose you think of it as a crusade!" Heinrich's voice had been ironic.

"To some extent, yes. From all one hears the Wehrmacht has had a good reception in many places. Churches have been reopened – "

"And synagogues destroyed."

A pause. Wolf said, "I suppose so. But, by and large, we are fighting a Christian battle."

Heinrich had smiled and said, "You have been in Africa eighteen months. I wonder how much you know of what has been going on in Germany."

An interruption than, and, somewhat to Wolf's relief, few opportunities for further discussion on those lines. But his brother's disillusion with, even revulsion from, the regime had come through quietly and unambiguously. Wolf's reaction had been troubled surprise, irritation and disapproval. Germany was at war, Germany needed the united, patriotic loyalty of all her sons. Germany was facing an implacable and barbarous enemy. His subsequent and reflective reaction, however, had been one of anxiety.

Now it was one of fear. With what or whom had Heinrich become involved – Heinrich the charming, detached, somewhat lazy sceptic? How had Heinrich died?

The second interview had taken place on the preceding day. The interrogator, a visitor to Army Group Headquarters, had worn SS uniform, but Wolf had seen with disdain that he had clearly never been in the Waffen SS, the armed formations of Himmler's private army who, fanatics as they largely were, had undoubtedly fought well. This man, opening his briefcase and sorting the papers in a file, was no soldier, whatever the pretensions of his uniform, his glossy boots, his meticulously snapped Hitler salute.

Wolf had acknowledged it perfunctorily – the raised arm was obligatory these days, had been made so since last summer. He had counter-attacked.

"I am a busy man, Herr— "

Wolf had affected to hesitate, uncertain. The interrogator had glared.

"Fogel. I hold the rank of *Sturmfuhrer SS*."

"Ah! Well, *Herr Sturmfuhrer*, I have a lot of work to do. Certain operations are imminent."

"I know that."

"Really? Well, what can I do to help you? Two days ago we talked and you asked me about my brother. I told you I hadn't seen my brother for some time before his murder in Spain. You failed to tell me why you were asking."

"No, *Herr Oberstleutnant*," the interrogator Fogel had said, "I did not fail to tell you. I chose not to tell you."

"I see. Why?"

"That is my business. I now wish to ask whether you were acquainted with a friend of your brother, a certain Karlsheim."

Wolf had frowned, glanced upwards as if remembering with difficulty. Karlsheim? Yes, he thought he had met a Karlsheim once, perhaps twice, initially with his brother. A member of the Foreign Service also, would that be right? No, he had not seen Karlsheim for a long time. Wolf's mind had been working fast. Kurt Karlsheim! Yes, he might well be in deep trouble. Wolf remembered. A contact at a Berlin party before he had travelled to Greece. Karlsheim's charming smile, his mention of Heinrich, his invitation to supper. Later, Karlsheim's impassioned, indiscreet, shocking words, quiet, intense. Wolf never forgot his voice . . .

"You are a soldier. You know as well as anybody that this war is lost."

"It's not going well, true." That had been at the end

of May 1944. The Allies had not yet invaded Normandy, the west wall was loudly advertised as impregnable. In the east, however, the Wehrmacht had already been driven back to only fifty miles from the line they had crossed at the dawn of the great adventure in June '41.

Wolf had gazed at the handsome, concentrated face across the table and said, "Not well. But the tide will turn."

"You don't really believe that. And is it right that it should?"

Then Karlsheim had talked urgently and fiercely about the internal policies of the Reich Government. He had spoken of whole sale deportations. He had spoken of camps – everyone knew that they were harsh and everyone regarded that as just, but this was different, unbelievable, horrifying – there were places where there was systematic and large-scale murder of inmates. Inmates sent to them, in fact, to die. Wolf had demurred.

"How can you know such things?"

"I have contacts."

Karlsheim had ended the evening by saying, "We must meet again. I'd like you to meet some friends of mine," and Wolf had bowed and said perhaps. He knew that he still experienced relief that such encounters had not materialised. Within the week he'd been posted to Greece.

Kurt Karlsheim! The interrogator had persisted.

"You have not seen Herr Karlsheim for a long time, you say?"

"That is so. I only met him socially, in Berlin."

"Did you have dinner with him in a Berlin restaurant in summer last year?"

"Perhaps. I was in Berlin at the time, before travelling to Greece."

"Exactly. And you would describe that as a long time ago, *Herr Oberstleutnant*?"

"Yes," Wolf had said with a hard stare, "I would."

The interrogator had then asked whether Wolf knew Karlsheim's sister, a certain Frau Carlucci. Wolf said that he believed he had met the lady once, long ago, also in Berlin. Perhaps before first meeting the brother. Wolf understood that she had been married to an Italian officer. And what a beautiful little creature, Wolf thought fleetingly. Long ago!

The interrogator had returned to the dinner with Kurt Karlsheim, God knew why.

"Of what did you talk at that dinner?"

"That is my business."

"No, *Herr Oberstleutnant*, it is my business. Or may be."

"I have no recollection of our conversation."

The man had certainly not believed him, and Wolf knew that that evening with Karlsheim had impressed him so powerfully, with so unwelcome an impact, that it had been hard to convey conviction when he denied all memory of it. The interview had continued, the probing, the mention of other friends, other acquaintances, some of them now disappeared. But no more mention of Heinrich. At the end of it, when Fogel had at last closed his briefcase, stood up, shot out his arm with a dismissive "Heil Hitler", Wolf had felt absolutely certain that Heinrich had died through the agency of the German Reich.

The attack had gone well, astonishingly well. A new technique had been tried. A whole battalion of tanks had been assembled for the assault on a straggling village, known to be defended by most of the infantry of a Russian Rifle Division. German *Panzer Grenadiers* were to attack the village supported by the tank battalion. The tanks had been given novel orders. Instead of moving with the infantry or ahead of the infantry they were to open on the village with rapid fire from their own main armament, their 75 mm guns, firing high explosive – rapid fire, regardless of acquiring precise targets; rapid fire for four minutes, sending high explosive shells from their high-velocity guns at point-blank range (the tank battalion was drawn up behind a fold in the ground only 400 yards from the objective).

It had been reckoned that this sort of devastating, concentrated, indiscriminate fire could be more effective at silencing, for a brief while, defenders against an infantry attack than all the conventional artillery you could hope for. And artillery, Wolf knew better than most, was in depressingly short supply. There had been mutters about tank ammunition consumption, but four minutes' rapid had not worked out at an intolerable bill.

It had worked – Wolf was due to report, for the Army Group Commander was himself interested in the technique proposed. It had worked, and triumphantly. When the Panzer Grenadiers had swarmed across the ground towards the objective in broad daylight not a single shot from a Russian carbine, not one burst from a Russian machine gun had met them. In the village were a large number of Red Army corpses, a greater number of wounded, and a far greater number still of Soviet soldiers wandering about in a state of befuddlement which owed something to vodka but a lot more to the terrifying four minutes' tank fire which they had survived.

Wolf drove himself into the village. The success signals had gone up only thirty minutes before. He approached a company commander, a tough-looking lieutenant who saluted and reported his company in the usual way. Wolf smiled and held out his hand.

"Well done!"

"Not much for us to do, *Herr Oberstleutnant*."

No answering smile. He's had plenty, Wolf thought.

And I expect he knows as well as I do that this attack, this offensive in Southern Hungary, can be no more than a flash in the pan. The Eastern front is cracking before our eyes. We've been told that this show of ours is going to throw the Ivans into total disarray, send them flying from Budapest, back into the Ukraine. The latest "concept" talked of this making a dramatic and favourable effect on the fuel situation within the Wehrmacht and the Reich. What utter nonsense! After a limited tactical success, like this one here, we'll run out of steam, bound to. Then the Reds will recover the initiative and come forward again, here as well as in Poland and Bohemia and into Prussia itself. They're bound to. There are twenty of them for every one of us. And behind us Germany is being broken into bleeding pieces by bombing.

Wolf looked around him and the lieutenant pointed and said, "We've left them, for the moment. We heard some foreign Press men were coming, but they've not turned up."

Wolf stared. He had seen plenty in this war but this was as bad as any. He said, "I see what you mean."

"There's another whole street like this."

They were standing in a street of small detached one story houses, each set back rather pleasantly from the wide roadway and separated from its neighbour by no more than five or six metres. To the door of every house which Wolf could see – three or four on each side of the street – human figures appeared to have been nailed.

Wolf walked towards the nearest. It was a broad double door, and from each of the doorposts was suspended a figure, clothes torn and hanging, soaked with blood. On the left-hand doorpost Wolf saw that the figure was male. He was attached to the post by two long nails hammered through his throat. He had not died quickly – the contorted face showed that very plain. His genitals had been hacked off. One arm, in a parody of crucifixion, had been nailed against the door itself. Dried blood caked the whole front of this appalling figure from forehead to boots. To the other doorpost was nailed a female figure, in ghastly symmetry. Her skirt had been torn from her, and it was clear that she had been raped with the violence and doubtless with the frequency that had distinguished every inhabited place in Hungary recovered by German troops from the Russians.

The lieutenant said, "Pity no Press photographers! These are the parents, one imagines. No doubt they were positioned to watch what happened to the family." He indicated two small heaps of rags between the house door and the roadway. Wolf took a pace or two forwards and saw that each heap represented the body of a child, a child of perhaps six, seven or eight years. One was clearly a girl and she, too, showed the marks of brutal rape. Both children had had their eyes gouged out. It looked as if, thereafter, their skulls had been smashed before the Red Army moved on.

Adam's first reaction on reading Beatrice Hardrow's letter, a reaction which later made him ashamed of his ingratitude, was one of irritation that yet another complicating factor had intruded into his life. The letter ran:

My dear Adam,
I have been thinking about Stonehead's future. You have often seemed to like it, our family's roots are in this district, there is a certain harmony here between land and sky and weather which one only feels, I fancy, (or at least only appreciates) if it's in the blood. Anyway, that's an elderly woman's conceit, and is the reason why I would like to insert

in my Will that Stonehead shall be yours on my death.

You know the place and you know that nobody, however energetic, would make a fortune farming here. But given care and economy and affection it can just about look after itself, and it might, one day, give you a refuge and a purpose. I shall do this unless I hear from you that you object. I hope that Italy is not proving even more disagreeable than was Holland, and that it may bring some happiness; as well, I daresay, as the grief which is inseparable from war and the loss of friends.

Your loving cousin,

Beatrice Hardrow.

"Bring some happiness— " Adam knew well that Cousin Beatrice appreciated his extraordinary state of mind when he left for Italy – wildly in love with an exquisite creature last seen over a year ago, in circumstances as unnatural as could be imagined; an exquisite creature who had sheltered for weeks at great personal risk a British officer escaping from the Wehrmacht in central Italy and of whose present whereabouts or even existence that British officer had no knowledge.

In those brief disjointed visits Adam had made to Stonehead when he had first returned to England, before D-Day, and again when in transit through England from the 5th to the 2nd Battalions, Cousin Beatrice had divined all this, and the uncommunicative old spinster had understood and sympathised and wished him all manner of well. Adam knew it. He felt an affection for her entirely different from that he felt for his Russian mother, Natasha, whom he adored but who exasperated him. Beatrice Hardrow with her silences and her gruffness and her total lack of emotional self-expression deserved affection of a different sort. It was well salted with respect.

And now she wanted to leave Stonehead to him! He was grateful and glad – grateful at the love he felt behind the gesture, grateful and glad because he loved the north, he loved thinking of its grey coolness, even of its wind and driving rain, of the rough dry walls of Stonehead, the solid stone gate posts and stone slates, the rhododendrons, flowering cherries and berberis untidily crowding the short drive, the yard with its open stone-supported barns, its feeling of half-farm, half-manor, the way it seemed to grow out of the hills. Stonehead might one day be a delightful place to live: but at present Adam's imagination could not possibly leap to a life at peace, a life in the north of England surrounded by sheep and grass and silence, a life without the sound of shellfire, without the rush and bustle of an army at war, without the imperatives of duty and responsibility, without the challenge of danger.

Stonehead – Adam never, in any case pictured himself beyond the end of war if he survived to see it. What he would do or where was a matter to which he never turned his mind. But a life at Stonehead – doing what? Farming? Working at some other profession, locally? Using the place as an occasional home while still in the Army? How could he possibly afford that? He switched his thoughts – this was ridiculous, Cousin Beatrice called herself elderly but she was only in her fifties, she was good for years yet. He'd write, nevertheless, a letter full of gratitude, genuine affection, and as much news as possible. She'd read between lines.

But the idea, somehow both enchanting and provocative, of Stonehead nagged Adam during the rest of the day which brought him the letter. He knew the underlying cause. Stonehead should surely be a family home. One day it might be. And the word "family" brought Anni's face before his eyes.

A few weeks back Ben Jameson had returned from Rome. Ben Jameson had said, "I found your Father Flynn," and had watched, with sympathy behind that curiously twisted smile, as Adam, face taut, had said, "Yes?"

"He was delighted to hear you're well. He hopes you'll get leave to Rome yourself. I said I was sure you would but that you've only just arrived and have got a bit of work to do first. I didn't of course tell him that the bit of work is a particularly big battle, and that it's going to start at the beginning of April!"

Adam stared at his Commanding Officer impatiently, and Ben said, "No, I just said that come May or June you might get away. By which time, no doubt, you'll be commanding this Battalion yourself."

A silence. Ben, tantalising, added, "So that local leave will be up to you!"

The silence continued, and Ben went on, "Assuming, of course, that the battle goes as intended."

His smile faded. He was considering Adam.

"About the other thing, Adam. The lady."

Adam nodded. His expression was very stern, his heart pounding. He wondered whether even Colonel Ben Jameson appreciated with what desperate impatience Adam had awaited his commanding officer's return from Rome. Ben was looking at him very steadily.

"It's not good, Adam. Uncertainty is the bloodiest thing to suffer in things like this and I'm afraid what you've got is uncertainty."

"So Father Flynn doesn't know where she is."

"What Father Flynn knows is that your friend was arrested by the Germans last May. Before the breakout from Cassino, before we got Rome. They took her away. They also took her boy away."

"With her?"

"Flynn wasn't sure. And he has no idea where they took her – his information was from local people. Because there's been no word of her since, the assumption has to be that she was taken to north Italy or Austria or Germany."

"Has he," said Adam grimly, "any idea why?"

"He spoke of her friends and family – she has a brother it seems, who's always been anti-Nazi."

"He has indeed. Kurt Karlsheim. I know all about him. But Anni was never involved with that sort of thing."

"How can you know?"

"I can't, I suppose, really know."

"I don't expect you can. Father Flynn had, it seems to me, quite a lot of contacts in the German Army. He'd had word – God knows how, because by last July when it happened we were already north of Rome and Flynn was in, so to speak, liberated Italy, but he'd had word of wholesale arrests, executions of individuals he knew, of people thought to have been involved in plots against Hitler, in the plot to bump him off. That was widely reported, of course, our own Intelligence has broadcast it. In all the papers. No secret."

"Does Father Flynn think that Anni's arrest was connected to that? Because of her brother or her friends?"

Ben stared at him. "No, I don't think he does. The dates don't fit. The attempt on Hitler was made in July, and your friend was pulled in in May. No, the general impression round her home – sorry about this, Adam, but you've got to know – is that she was arrested because they guessed she'd helped you get away."

"I see."

"But Father Flynn," Ben said, keeping his voice carefully conversational, doing his best, "reckons the odds are she's alive. Don't ask me why he thinks so, but he reckons he'd have heard if they'd shot her." He knew it was best to be clear, not to fudge it, to call spades spades. Anyway what else could you expect in this war? He went on, "Father Flynn thinks he'd have picked it up. It's what one would expect, but he believes it's reasonable to have hope. Naturally the Jerries would shoot anyone convicted of helping one of us escape, but Flynn thinks there's a chance it hasn't happened. For whatever reason."

That conversation had been three weeks ago. In those three weeks the gale of the war had blown even more strongly. In North-West Europe, they learned, the Allied Forces had crossed the Rhine on 23rd March and Adam's heart had leapt with exultation and concern as he thought of the old 5th Battalion and his Company. Very soon, almost unbelievably, the Allies would surely be streaming into Germany, liberating prisoner-of-war camps, bringing the nightmare to an end. In Natasha's last letter she had written again of Uncle Alex Kastron, beloved White Russian Paris-dweller, once "The Czar's youngest Colonel" who Natasha had hoped would once again be in touch when the Armies of Liberation reached Paris but who had mysteriously and alarmingly "disappeared". Natasha prayed, she wrote, that darling Uncle Alex would prove to be somehow alive, perhaps "in one of these dreadful internment camps", and would one day be found, resilient, indestructible. But of course he might, she wrote desperately, have been murdered, like so many. But hope was in the air.

And here in Italy the props were being arranged for yet another scene, a scene which it was permissible to suppose might be the last, or one of the last. Word had come that it would certainly be Ben Jameson's last battle commanding the Battalion, and men were already eyeing Major Adam Hardrow curiously. It still wasn't official but there was no doubt he was going to command next. The older ones remembered him as a lieutenant, but long, long ago. Odd sort of bugger, gave you a funny feeling, electric-like, you certainly knew when he turned up. Handsome, too. But would he take care of them? DSO and two ruddy MCs – nobody wanted him to try to add to that row of medals with the lives of 2nd Westmorlands! The bloody war must be nearly f— ing over, and nobody wanted Hardrow indulging in heroics before the end – except by his ruddy self. Anyway he'd be under old Ben's eye to start with; except that as Second-in-Command he'd probably be left out of battle for this next show and not learn a ruddy thing. Italy wasn't bloody Belgium.

"The Battalion," Ben Jameson said to his assembled order group, "is being divided into two waves for this next attack. Two companies in each wave. That is my present intention, although it may be modified after the opening phases, conducted as you shall hear, by others. No reserve company. Pembrokes are in brigade reserve."

The Battalion had received reinforcements and was fielding four strong rifle companies. Captain Tom Abel had recently arrived to command A-Company, to Ben's private satisfaction. Tom Abel had been Battalion Signal Sergeant in 1940, had been commissioned in the 1st Battalion and had now been posted across. Otherwise the team of Venables, Entwether and Andrews was complete.

"Two waves. I shall command the first wave, of B- and D-Companies. Second wave, A and C, will move under the Second-in-Command, Major Hardrow. We've got two days, and before giving detailed orders I want to talk about the general plan. It's rather a peculiar operation."

CHAPTER VI

In being given an outline of the Allied concept of attack nearly two days before themselves being committed, the Westmorland company commanders, Adam knew, had been privileged. Rather like the Normandy invasion, rather like that D-Day which still sometimes returned to Adam in dreams, the details of this attack in the broad valley of the Po in April 1945 were kept under wraps until the last possible moment. The fact that the 2nd Westmorlands were not to go into action at the very start of the first phase of battle enabled Ben Jameson to give his men an idea of what awaited them rather longer ahead of Battalion H-hour than less – or more – fortunate others. Battalion H-hour! That hour, so often experienced or anticipated, when, to the orchestrated thunder of the great guns, men of the Westmorlands would move from cover, from comparative safety, to exposure, to comparative danger.

Or extreme danger.

In this case Ben Jameson had helped their spirits not by making light of the hazards ahead but by talking about them amusingly and indicating, with whatever sincerity, that he felt thoroughly nervous and hoped that the Battalion's corporate sound sense and his company commanders' competence would help him and all of them get through.

"You've probably had to do with these Fantails, Adam. You can reassure us about them."

"No, sir. I've never seen one."

"I thought they were all over the place in Holland! I gather that was where they were meant to be used."

"Probably. We never saw them in the 5th Battalion."

"Ah," said Ben, "well, we're familiarising tomorrow. I don't care for the thing myself. Awkward to get in and out of! Doesn't look very thick-skinned to me! And although, God knows, I'm not a vehicular or mechanical expert the wretched object's tracks look awfully narrow! I suspect plenty of them will get stuck in the mud. Assuming, of course, that they actually float."

The "Fantail" was a tracked amphibious, lightly armoured troop carrying vehicle. A number had been allocated to the Westmorlands for the forthcoming operation. The idea was to break into and smash the German left flank by crossing the flooded waters west of Lake Commachio and the lake itself; and by seizing a bridge across the Reno river. The bridge was a door to a north-running strip of dry land lying between lake and flood.

If the Allies, Ben pointed out to them, could force their way up this strip, through this gap, not only would the Jerry positions facing south-east between Appenines and Po be turned but Allied mobile forces could have it all their own way in the open country south of the Po; could utterly destroy the Jerries running for the great river, surely their last remaining defensible line south of the Alps. A lot, Ben said in his amused, unemphatic way as he affected to shudder at the discomforts and vulnerability he expected in a Fantail, a lot depends on this battle. I know, he said, that we've often been told this before but if this comes off the end really can't be awfully far away. His company commanders watched him, responding to his mood, smiling at his smiles, thoughtful. They disliked feeling that these were the last Battalion orders they'd hear from Colonel Ben – or for his last battle with them, anyway; there'd be further orders, detailed orders, before kick off, that was clear. Nobody yet knew exactly when the CO was leaving them. Nobody looked at Adam Hardrow.

Ben told them about the air programme and the fire programme for the main attack. The German gun areas were to be bombarded from the air with nearly 200,000 fragmentation bombs, and soon thereafter a further 200 bombers would visit those same gun areas. It didn't sound as if much would survive but Adam, watching their faces, knew that, as in Normandy, as in Holland, they'd all heard this story before and received it with a degree of scepticism. All very lethal, no doubt. All very comforting. But although generals and others were prone to explain that this sort of preparation meant that not a single Jerry gun would be firing, when it came to the crunch there always, somehow, seemed *some* Jerry guns left. And they, God knew how, *would* be firing. Accurately, too.

"Then," Ben said, "we get five waves of fighter-bombers going over – about 500, attacking the Jerry positions five times. Every time, after they've been over, our own guns open up on the Jerry front line and depth positions. Each artillery programme – four of them – lasts forty-five minutes, about a thousand guns, I fancy. The whole thing, fighter bombers, guns, takes about three and a half hours. Not much fun if you're a Jerry sitting behind the Santerno or the Senio or anywhere else."

They nodded, expressionless. A devastating preparation, and in the history books, one day, people would doubtless marvel that the defenders had found any stomach for resistance thereafter, would suppose that an attacking army supported by such a brutal mass of high explosive and with complete domination of the skies would have been able to walk or motor forward with total immunity. They'd experienced this sort of thing before, albeit on a smaller scale. And here, too, they knew that there would still, in fact, be handfuls – if no more – of brave Germans, manning their Spandaus, their Panzer fausts, crouched in their foxholes, in banks, in the ruined outbuildings of farms, in the outskirts of villages; brave Germans, dazed, hungry, long disabused of any hopes of victory and in some cases happy to give up, to pack it in. But in some cases – perhaps in many cases – still selling life dear, still ready to go to another world taking a Westmorland or two with them. Still defiant. Still faithful to the Fuhrer.

"On the fifth pass of the fighter-bombers," Ben said, "they won't actually attack. And that's the signal that the artillery programme's over, and our chaps advance."

There were a few, a very few questions "on the general outline" before Ben turned to the Westmorlands' own role, to the right-flanking operation as part of a detached division.

Harry Venables suddenly said, "Do we know how they're getting on in North-West Europe? In Germany?"

"Pretty well. I gather we're across the river Weser, if anybody knows where that is. And moving towards Bremen."

It all sounded extraordinary; so bewilderingly, so suddenly, after nearly five years, were the Germans being penned and pounded to death in their own heartland.

"What about the Russians?" It was Bill Andrews, knowing, pointed. Ben told them he knew no more than the newspapers and radio bulletins conveyed. The Red Army would soon be fighting in the eastern suburbs of Berlin itself, had driven the Germans from Hungary and already occupied Vienna.

"I suppose, sir, there's no question of them getting on so fast that this attack down here is called off?" It was Simon Entwether's voice, and it wasn't, Adam reflected, a stupid notion although its propriety might be questioned. If, north of the Alps, the Russians were approaching the German capital and ravaging Austria, while the Anglo-American forces were, it seemed, approaching the Baltic, did it necessarily make sense to spend time, ammunition – and blood, including Westmorland blood – on a battle against German divisions who must, in the logic of things, shortly surrender in any case? But Adam was unsurprised by the curtness of Ben's response and the lack of warmth or humour in his voice as he answered Entwether with a "No, no question whatsoever. Any other questions?" And then dismissed them until a further order group twenty-four hours later – after the first phases of the massive attack would have started and when their own objectives and their own timings should have hardened into certainties.

Ben Jameson had described the Westmorlands' operation as "rather peculiar" and had looked quizzically at his subordinates when telling them that the Battalion was to be divided into two more or less equal waves for the attack. It was, certainly, unusual – usually there would be two, even three, assaulting companies with a reserve kept firmly under the CO's hand. The idea of attacking in pre-planned "waves" seemed, on the face of it, to commit the whole Battalion to a mechanistic-seeming concept of battle, rigid, drill-like, with the CO unable to affect the issue by the use of his reserve or reserves.

Adam understood. Adam had talked for a long time to Ben Jameson, and he knew that Ben was uneasy about the entire thing. He was particularly uneasy about the characteristics of the Fantails, although, being Ben, he made light of it. He felt that once embarked the Battalion, his beloved Battalion, would or could be at the mercy of elements completely beyond his control. He mistrusted the protection the light armour of the Fantails would afford while the men were moving on the water – or beached.

More, he was unconvinced of the ability of these same Fantails to move with the agility promised in the muddy areas of the Reno Valley.

And he had, therefore, decided to leave half the Battalion, under Adam, well clear of embroilment in the initial phase.

"Let's see how we get on, Adam. If it all goes well I'll call you up to join us damn quick, don't worry. And I'll know where I want to put your companies by then." The Battalion objective was a village, with two outlying farms, in the low ground east of the north-running road from the Reno bridge. Another whole battalion was being simultaneously launched at the bridge itself, thought to be strongly defended and due to receive the attentions of a formidable force of fighter bombers.

"Of course."

"While just supposing all *doesn't* go well –" He had let the sentence hang in the air. Just suppose it doesn't go well, Adam thought, the CO will only have written off half as opposed to the whole of his Battalion. And himself, of course.

But Ben's concern, Adam knew, was not only with the performance of these unfamiliar vehicles with which the Westmorlands were to make this aquatic foray. It was, and perhaps more seriously, with the situation thereafter. If, Ben had said softly – as if to himself, with Adam his only companion, friend and listener – if that bridge isn't taken we'll be isolated north of it, on the German side of it, the German side of the river. We'll have arrived by water, we'll have artillery support from the south bank, OK, but we'll be pretty vulnerable to any Jerry armour which decides to come trundling down the road north of the bridge. No heavy weapons. No anti-tank guns to speak of. No armour of our own.

The German armour, the Brigadier had said with

115

authority, can be virtually discounted. They have next to no petrol and our air attacks have made their movement all but impossible. Ben quoted this to Adam.

"I don't like 'virtually' discounting things, least of all German Panzers. He knows I'm uneasy about it. He thinks I'm windy, I can see that. I don't in the least care."

That had been yesterday, and now Adam was sitting on the ground beside the tracks of the Fantail in which he, personally, would travel forward when called on the radio by Ben Jameson. They had watched the two leading companies, Harry Venables with B and Bill Andrews with D, grinding forward in the pale dawn light. They were not due to move forward themselves until bidden. Adam had the two follow-up company commanders with him – the newly joined Dick Abel of A and Simon Entwether, the ever-confident, dislikeable Simon Entwether. A headset of a radio on the Battalion net dangled over the side of the vehicle and they could hear the traffic on the air and hoped to read something of the course of the battle. If there were a battle – this operation, at this stage, was simply designed to place the Westmorlands – 2-West R in the unlovely official abbreviation used in brigade orders – in a concentration area behind the enemy's front line, behind the key bridge, to be attacked by others: place them there, having, to the assumed astonishment of the Germans, navigated the flood water which protected the German left flank. Then a straightforward northward attack.

It was a perfectly beautiful morning, and once again Adam marvelled at the similarity between this flat, low-lying land and the Netherlands where he had left the old 5th Battalion, battling from dyke to dyke between Maas and Rhine. In the same way the landscape was marked, and only marked, by long, straight banks – parapets to a defending force – along the tops of which ran roads or cart tracks, and between parallels of which ran narrow rivers and occasionally canals. Even the tiled farm houses – battered, like those in Holland, by war – bore a certain resemblance; long, low buildings ending in massive, attached barns. No wonder Ben Jameson, with his crooked smile, had said that Adam, fresh from Montgomery's British Liberation Army, ought to feel at home.

The radio crackled undramatically. Adam, inwardly amused, saw how Dick Abel's ears were automatically cocked towards it, quicker to receive and interpret noises than the others. Signal Sergeant Abel, Adam remembered – how completely reliable he had been in the old Second Battalion days, 1940, the old Whisky Wainwright days, running from the Germans like spring rabbits and like even smaller ground game cowering from the stooping hawks of the Luftwaffe above! Things were mighty different now! A massive preponderance of ground forces, ammunition unlimited and 500 fighter bombers giving the Jerries full treatment again and again and again. These last two and a half years had certainly seen a wheel come full circle. Greater Germany shrunk to a small beleaguered fortress north of the Alps, with nothing impeding the roll towards it of the Anglo-American and Russian forces, while south of the Alps this futile, last-gasp resistance was being put up in North Italy. God knew why.

Following the invariable instinct of every soldier of whatever rank Adam dozed while the situation allowed. There was nothing to do until they were called forward. Everybody knew the orders. He leant against the bogey wheel of the Fantail and closed his eyes.

"Hullo, Ullo!"

It was Dick Abel, exclaiming. Adam was awake instantly.

"Hear that?"

"No."

Abel said "Sh, sh," and the easily recognisable rather high-pitched voice of Peter Jarrett, the Adjutant, came through on the air. He was talking to B- and D-Companies. He was telling them that Sunray – the CO, Ben Jameson – had been hit "not badly". Were they ashore? After a brief pause the Harry Venables voice said "More or less. Out," and Bill Andrews, meticulous, reported that four vehicles were bellied, one had been hit by a mortar bomb, there had been seven casualties in D-Company, none of them serious and that otherwise his sub-unit was moving, mounted, towards Clapham.

Clapham was the codeword for the area, well east of the north-running road, where the whole Battalion was due to assemble before its approach march and attack on the Battalion objective 2,000 yards further to the north. Codeword Wandsworth. Air photography had shown the entire area of Clapham and and between Clapham and Wandsworth completely clear of enemy positions. In this sector of the front the Germans were, it seemed, relying on a powerful close defence force for that damned bridge over the Reno river, that bridge over which would run the Westmorlands only southward line of communication; and on flood water.

Peter Jarett's voice said, "One seven, did you get all that?" One seven was the call sign for Adam's follow-up wave of the Battalion.

Adam was on his feet. He caught the microphone with its rubber mouthpiece and said, "Roger. Is Sunray coming back?"

A pause. Then the Jarrett voice, slightly hesitant, Jameson no doubt beside him, said, "A bit later, probably."

Ben Jameson would never in a thousand years have allowed a message to announce his wounding if he were fit to remain at duty. It didn't sound as if the forward companies were as comfortable, or had arrived as unscathed, as had been hoped. And until that bloody bridge were taken by the rest of the brigade there was no way south by road – no way south, in fact, except by water and amphibian.

Adam said, quietly, conversationally, "Sunray Minor here. I'm moving up to join you now."

Again a pause. Adam could imagine Ben's irritated shake of the head. That wasn't the plan. He could cope. Tell Major Hardrow from me to stay where he is. Adam could visualise but at the same time knew that on this occasion, rather than conform to orders whether in letter or spirit, he had to do exactly what he thought right. It wouldn't be the first time. Shouting to the crew of his own Fantail, and calling to Abel and Entwether that he'd keep them informed by radio, he climbed over the thin armour-plating and eased his binoculars on to his chest.

Some of the men of the Battalion's leading wave seemed to be sheltering under the lea of a dyke, immediately on the edge of the flood water, itself in this sector an extension of Lake Commachio. Adam's own Fantail had moved with comforting speed, but as they beached on the shallow muddy slope of what was in theory dry land the tracks began to spin and the engine roar. The Service Corps driver swore.

"Too many ruddy boxes aiming at the same effing place! Hang on, sir!" He attempted to reverse into the water again.

Adam said, "Forget it!" and jumped. Soaked and splashing he made his way towards the dyke. As far as he could see a lot of the Battalion was strung out in a long line, right under the dyke. B-Company? Bill Andrews had reported he was moving "mounted" towards

Clapham, presumably on dry land, and beyond his right shoulder Adam could see Fantails moving in a northerly direction about 500 yards away. Among those under the dyke he identified a group which must, he thought, be Battalion Headquarters. Behind him he heard shouts and the renewed roaring of an engine. His Fantail, he saw with a quick glance over the shoulder, was winning the battle. It might even reach Battalion Headquarters before he did.

The Regimental Sergeant-Major, Quidding, intercepted Adam as he waded over. Quidding had been a young sergeant in the 1st Battalion in Crete when Adam had commanded A-Company. He hadn't known Quidding in those days but in these weeks of return to Italy had come to like and value him highly. Sergeant-Major Quidding was not particularly quick-witted but he was thorough, decent, loyal and straightforward. The senior Warrant and non-commissioned officers of the Battalion respected him and if you'd got that, Adam knew, you'd got ninety per cent of the necessary.

The RSM saluted and Adam said at once, "How's the CO?"

"Won't be pleased to see you, sir."

"I guessed that. But how is he?"

Quidding smiled and said, "I'm glad you've come, sir. Colonel Jameson ought to go back as soon as we can organise it, but he's being obstinate. The MO's with him now." The Battalion Medical Officer and a small section from the Regimental Aid Post, again unusually, had travelled with the two leading companies. Casualty evacuation was never going to be simple. Until that bloody bridge was clear.

Adam nodded. Delaying for a further minute his report to an infuriated Commanding Officer, who would chastise his errant Second-in-Command for disobedience as cuttingly as he would anyone else, Adam said, "What happened?"

And Quidding said, "It was real rotten, sir, real rotten. Rotten luck. One of these Fantails, not the CO's own one, another one, slipped back in the mud and the CO had dismounted, as his was stuck, and he couldn't get out of the way. It's crushed his foot."

"Christ!"

"The Colonel's in a lot of pain, I'd say."

"I bet he is!" And so the gallant, quizzical Ben Jameson, survivor of Sicily, Salerno, Cassino and the long slog up Italy had received his first injury in battle since being rescued, leg smashed, by Lieutenant Adam Hardrow on the grim road back to Dunkirk in 1940; an injury inflicted not by German shot or shell but by an awkward British vehicle slithering and lethal in the mud of the Po Valley! How enraged he would be!

But a crushed foot . . .

"I bet he is! I'm glad the MO's here, anyway." Captain Bruce Winton, Royal Army Medical Corps, had a very good name within the Battalion as Adam had instantly perceived with relief. A good Medical Officer not only saved lives and reduced suffering; he had an inestimable effect on morale. Men had confidence that the best would be done for them if it came to it.

"Captain Winton says the CO needs to get to CCS as soon as maybe. CO says later, after the Battalion's assembled, gets going, gets to the objective."

"That won't do. Of course it won't do."

"You'll have to tell him, sir."

Adam strode towards what he recognised as Ben Jameson's Fantail. There wasn't a cloud in the sky, no German shells were falling, temporarily, there weren't even British aircraft disturbing the day's tranquillity, and the periodic rumble of British artillery was a long way to their west, where the main frontal attack across the rivers was making whatever progress it was. A lovely morning, almost peaceful. And Ben Jameson's foot crushed.

Ben was sitting on the ground, his back against a Fantail bogey, his eyes narrow. He had watched Adam's approach. He knew that this bloody foot would create hell again when the morphine effect diminished but meanwhile, and surely until 2nd Westmorlands had completed this essentially simple little battle, he had no intention of leaving them. It wasn't as if he were going to need to walk, run, jump. He turned his mind away from the inevitable requirement to climb again into a Fantail. It was, regrettably, a cross-country armoured vehicle as well as an amphibian and it was going to be needed for the next phase and beyond. But he'd manage. If a CO had his wits about him and his radio was working he could cope with this sort of battle. And his wits, he told himself with anger, *were* working. God, to be one of the very few Battalion casualties in his last fight with them, simply because he'd failed to get out of the way! God!

"Why are you here and not with A- and C-companies, Major Hardrow? I haven't called you and them forward yet. Deliberately."

"I heard you were hit, sir."

"I was not hit. I had a minor accident. It may well be that since you're here— "

"I assumed, sir, that you probably wanted my half-battalion up. Since the first wave are now all here."

"I didn't," said Ben Jameson, rather slowly, his head shaken at Adam in a curiously unreal way, "I didn't intend— " At that moment he slithered sideways. Sergeant-Major Quidding darted forward and caught him, saying, "MO here again, quick." Colonel Jameson had fainted.

Adam had quietly told Peter Jarrett to order A- and C-Companies forward. He had no idea how all this was going to turn out but there was by now no point in leaving the Battalion divided into two. The first wave, despite Fantail trouble, had arrived without disaster. Except for the disaster of crushing Ben Jameson's foot. The other casualties in D-Company were, Sergeant-Major Quidding said briefly and unsympathetically, "Walking wounded at most." Adam had the impression that Quidding was a shade contemptuous about something. Why?

There was no time to ponder such matters. Peter Jarrett was talking on the rear link set to Brigade Headquarters. Adam looked a question at him and Peter mouthed, "Change of plan," and returned to the set. Adam left him to it. Peter was a clear-headed, quietly competent young man – again, unusually, Ben had brought him and a sort of advance Battalion Headquarters with the first wave. Normally the Adjutant would remain at main Battalion Headquarters, near their original starting point. There was no point in Adam demanding to hear any new orders himself. If the Brigadier wanted to speak to him personally he'd say so.

Ben Jameson had been ferried back by a "DUKW", an amphibious logistic vehicle, to the Regimental Aid Post established next to main Battalion Headquarters well south of the Reno river. Soon he'd be moving by ambulance to the CCS, the Casualty Clearing Station, and thence, very probably, to a dressing station, a field hospital, even England perhaps. A crushed foot – Adam hadn't seen it – sounded bad but the language might be exaggerated, the damage relatively trivial. Ben might be limping in within weeks to take command of the brigade he so richly deserved.

Or he might be hobbling, foot amputated, round some rehabilitation centre at home, snarling, sardonic, seducing some of the nurses without excessive difficulty very probably. And Felicity would visit him, cool, unemotional.

What sort of a wife would she be in circumstances like that, Adam fleetingly wondered?

"New orders, sir," said Peter Jarrett. Battalion tactical Headquarters consisted of two Fantails, one or two signallers, Sergeant-Major Quidding, Fred Barstow the Intelligence Officer, and himself. And Major Victor Knott, their affiliated Battery Commander, the man who could, with luck, summon British shells from afar to their support. And the CO, of course, but the CO was now the Second-in-Command. Major Hardrow. Major Hardrow had been due for Battalion Command shortly in any case, it was said, so perhaps Colonel Jameson's mishap had merely brought matters on a bit. Peter had loved Colonel Ben although certainly in awe of him. He wasn't sure what he'd feel about Major Hardrow. Bad luck on his having to take over in the middle of a battle. And he hardly knew the Battalion. It was such a different Second Battalion from the old pre-war outfit he'd known in '39 and '40 . . .

"New orders, sir." The map was spread on the ground and they knelt beside it. Peter, on his own initiative, had told Bill Andrews to stop D-Company where they were – he knew they'd be needed in this direction rather than that in which they were moving, towards Clapham, the original assembly area. Harry Venables, rather silent these days, had his Company near them, under the dyke. A and C were moving by Fantail towards them across the water, ordered up by Major Hardrow before this revised plan had crackled across the air but certainly still desirable in these new circumstances.

"New orders, sir. I think I've got everything."

The bridge was still in German hands. The bridge behind them, south of them, was apparently defended more strongly than expected. For whatever reason it hadn't been taken. That meant that there was no land communication to 2nd Westmorlands. Communication was across water.

Until, of course, the Jerries withdrew from their main positions south-west of them, withdrew towards the Reno and the Po, scarpered. Which, under the fury of British air and artillery attack and the assault of three divisions on a narrow front they surely soon would. Then all this would be irrelevant. Then the German garrison of the bridge would find itself besieged on all sides, would pack it in.

Meanwhile, however, the German front line was still anchored on this infernal expanse of water. And 2nd Westmorlands, scheduled to play their part in securing the only dry passage northward from the bridge for the exploiting armour – 2nd Westmorlands now found themselves largely surrounded by water, on the enemy side of a river with an enemy-controlled bridge behind them, and feeling extraordinarily lonely.

The new orders were simple. 2nd Westmorlands were to turn about and attack the bridge from the north. From the enemy side. It made, thought Adam, sense. It was the only thing which could make sense. But were they strong enough to do it?

Peter sketched in the details. A plan, inevitably, made off the map. A plan which sought to coordinate the movement of troops from different directions against an objective. A convergent movement, where only part of the troops converging were starting from friendly-held territory.

A movement of men on their feet. Or men in these deceptively thin-skinned Fantails.

A movement which would be supported by artillery, provided artillery communications worked, as they almost invariably did. A movement preceded – Peter had scribbled the details – by yet another massive air strike on the Jerry garrison around the bridge. Why, Adam wondered, were any of them alive? He knew, however, that some were alive, enough to hold off another battalion's attack. He also knew that there would still be some alive after the next air strike. He knew, too, that the accuracy of that strike, impressive though it might be, would not be such that the assaulting British infantry could form up sufficiently close to take instant advantage of it. There would be a fairly long, a fairly protracted advance and assault. Supported by artillery alone.

A movement over flat, featureless, water-logged country, with the land round the objective bridge seamed with rivulets, ditches and dykes; land difficult to move over, to manoeuvre over. How well, Adam wondered, did 2nd Battalion companies now move under fire? Ben Jameson was a fine trainer, but during the last year they'd been pushing up through mountains or sitting defending in freezing foxholes. They might move with skill, using such exiguous cover as there was. Adam rather doubted it. Tactical movement, covering ground in small parties with minimum exposure, "dribbling forward" as Adam named it, had never been the long suit of the British Army. Even in the Westmorlands. Even in the old Second Battalion.

And now they were inwardly exhausted – not tired in the conventional sense, they'd had months of rest and recuperation. Training, even. No, they were inwardly exhausted, they'd been out here long enough. And – of immense significance – they knew very certainly that the war was almost won, that on other fronts the Reich was crumbling.

So would they move, not only more or less skilfully, but with much determination? In approaching and assaulting this bloody bridge?

In the ensuing forty minutes four things happened, the first three of them as ordered by Adam. Bill Andrews brought D-Company back from their abortive foray towards Clapham, dispersed them astride the road south of advanced Battalion Headquarters as directed, and reported. Good. Stay here, Bill. Harry Venables, as ordered, had disposed B-Company facing and watching north, also astride the road, and had been summoned.

Then A- and C-Companies had joined the rest. There had been Fantail trouble and some mishaps but the men had arrived although only a proportion of the Fantails were reported fit for further immediate service, in their role of armoured troop carrying vehicles. Dick Abel and Simon Entwether were exchanging ribald reminiscences about their voyage. They seemed unconcerned, unhurried. Adam eyed them as they walked up, glad that they were still light-hearted but knowing that a trial awaited them. It might be almost the end of the war but Jerries were still Jerries and there was unlikely to be anything easy about an assault on that bleeding bridge three miles south of them.

Third – and he knew that he had, as ever, less time than he would have liked – Adam started to give out orders. There was a change of plan. The Battalion, in conjunction with one other which would attack from the east, also north of the river, and with yet a third which would also attack from the east but south of the river and parallel to it – the Battalion was to assault the garrison of the bridge and in particular clear one small village, a railway station and a farm, all on the northern outer perimeter of the bridge's defences. Map references were given. Company objectives were given. All movement would be on foot.

A few eyebrows were raised. Adam said, "On foot. Distances from here are short. The going's soggy, we know that. The protection Fantails give against direct fire is minimal."

He could see they were sceptical. The fact of armoured walls around them could be comforting and they expected it. Adam said again, firmly, "Minimal. They're all right for an approach march but in the assault – and the forming up place is only a thousand from here – we'll move on foot." He gave them the timings and the fire plan and instructions for the Fantails. He suddenly realised that he was commanding a battalion for the first time. Well, he'd seen it done well before – and badly done, for that matter. But he could remember such as Whisky Wainwright, the great and good Whisky Wainwright with this Second and then, later, with the Fifth Battalion – and others. He'd seen it done well, the team seemed on the whole a good one, and Adam knew – and knew he must grip the knowledge firmly for there'd be temptations to neglect it – that once companies were launched on a clearly defined operation nothing but harm would result from a CO trying to command each of them in turn.

There was time to let them express their queries, their anxieties – time, but not much. There was no question of reconnaissance or objective recognition – this flat terrain and the circumstances made inevitable a plan conceived from the map alone.

"Yes, Harry?"

Harry Venables, Adam had noted for some time, was uncharacteristically quiet these days. Adam knew that for Ben Jameson Harry was without doubt the most gifted of the Rifle Company commanders. He was leisurely, rather indolent, brave and charming; and he had tactical flair, an eye for country, a sense of where the Germans would deploy men, which way they'd come, where a Spandau would start snapping on the flank of an attack, or having infiltrated into a defensive position. Harry had form. He was also Adam's senior and a very old friend indeed. An old 2nd Battalion man, Adjutant in 1940, one of the original band of brothers. With Ben and Adam. And apart from a stint instructing at an Officer Cadet Training

Unit in England in 1942, with the Battalion almost without a break.

"Yes, Harry?"

Harry Venables, oddly shifting his shoulders inside his jacket, said,

"Oh it's nothing, really."

A tiny pause, an imperceptible corporate catch of the breath. Adam waited. It was worth thirty seconds' wait to see if Harry really had something to say. One didn't, couldn't, hustle or snub Harry. The others were waiting too.

Into the silence Harry said, "It's really what Simon said to Colonel Ben. I suppose all this is worth while? In view of what we understand is going on elsewhere?"

Adam said, very quietly, "I'm afraid that it is, Harry. We've got our orders." And Harry said no more, but gazed at his map, and Adam looked at his watch. And at that moment the fourth particular event of Adam Hardrow's first forty minutes in Battalion Command occurred, the event he'd not intended. A Battalion signal corporal, minding the Battalion net, was heard calling "Roger out," and again "Roger out" with a particular note in his voice; and then to shout "Sir, sir!" although he wasn't far away.

It was B-Company, who had a post established well to the north of them, the most northerly point of the Battalion. And towards that point, from the north, was apparently rumbling a strong force of German Panzers.

"Frau Carlucci, a word please."

Dr Wemmer was always courteous, formal. In a sense they all were. It was part of their defences, unspoken. Decent manners in a nightmare world of privation, violence and squalor provided some sort of obscure boost to self-respect.

"Frau Carlucci, I heard two of them speaking, mentioning your name. I listened."

They had arrived in this latest place of confinement the evening before and from a psychological point of view this was the worst. The word had passed that they were now back in Austria, surprisingly they seemed to have travelled south again. The place itself was, very clearly, a purpose-built concentration camp, the sort of institution of which they had only whispered to each other; and by now, the afternoon of the second day, they had seen a little of its workings.

By a bizarre sort of privilege they had been pushed along an inner corridor between barbed wire walls. Yells of "*Nein, nein, nein!*" had pre-empted the ordinary human instinct to stare at what was on either side of the corridor, but Anni and all of them had seen enough to confirm that this was a place of fear and horror. The corridor had been long, leading to one isolated hut, not unlike many huts they had experienced in the previous six months – bare boards as beds, filthy barred windows, an unlit stove, two buckets, an iron bar across the double doors. But the corridor had been long enough, despite the yells of the guards, for certain vignettes to print themselves on Anni's mind. And if I saw that, she thought, when shuffling along 500 metres with my threadbare old knapsack, shuffling along for perhaps ten or twelve minutes, if I saw that in so short a time it must go on always, incessantly. That and worse.

She had seen enormous numbers of human beings, wearing striped pyjama-like clothes, their heads covered by flat caps of the same material, moving in groups, carrying what looked like immensely heavy loads. And Anni, almost immediately after entering the corridor, had seen one man, one of a pair, collapse and his load – the loads looked for the most part as if they were concrete slabs

– crash to the ground. That particular load appeared to have, incidentally, fallen on his foot. His mate, the second man with the load, a two-man load, had been unable to help. Now he stood, immobile, helpless.

Anni then saw two other figures approach the fallen man and his erect comrade. They were curiously dressed. They hardly had the appearance or uniform of guards but, equally, they didn't look like the other prisoners. One had the usual pyjama trousers but topped it with what appeared to be some sort of blue tunic, not unlike that worn in Germany by railway staff. The other had a brown uniform-type jacket, open at the neck and, incongruously, trousers of grey serge, as if part of a tidy city suit. The trousers were tucked into huge, high felt-topped boots.

Each carried a long cutting-whip. And, without a word, each started to work on the recumbent figure. Anni saw him writhe and attempt to bring up an arm behind his neck. One of the two tormenters looked carefully and then swung an accurate blow at the wrist of the arm, which fell limply as if independently manipulated. They then returned to their flogging. The whips rose and fell, rose and fell. After a little they stopped.

All this time the second figure had been standing erect. After one or two minutes of this performance one of the two men with whips seemed to scream words at the standing figure and Anni saw him stiffen to a parody of the position of military attention. The two men began walking round him, looking at him, and Anni could see but not hear that they were exchanging remarks and laughing.

She had witnessed this, standing within the barbed-wire corridor, because the little group of prisoners to which she belonged had temporarily halted and individuals, gratefully, had set down their loads to relieve their aching and exhausted limbs.

Immediately ahead of Anni was Dr Wemmer. Anni

glanced at him and saw that he had averted his eyes and was gazing straight ahead, at the back of the woman in front, a lively and indomitable young widow from Silesia by name Inge Barten. Nobody knew why she was in their company, but she had greatly assisted in keeping their spirits up. Anni looked at the dusty-floored compound again. The man who had been beaten lay still, contorted, a pile of dirty rags.

"Dr Wemmer, did you see that?"

Dr Wemmer didn't turn his head. He said, "Yes. Of course."

The queue started to shuffle forwards again. Anni couldn't resist looking once more at the compound, scene of cruelty and suffering. She saw that the two men with whips had stopped walking round the standing prisoner, still erect and at attention: had stopped walking round him, and were standing back a little, giving themselves room for action. Then Anni, as she lifted her knapsack and began to move her aching legs forward, saw one of the men raise his whip and deal the prisoner a mighty slash across the face. She turned away, and perhaps only imagined she heard the screaming.

That had been yesterday evening, still light. And now Dr Wemmer, serious, concerned, was at her elbow.

"Frau Carlucci, I heard your name. They said, I must tell you, it is only right to tell you, they said that your name is on a list to be moved from here."

"Moved?"

"From our party."

"Why me? Any more detail?"

"They said," whispered Dr Wemmer, "that the intention is to move you into the main camp."

For a moment Anni could hardly take it in.

"You mean— "

132

"Yes, it is a – a standard place of confinement. With hard labour."

"I see," said Anni. Dr Wemmer was looking at her with pity and she drew on every inner resource she still had. There were few remaining.

"Thank you, Dr Wemmer. I don't expect I'll be able to avoid it. I shall ask for an explanation, of course."

"Of course." And a whip across the face, thought Dr Wemmer. And worse.

"Perhaps you'll get a chance to wave to me from time to time!"

"I think not," said Dr Wemmer seriously, "I think not. We are, ourselves, being moved tomorrow. Or so I gathered. I do not, of course, know where. We have never known where, have we?"

"No. You're very well informed today, Dr Wemmer."

"I heard more."

"Really?"

"It is obvious – I am guessing a little here, Frau Carlucci – that we are not far from the German front line."

"I see."

"The inmates of this place are being, as it were, shifted to and fro. As the line itself comes back."

"Which line?"

"The East Front, Frau Carlucci. I think. I am not sure where we are, but I think, I am almost sure, that we are somewhere south, perhaps south-west of Vienna."

"So what else do you know, Dr Wemmer?"

"I know, or I heard, that we are moving, our group is moving, tomorrow. As I told you. But I also heard that the whole camp is being evacuated. Which I presume will include yourself, Frau Carlucci."

"Why bother to move me to another category, if everyone's running?"

"I presume," said Dr Wemmer, "that different –

er – categories will go to different destinations. Perhaps."

"And why change my category after what must be nearly a year?"

"I cannot say, Frau Carlucci. I cannot say." He had spoken his warning just in time. At that moment two uniformed guards marched into the hut. One was carrying a piece of paper. The other stood beside him, a carbine in his hand. Both, Anni remembered afterwards, were grinning. For some extraordinary reason the one with the piece of paper muttered something to his companion who bent forward, ran his eyes down what appeared to be a list in the other's hand and then stubbed his finger at it. Perhaps the first one, Anni thought, can't read.

She knew now what was coming and had composed her face when the man holding the paper yelled out, "Carlucci!"

CHAPTER VII

The ditches gave some cover. B- and C-Companies were down astride the road, a thousand yards north of Adam's dyke-side Battalion Headquarters. The road itself ran south-eastward from the village christened "Wandsworth" which had, only an hour ago, been the Westmorlands' objective of attack. Now Wandsworth was, it seemed, not so much an objective as a launchpad for German armour – that German armour which was meant to be incapable of movement, so starved was it of fuel, so exposed to Allied air attack and bombardment.

Wandsworth was just under two miles away. B-Company's post which had reported the enemy's tanks was a little over one thousand yards away. German Panzers could cover the intervening 2,500 yards in five minutes. And B-Company's Projectors Infantry Anti-tank, hand-held weapons of low velocity, questionable both in accuracy and lethality, were just about all that existed between those German Panzers and the whole of 2nd Westmorlands, deploying for a southern advance. All movement, Adam had ordered, should be on foot. The Fantails, beached monsters, were standing about in the fields on either side of the road.

Adam found, and could never afterwards remember exactly what decisions he'd made or how, that he had jumped aboard the Fantail that had once been Ben Jameson's, that he had grabbed Harry Venables and

Victor the Gunner and an assortment of signallers, and that he'd directed the driver, yelling a need for speed, on to and straight up the road towards B-Company – there was, Adam knew, easy access to the road from the lower ground at a point two hundred yards north of where they'd been sheltering in the lea of the dyke. All that mattered now was to move, flat out, towards the threatened point and discover what in Hell really was happening. As they moved, the Fantail tracks noisy, Adam bent his mouth to Victor's ear.

"Everything you can get *quickly* on the road between Wandsworth and here!"

Victor nodded.

Adam bellowed, "And air!" There were complex drills for requesting air support but Victor would be talking to people who knew the form, who'd realise what "Panzers on the road south of Wandsworth" portended, who'd do their damndest.

Along the road, vulnerable very soon now to a German tank gun from a German tank trundling south on the same road, Adam's Fantail moved and Adam's binoculars were up. He could see the road beyond the northern-most point of B-Company now, he could see that so far it was empty. It curved, tree-lined, but he could see it to a point which must be only a quarter-mile south of Wandsworth. Still empty! The flat fields on either side of the road were low-lying but in many cases could probably bear tanks. If the Jerries were really motoring down this road, however, motoring into 2nd Westmorlands, motoring to the relief of their beleaguered bridge garrison to the south, at least some Panzers would probably be coming down the road itself.

Faster! Obstacle free! Exposed, yes, in those places where the banked-up dyke which supported it rose clear of the neighbouring land, but exposed to what? Jerry knew that there were no British heavy weapons north of the bridge, north of the Reno. Jerry, in fact, probably imagined there were no British of any kind on this vulnerable neck of land between the waters.

Until he bumped into the exceptionally vulnerable Westmorlands.

"Stop here!" Adam yelled the command, jumping clear of the Fantail at the same time. Instinct had chosen the place. The road ran across a culvert, and a Fantail could drop off the road itself down an easy slope and grind in, if need be, sheltered by the culvert's concrete. The ground was apparently dry. A shallow bank, affording minimal cover, ran at right angles to the road, northward.

"Get down there and wait!"

For speed regardless of the imprudence Adam, gesturing, pulled the others behind him and ran northward up the road. No sign yet of any enemy whatsoever, thank God, thank God, and the forward B-Company position, consisting of a section with a very young Lance Corporal whom Adam didn't know, behind a bank a hundred yards from where they'd left the Fantail, another bank running at right angles to the road. "Wandsworth" was clearly visible – about 1,400 yards. At this point the river ran parallel to the road on their left and very near it, with only one field's width of dry land between. If the German Panzers manoeuvred off the road it would be on the other, the northward side.

On the young Lance Corporal's right another very young soldier was, Adam noted, grasping a PIAT. He looked absolutely terrified. Behind Adam he was conscious of Victor Knott dropping to his knees and saying, "I got through. They'll do their best."

"May be premature. Corporal – I don't know your name— "

"Corporal Neave, sir." The voice was uneven, slightly choked. Frightened.

"Corporal Neave, you reported Panzers coming down the road."

"I heard 'em, sir. In the village."

Different, Adam registered, but so what? The boy reckoned, very fairly, that if there were German tanks in the village they'd be likely to come this way. Jerry knows there's a battle going on at the bridge behind us. And here young Neave is, with six Westmorland soldiers, a Bren gun and a PIAT!

Still talking quietly to Corporal Neave, Adam said, "Where's the rest of your platoon?" And Corporal Neave, his own voice quieter now, a little calmer, said,

"Over there, sir," and jerked his thumb.

"By that hut?"

"Yes, sir. Think so."

There was a long low hut, about two hundred yards from the main road and north of it. It looked like some sort of farm store. The rest of Harry Venables's northern-most platoon must be there, and the rest of the Company, presumably, somewhere not far from the road, and further back. Bill Andrews, Adam dimly remembered, had his D-Company on the other side of the road, the river side. A lifetime ago, all of twenty minutes ago, he'd been giving out orders for a completely different operation and he remembered Bill saying as an aside, "My chaps are down between the road and the river."

Adam, binoculars up, watching Wandsworth intently, mind racing, Corporal Neave beside him, realised very clearly a number of things. The first was that he, the Battalion Commander, was with the point section of the Battalion, and was close to cutting out one of his company commanders and doing that company commander's own job – doing, very possibly, one of that company commander's platoon commander's job! It was, a signal flickered to his brain, a familiar feeling, a familiar self-reproach. How often, as a company commander, had he not, in exactly the same way, found himself fighting like a junior at the most exposed point, shouting orders, diving into detail, grabbing a weapon? And now, as a CO!

But Adam, secondly and unhappily, realised another thing, had been conscious of another thing for some little time. Harry Venables wasn't functioning. Harry Venables had done and said nothing, was acting as a passenger. Harry Venables was tagging along.

The Venables nerve had gone.

Adam was sure of it. Harry Venables, so debonair, gallant, gifted, Harry Venables whose eye for country, whose sense of soldiering, whose unfussy rather lazy competence made his company love him, feel safe in his hands – Harry's nerve had gone. And there could be no question of sensitivity or niceties. Harry Venables, Adam's senior, once Lieutenant Hardrow's Adjutant and boss, was a liability in present circumstances, and someone else was going to have to cope with whatever happened in the next three minutes. But something, perhaps weakness, perhaps a sense of propriety, made Adam draw Harry into decision.

"Harry, it's when they come down the road and across these fields to the right of us, I want to plaster them with everything you've got. PIATS, Bren guns— "

"What good will that do?"

"— Rifle fire. Everything. Just throw everything at them. From all three platoons. Simultaneously."

"Hmm— "

"So get Corporal Neave back to the rest of his platoon, and bring the other platoons up to that same bank, and the area where we've left the Fantail. And throw everything at them. Never mind how much bounces off them. They'll stop. For a bit."

"Not for long."

Adam knew that he'd wasted thirty seconds.

"Corporal Neave," said Adam. "Double with your section *now* to where the rest of your platoon is and tell your platoon commander to meet me on the road, a hundred yards behind us. Move now!" I've got to command this company, Adam thought, even if Harry goes through the motions he won't believe in what he's doing. He's had it.

To the others he said, "Come on!" and four minutes later was speaking to Corporal Neave's platoon commander, a certain Second Lieutenant Michael Raft, with urgent orders. Then—

"We should," Victor Knott gasped, "get the whole Regiment's fire on the near outskirts of Wandsworth. In one minute." A plump officer he was puffed from the run.

"Can we hold it?"

Victor nodded and grabbed a microphone. Once again they were off the road, by the culvert. Adam had sent word to Harry's other two platoon commanders to move instantly, to move now, up the road towards him. He intended to throw them into fire positions behind the bank which ran at right angles from where they were now gathered. The hut which now sheltered young Raft and his platoon, Corporal Neave and his section, would lie behind their right, when they were all deployed. B-Company, 2nd Westmorlands, lying down behind a bank in the open. A handful of PIATS, perhaps three; nine light machine-guns; maybe fifty rifles. German Panzers 1,400 yards away, having, by the grace of the God who occasionally seemed to protect undeserving Englishmen, not yet advanced to overrun them. And the CO, Corporal Neave said to himself, relieved to be back nearer some of his mates again but only slightly less frightened than he had been as outpost section commander, the bleeding CO, because I suppose Major Hardrow's acting as such, right up here commanding the bleeding company! The bleeding platoon! Christ, what a do!

Adam had sent a man back to find Bill Andrews and bring him, personally, up. Having, he grimly recognised, virtually abandoned his communications as well as his headquarters, commanding his battalion was going to be a hand-to-mouth affair, a matter of runners and shouting and of Peter Jarrett picking up the sense of it somehow, when he could. Oh, I know this is *not* the way to do this job, Adam heard his mind whispering, just as it had often whispered similar messages in the past about company command, platoon command – even when not reinforced by the explicit tongue-lashing of a critic like Colonel Whisky Wainwright. But old Whisky, he thought, would be up here with me, come what may. Perhaps he is.

Adam wanted to tell D-Company, too, to deploy so that every weapon possible could plaster the advancing tanks with fire. Adam knew, every sense told him, that if met by fire, lots of fire however materially ineffective, tanks, even tanks handled as boldly and confidently as were, generally, the German Panzers, would stop, look, hesitate. And artillery fire, perhaps also ineffective in terms of damage, could have a similar effect.

"Yes, sir?" said Bill Andrews, out of breath but scrupulous, saluting. The Second-in-Command would probably be actually confirmed in command now. Bill proposed to act accordingly.

Adam turned his head, "Bill," he said, "I want— "

But at that moment Victor Knott, binoculars up, said, "Here they come!"

A camp inmate now, an ordinary camp inmate, Anni supposed that by some obscure bureaucratic process within the surely disintegrating Reich it had been decreed that her "category" no long matched that of her former companions. Presumably – she removed – this meant that she was relegated to a criminal rather than political list. Because "they" were now sure she had helped an enemy prisoner escape, over a year ago, in Italy? But that was a shooting matter and she'd always stoutly denied it, they had no proof.

Or was it the other way round – they'd dropped the criminal charge and now held her with others of suspect loyalty? Because of Kurt? Nobody said anything. One couldn't tell. One certainly couldn't ask.

Anni knew that the other prisoners regarded her with suspicion, probably with hatred in some cases. She knew, with shame, that although the conditions under which she had existed for the last twelve months had plumbed, in her experience, the depths of deprivation, she had been incomparably better off, better fed, better treated than most of those unfortunates with whom she now found herself. With them life, for longer, probably, than many could now count, had been a matter of surviving from the morning roll-call to the miserable, exhausted collapse at night. Surviving one more day. The marvel, Anni thought bitterly, was that they could want to do so.

Anni knew, too, that the fact that she was wearing her own clothes, rather than the degrading, striped prison garb aroused vicious resentment and distinguished her undesirably. Her "transfer" to the other part of the camp had been in the late afternoon and soon thereafter had come the yelled orders and warnings: they were moving next morning, early. There was, clearly, no time for the ordinary processes of reception, delousing, issue of prison number and uniform. She existed and would march in what she had worn for much of the previous year – her "luggage" was snatched from her, and something recorded in a ledger with a cynical appearance of scrupulosity. She wore a threadbare woollen coat, poor protection against April frost but better than anything on the backs of others, and she felt the glances, the whispers.

It was on the march that the real animosity of others hit her first and hardest. They had all been paraded in the cold of that April morning. They had stood waiting for nearly two hours while whip-wielding tormentors moved up and down the ranks, yelling, counting, pushing, pulling, appearing to hunt for any excuse which could lead to physical violence. Anni had never experienced anything like this before and was stunned.

This was the nightmare she had witnessed on arrival at the camp the previous day, had witnessed, appalled, through barbed wire on the way to her own and the little group's own "privileged" corner, aloof from that nightmare. Now she was part of it, it was all round her. Here a woman was shrieked at to get back into line, mistook the command and stepped forward with a parody of parade-ground promptitude and was instantly slashed across the face; and then, screaming, dragged out and thrashed again and again until pushed back into her place, collapsing, bleeding, a huddled bunch of rags unable to stand. There a woman was formed up with her feet, seemingly too far forward, imperfectly aligned; a "Kapo" – Anni had learned that these vicious overseers, drawn from the prisoners themselves, accorded privileges on sufferance and, from their accents, few of them German, were known as Kapos – ran up, thrust her face (there were women as well as men among the Kapos) into the prisoner's, held her firm with a hand on the front of the uniform, over the breast, and then stamped, brutally, on the woman's feet with her heavy Kapo boots. All Kapos held and used their whips – badges of office and power – at all times.

Then they had shuffled off, four in each rank, parody of a marching army. Failure to keep up, to keep decent alignment, could, it was clear from the start, mean the whip. As they trooped out of the camp, place of misery for many of them for years, Anni supposed, she wondered where Dr Wemmer and the others had been taken. The little group with which she'd passed the preceding months now appeared unimaginably desirable. On the flanks of the limping line of marching prisoners the Kapos moved up and down like menacing sheep dogs. They were, Anni realised with savage misery at the realisation, the lowest of the low, in human terms. They were cruel, devoid of human feeling or decency, exultant in the most primitive and debased exercise of authority. But they were also, themselves, frightened. It took little to sense it. Only gratuitous and ostentatious ferocity could earn them a little latitude from their own masters.

A voice from the rank behind Anni hissed, "Where's she been?"

Anni looked to her front and trudged on. A moment later she felt a feeble blow between the shoulder blades.

"This one! Where's she been? She's new and she's been eating! Look at that neck!"

Anni turned her head, and tried to smile, an ingratiating smile as she remembered later, ashamed. She knew how different she looked, thin, dirty and haggard though she felt, from these pathetic, yellow-faced creatures, with their skeletal forms, their wild eyes.

"I've been a prisoner for over a year!"

"A prisoner!" it was another voice. "Some prisoner! She's had it good! Why?"

"No need to ask!" It was the first woman enlightening the others, her words greeted with grunts "*Ja, Ja*". "No need to ask! She's here to keep an eye on us!"

"No," said Anni strongly. "No, most certainly no! I was transferred from another prisoner unit."

"Transferred from another prisoner unit!" The first woman mimicked Anni's educated voice. A snigger or two went up, and then the second woman muttered, "Watch it" and a female Kapo strode up the line near them and passed.

When the Kapo was a little distance away the same woman said, "Look at that coat! The Countess's coat!"

Another snigger. A different voice said, "A Kapo'll have that – would have already if she wasn't in with them!"

"That's right!" There were several mutters of assent and the first woman's voice said, "I'll have it myself tonight, unless one of you's got a better claim! The Countess won't need it after we've finished with her!"

More sniggers. Anni knew that the wretchedness of the women in the rank behind was finding outlet in bitter resentment of herself. She felt utterly alone.

They were marching painfully up a steep, mountain road. There was low cloud obscuring the peaks. An attempt by Anni to make friends with her right-hand neighbour had failed utterly.

"Do you know where we are?" They had been marching for two hours, with one fifteen-minute halt, just ended.

The woman, a woman who might be quite young Anni supposed, had been gabbling to herself almost the whole march. She seemed incapable of stopping it. The steep walk was demanding their breath and, mercifully, precluding conversation or mockery but this one nevertheless muttered incessantly, Anni repeated her question, more to attempt human contact than in hope of a coherent answer.

"Any idea where we are?"

Gabble, gabble, incomprehensible. On Anni's other side an older woman, a woman with a lined, shrunken face, who had not joined the chorus of animosity, muttered, "She can't talk. She's touched."

Anni said nothing and the same woman said, "She's from Hungary. Budapest."

"She was arrested in Budapest?"

"Sh-sh!" Anni realised that to speak of arrest or anything like it was dangerous, although there were no Kapos near.

The woman hissed, "No, she got away. Got put in some sort of hospital, walked out of it, did something, you know, disorderly. Got picked up. Clapped in with us. Only two weeks ago."

"She was in hospital? She doesn't – she doesn't seem well."

Women in the rank in front of them were turning heads, listening to the conversation. The rank in front, unlike the enemies in the rank behind, had not yet marked Anni and her coat with aimed venom. They all spoke about the wretched gabbling young woman without reserve, as if she weren't there.

One of the women said, "I got a bit of sense out of her when she first came in. She was in Budapest when the Ivans got into her bit of the city – Pest. She was rounded up – all the women were rounded up, every one from eight to eighty they said. Boys too. Then the Ivans got to work on them – you know. Till they were unconscious or dead or something. This one survived somehow."

Organised mass rape, or spontaneous individual rape or a mixture of the two; crowned, very often, with mass murder. It had been a constant theme of Berlin's propaganda as the inevitable consequence of defeat on the Eastern Front. Well, the propaganda was no doubt well-based on fact and here was one of the victims. The woman in the row in front of them who'd first mentioned "Budapest" was still muttering away as she trudged, almost with relish.

"Know what? The Ivans are very near us here. That's why we're on the move. Hear the guns?"

They could indeed hear the guns. There had been a rumble of artillery, a background noise like distant thunder from the east, throughout the morning's march.

"The Ivans may catch us yet!"

They marched on in silence, a new fear drifting like a stink through their ranks. Could it be worse to be caught by the advancing Red Army? Worse than the Kapos with their whips, the threat of instant execution by the guards if anybody stepped out of line, the hunger, the exhaustion, the uncertainty? Could it be?

Yes, Anni recognised, yes, it might well be. Even worse. One might end mad, like this poor creature beside me. Or dead of course.

It was at the next halt that the Kapo incident, as Anni thereafter thought of it, occurred. They had climbed some way up the track, painfully. They were halted – a shrill yell of command, another yell which ordered them to sit down where they were. Despite the frosty April morning everyone was sweating and thirsty. The halt was at a point where the road ran through woods and on one side a steep bank dropped to a stream running over stones. The sound of the water was tempting and delicious. Nobody dared move from the point on the road where they were squatting.

Suddenly a male Kapo appeared. Anni had noted him several times on the march. He was dressed in particularly bizarre clothing, even for a Kapo, with a short woman's fur coat atop a pair of white flannel tennis trousers, tucked into stout calf-length black boots. He wore a chauffeur's cap. He looked absurd; but in this atmosphere the absurd was itself sinister. The women had muttered, "Leo", naming him with particular fear in the voice as he passed.

Leo was striding up and down in a leisurely way. Suddenly he stopped opposite Anni's rank. He shouted something at the girl who gabbled, the girl from Budapest, the girl the Ivans had caught and used until she lost her reason.

"You!"

Anni saw the girl look at him. Then she stood up. They were all squatting on the road.

"You! Out here!"

The girl shuffled past one other woman, the outer file, and stood looking at the Kapo, submissive, without expression. He grinned. Then, out of the pocket of his feminine fur coat he pulled a metal flask. He pointed down the bank at the stream with his right arm and pushed his face into the girl's.

"Down there! Fill it! And if you spill any or take a sip— "

He pushed the metal flask into her hand and gripped her upper arm.

"One spill, one sip! You know what you'll get!" His whip was dangling from his wrist and he gathered it and swung it through the air.

"You understand all right! Now move fast!"

Leo gave a roar of laughter and pushed the girl towards the bank. She said nothing but seemed to understand. Anni saw her move to the edge of the bank and slither down it. Leo, the Kapo, laughed again.

"Hey!"

This was a new shout, a different shout. There had been no uniformed guards visible with the column since they had shuffled out of camp in the early morning but now two guards, materialising from God knew where, had appeared and yelled at the Kapo to come over to them. Anni saw the Kapo, Leo, standing to attention in front of them, having whipped off his chauffeur's cap. The little tableau was about twenty metres from where she was sitting in the roadway.

Anni saw one of the guards gesticulating as he shouted. It was not difficult to guess that he was pointing at the girl from Budapest, the girl dispatched to fetch water. Not difficult to guess, either, that he was asking the Kapo what the hell was going on. A prisoner leaving the line of march! Strictly against orders!

Nor, Anni remembered afterwards, was it in the least difficult to supply words for the rest of the little drama, although the women squatting in the roadway and surreptitiously watching it were out of earshot. Leo was seen to turn and peer. And then to express surprise! Astonishment! Whatever could she be doing?

The next ten seconds would be impossible ever to forget. Anni was conscious of Leo the Kapo kneeling at the side of the road. Then she watched, could not prevent herself watching, while one of the guards unslung his machine carbine and fired a short burst into the back of Leo's neck and head. There was, through the ranks of the squatting women, a hissing exhalation of breath. Leo crumpled forwards and lay in a spreading pool of blood. His fur coat had rucked up to the waist and his large bottom in the white tennis trousers looked gross and ridiculous.

Then they saw the same guard walk to the top of the bank, take careful aim and fire another two bursts, downward towards the stream. A moment later a shout from both guards, instantly taken up by a female Kapo, who had come running on the other side of the column, brought them all to their feet, and the march resumed. Anni found herself now marching as outer file – the woman previously there had smartly taken the place of the girl from Budapest and elbowed Anni roughly to the position outside her.

The woman in the rank in front of them who had told

them the dead girl's brief, awful history, said grimly, "Just as well. She was off her head. They'd have done her in for that if nothing else sooner or later."

And as they marched on, silent now, Anni realised that she and her coat were particularly visible and vulnerable to the escorting Kapos. She was also increasingly aware, as she had been for several days, even before her "transfer", that she felt terribly ill, found it difficult to focus her eyes on objects, found walking curiously awkward as if her legs had no connection with the rest of her body. Her head felt hot and feverish. But a resolution began, too, to burn inside her.

They were all, Adam reckoned, Mark IVs. About seven of them and the noise of more further back. A Panzer company or what was left of it; a Panzer company, presumably spearhead of a Panzer battalion, a Panzer regiment. Ordered, no doubt, to shoot out of the way any inconvenient British troops attacking that key bridge from the north, or interposing between the place called Wandsworth and the garrison of the bridge. A Panzer company with almost no fuel, if British Intelligence had any substance. But a Panzer company ready, nevertheless, to do its best, to sting mortally, to make a mess of 2nd Westmorlands before the end came.

The German tanks had fanned out to the right of the road as Adam looked at it from his position on the lip of a ditch, near the road. Two tanks appeared to be on the raised road itself. They would, Adam knew, feel vulnerable. Unfortunately the Westmorlands had little with which to bring that vulnerability home to them.

The tanks came on slowly. Off the road, Adam reckoned, the going would be soggy, difficult, slow. So it seemed – they could all see the enemy's armoured monsters moving, crawling almost, with what appeared considerable caution across the flat fields to the northward. When we open up, Adam thought, his heart beating very fast, sweat pouring down his face, when we open up they may, they just may, decide to pin us here from the front and send part of the company or whatever it is round us, round our right. And that won't be easy, the ground on that side slopes down quickly into the floods we've just crossed in our Fantails. It won't be easy, it will take them time. But it's just as likely that they'll come brassing down the road, shooting us out of the way like rabbits.

There was no doubt that the tanks deployed off the road were having problems in movement. The nearest were about seven hundred yards from where Adam lay and he thought he could hear, faintly, the roaring of a tank engine, the futile, grinding roar which might, just might, betoken a monster bellied and immobile. It was certainly bad going for armour, no doubt of that and a seed of hope as well.

"Should get some shells down any minute now," muttered Victor Knott.

"Won't put 'em off, unless we're lucky." Adam kept his voice as slow and business-like as he could. He realised he was extremely frightened. I've been in worse spots than this, he thought, but there's no doubt I'm as windy as hell. I suppose I'm particularly windy because I realise that at any moment this battalion, my battalion, or anyway the foremost two companies of it, may take to their heels, may reckon that there's nothing they can do to halt Jerry armour or not enough, anyway. May take off. And the responsibility's mine.

Victor Knott said, "Roger out" on his man-ported radio and looked up at Adam.

"They *hope* to get some air over. I've just said, 'Jerry Panzers on the ground immediately south of Wandsworth. Either side of the road.' I know they're actually only one side of the road but – "

"He's coming on!" said Adam. His binoculars were on the two tanks on the road. They were now moving – slowly, exhaust smoke very visible in the morning air. Adam was conscious of Harry Venables beside him. Harry was talking.

"4-Platoon are completely exposed!"

Harry's voice was still high, jerky, excited. 4-Platoon was, presumably, the platoon Corporal Neave had rejoined, the forward platoon, near the farm hut previously indicated. Yes, Adam recognised, they're completely exposed, of course they are, we all are. So bloody what? There's not much cover on this bit of territory! But bolting isn't going to make us much safer!

He said, "I expect they've got themselves decent positions, Harry. And we've told them to open up with all they've got."

"And give themselves away, for certain," Harry said. His voice was shaking.

Adam shot a look at him. "Yes," he said harshly, "and give themselves away for certain! Now— "

"Shooting now," said Victor Knott conversationally. The sighing of shells overhead came seconds later, and they could see the spurt of shell-bursts well behind the leading tanks, between those tanks and Wandsworth. The leading tank on the road was now 400 yards away, and, Adam reckoned, less than 200 from 4 Platoon on its left flank. Turret and gun were pointing straight down the road. Four hundred, Adam thought, to hell with Harry talking about his lead platoon being exposed, we're as exposed as anyone where we are, right here! But tanks were remarkably blind to decently concealed infantrymen and Adam's little group, like most of 2nd Westmorlands, he hoped, would not be easy to spot. The lead tank on the road having stopped and its commander, no doubt, having inspected the landscape, began lumbering forward

152

again. The tanks north of the road appeared stationary so far as Adam could see. He heard Victor Knott, quiet, professional, correcting fire, attempting to bring shell fire in nearer to themselves.

Then three things happened almost simultaneously. First came a rattle of rifle and machine-gun fire from the area of the farm hut and from a point near the road and south of it, behind yet another ditch, where Adam had pushed in Harry Venables' second platoon; the third platoon was all around where Adam and Harry now crouched. There was a satisfying and sustained fusillade and Adam saw that, even if momentarily, the leading German tank had again stopped. He can't get off the road just there, Adam remembered, good luck or good judgement, it doesn't matter which! Well done 4-Platoon! Then he saw the Panzer turret starting to traverse left. Pray God, thought Adam, they're tucked away as well as they can be, there were some solid-looking walls and a stout dyke there although it won't really help them much against a shell from where that Panzer is now! Pray God, Pray God!

The next Panzer on the road was about a hundred yards behind the first, and the second thing which happened, and happened before the leading tank's turret had fully traversed so that it must, Adam afterwards supposed, have been within seconds of 4-Platoon first opening up, was an explosion which seemed to come from the second tank. For a moment Adam thought an artillery shell had hit the tank itself. Then he realised what had happened. The tank had been hit by a PIAT! A 4-Platoon PIAT, at extreme range and lucky! There was no doubt the tank had been hit. Damage, through Adam's binoculars, was impossible to assess, but a few seconds later he saw the unbelievably welcome sight of black-garbed figures scrambling out of the turret and he thought – while grimly discounting it as probably wishful thinking – that he saw at least one of them fall.

There was a vigorous storm of small-arms fire still coming from the area of the farm hut, as well as from B-Company's second platoon, in makeshift positions between the lead tank and where Adam lay. Adam could almost hear the bullets ricochetting uselessly off the Panzer's armour. Never mind, he thought, the bugger's still halted! He saw the leading tank's gun fire at that moment – a louder roar than any heard in this little battle so far. Then he saw, almost instantly, the smoke and flash of detonation as the tank gun's shell smashed into the roof of the farm hut near which 4-Platoon were deployed. Then another! Then another! Point-blank range, under two hundred, God help them! Adam heard Harry, beside him, mutter something he couldn't catch.

At that moment the third thing happened.

Quietly at first, undramatically, but with sound increasing very fast, second by second, Adam heard approaching aircraft. Coming in from the south-west. At the same time he was conscious of shells, British shells, now falling mercifully near the spot on the road reached by the leading tank. One tank, Adam thought, one bloody tank with the others well over to his left rear, but at least we're giving him something to think about! God knows he's put the wind up us!

A whoosh and crump, whoosh and crump as more shells fell. Victor Knott said, softly, "Here they come! God help us all!"

Adam and the rest of them had the same thought at the same moment. It was one thing to request air support, urgently. It was another, in what military commentators lightly described as "a fluid situation", to ensure that the attacking aircrafts' attention was paid to the enemy rather than oneself. They'll see the Jerry tanks, anyway, Adam thought, heart in mouth, Victor made clear that's the target. Pray God they don't mistake our beached Fantails, all round us here, for Panzers! Victor told them "advancing from Wandsworth" – one can only hope and cower!

The screech of the leading fighter-bomber was intensifying now. Adam, levering himself as deep into his ditch as he could manage, watched. It was a Spitfire – British! Supporting aircraft might be Kittiwakes, square wing-tipped Mustangs, many differing types and many different nationalities of pilot, but the Spitfires, the wonderful old Spitfire with its heroic mythology rooted in air defence over England in 1940 – the Spitfire was British and Adam felt a spasm of chauvinistic relief. Probably unfairly, the Royal Air Force had the highest reputation for hitting the enemy rather than ourselves.

Low, but not very low, a steep dive but not a very steep dive. Well clear of where they were sheltering, much nearer "Wandsworth". The bombs could be seen in mid-air and Adam saw with satisfaction that they must be falling in the general area of the tanks which had deployed off the road, in the low-lying fields north of it. The odds were against a hit, of course they were, but this should have an inhibiting effect if no more. The second aircraft pass followed almost exactly the route and pattern of the first. More little black bombs in mid air, more explosions. 4-Platoon should be having a grandstand view.

There were four attacking aircraft and Adam never knew afterwards what happened to the third, but the fourth and last selected a slightly different line and came in over a point between the lead German tank, halted on the road, and the spot where Adam and his companions were taking shelter. There was a whistle of bombs and Adam, shouting quite unnecessarily, "Keep down, keep down!" saw one, two, three bombs explode on or very near the road itself. Through the dust the silhouette of the tank was visible and Adam, with gratification, heard the rattle of at least two Bren guns from down the road. 5-Platoon, Harry's second platoon, stuffed into some sort of fire positions, completely unprotected, vulnerable whether to the fire of a tank gun looking straight at them from a few hundred yards away, no more, or from the attentions of the Royal Air Force! 5-Platoon, the excellent 5-Platoon – Adam didn't even know who commanded it. 5-Platoon had the sense and the courage to keep plastering that tank with fire. And, from whatever cause, the Panzer had stopped and hesitated. And now he'd had the benefit of an air strike as well, which might have indicated the sort of thing he and the rest of that Panzer company could be in for if they hung about in this bit of the Reno valley.

Victor Knott said, "They're coming round again!" And Harry Venables said, "I wonder how much damage has been done to 4-Platoon."

"Probably not as much as appears. We'll get a Fantail up there as soon as this is over. Use it as an ambulance."

"I think perhaps, I'll go— "

"Stay where you are! Here they come, here they come!"

The four aircraft were coming in from a different direction, from the east, over Lake Commachio. The leading pilot seemed, this time, to have decided he could and should conduct a vendetta with the lead tank itself. He came in lower than on the first pass, lower and even less steep so that he must be taking a tank hull, if that were the hope, from a near-horizontal position. Adam could see the second and third swooping in on the same trajectory – he again lost a fourth aircraft.

The attacker, this time, was not bombing but firing cannon. Armour-piercing shells, Adam remembered, constituted a proportion of what each ammunition belt carried.

The leading aircraft machine cannons opened. Next moment Victor Knott exclaimed, "The others are scarpering!"

"Can you see, Victor? Really?"

"Yes, really. They've turned round. There are two, no three, still there. I bet they're stuck."

And one brute on the road, four hundred yards away, one only. Turret now traversing slowly, deliberately, back to the twelve-o'clock position, to a line towards us, down the road. The aircraft had all passed now, their cannon fire no doubt alarming but as far as the Germans were concerned, unlethal. If further demonstration had been needed that the Panzer company, battalion, regiment, whatever it was, could not advance to the bridge unopposed the Royal Air Force had provided it, but beyond a formidable demonstration not much had been done. Still, some had apparently turned back. It might, it just might, have been enough.

As Victor the Gunner said, "More shells, I think— " the sorely tried Battalion signaller, Private Pell, said, rather more loudly than Victor Knott, and careless of his acting Commanding Officer's presence, "Fucking hell!"

It was another PIAT round. It was another PIAT round from the same place as the last, from near the farm shed, from Corporal Neave's mates or Corporal Neave himself, from 4-Platoon. And it struck the lead Panzer, perched like a range target on top of the raised road, fair and square. Adam watched, fascinated, as what appeared to be an internal explosion convulsed the Panzer. Three seconds later two more black uniformed figures leapt from the tank on to the road. 5-Platoon's small-arms fire cut into them and they both fell.

Pell said again, "Fucking hell!" He was gazing up the road towards Wandsworth. It was clear. The road was clear.

Adam, speaking for anyone within earshot, said, "Fucking hell, indeed!"

"Well done, Harry."

Harry Venables looked at Adam Hardrow silently. He knew Adam, his junior by three and a half years, well enough to be sure that there could not possibly be sarcasm or irony in the compliment, but he also knew that the air between them was far from clear. Harry was incapable of jealousy or resentment that the Hardrow rise in the wartime army, the wartime regiment, had been so meteoric, that his one-time junior as a subaltern was now commanding him. But Harry was also incapable of self-deception.

Adam said again, "Well done for yesterday! B-Company did jolly well. Its extraordinary how often it happens that if you throw everything and the kitchen sink at the Jerries they'll stop, at least for a bit. And, of course, they're windy of the air and our planes came over at a good moment. But it was a nasty few minutes and your chaps were stout-hearted. And two PIAT hits! Marvellous!"

It was the evening of the following day and the situation had changed yet again. After the withdrawal of the German tanks from their short-lived foray southward towards their beleaguered garrison at the bridge there had been no further enemy moves southward from "Wandsworth". 2nd Westmorlands had been ordered to move, with their Fantails, to an area to the north-east, well clear of the recalcitrant bridge and well clear, too, of the scene of the morning's encounter – an area safe, because of water, from German attack.

One must, Adam thought, recognise that today's efforts by this battalion have helped the main battle not at all; but I don't think it was our fault. One man of B-Company had been killed and two wounded when the lead tank had swung its gun on 4-Platoon, but that, with the men peppered or injured during the Fantail approach march, was the sum of casualties. Too many, every man dead or damaged was one too many, but considering the nasty corner the battalion had found itself in it might have been worse, Adam knew.

How right Ben Jameson had been to be sceptical of this operation, Adam said to himself! He still supposed he had behaved with a good deal less than a mature commanding officer's skill and discretion but he couldn't yet entirely perceive where he'd gone wrong. And now here was Harry Venables, clearly in an awful state. The Battalion's best and most experienced and most popular Company Commander, and in a nervous and suicidal condition because he realised he'd been utterly, bloody useless. Because he realised his nerve had gone.

Adam marvelled that B-Company had put up the good show they had. When he'd first appreciated that Harry Venables had cracked he'd imagined that his whole company was probably equally unsteady – the whole battalion, for that matter, was edgy, looking over the shoulder, asking whether the Jerries in Germany had surrendered yet, calculating primarily how to survive. How not? Adam understood as fully as any. But meanwhile the war happened, right here in Italy, to be going on.

And now, a day later, they'd all learned that the Eighth Army battle south of them was meeting with considerable success, and that the Yanks were advancing, far to the west, from the Appenines into the valley. Indeed there was talk of the Yanks soon joining up with Eighth Army, there was talk of the Poles, who were fighting with the Yanks, being nearly into the city of Bologna, miles ahead.

Adam wondered. Harry Venables needed a rest, he needed change, he needed his nerve restoring. He'd probably reached the point where he simply couldn't face another bend in the road round which might appear a German machine gun, couldn't make himself propel his limbs forward across a field knowing that it might still be swept by enemy fire, couldn't even sit in a slit trench without reckoning that the next shell was bound to hit exactly that spot. And couldn't encourage, inspire, bully or cajole men under his command into doing any of those things either. Yet Harry was a brave man. Adam had talked long to Ben Jameson about him, heard his record – especially here in Italy – from Salerno onwards. Harry was a brave, skilful officer. And, now, a menace to his men.

Adam had decided to visit Harry's company area, a large field around one of the long barns which marked this part of Emilia and which so reminded Adam of the Low Countries. He didn't know what to do but he knew he had to do something. The Brigadier had visited an hour ago. The front was loosening up, it looked as if "exploitation", that ultimate mirage, was almost within grasp. Exploitation. Encirclement. Pursuit.

Victory.

And 2nd Westmorlands, the Brigadier said, was probably going to be "lent" to an armoured division, mounted in their Fantails, up with the hunt. If the hunt took place. Any day now. Meanwhile, get a bit of rest.

Adam was sitting on the ground beside Harry. Harry had produced from somewhere a bottle of Italian wine and two mugs. This was a social visit, a human contact, a pleasant reminiscence of the day before, a recall in safety of dangers now past – one of war's more agreeable facets.

And what on earth to do with Harry? If he were removed from Company Command on some pretext – which surely must be right – his morale would be destroyed for ever, his failure would crack him beyond repair. Very possibly the men of his company would themselves fail to understand, would resent their Commander's removal by this newcomer who thought he knew everything and actually knew Italy not at all. Again, might not Harry's utterly out-of-character feebleness of touch have been a passing phenomenon, a thing to forget? Perhaps he wasn't feeling well. That must be it! A flu germ of some sort . . .

The only germ around here, Adam thought miserably, is the germ of a new, unconfirmed young Commanding Officer lacking the moral courage to do what has to be done! How often have I not seen and despised exactly that in others! Adam took a swig from his mug of wine. They were sitting side by side, looking towards the glassy waters of Lake Comacchio.

Suddenly Harry said, "I'm afraid I'm perfectly useless. Just at the moment."

A pause. Adam said softly, "Explain."

"I've completely lost my nerve. I can't explain. There's nothing to explain. One's always frightened— " you, at least outwardly, less than most, Adam thought "—always frightened but I now find being frightened simply immobilises me. I can't make myself think straight or act decisively or even move. I'm sorry."

When he said, "I'm sorry," Adam felt his throat constrict. Harry said, "I know everything you're thinking. And were thinking yesterday. I repeat – I'm perfectly useless. You ought to put in somebody else. To B-Company."

"Harry," said Adam, "listen."

"Yes?"

"What you've just said is extraordinarily brave. All this is temporary, but to see oneself clearly and face it and come out with it like you've done – I think it's very, very good. I really do."

Harry Venables shrugged his shoulders. He's past comfort, Adam thought, but he'll recover. He told Harry, briskly, that he wanted him to take over Headquarter Company, young Will Barker, the captain commanding it, should be given his chance with a rifle company. He'll come over tomorrow, Adam said. It will work very well. Tell him all you can, help him, won't you? And Harry, voice a tiny bit lighter said that yes, of course he would.

CHAPTER VIII

The small mountain village of Pustenau, peacetime population 371 souls, had been jangling with rumour for many days now. There were few young men left in the village and Willi Strosser, eleven years old, had got used to life being dominated by the chatter of women and the sour grumbling of old men. Life in Pustenau was overshadowed by the mountains and the weather, and although the really high peaks were some way off the valley felt enclosed, remote and in a curious way secure. The nearest large town, Willi had learned at school, was 19 km away and he'd never been there. Vienna was incredibly distant, a name, incomprehensible, another world. The small road running through the village wound on up higher, into the bigger hills.

Few cars or lorries came through the village in the normal run of things, and because there was a narrow bridge across a stream in the village centre a track – rough but just negotiable by lorries – ran round Pustenau, by passing the place. On the previous day an extraordinary thing had happened, providing talking material from now to eternity, Willi supposed. An enormous column of people marching on foot had climbed up the hill road to Pustenau. Then, instead of moving through the village itself, they had made the detour, walking along the lorry track, by-passing. This track started 300 metres outside the village, rejoined the road another 300 metres beyond it and was at no point nearer the houses than 150 metres. The marching column, therefore, had passed Pustenau and completely avoided the observation of its inhabitants. The bypass track, furthermore, was rough and stony.

Nor was this all. When some of Pustenau's inhabitants, including Willi's grandmother and Willi with her, had naturally darted out of their houses and started to climb towards the bypass track to investigate this remarkable visitation, a number of soldiers – they looked like soldiers, Willi supposed, grey uniforms anyway – had begun shouting angrily, and gesticulating. "'Raus, 'Raus!"

The soldiers had guns and were pointing people back to the village in a most disagreeable and threatening manner. It appeared that the villagers of Pustenau were not even allowed to see who was marching round their own homes! And the glimpses they'd caught of an immensely long, unimpressive snake of humanity had not been prepossessing. This was not a column of soldiers marching back from the not-very-distant front, as the old men asserted. The marchers were shuffling along wearing extraordinary, ill-fitting garments. No weapons.

"Raus! Raus!"

The Pustenauers had scampered back to their houses. The men with guns looked as if they meant business, and their voices had been loud and hostile. But conversation was excited and speculative later that afternoon when the column had passed – over 2,000, one old man estimated, an ex-soldier from the Italian campaign in the last war; Konni Reser with a stump for a left leg.

"Over two thousand! And a lot of them women!"

Konni was presumed to be able to tell a woman, even at 200 metres, in shapeless garments and viewed momentarily; few girls in the village were safe from him, even now, and he over sixty! But it had been a long, dragging column, no question. And nobody contradicted old Konni in asserting that some if it had been female.

There were, however, other rumours abounding and the people of Pustenau spent much time trying to put all they heard together and make sense of it. One faction – not strong but vocal – was in favour of piling possessions on to carts and moving off westwards over the ridge and along the next valley. Of actually abandoning their homes, migrating. Their reason was loudly given.

"The Ivans are coming! Everybody knows it – they've broken through our boys in Hungary long since— "

"They're in Vienna! They've slaughtered half the population!"

"And as for the women— "

"They're savages! And— "

The larger faction, fatalistic, wedded like all peasants to land and possessions however simple, shrugged their shoulders.

"It may not be too bad! And they may not get here! There are plenty of Wehrmacht boys still between us and them, the papers show it!"

"The papers!" Old Konni's voice was scornful, "the papers! The official communiqués! You can't believe a word! I tell you— "

This conversation or something like it had taken place on many occasions in the last twenty-four hours, Willi Strosser listening, puzzled. People looked away when old Konni or anybody else said you couldn't believe the official communiques – even in isolated Pustenau that was dangerous talk, but Konni had not been harassed so far. But to pack up and leave, trek into the unknown! Willi's imagination caught at the idea. A long walk alongside a cart on the way to Heaven-knew-where sounded rather fun! His grandmother however – both Willi's parents were dead, his father had never returned from Russia and his mother had died in childbirth in '39 – grumbled and wept alternately, and the atmosphere was difficult. Meanwhile nobody had actually left the village, while talk and rumour continued.

Talk, moreover, was generally stilled if the Pustenau blacksmith, Herr Krandt, joined a gossiping group. Herr Egon Krandt held an official position. He was *Parteileiter* Pustenau, the local Nazi Party bigwig. He had had an accident in the forge when quite a young man and as a result part of his spine had been severely injured, and he walked with pain. He had, nevertheless, been able to keep the smithy going, with a younger assistant (now, regrettably, serving in the Wehrmacht far from home).

Krandt derived compensatory satisfaction from his political work and local political power. It was obligatory to report to him untoward circumstances which might, as he put it often and portentously, "affect, even to a small degree, the security of the Reich". Not many occurred in Pustenau. Krandt had, however, a duty to support the morale of the population in his charge, to denounce disloyal talk, dispel harmful rumour and generally keep an eye on things.

In recent weeks Krandt found diminishing respect accorded, but a tremor of unease still rippled through a gathering when he appeared. In the aftermath of the marching column – and, to tell the truth, Krandt had no more detailed ideas than anyone else about them, but thought that they were convicts – Krandt spoke with authority to anybody listening about the war situation. It so happened that the local Gauleiter, a great man, had sent a roneoed flimsy piece of paper to all Party functionaries, however junior, and Krandt had just received his through the highly erratic post.

"You should know," he had announced in the Pustenau inn, a tiny place, "that a strong defensive line has been established east of here. A line running south from Vienna. This whole region is a fortress. No enemy troops will be able to penetrate it. That is the Fuhrer's policy."

There had been other snippets in the Gauleiter's letter, but since it had been written ten days earlier Krandt had a terrible suspicion that some of it had already been overtaken by events. Even the official radio . . .

His task, nevertheless, was to maintain discipline and spirits. Talk of fleeing in front of the Ivans was defeatist, disloyal talk and he made that clear, with a menacing brow. The talk went on all the same.

All this had been yesterday and now young Willi Strosser was strolling along the woodland path which ran beside the stream, upwards from the village. The trees were just coming into leaf and although Willi didn't consciously think in terms of beauty he felt that the day was, somehow, good. The sun was shining. Great adventures perhaps beckoned. The stream sang as it rippled down towards the village, over the stones. Willi loved this wood with its trees to climb, its secret places, its patchworks of sunlight in the clearings. He felt hungry, but then he always felt hungry and in most ways life was smiling today. Willi tried a yodel.

"Hello!"

Willi stopped in his tracks. It had been a voice, a human voice, no question of it. The wood was shared. The voice had seemed to come from a dark place by the roots of a fallen tree. It had been unnerving. These were, after all, difficult, dangerous times; his grandmother spent the day saying it.

"Hello!"

Unmistakable. Soft, not unfriendly. Almost certainly a woman's voice. Willi, daring, took a few paces towards the uprooted tree and said, "Hey!"

A woman's voice, unmistakable now, said, "I am hurt and cannot move. Will you help me please?"

Willi could still see nothing. The voice was distinctive, gentle. The German of the voice was not local German at all, barely comprehensible in fact. The intonation, too – Willi sought in his memory – it was as he'd sometimes heard spoken by the *Herrschaften*, the bosses, the lordly ones. He'd heard it when helping old Konni Reser look after a Count who'd come once for the fishing and needed rods and baskets carrying. There'd been others, too. And what was a lady of the *Herrschaften* doing, lying or sitting injured by or beneath an uprooted tree in the wood near Pustenau?

A few more steps and Willi saw her.

She was sitting on the ground, almost hidden by the great roots – almost as if she'd in fact been deliberately hiding. She looked small and pale and was wearing a woollen coat, none too clean and certainly not new. If this was one of the *Herrschaften* it was a pretty poor specimen of its kind. She looked quite old, Willi thought. She was apparently nursing her leg which was bent under her. Her eyes were very bright, glittering in fact. There was, however, no menace in her that Willi could perceive. He said again, "Hey!"

The woman said, "Will you help me, please? I've twisted my ankle and I can't walk. I've tried and it gives way. If you could walk and let me lean on you I can manage, I think, for a short way."

"All right. How far?"

"What's this village?"

So she knew there was a village. He said, "Pustenau. Where've you come from?"

She didn't answer this but said, "I need to get somewhere where I can rest and perhaps get something to eat."

I bet you do, Willi thought. He helped her up and she put her arm round his neck. She was very light. He said, "Where are you going?"

Again no answer. They hobbled towards the path by the stream running to Pustenau. This is an odd one, Willi thought. He wondered what his grandmother would say, and whether he'd catch it. Their house was at the near end of the village and it was the only place he could think of to take his peculiar charge.

Pustenau was most unusual in one way for so small a place, and most fortunate. A retired doctor, Dr Emil Parsfeld, had selected it as the home of his declining years. Dr Parsfeld, aged sixty-seven, had had a lucrative practice in Graz but had always intended one day to retire to mountains, solitude, books and fishing. He was a kindly, courteous bachelor, respected in the village as the one educated man therein. A housekeeper looked after him in a fine, modern balconied house up the hill, above a meadow, some 300 metres from the village proper. Dr Parsfeld was invariably accessible and friendly. Although retired he was always ready to be consulted "in an emergency" and he shrugged off suggestion of payment – not that many in Pustenau could have afforded payment. The "official" medical centre for the valley was in Larstein, 12 km distant.

When Willi's grandmother saw Willi supporting a strange woman who looked, Frau Strosser thought, extremely ill as well as lame, she was at first completely silent. Her mouth dropped open. Her silence was uncharacteristic, and Willi wasn't sure whether it boded good or ill. He was starting to explain this visitation when, equally uncharacteristically, his grandmother hauled him and the strange woman in through the door of their cottage and banged it to. Her noisy conversations, including ferocious rebukes of Willi, often emphasised with a stick, were usually carried out half in the doorway and half in the road with most of the village listening. Once inside Frau Strosser stood rooted, her face an image of astonishment.

"Who's this?"

"I found her in the wood, Grandmother. I think she's ill. She's hurt her leg anyway. I had to help her get somewhere, she couldn't walk."

"Who – who— "

The strange woman started to talk, a soft voice, trembling slightly, rather high-pitched. She's sick, whoever she is, thought Frau Strosser. I don't want her here. Heaven knows what she's got. And where does she come from, alone in the woods like that? Something wrong here, no question. And her voice – a *Herrschaften* voice, worrying.

"I am sorry," the *Herrschaften* voice said, "to trouble you. Your son has been very good— "

"My grandson." Frau Strosser was eyeing her, trying to think.

"– very good. If I could just rest here for a short while. And if, perhaps, there were some water. If you have something to eat I will pay for it, although it may have to be later as I have no money with me."

No money! A lady alone in the woods with no money!

At that moment the strange woman gave a little cry and fainted, crumpling to the cottage floor. And Frau Strosser, doing the only thing she could think of, ordered Willi to run to Dr Parsfeld and ask him if he could possibly pay a visit. And don't forget to take your cap off and bow, she snapped at him, as he moved towards the door; and don't speak to anybody about this on the way there or back, she hissed as he passed through it.

Emil Parsfeld was at home and agreed to accompany Willi. On the way he asked what was the trouble and was somewhat mystified by the response. A small, worrying idea, however, started in his mind, and when he saw Frau Strosser's unbidden guest, now restored to consciousness, the idea was not dispelled. He examined her, took her temperature and looked at throat and eyes. He then said briskly, "You have torn a ligament. It is nothing. I will strap it up and you need to rest it. You will not be able to walk, except with difficulty for a few days. And how are you feeling?"

"It is nothing. My leg— "

"I do not mean your leg. You are ill, you know that?"

"I feel – perhaps I have a touch of influenza?"

"More than that, Frau – I do not know your name."

After a pause she said, "Frau Carlucci."

"I see. You are from Sud-Tirol, perhaps? From the province taken by Italy?"

"No. My husband was Italian. I am German, not Austrian."

"And may I ask, Frau Carlucci, what you were doing with a high fever and a twisted ankle, lying in a wood near Pustenau, all by yourself on an April morning?"

"I was lost. I was trying— "

"Trying?"

Anni burst into tears. Her powers of invention had completely left her. Dr Parsfeld said, "You need attention. You should really be in a hospital. The nearest is twenty-five kilometres away and in these times it will be difficult. In a hospital, of course, full particulars will be taken."

He was watching her.

"You are seriously undernourished, Frau Carlucci. We will get the fever down, that will not be too difficult, and we will see if we can feed you a little better than seems to have been done for some time. It is not easy to get things now but we will do our best."

Anni said, "We— " interrogatively, and Dr Parsfeld

said quietly, "I suggest you move to my house. I have a small pony cart and an old beast not taken by the army and I will fetch you and help you. I have an elderly housekeeper who looks after me and will help look after you."

Anni muttered, "Thank you." She had only taken in part of this. She was unsure where she was. All she could remember was that on no account should "the authorities" find her and take her back to that terrible, terrible marching column or whatever hell they were tramping towards. She could also just remember the relief which the sharp agony of a wrenched ankle had in no way lessened, when she realised that her plan had succeeded, that there had been no guard or kapo within sight for a brief, terrifying instant when passing through the wood, and that she had managed to do as she intended, to drop to the side of the column as if fainting and then to roll, like one dead, over the edge of the slope to trees and cover.

Dr Parsfeld spoke some brisk, reassuring words to Frau Strosser, gave a few brief instructions and departed. One hour later his pony trap headed from the Strosser house to the bypass track and thus to the Parsfeld house. Only the eyes of Egon Krandt followed it inquisitively on its way.

It was 24th April. Adam Hardrow was giving out orders. 2nd Westmorlands were to cross the river Po.

The Battalion, using its residue of Fantails for the actual crossing (many had been re-allocated elsewhere within their brigade) was also assisted by twelve soft-skinned amphibious vehicles, the capacious DUKW – "Ducks" to the soldiers and invariably spelled as such. The river was wide, and the swim would be a long one. It would be undertaken in darkness.

The river was edged on both sides by a steep artificial bank, along which ran a road. Behind the near bank troops and vehicles could assemble, it was hoped undetected;

they could only reach the water itself at particular points through or over the artificial bank, points used by and certainly familiar to the Germans. And on emerging from the water the far bank would have to be negotiated. Lines of poplar trees fringed the banks on both sides. It was, Adam had decided, not an operation which would be particularly attractive if the Jerries were not on their last legs.

But they were.

The concentration of troops near the river, in entirely predictable forming up places, was appallingly vulnerable to the Jerry guns and mortars. But they didn't have much, if any, ammunition left, it appeared. And since the Allies had complete control of the air, Jerry had virtually no way of acquiring targets, even if he had guns and shells. Or way of observing fire.

Nevertheless on debouching from the water on the far bank the Westmorland companies would be, must be, vulnerable. A few well-sited Spandaus, a few brave and desperate soldiers ready to die for the Fuhrer, and the leading companies could be slashed to bloody pieces. Adam's mind went back to a certain beach in Normandy on 6th June last year. Bobbing about on water or emerging from it if bullets were cutting into you and your companions was no fun. He knew this better than any of them.

He smiled confidently at his company commanders.

"First phase, crossing by two companies, left C, right D. Here are the objectives."

The Battalion Intelligence Officer indicated them on the map. They involved climbing over the northern bank, having negotiated the river, and assaulting across what appeared from the air photographs to be a cluster of small fields, in order to make good a lateral track and take a village only 200 yards from the Po. It was a straggling east-west village. Once C and D were secure on these objectives they could sweep the ground behind the northern bank for several hundred metres in both directions, and under that cover A- and B-Companies, Dick Abel and the untried Will Barker, would cross in "Ducks" and move north from the northern bank to deeper objectives about 600 yards beyond. The Westmorland bridgehead would then be used by another battalion of the brigade, and when the bridgehead had been expanded and secured a regular ferry service would start, and armour cross. And then, of course, there would be bridges built. Adam hoped he exuded confidence.

The hope was justified. Adam didn't hear Will Barker with Dick Abel as they left the Order Group but he would have been gratified. Will – secretly immensely relieved that his was to be one of the second wave companies, while sufficiently nervous of the thereafter – murmured to Dick Abel,

"Pretty clear, isn't it!"

"Perfectly clear. The air photos were good."

"Colonel Adam was first-class, wasn't he!" Adam had been confirmed in command and the signal appointing him acting Lieutenant-Colonel had been received the day before.

"Yes," said Dick Abel non-committally, "he knows what he's on all right. Always did."

At 3 am on the following morning Adam's own Duck slipped into the water.

Simon Entwether's Company on the left and Bill Andrews with D on the right appeared to have got across with next to no opposition. There had been one short burst of Spandau fire in the Entwether sector, as far as Adam could make out well after they had beached – probably when they were crossing the northern artificial bank. C-Company must be over that now and swarming towards the village objective. Soon, if all went well, there would be a success signal showing objectives taken. The follow-up companies were only to launch on that signal.

Adam's instinct had been to cross with the two leading companies and he had resisted that instinct. Now he wondered whether he had been right. He had told himself, trying to be objective, that his besetting fault was that of seeking to command the point section, seeking to influence from the tip of the arrow. You couldn't influence from the tip of the arrow. It might gratify some sort of need for self-proving to be there, but all too often that gratification meant doing a subordinate's job and not your own. There was, of course, always the nagging feeling that you were committing others to risks you weren't sharing, but so what? That was part of the business of command, at every level. You had your own job to do. Conscious of all this, as well as of the fact that he was a novice, Adam had decided that he and his small command team of Gunner, Intelligence Officer and signallers would not cross until the leading companies were well under way.

And now he wondered and was uncertain, an uncertainty he recognised none must perceive. Was he not, in fact, ineffective where he had placed himself? He could divert or cancel the crossing of the second wave of companies, of course, but he could do that as well from the far bank, from up with the lead companies, and would have, perhaps, a clearer picture of what change of plan might be appropriate if things went wrong. Might it, on the other hand, have been better to move with, or behind, the rear two companies? Some old adage had stuck in Adam's mind, perhaps from the lore of Whisky Wainwright, perhaps from some forgotten textbook – "You command everything behind you, nothing in front of you."

Might it not have been wiser, after all, to obey instinct

and move with the leading companies, share their hazards in the darkness, draw on their strength and lend them whatever he had of his own? And here I am, Adam thought, controlling this historic movement, commanding the Battalion for my first set-piece operation and I'm fussing about where I, personally, ought to be and what I, personally, ought to be doing! I've got an awful lot to learn! The two Ducks of Adam's party gathered speed and at that moment he saw, with profound relief, the first success signal go up, the Verey lights from Simon Entwether's Company. Before he reached the far bank the sky was lit by more Verey lights from Bill Andrews's company, and looking back through the darkness Adam could see the silhouettes of Dick Abel's and Will Barker's vehicles top the southern bank and lose themselves from sight as they ground down towards the water. And so far, Adam said to himself, hardly any opposition! Hardly a shot fired from behind one of the largest rivers and most defensible obstacles in this part of Europe! And like almost every man in 2nd Westmorlands, he also allowed himself to reflect that the end couldn't, really couldn't, be very far away.

Twenty minutes later Adam, with an alarming sense of success too cheaply earned, started moving in his Duck, the novel base for Battalion battle headquarters, towards C-Company's objective, the village of Prova. The light was thinning and Adam was able to see that the ground looked exactly as the air photographs had shown – small fields edged by ditches, flat, treeless except for the belt of poplars along the river bank, now etched against the sky.

The track he was moving along ran straight to Prova; it had shown clearly on photographs and had been the axis for C-Company's advance. C-Company had, Adam thought with satisfaction, made damned good time from the crossing. Artillery tasks had been "on call", gunfire to be invoked if opposition were met. None had sounded – the night had been marked by the original roar of artillery shooting in greater depth, shooting at known German gun positions. There had been no Jerry response, no Jerry response whatsoever, and there had been no calls for fire from C- or D-Companies. The Po had been crossed and close objectives taken with hardly a shot fired, save one isolated Spandau burst. The whole thing was uncanny.

Looking back Adam, straining his eyes, thought he could already make out the shapes, and equally straining the ears he believed he could catch the shouts and vehicle clatter, of A- and B-Companies emerging from the river and making for a marked gap in the northern bank before their own dismount and advance northward. The actual crossing and form up should be covered by Bill Andrews's D-Company, if Bill had reached his objective and were in the right place. And old Bill – for the first time in their long acquaintance Adam found he was referring to Bill Andrews in his mind as "Old Bill" – Bill Andrews, whom he had never cared for, Bill Andrews the know-all, the ambitious, the over-zealous-at-the-wrong-time, was competent; and Bill Andrews would assuredly be at the right place and the Jerries would not be able, whether by accident or design, to march through the night towards the north bank of the river and shoot up A- and B-Companies as they debouched from it.

Adam planned to visit Bill Andrews next, by which time A and B should be legging it towards their own objective and he could follow them up, join them, tidy up the northern perimeter of the bridgehead. It would be dawn by then. Just for now he'd see Simon Entwether, the cocky, somewhat insensitive outsider Simon Entwether, whose company, once in position, held the Prova key to the security of the bridgehead from the west. It must be a weakness, Adam thought, to find in myself no particular liking for two of my own company commanders, efficient though they may be; but perhaps it doesn't matter as long as I'm fair and they respect me and do their jobs. Command isn't about affection. Or is it?

The shape of the low roofs of Prova showed clear ahead now. Dark shapes in the grey dawn, helmeted Westmorland sentries beside the track. A wave from Adam's signaller, a wave back from two soldiers by the roadside, giving a thumbs-up sign, relieved, cocky. The Duck checked at a righthand bend round the first houses and Adam shouted, "Halt here, we'll get down!" He dismounted with his little party, in search of Simon Entwether. It was a small place and he knew exactly where Simon would have planned to put his platoons.

Victor Knott said suddenly, "There's Simon, I think." His eyes were better than Adam's. The dark outlines of a small group standing beside the most westerly house in the village, a house presumably on the outer perimeter.

Adam's signaller said conversationally, "That's Major Entwether, sir."

Adam nodded and walked towards the small group.

When he was fifteen yards away the tallest figure in the group, the unmistakable figure now of Simon Entwether, detached itself and started to saunter towards him. Entwether all right! Confident, a bit supercilious! This hasn't really been a battle, has it! Compared with the various shows we experienced before it all got easy, before you joined us! It was light enough now to see, or at least guess, the Entwether expression.

At that moment Simon Entwether let out a piercing, fearful scream, an animal scream; threw up his arms as if to ward off something indescribable; spun round like a top and collapsed nearly at Adam's feet. His back was a mess of blood, bits of bone and scraps of battle dress. One tiny, terrible silence and then hubbub.

Shots rang out, and yells: "There he is! There he is, the bastard!"

Men were running and crouching. They were frightened, angry, shaken by this intervention of violence and tragedy at the very moment of easy triumph, a moment already on the frontiers of peace. A Jerry who had upset them like this had no rights, no rights! The bastard, the bastard!

"There he is!"

One glance showed Adam that someone had managed to sneak up to only yards away, unobserved; had chosen his target; and then, having selected Major Entwether, had given him most of a Schmeiser magazine between the shoulder blades. At point-blank range the murderous salvo had almost blown Simon's heart and lungs out through his chest. Simon Entwether would date no more girls.

Two more rifle shots. A man shouted, "He's not finished off, the bastard!"

Adam saw a German soldier about forty yards away from the village edge. A rifle shot had clearly hit him through one leg and he had dropped and appeared in a kneeling position.

"Finish him off, the bastard!"

It all happened very quickly. The German seemed to put his hand to the region of his stomach. Two seconds later there was a flash and a loud report, and men instinctively shrank behind cover. When Adam looked again there was a pile of cloth and a leather boot where they had marked the German who had shot Simon Entwether.

A grenade. A grenade with the pin pulled by himself. Private Pell said, wondering, "He's blown his fucking self up!"

"He seems to have been on his own." It was Adam's voice.

"You can never tell!" said C-Company Sergeant-Major Dodsworth. He was shaken to the core by what had happened to Major Entwether, whom he'd started to like as well as respect as a soldier. He called an order to two soldiers of the platoon, to keep an eye on that bloody Jerry and another eye open for his mates. To a third he said, "Tell Mr Bellew that the CO's here."

Roger Bellew, once Sergeant Bellew in the Pembrokes and coming on well, commanded 8-Platoon in C-Company. He had seen what had happened from a hundred yards away and was already running over. Out of breath and upset, he reported to Adam. He supposed he was the senior platoon commander – 7 was commanded by a young boy just joined from OCTU and 9 by a sergeant. There was no second captain. Bellew, Company Commander, he thought as he panted towards the new CO. Christ, I hope the war's soon over. But Roger Bellew had already done the needful.

"The Jerry must have been alone, sir. I've been right through these houses beforehand. They've been deserted, the Itis have scarpered. This one must have been lying up, hiding, waiting his chance— "

Men of Bellew's platoon were again going through the houses, searching, rifles and grenades ready. The men, Adam could see, were jumpy. It was fully light now.

"Mr Bellew, who's your platoon sergeant?"

"Sergeant Donner, sir."

"Hand over to him and take command of the company. I'm going round them quickly now. Join me."

"Right, sir."

Adam eyed Sergeant-Major Dodsworth.

"All right, Sergeant-Major?"

The Company Sergeant-Major was still on edge, Adam saw. It was natural. The whole thing had been so unexpected, in its curious way an outrage, unlike the normal infliction of casualty.

Adam said quietly, "See to Major Entwether. We'll have a decent funeral later."

"Yes, sir."

"And help Mr Bellew all you can."

"Yes, sir."

"I know you will. Now I'll go round the rest of the Company. Any news, Victor?" Victor Knott had been keeping in touch on the air and shook his head. Nothing, he said, from A and B, no calls for fire, no sounds of enemy fire either. They must be on their way.

"We'll get over there," Adam said, "we'll get over there, via Bill Andrews, when we've had a quick look round here." They had only been six minutes in C-Company area and in those six minutes two men had died very unexpectedly. One was a young major attached to the Westmorland Regiment who had never, Ben Jameson had admitted, quite fitted in. On an impulse, followed by the Intelligence Officer, Eric Raikes, and the faithful Pell, Adam walked over to where lay the bloodstained, mangled remains of the Wehrmacht killer of Simon Entwether.

Adam looked down. The grenade had obviously been held to the stomach and the mess, like the mess made of his victim Entwether, was gruesome. The face, however, had been completely untouched by the explosion and Adam gazed at it for a moment. It was a very young face – fair hair, a pale complexion despite the warmth of the Italian spring, a resolute expression. The German looked about fifteen. He looked as if he were at some extraordinary sort of peace.

The Army Group Chief of Staff said, "Look at the map," and Wolf von Pletsch, who liked and admired him, looked at the map as a conventional gesture of compliance, well knowing the map to have absolutely nothing new to communicate. The map was stuck on the wall of a large villa on the outskirts of a small town in south-eastern Austria. Out of the windows the Alpine masses should have brought joy with their beauty, snow on the high ground, spring flowers already carpeting the meadows. There was, however, no joy in the heart of the Chief of Staff or of Lieutenant-Colonel von Pletsch.

"Look at the map. Our so-called offensive in Hungary futile— "

"Inevitably, Herr General."

"The Reds in Vienna, and ringing Berlin. The Americans in Bavaria and the Danube Valley. These Yugoslav communists rampaging over the country south of here, cutting throats— "

And having had plenty of their own throats cut, God knows, Wolf thought without emotion. He said, "We're in a sort of Alpine sack, Herr General. The only route of escape is westward."

As if not hearing, the Chief of Staff continued, still gazing at the map on the wall.

"The British and Americans are in the Po Valley. They'll be across the river and moving northward soon."

"One imagines so. If not already."

"If not already. In this part of the world there's not much of the Greater German Reich left unoccupied, is there? Yet these insane orders continue to arrive – 'Hold this line. Assemble forces for counter-attack towards Vienna.' Mad."

"Of course."

"The Commander-in-Chief has no effective command any more. No viable communications and no troops one could possibly regard as ready for battle. Except small groups here and there, acting independently, poor devils. But for most it's a matter of getting the hell out of it, out of the way of the Ivans."

"Certainly." Wolf knew that, as they talked, wretched

columns of underfed men and underfed horses, thousand upon thousand of them, carts laden with bandaged wounded, spirits utterly dejected, were crawling along every available road or track westward and northwestward. To avoid, somehow, the Red Army surging westward from Hungary, westward and southward from Vienna. To avoid the Yugoslav partisans, swarming into Slovenia, not far to the south. To get away. Without information, resources, defensive capacity or anything remaining but fear itself, to get away. It could only be westward, mountains or no mountains.

The Chief of Staff said, "And virtually no petrol. Now listen— "

Wolf listened.

"If the Anglo-Americans advance quickly the Commander-in-Chief proposes to make contact with them."

Wolf stared. "Independently?"

"If necessary. But that may be made impossible by the Yugoslavs. Meanwhile, as you say, the escape route is westward."

"Certainly."

"So that in present circumstances there's only one thing to do. I won't describe it as a chance because it isn't a chance but at least it's better than sitting waiting for final disaster, and it's an alternative to shooting ourselves. Shooting ourselves may be honourable but it doesn't exactly help the troops. Pletsch, I want you to take a car and work your way westward and make contact with the Americans."

"Do we know where they are?"

"No. Pletsch, you must somehow get it across that the Commander-in-Chief wishes to surrender the whole of this Army Group. He wishes the American Army to receive this surrender and take position as far to the East as possible, in Austria. They will not be opposed."

"Can we guarantee that? Have we the communications to ensure such a thing?"

"Leave that to me. I intend in any case to give such orders, whether you've made contact with the Americans or not. But we must try to gain the credit for them. If you understand me."

"I understand you, Herr General."

"Pletsch," said the Chief of Staff. "You're in no doubt that further resistance is an utter waste of men's lives, aren't you?"

"None, Herr General."

"I want you, on the way, to do all you can to stop, in the areas you pass through, this miserable Volksturm business. As you know there are, on paper, God knows how many so-called Volksturm battalions spread across the so-called front. Old men, children, with nothing but an armband and a last war rifle! Volksturm battalions! Volksturm divisions! It's murder – against the Ivans! Against the Yankees!"

Wolf von Pletsch nodded and the Chief of Staff said heavily,

"But, as you know, the Volksturm has been raised, organised, by the local SS. They've been administered, if you can call it that, through Party channels, under the direction, God help them, of the Reichsfuhrer. That means that you may find yourself, if you're unlucky, having trouble with the local SS people. If any are still hanging about – the odds are that they're running faster than anybody. If you have trouble, Pletsch, don't hesitate."

They eyed each other.

"I won't, Herr General."

"Here is an order, directing you to liaise with local Volksturm formations, to improve their operational coordination with units of the Army Group." The Chief of Staff gave something like a smile, puckered. He said, "That will, or might, at least help you poke your nose about. Help you keep it clean, too. We all know how trigger-happy the SS are, and how the so-called authorities protect them."

Wolf nodded. The General added, "And do your best, if you're successful, to reach me. We'll try to take the operations branch to somewhere here," he tapped a point on the map many kilometres west of where they were talking, "as agreed. Find me there. Good wishes, Pletsch."

"Thank you, Herr General."

Wolf travelled alone with a driver, a Ukrainian boy who had made a name at the Headquarters as being exceptionally skilled as a mechanic, as well as by now fluent in an idiosyncratic sort of German. His name was Vlasko – or that, anyway, was how he was universally known. Wolf had been driven by Vlasko before and liked him. Vlasko had remarkable stories to tell of the Ukraine, the Bolshevik times, the mass murder, the starvation. Vlasko had joined the Wehrmacht with enthusiasm in 1941 after the first arrival of German troops, when volunteers had been invited, and had since served with enjoyment in Greece and, latterly, Yugoslavia. Vlasko stood by the car, hand at the salute, with his wide, endearing smile on his broad, equally endearing face. However desperate the situation Vlasko always seemed capable of a grin, and perhaps would be until the end.

Wolf gave directions. He knew Austria and these mountains well from pre-war-days – Wolf had never until 1939 missed a skiing holiday and in the old Reichswehr such activities had been encouraged.

"We'll go by small roads as much as possible, Vlasko. The main roads are so clogged with troops and horses and refugees that we'll make better time by keeping off them, longer though it may be."

"*Jawohl, Herr Oberstleutnant.* How far are we trying to get today?"

"As far as we can, Vlasko." Wherever the American leading troops have got to, Wolf thought. It was unclear where, exactly, the Wehrmacht's west-facing positions now were, south of the Danube. If, indeed, they existed at all. He said, "We're aiming at Innsbruck, know it?"

"No." Vlasko was driving along happily. He had three cans of petrol and some food from the field kitchen in the back of the car. They were going westward and with luck wouldn't ever turn round. Vlasko had no illusions about what would happen to him if he were caught by the Red Army. He realised, wretchedly, that it was a fate which had probably already overtaken his family, because of him. A bullet in the back of the neck if you were very, very lucky. Being, however, a sunny soul he never let his mind rest for long on such matters – he lived in the present and as often as not the present had been good. And it was a fine April morning, they were going in the right direction and Lieutenant-Colonel von Pletsch, a much more agreeable man than many of them, would look after him. He knew that Lieutenant-Colonel von Pletsch would want to take a periodic turn at the wheel – just for now he was studying his map and occasionally giving Vlasko directions.

They twisted and turned, Wolf directing Vlasko from the map first up one minor road, then another, climbing, dropping, always somehow working westward. The hours passed. They had certainly managed to dodge the main roads and any serious military traffic. Vlasko supposed they were going the right way. The sun still seemed to be behind them and at this time of day that was what mattered.

It was, Wolf saw from his watch, approaching midday when, having climbed for nearly an hour, they drove over a low ridge and saw a small enclosed valley lying ahead.

Their road, a rough but driveable road, had run through woods and at the near end of the valley, almost touching the edge of the woods, was a village, a small place with what looked like a dirt track running round it, clear of its perimeter and crossing a stream outside the village and well beyond it.

Wolf guessed that there was a narrow bridge in the village itself and that heavy traffic could bypass it. He reckoned from his map that the road ran north-westward from the valley, climbed narrowly over another ridge to the north, and joined a slightly larger west-running road thereafter. Progress was slow and winding but they were getting on and it was better than jolting along for hours on end past the horses and carts and occasional lorries and marching, shuffling columns of the Wehrmacht. Columns likely to be by no means well-disposed by now, even particularly respectful, to lone staff officers with maroon trouser stripes and clean tunics, travelling in comfort in staff cars and doubtless looking after their own safety and comfort and not much else.

Vlasko edged the car bumpily forward.

"We can bypass this place, *Herr Oberst leutnant*. If you wish."

"Yes. No – wait, Vlasko. Stop here a minute."

They were 200 metres from the first houses of the village. Beyond it sloping meadows rose to several attractive looking balconied houses. The village itself seemed a poor place, but the valley, Wolf thought was charming. He consulted his map. It should be called Pustenau.

His eye, however, had been caught by the rather surprising sight of another car, unquestionably another official car. The other car must have been driving along the same road as themselves, some little time ahead of them. It was halted on the near edge of the village and standing beside it Wolf saw a man in SS uniform. A second man, a civilian, was standing with him in an attitude which even at a distance indicated deference.

Wolf said, "Drive up to that other car, Vlasko, and stop. I think I'll ask what, if anything, is going on."

Vlasko did as he was told and Wolf dismounted from the car in a leisurely sort of way, Vlasko standing smartly by the door. The two men Wolf was approaching eyed him carefully. The man in a civilian jacket, trousers and boots, Wolf saw, was wearing a Party armband. A local functionary of some kind no doubt.

As he reached them both raised their arms in the Nazi salute.

"*Heil Hitler!*"

It had been obligatory in the Wehrmacht, too, for the last eight months. Wolf flapped his wrist in a somewhat disdainful gesture towards conformity. He said, unsmiling, "*Von Pletsch, Oberstleutnant, Generalstab Armee Gruppe E.*"

The civilian looked, if possible, even more obsequious than he had before. What a morning for Pustenau! Two uniformed Party men to discuss and delegate responsibility for a special Pustenau Volksturm unit, although previously this had been decided against by the Reich authorities on the reasonable grounds that there were no able-bodied men left in the place of what could remotely be described as military age. Now, however, there had been second thoughts and considerable responsibility was thus likely to accrue. Some people who thought themselves too old or too grand might yet find themselves marching and digging, a spade and an old issued carbine over the shoulder, an honourable Volksturm armband round the upper arm! And as if this were not enough a Lieutenant-Colonel of the General Staff! A nobleman, too! Pustenau was certainly in the news.

The SS man spoke. A Hauptsturmfuhrer, Wolf observed.

A sort of captain. He felt the aroma of dislike and mistrust float towards him and returned it.

The Hauptsturmfuhrer introduced himself as named Buhler.

"*Herr Oberstleutnant*, we are giving the local *Parteileiter*, Herr Krandt, orders for the formation of another Volksturm unit in this valley. Together with the three neighbouring villages a further battalion, 955-Battalion, is to be formed. We have been explaining the details of weapon drawing and reporting. There will be eleven men mustered from Pustenau."

"Some very young, of course," said Herr Krandt, with an apologetic, obsequious smile. Hauptsturmfuhrer Buhler ignored him. Wolf knew that this absurd little scene should not delay him. The whole thing was so ludicrous that it would no doubt be best to leave it and drive on as fast as he could. On the other hand he was mindful of the Chief of Staff's words, and quite suddenly the reality of a handful of children and dotards, being marshalled tomorrow and thrust somewhere into the path of the Red Army, made his gorge rise. Pustenau might be a tiny segment of the whole ghastly picture but if he could correct this iniquity at Pustenau he would.

With deliberate abruptness he said, "Sturmfuhrer, as it happens I have orders, written orders, to coordinate the actions of the Volksturm, to take steps to ensure they conform to the operations of the Wehrmacht."

"The Volksturm are raised and commanded under the orders of the Reichsfuhrer SS."

"Possibly. But if they are to fight it must be in conformity with the plans of the Wehrmacht commanders."

They stared at each other, and Buhler said, "Well? Well, *Herr Oberstleutnant*? They must still be armed and organised before they can conform to anybody's plans, must they not?"

"In some areas," said Wolf, speaking carefully, lying with the clearest of consciences, "in some areas the Army Group Command do not wish Volksturm units deployed. In any way. It would complicate operations. This is one such area."

"I have orders, SS orders, Home Army orders under the Reichsfuhrer's authority, that in this region further Volksturm— "

"So you said. But that is against the operational policy of the Wehrmacht. Which must have priority. This is an operational area."

The Hauptsturmfuhrer SS said, his voice sounding slightly choked, "No, *Herr Oberstleutnant*, the policy of the Wehrmacht does *not* have priority over the orders transmitted, through Gaus and regions, of the Reichsfuhrer's headquarters! You will recall that the Gauleiter is also Reich Defence Commissioner!"

I'm not going to stay here arguing, Wolf thought, the whole damned business will be over in a fortnight anyway. I'll give them a chance to save their faces and buy time. He said, "That is a matter for higher authority. I have my orders. You have yours. I will report this incident and ask that the Army Group Command resolve it by direct contact with the civil authorities at Gau level."

"With the SS authorities."

"Very well," said Wolf, trying to keep his voice comparatively agreeable, "with the SS authorities." He knew that the others realised as clearly as he did that nobody would make direct contact with anybody. It was all a farce. They stared at each other in silence. The Hauptsturmfuhrer, wondering whether he was being culpably weak, said, "I will report that the Army Group will seek clarification on the policy relating to local Volksturm."

"And that meanwhile no new units will be formed in this region."

"Until clarification."

"Very well, until clarification." To Krandt, directly and very sharply, Wolf said, "You can stand down your eleven men Herr Krandt!" He then smiled. Krandt was perplexed. The Sturmfuhrer said, "When the order is reaffirmed, Krandt, you will know what to do."

"Yes, Herr Hauptsturmfuhrer."

It might, Wolf supposed, delay this ludicrous sacrifice a few days. The Russians might well be here by then, and the unfortunates of Pustenau victims of one kind or another anyway. To Buhler he said, again trying to reduce hostility,

"You have a long journey ahead?"

"Yes. Meanwhile we have further business here. A judicial matter." Buhler turned and shouted a command down the village street. Fifty metres away Wolf saw another SS man, pushing towards them a woman, a woman stumbling, whose hands appeared tied behind her back.

Krandt, feeling that a Lieutenant-Colonel on the General Staff was owed an explanation of untoward circumstances in Pustenau, said, "It is a prisoner – a civil prisoner. Escaped."

"Escaped?"

"She was being sheltered," said Buhler, "by a so-called doctor. It was clear that he knew that he was hiding an enemy of the Reich who had escaped from custody. Deplorable. Fortunately Krandt, here, was vigilant."

Wolf said, "I see. And where is the doctor?"

"We have dealt with him."

"Do you mean you've shot him?"

"Now this," said Buhler with something like a sneer, "now this at least is not, emphatically not, a matter for the Wehrmacht command as I am sure you would agree,

Herr Oberstleutnant! This was a case of a woman who escaped from a prisoner convoy, a convoy of men and women convicted of working against the security of the Reich, men and women fortunate to be alive. And having escaped and reached this place and found this doctor she was helped by him, although he admitted she told him where she'd come from – "

"And Dr Parsfeld," said Krandt unctuously, "never reported it. It is known that any strangers, unknowns, must be reported at once to me. At once! But not a word."

"So Krandt mentioned it when we announced our visit," said Buhler pleasantly. He added, "There are a number of escapers at large in the countryside. Headquarters orders are to deal with them summarily. They represent a real threat."

The woman and her escort were now halted five paces from them. Buhler turned and took a step or two towards them. Then he screamed something and the woman sank on to her knees. Wolf thought there was something, he couldn't say what, familiar about her face. The escorting SS man stood clear. He was grinning.

Buhler raised his gloved hand and struck the woman very hard first on one side of the face then on the other. He turned and said to Krandt, "Here, I think. Why not?" This will be good for red-stripes, he thought. This will show these dressed-up snobs from the Army General Staff what real men have to do, real men, capable of being tough with themselves and tough with others. The village street was deserted. Not even a dog or a cat peered. They were all standing in the roadway except for the woman who knelt, head bowed. She was shivering but silent.

Buhler said, sharply, "Lensky!" And the second SS man stiffened to attention and began to unsling a carbine from his shoulder. At that moment, however, he stared past the Hauptsturmfuhrer and started to speak, incoherent.

Buhler spun round and saw that he was looking straight down the barrel of Lieutenant-Colonel Wolf von Pletsch's Luger.

CHAPTER IX

"Harry," said Adam, "I want you to act as Battalion Second-in-Command. Fred Barron will look after Headquarter Company in so far as it needs it." Fred Barron was the rather elderly Battalion Transport officer, a Newcastle wholesale ironmongery merchant in civil life who had very gallantly volunteered for service early in the war although of an age easily to plead exemption. He had, for most of the years since 1939, been employed on training duties at home but to his great pride had been sent as a captain to the 2nd Battalion just before Christmas. He was expert at organising transport, a meticulous administrator and loyal to the Westmorlands beyond reproach. Everybody liked him and although the men knew that he wasn't exactly a soldier, they also knew that he was an honest, fair-minded man and efficient at his own job. He would act for a while as Headquarter Company Commander perfectly competently, Adam knew.

There was no Battalion Second-in-Command. Adam's promotion had occurred prematurely and although in due course the position vacated by him would doubtless be filled by the posting authorities this was unlikely to be done at speed. Adam felt no urgent need for a second-in-command; but he felt that the mark of at least superficial elevation would be good for Harry Venables. Also Adam needed a companion. Harry knew the Battalion much better than Adam. Harry was sound as a bell. Harry would soon recover from the temporary attack of nervous exhaustion which had overtaken a brave man. Harry had the sort of genial and relaxed temperament which wouldn't resent two quick moves in succession – first to Headquarter Company, now back to Battalion HQ. And Harry was a very old friend.

Harry said, "If you say so – sir!" But he smiled as he said it and Adam thought he was pleased.

"We move at four tomorrow morning, Harry, unearthly hour. I've told Peter I'll give out orders at seven, quite soon. The powers-that-be seem to think the brigade won't find much holding it up, but we've all heard that sort of thing before and I reckon there may be a few excitements on the way."

"On the way to where?" They were sitting in a large Italian café, untouched by shellfire from either side, its windows intact, its proprietor anxious to ingratiate. For a few hours the Westmorlands had appropriated it as Battalion Headquarters.

Adam shrugged.

"Treviso. Beyond, maybe. The mountains. The sky, as they say, is the limit. They, the Jerries, really are cracking up, Harry."

Harry nodded. He said, "There are some big rivers to cross."

"Certainly – Piave, Tagliamento. Bridges blown, one imagines."

"I hope the sappers get their bloody bridging stuff up to the right place, this time," said Harry. For the previous twenty-four hours it had been a matter of some grievance with the Battalion that although raft ferries had been plying within the bridgehead they had won over the Po, no bridge had yet been built. The movement of bridging equipment had, it seemed, been subject to especial difficulties. In consequence most, though not all, of the heavy armour was still south of the river. The Germans, however, had taken no advantage of this circumstance and Adam was certain they were in no condition to do so. He glanced at his watch and nodded towards a large *Daily Express* map of embattled Europe which Eric Raikes, the Battalion Intelligence officer, had cut out. Whenever possible they listened to the BBC news on one of the Battalion radio sets.

"If the BBC have got it right, the Yanks are running free to the west of us. The Jerries are hemmed in to the north-east corner of Italy, between us and the Alps and the Adriatic."

"Where," Harry said, "one imagines they'll hang on like grim death."

"Grim death indeed. And the other side of the Alps – or in them for that matter – the Americans are moving through Bavaria. And the Russkies have cleared Hungary, got into Vienna weeks ago and are moving towards Prague."

"And Berlin."

"And Berlin. It can't be long, Harry."

"No, it can't be long."

It was five o'clock in the afternoon two days later, a hot afternoon. They had been moving, checked by nothing but the periodic need for rest and fuel, for twenty-four hours and they had already covered 70 miles. It was incredible.

The Westmorlands were now part of a mounted column and Adam, marvelling at the course of the war, was travelling with Eric Raikes in an open jeep behind the leading company group, Bill Andrews's D-Company. Adam had tried to go out of his way to be warm and trusting to Bill Andrews since the river crossing – Bill, after all, was wholly reliable and the irritation he sometimes evoked from all ranks was richly compensated by his steadiness and commonsense. Bill, Adam had decided, should lead the column.

They were told that the enemy "were now offering no serious resistance" – there had even been rumours of surrender feelers having been put out here in Italy – but no chances could be taken. Adam's mind went back to tea with General Sir Mason Vine back in the Cumbrian cold. Chatting of days gone by and other wars the old man had said, "Well, it can't be long now, but don't let your people get careless. *You can never take chances with the Boche!*" Adam smiled at the memory, but the Colonel of the Regiment might not be such a fool after all.

Meanwhile the leading company group was carefully constituted – a troop of Sherman tanks from the Yeomanry Regiment with which the Westmorlands were working, D-Company in lorries now (the Fantails had long departed, to nobody's great sorrow), Bill Andrews well forward in the column in a jeep accompanied by an Artillery Forward Observation officer, two of the Battalion's own six-pounder anti-tank guns, a section of the Battalion three-inch mortars under Corporal Fairbrother, a mortar fire controller, and a reconnaissance party from the Divisional Royal Engineers, travelling in a capacious truck under a Sapper staff sergeant. Immediately behind this all-purpose little party rode Adam and Tactical Battalion Headquarters as he grandly described it to himself, Victor Knott, Eric Raikes, their drivers and their signallers. It had been thus for twenty-four hours.

Adam had also added to his party the Regimental Sergeant Major, Quidding. Quidding was usually behind at Battalion Headquarters proper, seeing to the ammunition re-supply and a hundred other things. He might not have anything useful to do with the CO's tactical advanced group but Adam thought, rightly, that the RSM would enjoy the change and appreciate the experience. Hell, the war must be nearly over!

Eric Raikes spoke Italian. The Brigadier had smiled agreeably at the fact and said, "One's no idea of what sort of conditions one will find among the locals. Partisans are *meant* to have been active in that area and of course as we get on we'll be near where Tito's boys have also been active although that's some way away. Play it by ear."

"Yes, sir." "Play it by ear"! "Use your wits and your initiative, both are likely to be as good as mine! And I can always have second and better thoughts, after all!"

The winning of their bridgehead over the Po, in fact three days ago, seemed an age. Somebody else had, without difficulty, secured the crossing of the Adige river a few miles to the north. And now 2nd Westmorlands were having, it appeared, a clear run. Occasionally reports came through on the radio of particular places clear of enemy; of a large number of prisoners having surrendered in one town, and even larger in another. The Corps armoured car Regiment was ranging the countryside, nobody was ever at any one moment entirely certain exactly where. The Battalion's own route – to the disappointment of all – ran clear of major cities, whose reception of the advancing Allies was reported, again on the radio, to have been in many places rapturous; and it appeared that the only Germans found were giving themselves up in droves. Victor Knott, who was listening on his radio in his own vehicle, strolled over to join Adam at one of their occasional halts.

"Sounds as if we're missing most of the fun!"

There were other columns on parallel routes, to both East and West. Adam smiled.

"Our turn will come."

"Chaps are in Venice, can you imagine!"

"Hardly. Well, off we go again."

The column was moving and they both jumped aboard their jeeps. Five minutes later Bill Andrews's voice, meticulous as ever, crackled through the headset. The Battalion axis ran over a canal, a negligible, thin blue line on the map compared to the great river they had passed, the Brenta, with bridge unblown. In this case, however, it appeared that the canal bridge had been destroyed, or damaged anyway. "Locals", Bill's voice said, had reported an alternative route two miles to the east. He gave a map reference and said he was about to reconnoitre.

Adam considered, looking at the map. The ground was still low-lying and ditch-filled. Roads mattered. The place indicated by Bill would necessitate a rather laborious diversion if Bill's Company were to retain the lead.

"Roger, I'm coming up to join you. Out."

If the column is to cross by an alternative bridge, he thought, I'll put Dick Abel, who's lying second, into the lead and divert him at the fork in the last village. The tank troop – only one was accompanying the Battalion – would need to move across country or by tracks, there shouldn't be a problem. But would the newly discovered bridge bear Sherman tanks? That Sapper Staff Sergeant would be there and he looked as if he knew his business.

"Come on Victor!"

Private Pell, driving now, swung on to the road and forward.

At that moment a considerable salvo of shells fell in what must be the area of the apparently blown canal bridge.

They're not ours, Adam thought as he urged Pell on faster, they must be Jerry's! Well, well, well!

They were indeed Jerry's. The bridge over the canal had been partially destroyed and would need work for it to be made viable for traffic, let alone tanks. Beyond the narrow canal the ground rose steadily towards a small town, crowning the next ridge about two miles away. On the near bank of the canal were Bill Andrew's jeep, several lorries backed behind buildings off the road, Bill Andrews, his Company Sergeant-Major Brierly, and the attached Artillery Forward Observation Officer. Protected from the front by one of the houses, they were standing, talking rather loudly to each other. Two men carrying a stretcher were moving towards them as Adam arrived. On the ground by the near end of the damaged bridge was a body.

Bill said, "It's Sergeant Pardoe. He was having a look at the canal."

Adam, as it happened, hardly knew Sergeant Pardoe but he had heard his name often mentioned since returning to the 2nd Battalion, and always with an appreciative chuckle. Sergeant Pardoe had not been in the old 2nd of Adam's memory in 1940. He was a reservist and had at first been an instructor at the Depot, posted to this Battalion in time for the Sicily invasion and one of its most renowned platoon sergeants thereafter. He was spoken of as a "character", mentioned with a smile. Ben had told Adam that he had put in Pardoe for a Distinguished Conduct Medal and it was, the Brigade Commander had said, about even chances that he might get it. Any day now, Ben had explained, before these last battles, before Lake Comacchio, before the Po crossing. Nothing had yet come through, and now Sergeant Pardoe lay with a groundsheet over his face.

Adam said, "I'm sorry, Bill. I know what a good chap— "

"The Company will take this very hard."

"Of course."

Adam had never seen Bill Andrews so obviously disturbed. Any casualty in one's company was a bereavement but in this case Bill looked more than ordinarily distressed. Not himself in fact.

"What happened, Bill?"

"Just the one stonk. Had the canal registered, obviously. We've had no shelling for ages— "

"Quite. Well, they must still have the odd gun and I suppose we've got to expect that they'll get rid of their remaining ammunition. I'm very, very sorry about Pardoe, Bill."

Bill said again, "The Company will take this hard. They thought the world of him." He looked miserable. Adam saw RSM Quidding having a quiet word with Company Sergeant-Major Brierly.

Adam reckoned that tough though it might be the day had to be moved along. He said, "Your Sapper— "

"I've sent him to where they say there's an alternative bridge. There's a track along the canal bank and he's gone in his own truck, the whole Sapper section's gone. He'll signal when he gets there. Should be within five minutes, I hope. I told him to watch out, I bet the bastards have got that bridge registered too, if it exists."

"Probably. Now listen, Bill— "

At that moment Victor Knott said, "Christ, look at that." His binoculars were on the next ridge, the small town whose roofs broke the skyline. Its name was Bastone. Adam looked.

Clearly visible through binoculars, crowding into the town along the same road the Westmorlands were following, was a huge concourse of traffic and what looked like human beings on their feet. Adam could see the occasional black eddy of smoke indicating motor vehicles and poor-quality fuel, but it was obvious that most of the traffic consisted of horse-drawn carts and marching men. And perhaps, Adam thought, horse-drawn guns. And one of them recently in action.

Oh, to have got armour across the canal somehow! Victor breathed, "What a target, what a target!" and started talking rapidly into his microphone, his map on the jeep bonnet, his eyes drawn irresistibly to the crowded road climbing gently into Bastone.

Three and a half minutes later Bill Andrews and, again, Victor Knott started speaking into their respective microphones at the same time. Bill looked up and addressed Adam.

"It's Staff Sergeant Wilson, sir, the Sapper. He says the bridge could be made good in one hour. It could take tanks, he says, in one hour. There's only one span damaged and he reckons he and his chaps can cope with it on a temporary basis. Enough to get our people across anyway. He's reporting it, of course, and his Squadron Commander's coming forward— "

"Good." One hour, thought Adam. I'll switch A into the lead and hope we can improve on one hour.

"Good. Now Bill— "

"Shooting in one minute," said Victor Knott, looking happily at his watch. He knew, with gratification, that his Regimental Commander had managed to so plan the movement of the close-support artillery that for most of the time there were trails on the ground and barrels pointing towards the enemy. It wasn't easy – with the brigade's advance going at a canter like this it meant being pretty adroit, and pretty firm with the brigade staff about when and how the guns moved. From his knowledge of the Regimental movement order Victor reckoned that Bastone must be at just about extreme range. Then, with luck, the rear battery would leap-frog forward and the lead batteries deploy.

"Half a minute now!" A-Company would be starting to move towards the alternative bridge in lorries, and the tank troop was already making its way thither. Adam decided to join them. The alternative bridge would become the axis of the Battalion's advance. Regrettably, however, there was no hurry. He glanced at his watch. The Sappers had had seven minutes. Fifty-three to go. Perhaps there was some labour which Dick Abel's men could provide to speed things up.

"Firing!" Victor Knott's voice sounded intensely happy. The thunder of the twenty-five pounders sounded very remote indeed and Victor said, as if to himself, "Just about the limit, I fancy," and smiled. To Adam he said, "Just made it, Colonel. You've been going almost too fast!"

"Well done, Victor."

"Look at that!"

The familiar sighing of shells overhead. Then they all saw the dust and earth spurting on either side of the road near what was presumably the beginning of the little town of Bastone. An instant later they heard the explosions.

Victor's eyes were glued to the target area. He said,

"Fair and square, I'd say! Glad I don't own any horses among that lot! Its hard to tell effect, but there's a lot of bustle and scatter, that I can see!"

Another salvo of shells came over. Followed by another.

"Yes," said Victor contentedly, "that was certainly a piece of luck! We're unlikely to get another shoot like that!"

Adam nodded.

"We'd better cut across to the other bridge now. All right, Victor?"

"Very all right." Victor had been talking again on his own net. Bill Andrews was standing, watching them. His Company would be taking their place now as the rear company of the Battalion. Their moment of glory in the van of the liberation of northern Italy was over. Adam mounted his jeep and indicated the canal track to Pell. RSM Quidding climbed into the back. Adam turned and smiled at him.

"The Gunners had a pretty good shoot, didn't they, Mr Quidding?"

Quidding said, "Yes, sir." A moment later Adam heard him say, very quietly, "And every one of those Jerries was someone's son. Same as old Pardoe." And as they jolted along towards the newly discovered alternative canal bridge Adam felt humble and ashamed.

"Will you get into trouble for this?"

"No. If questioned, Frau Carlucci, I shall say, truthfully, that you are a refugee. But I will not be questioned."

Anni was sitting in the front seat of the car, beside Wolf von Pletsch who was driving. Vlasko was perched in the back, dozing most of the time. The Colonel knew what he was doing. He'd been quick, too – bang, bang, two of them, just like that! Vlasko hadn't been able to hear their exchanges but he'd seen the action.

"I didn't mean trouble about me. I meant trouble because, because— "

"Because I had to use my pistol to prevent the committal of a crime. The answer, Frau Carlucci, is that if the German Reich were not about to collapse in total defeat and the institutions of the SS and Nazi Party with it, yes, I would certainly be in trouble. That little Party functionary who betrayed the doctor and betrayed you is alive, of course, and will report the matter."

"And so?"

"He will then spend the next weeks or months explaining that he was never really a Party member! And that he was relieved at the execution of two SS men who were about to murder an innocent woman and had already murdered a distinguished doctor, both in his village!" Wolf smiled bitterly. They were making good progress and were already 25 km west of Pustenau.

Wolf glanced at his companion. How lovely she once

was. He remembered a young girl in Berlin, smooth-skinned, dancing eyes, confident. Now she looked twice her actual age. He had established her identity without difficulty as they drove at speed away from Pustenau. Anni had hardly seemed to take it all in. She was, he thought, undoubtedly pretty ill.

A little later she had said, "What did you say your name is?"

"Pletsch, Wolf von Pletsch. We met in Berlin, and later I knew your brother, Herr Kurt Karlsheim. As I told you just now."

"Ah. But Herr von Pletsch, what are you doing here?"

He had explained briefly. He had said, "It is a curious coincidence, but such things happen in war."

"I suppose so. Where are you taking me?"

Wolf said kindly, "We can talk about that as we drive along. I'm afraid you are not very well, Frau Carlucci."

"Are you taking me to prison?"

"Certainly not."

"Or to a camp?"

"Very certainly not. I imagine you were in a camp, Frau Carlucci, and we will make sure that all that is behind you. As far as we can." Which may not be all that far, Wolf thought. Red Army behind us, Nazis running all over the place, wreaking revenge on whoever they find who's opposed them. Still living in their own idiot world. Americans somewhere or other. The whole fabric of society torn into pieces and the pieces scattered all over Europe. And all over Austria.

They drove on in silence and after a little Anni whispered, "I had never been so near to a dead man before. It is curious – in the middle of a war, and all the bombing and so forth. And I was a prisoner, you see, arrested at my home in Italy and deported. All that, and I had never been so near a dead man before. Before this morning."

Wolf said nothing, and glanced at her. He was sure she had a high fever. Those eyes! And the trembling . . .

"The doctor," Anni said, "the doctor. His name was Parsfeld. He was a good man. He took me to his house. And he gave me some medicine, and he bathed my ankle."

"I saw that you had hurt your ankle. A sprain, I suppose."

"It's nothing. Painful but nothing. And the medicine was good. I felt better this morning. Then, this morning, they came."

In the back Vlasko gave an enormous yawn. He wondered when the Colonel would decide a short meal halt was in order. He also wondered for how long they'd have to share rations with this female. Who was she, anyway?

"This morning they came. They shouted at Dr Parsfeld. They ordered him out of his own house, yelled questions at him. Questions about me. I was on a sofa in the sitting room, I heard. I couldn't see, I heard. Then there were two shots and they came back into the house and screamed at me to come out. My leg hurt, I moved slowly, they got angry and screamed again. One of them, I'm not sure which, hit me, hard, very hard. Then they tied my wrists."

They were crossing a sort of natural viaduct, at dizzy height. The day was still beautiful and the view breathtaking. Wolf said, "We come to quite a large town in about an hour, in the next valley. I want to be a little bit careful there, I don't want too many questions."

As if not hearing him, Anni said, "Then I saw you, I remember that. I thought you were another of them. Or a guard come from the camp, perhaps. Then that man hit me again. The next thing I remember was another shot and another and another."

"Frau Carlucci," said Wolf, "I had to do it."

"And two bodies. And the other man, the one in civilian dress, local costume— "

"The local village *Parteileiter*. We spoke of him. I could have shot him too but I believe it would have complicated matters. He had not, as far as I could tell, committed a crime. The others had."

"Yes."

"And were about to commit another. So I had to do what I had to do. The times are difficult and dangerous, Frau Carlucci."

They drove on in silence for another half-hour. After it Anni said, almost inaudibly, "They arrested me in Italy. They thought I helped a British officer escape, sheltered him. They've no proof."

"I see."

"His name was Adam Hardrow." And you helped him all right, Wolf thought. And it – or he – did something to you, the tremble in your voice isn't just sickness.

Now Anni said,

"You said you have met my brother."

"Indeed I met your brother, Frau Carlucci— "

"Will you call me Anni?"

"Of course." He smiled at her. He's got a charming smile, she thought, I think I remember him, or someone like him anyway. Perhaps it was in Berlin, as he says. I can't remember very much just at present. I suppose I'm a bit light-headed. Astonishingly she didn't feel hungry although she'd felt hungry, she knew, for over a year. When he'd suggested taking something to eat, soon after they'd set off, she'd shaken her head and said, "Later please, later," and he'd acquiesced.

"Where did you meet my brother?"

He told her, and Anni, trying to think coherently, said, "I've not heard from Kurt for so long, so long."

Then Wolf stopped the car, and spoke some words to

Vlasko. To Anni he said, "I will help you from the car. You can sit on these logs and make your ankle comfortable and we will have something to eat. Put your arm round my neck." He eased her gently and strongly from the passenger seat.

When they had eaten and Vlasko had eaten and Vlasko had taken a short walk and then filled the car's petrol tank from two of his cans, Wolf, gazing towards a mountain peak, said, "Anni, I'm sorry, but I must say something difficult. It is about your brother, Kurt Karlsheim." I wonder how clear her mind is, he thought.

Very softly, Anni said, "You're going to tell me he's dead, aren't you."

"Anni, he was a friend of a brother of mine, in the German Foreign Service – who is also dead. I believe, although I do not know, that my brother was murdered by – by them. Not tried or condemned but killed secretly. After the attempt to kill the Fuhrer. Did you hear of the attempt to kill the Fuhrer?"

"Yes, we heard something about it. I don't know when it was, I'm muddled, I can't remember."

"It was July last year."

"I was already interned. And I suppose Kurt was also killed by them, at that time."

"Later, I believe," Wolf said, "later. They were still asking me – me, who hardly knew him – questions about him up to last month. As if they thought I had evidence to give."

"And had you?"

"No. But after the last interrogation of me – it was all very polite, very correct – the man, the Gestapo man, said, 'Well, your acquaintance Karlsheim, has unfortunately been convicted by a People's Court of treason.' One must, Anni, presume the worst from that. Some of – of those concerned – were, it is rumoured, sent to camps, perhaps only to be executed later. But it would be wrong not to fear the worst."

"When?"

"The conversation was last month, March. When the – the deed – was done I do not know."

Anni looked at him and looked away. She said, "I felt sure of it."

"I guessed you did."

"I knew his opinions. And I knew his courage."

"I am sure." What Wolf thought about that business, he by now could hardly sort out in his own mind. He had been fighting too recently against the Ivans to be clear. But those men, Karlsheim, the others, brother Heinrich for that matter, had certainly been brave. He helped her into the car again, very gently, and she turned and gave Vlasko an especially charming smile.

Anni told Wolf about Guido, her son.

"I don't know where he is, whether they took him when they took me—"

"You will find him. I am sure you will find him. The world will become straight again and you will find him."

"Do you really believe that?"

"Yes. I do."

At the large town which Wolf had forecast he drove carefully into the centre, looked around, stopped, dismounted and spoke to Vlasko.

"Stay here. On no account leave. If anybody challenges you say that a Colonel from Army Group E is here on very important business."

To Anni, Wolf said, "There is a sign here, on that building, of a Divisional Headquarters. I am going to discover whether there is any news."

He was gone from the car over forty minutes. When he returned Vlasko thought the Colonel looked as if somebody had hit him on the back of the head. Stunned. Not exactly upset but stunned. Without a word Wolf climbed back into the driving seat but he didn't immediately start the car. He started to talk, very softly.

"Anni, there is news."

Anni had been dozing. She forced herself to remember where she was. Nightmares had kept intruding on the dozing and she had twice had to struggle into feverish wakefulness in order to dispel them.

"There is news. In Italy, it appears that the British and Americans have advanced almost to the Austrian border."

Anni's face bore no expression. To her exhausted mind it didn't seem particularly significant.

"There is a rumour here, but they weren't sure, they didn't want to say anything which might get them into trouble, a rumour that the German forces in Italy have requested an armistice. I therefore telephoned my superior, the Army Group Chief of Staff. I managed to make contact."

Anni knew she should try to follow what he was saying. It might, she supposed, lead to something actually affecting her. And he had saved her life.

"I made contact. As I guessed the situation in Italy has changed things. I am to return at once."

The Chief of Staff, using veiled speech, choosing his words with caution, had nevertheless made entirely clear that in the circumstances "to the south-west" the Army Group Commander proposed "at the appropriate moment" to make contact not westward, with the Americans, but south-westward, with the British. If humanly possible. Wolf knew the map, it was photographed on his mind. He knew that if the British really had advanced towards or across the Italian – Austrian frontier they would be the nearest Allied troops. He also knew that the Army Group was not part of the Wehrmacht command in Italy and would not be included in any surrender that command might have negotiated.

He also knew that however near the British were, the Yugoslav Communist partisans and the Red Army were probably by now even nearer.

"Anni, I am to return at once. Eastward. Back the way we have come."

In the back Vlasko listened to all this with a sense of despair. After a moment Anni said, "So you have wasted a whole day!"

Wolf looked at her. Then he smiled, only for the second time. He said, "How can it have been a wasted day if I have managed to help you?"

"Not help me," Anni said very softly, "not help me. Save me."

They looked at each other for a moment and Anni said, "Can I still stay with you?"

Wolf had been thinking hard, and asking some questions within the Divisional Headquarters. It also, he found, served as District Headquarters and he had identified one officer who was a local and knew the area well.

"Anni, you are rather ill. I don't mean your ankle, but you really should be in the care of someone rather than driving through Tirol with a General Staff Colonel for hours on end!" He smiled at her again, an anxious smile. He could see all the beauty he remembered now. It seemed to have been reborn.

"I don't mind."

"The truth is, Anni, that the further east we go the more difficult it will now become. People are leaving their homes, trekking westward and north-westward." And especially, he thought grimly, women and children. He remembered Hungary.

"Now, there is a small convent three miles from here. I explained to an officer here, a very decent fellow, that

I have a refugee in the car, a German lady who is ill. He believes they might give you shelter and care for a while."

"Would it not be better to stay with you? Suppose people come to this convent, looking for me – "

"In present circumstances, Anni, I think that is very unlikely— "

"They will take me away— "

"I will explain everything to the Sisters, Anni, everything. From what I hear of them you will be better and safer with them than anywhere else. Anywhere else at all."

"It's called San Stefano," said Eric Raikes, "yet again, sir. There are a lot of San Stefanos."

"Of course. I remember one in the south."

"Near Salerno, sir?" Eric bit his tongue. Colonel Adam wasn't with us at Salerno, or any of the other places until a few weeks ago for that matter, what a bloody silly thing to say, sounded like a bit of deliberate cheek, rubbing in what a newcomer he is!

But Adam just answered, seriously, "Not very near, no. North of Cassino. When I was on the run."

Eric said nothing and at that moment the radio crackled again. It was Will Barker, still commanding B-Company and doing so adequately, Adam thought. Will, cautiously, had entered the hilltop village of San Stefano. The country was broken and beautiful now, the Battalion was already approaching the foothills of the Alps and the air was cold and clear at dawn and evening.

Will was reporting a "somewhat confused situation" in San Stefano.

Adam grabbed the microphone.

"Hullo two. Enemy there? Over."

"Hullo two. No, just quite a party of prisoners, sitting in the square. Over."

There was nothing surprising in this, by now. Italian partisans had been delivering to the advancing Allies droves of Wehrmacht prisoners who had been only too glad to find themselves in the more reassuring custody of the British Army. Those in San Stefano would be directed to walk westward, back down the centre line. Cages were being established.

"Hullo Two," said Adam. "Are there problems? Over."

Will Barker, at two, said that there were indeed problems. "It's a bit hard," he said, "to know who's in charge, who to deal with." He sounded harassed and Adam said Roger, that he was on his way up. Driving forward with Eric Raikes a minute later he reflected that so far there had been mercifully few of the political complications and dangers of which they'd been warned. San Stefano looked like breaking the record.

San Stefano did indeed look like breaking the record. As Adam's jeep drove at speed into the small square he took in a number of simultaneous impressions, photographs on the patina of his mind and subsequent memory.

First were the prisoners. There were about two hundred men in motley Wehrmacht uniforms sitting on the ground looking with a good deal of apathy at the British soldiers, and – as Adam perceived on closer inspection – with a certain scornful hostility, a quite different impression, at the next main category of individuals in the square, the armed Italian Partisans.

These made the second and vivid impression. Partisans had been sighted in small groups in previous places on the route but in San Stefano there appeared to be a huge mass of them. The Partisans were hung with bandoliers of what seemed, in most cases, to be British ammunition and in many cases had what looked like British rifles slung over the shoulder although here and there Adam saw an American carbine and in several instances a

German Schmeiser machine pistol. A number of the Partisans were also festooned with grenades. Almost all wore berets, almost all had cigarettes hanging from the lip, and almost all had red armbands with the hammer and sickle roughly printed thereon. Most of the Partisans were shouting, although by no means in unison. Argument seemed vigorous, and at least six of the comrades were shouting at Will Barker.

The third impression was made on Adam's senses by the Westmorlands themselves and Adam felt proud of them. They were standing in ones and twos, expressions of amused incomprehension on their faces, rifles at the ready under arms, the British Army's unbecoming beret-like headress pushed in most cases somewhat to the back of the head, a style Adam disliked and corrected in quieter times. But he felt proud of them. They were unaffected by whatever turmoil was brewing. They were impartial, with the impartiality of total lack of interest. They were minding the Jerry prisoners as potentially recalcitrant children, but without rancour.

They presumably, Adam thought and profoundly hoped, had most of B-Company deployed somewhere forward, reasonably watchful for any astonishing, last-ditch German counter-stroke. B-Company had been ordered to "make good" San Stefano – another company would take the lead thereafter. Of the Yeomanry tanks there was no sign in the square – they often, Adam had found, had a usefully quelling effect on over-enthusiastic natives, who seemed to credit them with almost magical powers.

Will Barker broke through the circle of gesticulating Italians, approached Adam and saluted. He was unsure how well he'd done in San Stefano so far.

"When we first arrived, sir, a chap who appeared to be some sort of mayor met us, something like that. Wore a sash in Italian colours. Very friendly indeed, I got the drift, he said how glad the people of San Stefano are to see us, that sort of thing. Welcomed the British who had liberated them from the Germans and the Fascists. I got most of it."

"Well?"

"We'd pushed most of the company and the Shermans to the far side of town where they are now. Half the population seemed to be moving with them, offering them vino and so forth. Then these chaps turned up— " Will indicated the Partisans and, seeing that they were clearly under discussion, a very stout, unshaven man approached Adam. He was one of the Schmeiser carriers, and the little knot of his immediate cronies stood aside to let him walk forward. A man of authority.

As he moved towards them Will continued, "This chap who's about to talk to you seemed to be their boss. They brought in more Jerry prisoners – about half the total in fact."

"Very good."

"Trouble was they grabbed the mayor or whoever he was I'd been dealing with. Started shouting at me that he was no good. A Fascist."

"I see."

"And he started screaming back. Again, I think I got most of it. He said it was a lie, he was no Fascist, they were bandits – I got that all right. And *assassinine* – that's not hard either. Of course obviously they're mostly Communists, but he didn't say that, hardly advisable I suppose, it's meant to be a good idea. Anyway there was a real shouting match. Then they grabbed him."

"You intervened?"

Turning towards the Partisan who was trying to attract his attention Adam, not speaking to him, said to Eric Raikes, "tell him I will speak to him in two minutes. Ask him to wait, please, until I have received a report."

"Carry on, Will. So you intervened?"

"Yes, I'd no idea who was right or wrong or where we're meant to stand, but I thought I couldn't let them shoot the poor little bugger, with B-Company just looking on. They certainly intended to. They'd dragged him over against the church wall over there, and were talking to me, jabbering, explaining, all the time hoping I'd do nothing I suppose. Anyway I started shouting myself, I got 5-Platoon, who were standing about, to double over, and I got them to grab the poor little mayor, Fascist or no Fascist, and I yelled at this chap who's trying to have a word with you now that I was in charge and these were my orders, that sort of thing. I'd no idea what orders I was going to give but I thought what you might call a show of authority was required."

Will had looked progressively more happy as his recital had run. The stout, Schmeiser-toting Partisan, clearly understanding that recent events involving himself were being explained, stood a few yards from Adam, awaiting his moment. Adam deliberately deferred, looking and speaking to him. He gave himself a full half-minute's deliberation.

"You did right, Will."

"Thank you, sir."

"Absolutely right. I'm going to hear what your friend here has to say, and Eric will translate with a good show of formality. And then I expect we'll have to treat him as if he's in charge. He's got the guns, after all, and unless we disarm his people or something like that we've obviously got to play along with them. They've been fighting the Germans, like ourselves, and what happens to their country now is up to Italians, not to us."

"Quite, sir."

"But we won't allow murder or bullying. Not while we're in possession, so to speak. You did right. I suspect I'll have to look fierce and say we have orders to arrest your little mayor. Where is he now?"

"I've placed him in the care of 5-Platoon, over there." Will pointed. "The Partisans are looking at him like cats walking round a canary cage."

"I daresay. What attitude did most of the people here take up, do you think, when all this was going on?" And Will said that it was impossible to say. They'd all been screaming, gesticulating, shouting at each other and at him. It was impossible to say. Adam nodded and then turned towards the Partisan leader, making his movement deliberately abrupt. Then he stopped and stood very still. Next he shot out his hand, and for the first time, very deliberately, smiled the charming and renowned Hardrow smile.

Later that evening, when they had left San Stefano ten miles behind them, rumbling but apparently quiescent, with some British gunners occupying it, Adam was summoned to the radio set.

"Brigade Commander wants you, personally, sir."

They had set up Battalion Headquarters in a doctor's house in a small and rather dirty village. Adam presumed that, contrary to previous orders, another battalion was about to be passed into the lead for the morrow's advance. He wished he had found a better place in which to spend what might turn into a day's rest before resuming the onward march, although the doctor, sulky and suspicious, had made several perfectly capacious rooms available. But the Brigadier merely said that he had something particular to communicate and was coming up to see them and wanted to find Adam himself. He would be with them within the half-hour.

It was, therefore, at nine o'clock in the evening of a day at the beginning of May, in a doctor's house in the village of Pastinia, not far from the borders of Italy, Austria and what had until 1941 been Yugoslavia, that Adam Hardrow heard his Brigade Commander say, "The signal's going out officially tomorrow morning, Adam, and its effective from midday tomorrow. But as I'd heard already and was near you I thought I'd visit and put you in the picture. Early warning."

"Early warning of what, sir? And what is effective from midday tomorrow?"

"Ceasefire, Adam. In this part of the world, at least, the Huns have surrendered. Packed it in."

CHAPTER X

"The Jerries have packed it in! Here in Italy, anyway, they've packed it in!" The word ran round 2nd Westmorlands like fire through corn. It couldn't, surely, be long now before the whole bleeding business of the Second World War was over, men said to each other and said to their officers, hungry for news, gratified, yet feeling an extraordinary sense of anti-climax. So it was over, was it. So what?

"Any chance of demob before Christmas, sir?" Pell asked Regimental Sergeant-Major Quidding, to receive an earful back.

"Demob, what are you talking about, Pell? You don't know the Germans have surrendered in Germany yet. Just because they've chucked it in in Italy doesn't mean they're done for everywhere."

"Can't be long, can it, sir?"

"How should I know? Anyway there's the Japanese, Pell! The war against Japan is going to take a lot of winning yet. And, no doubt, a lot of time!"

"They won't send this Battalion out there, will they, sir?"

"More than likely, I'd say," said Sergeant-Major Quidding unkindly. Pell, whose mind had already flitted to his wife and three small children in the outskirts of Penrith felt suitably depressed. The Japs! Bleeding Hell! Meanwhile they were on their way to yet another Iti town.

At least they could now drive into it without a division's worth of artillery brassing the bloody place up before it was safe to show your face.

The Yugoslav looked at Adam without friendliness. He was standing on the steps of what appeared the largest building in the little town of Menzano – Adam supposed it to be the town hall. Its double doors had evidently been opened with some violence: one was hanging on its hinges, the other had a large splinter of wood obtruding. Behind the Yugoslav, who Adam imagined was the commander of this considerable body of armed men and women, stood a half dozen of immediate supporters. Adam could see red stars displayed but no other recognisable insignia.

Very evident, however, were their weapons. The Yugoslavs were hung with assortments of arms, hand-grenades, bandoliers and knives which made the Italian Partisans look almost pacific. The Yugoslav commander had a Luger in a holster on his leather belt and slung over the right shoulder a sub-machine gun which Adam couldn't identify but suspected might be Russian. It looked rough and serviceable and heavy. It also looked as if it might go off at any moment. Across the Yugoslav's left shoulder was draped a bandolier of cartridges. He wore a soft, uniform-type cap with no peak. Adam found it hard to imagine him in genial mood. On his immediate right stood a dark-haired girl of perhaps nineteen or twenty, sporting almost as much armament as her leader. Her expression, too, was scowling and hostile although her features were fine and she was, Adam thought, intended by God to be handsome.

She stared grimly at Adam and said, "I speak English. I will translate."

"Good!" Adam tried a smile. No sort of response.

There seemed to be about two hundred Yugoslavs in

Menzano, perhaps more. There had been no warning of this. Adam had driven in, the Battalion in convoy behind him, ten minutes earlier. He had been warned that an Italian Partisan group had "more or less taken over Menzano", and had presumed that the Westmorlands might be in for the by-now-familiar experience of preventing excessive murder of Italians by Italians – or at least postponing it until 2nd Westmorlands had moved on. The San Stefano experience.

And so it had initially appeared. Adam's jeep had been stopped by a crush of Italians at the entrance to the town, yet another hilltop town. Partisans, by now fairly easily identifiable, had been clearly in charge. There had been nothing like the allegedly Fascist Mayor of San Stefano – no sign of any Italians claiming legitimate authority in fact.

But the Partisans had been shouting more than welcomes. Something was clearly upsetting them, and the hubbub had been so great that even Eric Raikes, whose Italian had risen to most occasions very commendably, had looked perplexed.

"I'm not sure what's eating them, sir."

Rather to Adam's surprise a priest had been among the yelling jostling crowd. Were not the Communist Partisans sworn enemies of the Church? Not invariably, it appeared.

"Try to get sense out of that priest, Eric." The Partisan pack, without hostility, were preventing Adam drive his jeep forward. Eric had had the same idea.

"*Padre!* *"cusi, Padre* – "

Conversation was conducted *fortissimo* since none of the Partisans had it in mind to quieten sufficiently for the words of others to be heard but luckily the priest's voice was at least as loud as anyone's and Eric gathered something, nodded, shouted another question, nodded again and turned.

"Something about foreigners, sir. Foreigners in the town. Not friendly I rather gather."

"Eric, you don't suppose they're trying to tell us the Germans are here, making a last stand, refusing to surrender? Germans who may not have had the surrender order?"

Eric shook his head.

"I think not, sir. *Tedeschi?*" he yelled at priest and Partisans together. There was a roar of "No, no" and much shaking of heads. Nodding to them all as if understanding all things, saying in uncomprehended English in a reassuring tone, "Very well, I understand, we'll see to things, just let me and my battalion by, thank you very much," Adam managed to edge his jeep forward. Behind him C-Company, led by a grinning Roger Bellew who was by now much enjoying company command, followed in vehicles, canopies down, red Westmorland faces gazing incredulously at the hubbub of Partisans. As the column inched forward towards what Adam rightly supposed was the main square and centre of turmoil, the Italians surged along, parallel to the trucks and shaking hands extended from the truck sides. It was all, Adam supposed, good-humoured. So far there had been no rifle shots, none of the indicators of civil feuding for which they were now more or less ready.

And then, in the main square, the Yugoslavs. In considerable numbers. Concentrated. And on the steps of the Town Hall their commander. Complete with interpreter.

Adam had approached him and said in English that he was Colonel Hardrow, Commanding Officer of 2nd Battalion, Westmorland Regiment, British Army, and that his orders were to occupy until further orders the town of Menzano, to do anything possible to assist the civil administration pending the installation of Allied Military Government, to take charge of any German prisoners of war and supervise their evacuation to British cages, and to be ready to take action against any enemy forces still resisting the order to surrender. He, Colonel Hardrow, now proposed to arrange the billeting of his men in the town.

The Yugoslav stared at him. His expression was full of distrust; indeed, as Adam afterwards reported, hatred would not have been too strong a word. He turned his head to the girl beside him and spoke rapidly and at length. She nodded, interjected a word or two, nodded again. She knows the message as well as he does, Adam thought. He tried to keep a courteous smile on his face. The girl started to talk.

"The Commander says you have no right to be here— "

Adam was expecting something like this. He realised that he would have to decide on very simple objectives and principles and stick to them. His objective, he reckoned, was to quarter 2nd Westmorlands in Menzano and to ensure that, while they were there, no violence erupted. It wasn't going to be easy. Meanwhile a position needed staking out. He interrupted the girl, holding up his hand politely.

"Excuse me. Would you please tell me who I'm talking to?"

She glared at him with, if possible, even more hostility.

"This is Colonel Pastovic. He is the Commander of the 77th Brigade of the Yugoslav People's Army."

Is he indeed, thought Adam, well we've both been promoted pretty young! The girl was continuing, "You have no right to be here. This is Yugoslav territory and it will be administered by the Yugoslav People's Army. The People's— "

It seemed that some of the Italian Partisans understood this. They were watching this scene from close quarters, forming an ill-assorted ring with a large cluster of the

Yugoslavs, and on the girl's declaration that Menzano was Yugoslav territory a roar went up from several hundred Italian throats. Carbines and machine pistols were unslung from shoulders and every partisan within range seemed to be yelling simultaneously at Adam and at Colonel Pastovic. At the same moment Pastovic shouted – he had strong lungs and a rather musical voice, very resonant – and Adam saw a group of the Yugoslav Partisans, perhaps thirty of them, detach themselves from the group on the Town Hall steps and double over to a point some twenty-five yards away where they immediately formed up in a line, weapons unslung. Pastovic ostentatiously undid the strap of his Luger holster. The girl spoke.

"Colonel Pastovic says that he has orders to suppress any Fascist or unruly elements."

At that moment they all heard first one, then another, then a third short burst of sub-machine gun fire. The bursts seemed to come from one of the streets leading off the little square. Pastovic said something which the girl did not translate. The tableau remained frozen for a little – Adam, very still, confronting Pastovic; Pastovic, with on either side of him his female interpreter-aide and six other immediate supporters; the surrounding circle of Italian Partisans, about fifty Adam supposed in the immediate vicinity, looking in both directions and quieter now; the single rank of Yugoslavs a short distance away and beyond that many more Yugoslavs.

Adam said, eyes on Pastovic, "Do you know what that shooting was, Colonel?"

The girl answered before Pastovic opened his mouth.

"It was some Fascists. Being executed for their crimes." At that there was another roar of response from the Italian Partisans.

Eric Raikes, at Adam's elbow, said, quietly, "They say they weren't Fascists, sir. Or not all."

Adam could see that Eric was extremely nervous. He turned his head back to Colonel Pastovic. Pastovic was watching him. The girl was watching him. The Italian Partisans, whose leader at this juncture had not identified himself, were undoubtedly watching him.

Adam remained rooted to exactly the same spot. He nodded his head very gently as if considering. Then, without turning, he said, "Eric."

"Yes, sir?"

"Go and tell Mr Quidding I want him. I want him over here. Tell him to report to me and not to come too close. Move quietly, without fuss, smile, don't push unless you have to. Go now."

"Right, sir." Adam felt rather than saw Eric slipping away. The Regimental Sergeant-Major had been riding in the companion jeep to Adam's. He wouldn't be more than forty yards away. Adam looked up towards Pastovic and puckered his brows as if puzzled.

Pastovic started speaking again and after two minutes the girl interpreter said, "The Colonel asks that you now order your column of men to drive out of the town by the way they entered. They have no right to be here."

"That," said Adam, patiently, gently, speaking as if a little puzzled, "that will be difficult. Impossible in fact." And at that moment he heard a distinctive noise, a different noise from any impinging so far. On hearing this noise most others in the little tableau, including Pastovic, looked towards whence it emanated. Adam, too, turned his head. The noise, he appreciated, had been caused by Regimental Sergeant-Major Quidding halting and coming to attention ten yards away. Quidding was saluting, with great deliberation and energy. There was silence.

"Yes, sir?" said Quidding. Loudly.

"Mr Quidding, please report to Major Abel and Captain Bellew and ask them to form up A- and C-Companies and march them immediately into the square here, in threes. Then get back here and direct them to that side of the square over there," Adam pointed, "and over there," he pointed again.

"In threes, Mr Quidding."

"Yes, sir."

"Quite clear? And tell Mr Raikes I want him back here."

"Yes, sir."

A- and C-Companies, four troop carrying lorries each, were leading the Battalion column. Closed up as they now would be, it would only take a few minutes for them to arrive. Adam knew that Quidding, sensible and sensitive when that was needed, would quickly convey not only the letter of his simple order but its spirit and origins. Quidding was no fool.

"Ask Mr Raikes to return to me as you pass him. And to bring Pell." Diversions, thought Adam, diversions, something a little different. Time. We need time. The girl with Pastovic was talking again. Adam had spoken fast to the Regimental Sergeant Major and, while not entirely sure, he didn't think she'd understood his orders.

"Colonel Pastovic asks when your men will obey orders to leave."

"You can tell the Colonel," Adam said carefully, "that I have just given my own orders. But, of course, I have also received orders, from my general. I'm sure the Colonel understands that. Doesn't he?"

She looked puzzled.

"Please?"

"I said that I'm sure the Colonel understands that I, like him, have received orders."

Another dialogue, incomprehensible, between Pastovic and the girl. I wonder how long he'll last before doing something drastic, Adam thought. He must be getting fed up but he's probably been told to secure his object without force if possible. Or has he? Pastovic made a rejoinder and the girl responded. Several minutes passed. Adam moved not at all.

Eric Raikes, panting, rejoined him at that moment. He muttered, "A formed up and about stepping off now, sir."

"Good." Adam kept his voice conversational. He smiled easily.

"There's six bodies in a side street by A's lorries, sir," Eric said, "and more further down the street as far as I can see. Looks as if someone's got busy on them with an axe or something. Mutilated. Beastly."

Adam nodded. And as Eric started to say, very low, "The Itis are out for blood, they say it was done by these— "

Adam held up his hand.

"Later, Eric." For at that moment Adam could hear, unmistakably, the rhythmic tramp of feet as A-Company 2nd Westmorlands, followed after a fifty pace interval by C-Company, marched into the main *piazza* of Menzano.

The effect on Pastovic was electric. He pointed, gesticulated, and started shouting. He yelled an order to the Yugoslav in charge of the detachment drawn up in single rank at a little distance. And he snapped what seemed to be commands at members of his immediate entourage who slipped away in various directions. To the girl he aimed a torrent of words, pointing towards Adam, a torrent of words so rapid that she couldn't translate until it was over. Then she turned to Adam, her face as angry as her master's. There was no "the Colonel says" in what she had to say.

"Why are your men here?" We have told you you have no right to be here. We have told you to take your soldiers away, at once. You are confusing the situation. You are confusing the Italians. You are to leave now. This is Yugoslav territory."

Adam nodded. He kept his voice courteous and slow, and at each sentence he waited for the girl to translate. After his first sentences she attempted to answer back.

"That is wrong! That— "

"Translate, please!" said Adam, his voice a touch louder, his face set. "Translate, please! I am speaking to the Colonel."

A moment's hesitation and then she did so. And Adam continued, very, very deliberate.

"Those men are two companies of my Battalion. There are two more companies. We have, as you can see, about forty machine guns and about three hundred rifles in Menzano. My men are now going to move into four different quarters of the town. Within those four quarters peace will be kept by my soldiers and anybody breaking the peace, using a weapon or assaulting any inhabitant will be immediately arrested. By my men. And anybody attempting to interfere with my men doing their duty will be shot. By my men."

The girl talked rapidly and Adam reckoned she was conveying the sense. Then there was a complete silence. Adam said out of the corner of his mouth, "Repeat that in Italian, Eric!" and Eric Raikes, prefacing it very loudly with "*Il Colonello Ordinate*", had a fair go at doing exactly that. Adam eyed Pastovic and the girl. He found he had taken an especial dislike to the girl. She started to talk rapidly in Yugoslav, and Adam raised his hand and said sharply "*Momente!*" Something like that might be comprehensible in any language he thought.

"*Momente!*" To Eric he said, "Try to get it across as I say it, Eric."

"Right, sir."

"Now," Adam said, conversationally, looking all the

time at Pastovic, "you have said this is Yugoslav territory. It is not Yugoslav territory. On my map it is Italian territory. What it becomes is a matter for governments and not for me. And not for you. Today – today, Colonel – it is Italian territory, occupied by the British Army and subject to the orders of the Commander-in-Chief of the Allied Armies in Italy. My men are here to carry out those orders and safeguard that territory; and anybody opposing them with force will be met by force."

To the girl, with a sudden change of tone and temper, peremptorily, Adam said, "Translate that!" He did not smile.

"You've got a visitor, sir," said Regimental Sergeant-Major Quidding, putting his head round the door of the room in the town hall Adam had appropriated. He was grinning. Adam looked up and then jumped to his feet.

"Ben!"

Ben Jameson was hobbling, his foot in plaster, a stick in his hand. He said, "I'm not in the least fit, don't make any mistake about that. I'm very seriously wounded and I am really due for return to hospital in England and a prolonged period of sick leave. Don't make any mistake about that, either. Nor you, Mr Quidding."

"No, sir."

"Not many people get run over by a Fantail. I may get a medal. I've written my own citation."

Adam smiled at him.

"Ben, seriously, should you be hobbling about rather than resting?"

"Its not actually very serious. My foot, I mean. When they got down to it they found the injuries to be more or less what doctors, so slightingly, call superficial. Likely to be almost completely mended in a month, and 'light duties' in another two weeks. I got bored in the hospital and thought I'd pay some visits. I gather you've been confirmed in Command, I'm so glad."

"You'd better have the Battalion back, Ben. When you're fit."

"I gather," said Ben, "that there are other plans for me, which will knock on the head my ideas about a long stretch in England."

"What other plans?"

Ben smiled. "This brigade, believe it or not."

Adam had never before seen Ben look even slightly embarrassed but he did now. "I'm glad," he said from the heart, "very glad. Everyone's being saying its mooted. I'm delighted it's not been changed by— "

"By the collapse of the Third Reich? Well, I imagine we'll all go down about three ranks very shortly but meanwhile, hard though it is to remember it, the war is still going on – and I suppose that at least some of the troops now in Europe will be needed to help polish off Japan. A truly ghastly thought."

"And not one," said Adam, "likely to commend itself very warmly to our men."

"Let's hope it won't come to it. Anyway, I'm due to take over from Brigadier Dick in three weeks' time and I've promised to rest my limbs as much as I can till then." Ben inspected Adam and said, "You look rather tired."

Adam said, smiling, that tiredness was hardly justified after Battalion Command of only a week or so but Ben nodded, watching him, and said, "and it's gone well, I gather."

"It's gone all right. I've been lucky."

Adam gave him news of the Battalion, news of individuals, deeds, errors, absurdities. Ben drank it in thirstily.

"You've had some tricky moments, Adam, with Partisans and such."

Adam told him about the Yugoslavs in Menzano and

Ben said yes, he gathered from Divisional Headquarters that this area was something of a bone of contention, he was sure the Battalion had done admirably, cooled things down.

"We had to be quite tough, Ben. But that was two days ago and there's been no trouble since. Things are pretty tense."

"I imagine our political masters are having a nightmare of a time. And while they try to sort matters out we may have some difficult times here on the ground."

"I suppose so. They're bloody people, Ben. Absolutely bloody. They murdered about twenty people here, for no particular reason as far as I can see. And they didn't just shoot them – they hacked them about, mutilated them. Before finishing them off, I suspect. Things are only just coming to light. Meanwhile all we could do was keep the various factions apart and shoot anyone who tried to shoot anyone else."

"What about the Italian Partisans?"

"They hate the Jugs. Like poison."

"In spite of both being Communists?"

"Doesn't make the smallest difference. Europe's bound to be in quite a mess, isn't it Ben? To say nothing of Russian behaviour, if the stories one hears are correct. And I expect they are."

"It's a far cry," said Ben slowly, "from the almost carefree days of September 1939 when you were a subaltern in my Company and your eyes shone with the excitement of going to war and with righteous zeal at the chivalrous notion of facing up to a bully at last. And defending Poland. Poor old Poland!"

"A far cry indeed, Ben. Six years and God knows how much blood, Still, it's over. And we've won, which didn't seem all that likely in 1940."

"Yes. We've won. Or something."

A small silence lay between them, each with his memories. Among Adam's memories, inevitably, was that of Felicity Jameson, Ben's wife, lying naked and compliant in Adam's arms. Odd, he thought, that it doesn't make me feel guilty in his presence now. And he still didn't know whether Ben guessed. Ben was looking out of a window at the strong spring sun in a Menzano street and saying that he supposed he'd have to go back to the tedious General Hospital.

"The Medic CO lent me his car to pay social visits. A nice man."

Adam smiled and said again how delighted the whole Battalion would be to learn of Ben's impending promotion and appointment. Could it be announced yet? Not quite yet, next week I fancy, Ben said. He swung his plastered leg awkwardly and said he supposed he was lucky still to have it at all.

"By the way I expect you'll get another visitor soon. Frank Fosdikes's out here – a bigwig on the Staff."

"*Colonel Frank Fosdike*! What's he— "

"I can't remember his exact title. He's something in political affairs, or civil liaison, or Allied something-or-other. He's a brigadier."

"Oh well," said Adam, staring at him, "we'll have to make him welcome. He's a Westmorland, after all." They looked at each other and then both burst into shouts of laughter.

The Westmorlands' stay in Menzano lengthened from two to three and then four days. On the fifth day orders reached them of an agreeable character: the Battalion was to move northward into Austria and undertake occupation duties. Advance parties were to leave on the morrow. The prospect of fresh countryside and mountains seemed particularly inviting as the Italian summer approached. Civil affairs in Menzano were now the province of an officer especially charged with them who had just arrived. The Yugoslavs had withdrawn as suddenly as they had, apparently, first appeared; moving eastward. Colonel Pastovic had sought Adam and, much to Adam's surprise, had shaken him warmly by the hand. There had been no trouble between his Partisans and the Westmorland soldiers since their first dramatic confrontation although the situation, Adam recognised, had always been fragile. He found the Yugoslav presence troubling and repugnant.

The day before the Battalion moved off, on the seventh day after their arrival in Menzano, Adam had another unexpected visitor. He had been stretching his legs walking round Menzano from company area to company area, an agreeable but hot occupation on that May morning. Menzano, thought Adam, could be a pretty place if it were in better repair, were cleaned up and were rid of both Partisans (all varieties) and troops (all nationalities). He suspected the inhabitants secretly felt the same although they were extremely friendly and Adam reckoned from his observation that a number of more or less romantic attachments had budded between some Westmorlands and the ladies of Menzano.

Adam had returned to the room in the Town Hall he had retained as his office. Peter Jarrett had set up shop in a sort of ante-room adjoining. Adam hung up his cap and belt. Orders about dress had recently gone out within the Battalion – the Brigadier had issued prompt instructions that one consequence of the coming of peace had to be revived concern for military appearance, a consequence Adam entirely approved. They could all, he reflected, do with a good deal of smartening up. Mr Quidding was already murmuring suggestions about parades.

Peter Jarrett put his head round the door.

"There's a padre who's asking to see you, sir."

"The Divisional Padre? Is he visiting Rupert?" The Reverend Rupert Findlay, a very agreeable and very idle clergyman of the Church of England, had been the Westmorlands' Battalion chaplain since Sicily days. Adam had not known him before joining them, and liked him very much. Rupert Findlay made no secret of his dislike for Army life and of his longing to find a rural parish in the north country, preferably one with undemanding duties; but he was liked by the men, who appreciated the fact that he never talked to them about anything but cricket and football, and that if they confided to him – which was rare – some family problem he listened politely and responded sensibly. In what might be called his official capacity they mostly saw him at burials, functions he performed with decency. A very adequate Battalion padre, Adam thought, not one to carry out mass conversions of those without faith but a good man.

"No, Rupert's not here, sir, this one's not from Division. He's a civilian."

The local priest perhaps.

"Does he really want to see me, Peter?" Adam had spent longer than intended walking round Menzano. He had planned to write yet more letters before lunch, those interminable letters a battalion commander owed to all and sundry.

"Yes, he says so. He knows your name."

"An Italian?"

"That I'm not," said the burly figure behind Peter Jarrett which now pushed past the Adjutant without ceremony and advanced on Adam with outstretched hand.

"*Father Flynn!*"

Fifteen minutes later Adam had seated Father Flynn in a chair in the small café the Westmorlands had taken over as

Battalion Headquarters Officers' Mess and had set a glass of wine beside him. Other Battalion Headquarters officers had observed that the CO had a somewhat unusual guest and had given them a wide berth. Adam was grateful for this. He wanted to entertain Father Flynn. He wanted to talk to him. He would be proud to introduce him to some brother officers. But a little later.

Father Flynn looked up with a slightly mysterious look.

"You'll be a colonel now, is that it?"

"That's it."

"Colonel, this wine here looks very nice, very nice. But I'm wondering— "

"Yes, Father?"

"There wouldn't be in this Mess of yours such a thing as a drop of whisky, would there?"

Adam said there would, there would indeed. It was a pleasure to be able to gratify a taste which conditions, even in Vatican City, might have difficulty in meeting. Mess Corporal Willey brought a glass over with a smile and Father Flynn looked up at him benevolently.

"That's a very big glass you have there, young man."

"Water, sir?"

"No thank you, young man, no thank you." To Adam, Father Flynn said that he had enjoyed meeting Colonel Jameson in Rome. Adam told him of Ben's mishap and sudden replacement by himself and Father Flynn said, ah, poor fellow, poor fellow, but it was fine to think he'd be all right and about to be a brigadier soon, would you believe it, and him a boy still.

"And you a colonel! Wonderful, wonderful!"

"It won't be for long, Father. I'll be going down to Captain soon, I expect. As I was when you first met me."

"Is that so, is that so? Ah well!" They sipped their

drinks. Adam knew that Father Flynn knew exactly what was in his mind. He would speak when ready.

Father Flynn sighed and set his glass down. He looked at Adam.

"That lady that helped you, the Carlucci one— "

Adam nodded. His heart was beating.

"It was a bad business. Sure, they'll find her but there's prisoners and wanderers and refugees and folk fleeing from these Bolsheviks, all over Europe, millions of them. It's a terrible business, a terrible business. Such wickedness everywhere."

"So you don't know, Father," Adam said, "whether Anni Carlucci is alive or not?"

"No. I've asked our people – the Vatican has I don't know how many thousands of enquiries, you can imagine, Colonel."

"Of course."

"We've got lines of contact and enquiry, of course we have. And we're hearing fresh things all the time."

"I suppose so."

"And many of the things we're hearing are terrible things, Colonel. Wicked, terrible things. The cruelties people are inflicting on each other in these times are terrible, terrible things. And it's both sides been doing it, I can tell you that."

"I know."

"So my answer to your question is I don't know, I can't say for certain, whether Anni Carlucci is alive or not, but I can say that I *think* she is. I say that because we've heard of the death of several that were in the same sort of trouble as her. But not of hers."

It was pretty cold comfort. There was a long silence and Father Flynn said, "There's one thing, though. Her boy's all right. The little fellow, Guido. He's OK. He's safe."

Adam had forgotten about Guido. He said dully, "Good. Where is he?"

"He's at home. He'd been taken off with a maid, a good woman, fond of him. Now he's back at the Villa Avoria. The Americans are in most of the house but the lad's there, he's all right. They're telling him his mother's had to go away for a long, long time but he's not to worry, she'll be back. Pray for her."

"I see."

"Pray for her."

"I will, Father."

"I know what's in your heart, Colonel."

"Do you, Father Flynn?"

"Yes, maybe I do. And there's nothing you can do about that. Whether it'll turn good or bad or neither there's nothing, just now, you can do about it."

"May I stay in touch with you, Father Flynn? You're the only person— "

"Whom you know, who knows her. Of course. Letters take a long time these days."

"And we're off to Austria."

"Tell me where," said Father Flynn, producing a large, disorganised-looking notebook. And when Adam told him, he said, "Yes, yes. That'll be near—" and mentioned two places of which Adam had never hear.

"I have friends in that part of the world, Colonel. I'll let them know you'll be around."

"Priests, Father Flynn?"

"Well," said Father Flynn, "they might be, they might be!" Adam looked at him, remembering that stern face and how it would suddenly be creased by the widest of smiles. He summoned Corporal Willey, and Father Flynn, eyebrows raised in mock surprise, held out his glass for replenishment and started to ask Adam's views on the future course of events in occupied Italy.

Father Flynn was not the last unexpected visitor to Menzano. A providential hour had elapsed after his unhurried departure when Mr Quidding appeared in Adam's room and saluted.

"Brigadier just coming in, sir."

"Our Brigadier? Brigadier Robbins?" Dick Robbins would be handing over to Ben Jameson and bidding farewell at some time, but surely not yet.

"No, sir. Not ours, sir."

"Adam!" said a well-remembered voice, enthusiastically. Adam stood up, peered and saluted with as sincere a smile as he could manage.

"Brigadier Frank! How nice to see you!"

"Wasn't going to let too long go by after the end of the war before visiting the dear old Battalion I started it off with," said Frank Fosdike, grammar unusually clumsy, smile wide as ever, eyes thoughtful. He wrung Adam's hand.

"My dear Adam! Wonderful to see you in command! Not surprising to those of us who knew you in the old days!"

This is terrible, Adam thought, it's already beginning to grate. He said, "Well, it's grand to see you here, sir. Ben told me you were out here and might be calling."

"Ah Ben, Ben Jameson! Getting this Brigade, I gather! Extraordinary, extraordinary! I gather a vehicle ran over his foot."

"He's much better, sir. He called here yesterday. Limping a bit but fit soon."

"Good! Good! I don't think I know the RSM, Adam. He wasn't here in the old days, of course."

"No, sir, he wasn't." Adam summoned and introduced Mr Quidding. Afterwards they toured Battalion Headquarters and Brigadier Fosdike spoke graciously to Peter

Jarrett, Eric Raikes and others before returning to Adam's office. Then they chatted and Adam talked of such few 2nd Westmorland personalities as had survived from the old days, the 1940 days. The Fosdike days.

"I expect you'd like a walk round the town, sir? We've got all companies in various quarters of it."

"I'm afraid I've not got time, Adam."

You never did have, Adam thought. He had already established that the Fosdike schedule was too tight to admit taking refreshment. Too tight, even, to wait to see Harry Venables who had been his own Adjutant and was away at a meeting at Brigade HQ, back "any moment".

Brigadier Fosdike said, "And how is little Saskia, my marvellous assistant in Cairo?"

Saskia, Adam's sister, had worked for Frank Fosdike, a circumstance which brought back mixed memories, some of them troubled.

"She's fine."

"And her wild Highland husband?"

"He's fine too. I saw quite a bit of him in Belgium before I came out here. Marvellous chap."

"Yes," said Frank Fosdike, without enthusiasm. He asked about Adam's mother, Natasha. Still in London, Adam said, still grumbling about the course of events in Europe, still very independent in mind and views. He smiled. They were both standing now, Brigadier Fosdike having intimated that he ought to leave.

"I gather you had a little trouble when you first arrived here in Menzano, Adam? The word's got round."

"You mean the Yugoslavs, sir."

"Quite. Tricky customers, they can be. Its a complex situation. Wheels within wheels, Adam. High politics."

"I expect so, sir. In this place they were murdering people."

Frank Fosdike said, "It's going to need a lot of tact,

Adam. A lot of tact. It's going to try our patience a good deal, I'm afraid."

"I suppose so, sir."

"We're all going to have to do things we may not greatly care for. Now and then."

Adam nodded, without much understanding, and Brigadier Fosdike said that he was trying to get "the Powers that Be" to send out better political guidance for commanders at Regimental level. It wasn't fair on them, he said with a fine show of sympathy, to expect them to show right judgement in circumstances completely beyond the experience or comprehension of the ordinary battalion commander. How could they? They must have help and guidance. Circumstances, Adam thought, like people hacking other people to death for the hell of it. Very perplexing to know what to do, very! He saluted Brigadier Fosdike away into his car from the steps of Menzano Town Hall.

CHAPTER XI

Adam wondered how bad it was for the Battalion to be so comfortable, so happy and so relaxed. The conventional wisdom of the Army was that soldiers in pampered conditions soon became good for nothing but Adam, by no means hostile to the conventional wisdom, nevertheless thought that a period of calm enjoyment would be no unwelcome thing for 2nd Westmorlands.

And calm enjoyment, on the whole, was what they were savouring. They had moved to this part of south-eastern Austria two days after "sorting out" Menzano. North of the Alps a ravaged Germany was being occupied with anger and astonishment by the victorious Allies – anger and astonishment because only now were the Nazi concentration camps being opened to inspection; they were for the most part overrun in the closing weeks of the war, and the enormity of the suffering inflicted by the Third Reich on its enemies was sinking in.

The horrors, and the photographs of the horrors, were indignantly devoured by the men of the Allied Armies and a general taste for retribution was widespread. What sort of a nation was it which could throw up leaders and administrators for this kind of corporate and institutionalised brutality, amounting in many cases to mass murder?

There was a good deal of discussion as to how much "ordinary Germans" had known of the horrors. Harry Venables gave voice to a commonly held sentiment.

"Look how many people must have been involved in loading the trains, for instance. Don't tell me they didn't know where the poor sods were going or what was waiting for them!"

"They may have thought people – Jews and so forth – were simply being resettled in the East or something—"

"I don't believe such helpers were without their inklings," Harry said robustly, "and if they knew or even guessed they're involved in the guilt. All of them, to some degree."

But in Austria, except through the newspapers, little of this impinged. Here the scenery was delightful and spring was in the air. Meadows, now clear of snow, surrounded lakes which had always provided leisure and recreation for Austrians and Germans alike. Charming villas and pretty villages abounded, all for privileged occupation by the victorious troops. Adam's Battalion Headquarters was in one such villa and his Battalion Headquarters Officer's Mess in another, one hundred yards away. To the surprise of the soldiers, the local population were eager to explain how welcome the British were and how much they had detested the Nazis, the Germans and the *Anschluss* by which they had, they said, been forced into Germany's disagreeable embrace. These assurances were, by the directions of the authorities, treated with a certain reserve; but human nature inclines to friendship when bullets aren't flying, Austrian smiles were infectious, the girls seemed pretty beyond the average, the sky was blue, local wine was on offer, the birds were singing. And there was no war.

British prisoners of war, several groups of them, appeared quite soon in the Battalion area and one man Adam found on their second evening chattering with animation to the Regimental Sergeant-Major. Adam stared at him.

"Good heavens, isn't it Corporal Blyth?"

"That's it, sir. 1st Battalion."

Corporal Blyth, in another company, had been taken prisoner in the Western desert, in that great run to and battle on Sidi Rezegh, near Tobruk. Adam grinned. What memories!

Corporal Blyth was eager to talk. They had been told they were due for repatriation at the weekend.

"Sorry to go, to tell the truth!" Blyth grinned. He said, "Of course I'm not a married man! It's been pretty good here. Working on a farm. They're nice folk."

Italy, he said, had been bad and Adam, an ex-prisoner of war in Italy himself, soon began exchanging reminiscences. Italy had been bloody, they both agreed, but Austria – now that was something different. Adam smiled his understanding. Blyth, it was clear, had, in soldiers' parlance, got his feet under the table.

So this was, and for a fortnight had been, peace. And Adam recognised that because he, personally, could not relax and enjoy it; because he, personally, was obsessed all the time with the need to find Anni somewhere in the chaos of Europe, to find what had happened to her, to rescue her, woo her, make her his – because of this obsession, he had no right to dampen the enjoyment of others and pretend that it was purely military rectitude which made him do so. They had been told, cautiously, that the likelihood of 2nd Westmorlands being shipped to the Far East was remote, at least in the short term. Everybody seemed to think it would take at least another year to finish off Japan but everybody, nevertheless, felt disposed to live for the moment. And for most the moment was good.

Duties, although no longer involving danger, wounding, death, were onerous. Within the Battalion area there were large numbers of camps established, in which to house and sort and attempt to administer the very large number of human beings of diverse nationalities washed up on this Austrian shore by the tides of war. A great number of these were Wehrmacht captives and Dick Abel had his company entirely occupied in guarding and administering a prisoner-of-war camp. Wehrmacht personnel were to be interned in these cages until policy dictated otherwise. Members of the SS were to be segregated for special treatment and, in time, reindoctrination. Others, divided by rank, were being gradually sorted by category and moved or shipped to more permanent establishments. It would all take a long time and much of it, as the authorities and the troops recognised without concern, would involve a good deal of suffering. So what? Look what they did to other people!

The prisoners of war in Wehrmacht uniform, the Germans and Austrians and ragbag of *Volksdeutsch* in Wehrmacht formations – these were comparatively straightforward. Less straightforward were the refugees of baffling diversity. And of these the most perplexing group were the Yugoslavs. Roger Bellew's C-Company was in charge of what had been designated a "transit camp" – in fact little but an expanse of meadow around which a wire fence had been erected to mark its limits. The expanse was huge and needed to be. What was less obvious was the significance of its designation. Transit to where? And transit by whom? For guided into this area, watched with stoical incredulity by the men of C-Company, came an enormous concourse of men, women, children, horses, farm animals, and carts of every description, carts horse-drawn, carts oxen-drawn and carts pulled by men, women and children. These were the Yugoslavs.

Why were they here? They had arrived on Roger's second day of duty, his first "customers", and they had not exactly resembled what he had been expecting. The Yugoslavs had been routed to Roger's camp by the decree of the military staffs and they caused considerable surprise. To begin with the men were all armed – a heterogeneous collection of weapons, but clearly serviceable. Orders on this subject came quickly.

"All Yugoslavs to be disarmed, without exception."

But why had they appeared? Adam, on hearing from C-Company that first evening, had supposed they might be captured Titoist Partisan prisoners of war, now liberated, but on hearing they were armed the picture changed instantly. These people had obviously not been German prisoners. They had been carrying on their own varying sorts of guerilla campaign across the border in Yugoslavia itself – a border only 20 miles away – and they had trekked, families, beasts, possessions, the lot, into Austria to escape. It was clear from Roger Bellew's first tentative explorations that what the Yugoslavs were trying to escape was the vengeance of the Titoists, the Communists. Adam drove over to the camp next morning – it was 11 miles up a winding and very beautiful road from Battalion Headquarters. He took the Regimental Sergeant-Major with him. The latter sighed.

"Good thing when we can get the whole Battalion together, sir."

"Yes. That won't be for quite a bit, I'm afraid."

"Pity, sir."

"I expect C-Company are happy. They've got a real job to do, as far as I can make out."

"Too happy, sir, I wouldn't wonder."

And Roger Bellew looked fit and cheerful. The astonishing complexity of Balkan politics and animosities seemed to serve simply to broaden his smile. It was clear he had learned a lot in the preceding twenty-four hours and he was anxious to instruct the CO.

"There are a lot of completely different races, sir. The Croats are the largest group. We've segregated them.

I've got a sort of senior Croat who talks English and I'm working through him."

"The Croats were pro-Italian. Pro-Axis. Or a lot of them were."

"This chap says not. He just says they were anti-Communist. Then there are the Slovenes – they're the tallest on the whole, and they seem to have about three wives each."

"Or something."

"Or something, quite sir! They seem pretty well at home here, it's quite near of course. And they're just as fanatically anti-Tito as the others, but they say they started fighting the Germans before anybody. And then there are Serbs. Most of the officers I've got are Serbs. They're adamant that they were the original Resistance against the Germans. Quite a lot of them have got photographs of the King. But they can't stand the Croats. I've got them segregated too, and another top Serb, a colonel. He's rather stuck-up, snooty sort of chap. Not like my top Croat, who's a very decent bloke. And my top Slovene is really grand, I wish we had him in the Battalion! Marvellous-looking chap, too!"

Roger was, clearly, already identifying with his charges. Adam smiled a question at him.

"The Serb, of course, equally anti-Tito?"

"Right, sir. He says that what we've got here is only a part of what he calls an Army Corps, and the rest were caught and murdered to a man or woman. Or child."

"Not impossible, Roger." Adam remembered Menzano. Not impossible indeed. Likely even.

"They all want to know what's going to happen to them, naturally. The administration's going quite well because the weather's fine and the rations have come up very smartly and the women are cooking and all that. We've got tents for about a third up already; and more arriving this afternoon, and all sited; and they've started digging latrines, rather reluctantly, and we've made them improvise screens from tarpaulins and so forth. Its coming on. We need more watercarts, of course, we could do with three times the number, I've reported that." Roger Bellew looked as if he was enjoying his work hugely. Mr Quidding looked disapproving. This wasn't really soldiering, and God knew what sort of habits the men might pick up. Mr Bellew, once a sergeant in the Pembrokes, might not have really acquired proper ideas yet. Roger was babbling away.

"Of course all they mind about is not to be sent back to the Titoists. That's what terrifies them. The Serb Colonel, not a chap I like much, told me, 'It's not just they shoot us. They torture us, all of us, and the women and children too, torture and rape!' He was pretty het-up and I told him to calm down, they're in British hands now."

"Quite right, Roger. God knows where they'll go, but I'm sure they won't be sent to Tito. They'd obviously be butchered – we all saw the form in Menzano. And there are plenty of camps like this – it's an enormous problem, with which, no doubt, the powers that be are wrestling as we talk."

Adam visited A-Company next day. Dick Abel had received orders to separate officers from men of his Wehrmacht charges, a separation enjoined by international law immediately on capture but which had been deferred until reaching this first, Austrian, stage of imprisonment. Dick had, when Adam arrived, just had a further telephone message, received and transmitted by Harry Venables after Adam's departure.

"I've got to keep all the officers here and the rest are to march to Wenstrich, leaving tomorrow."

"How many will that leave here, Dick? Officers?"

"About three hundred, and I've been told to expect about the same again tomorrow. We've got tentage enough for that lot, because they've been scaling me and delivering bivouacs for the larger number—" He talked on, like Roger Bellew, perfectly happy in his task. He asked whether Colonel Adam had any news of how long the camp would house, if that was the word, these people? There was a rumour they'd be transferred to England or Canada within weeks. No, Colonel Adam had no idea.

"Have you a reasonably competent-seeming senior German officer?"

"Yes, he's a Lieutenant-Colonel. Speaks English. Do you want to see him?"

"Not now," said Adam, "but as long as we're looking after them I've got a duty, I believe, to see the prisoners' 'representatives' at intervals, on a fairly formal basis, ask if they've got any complaints, that sort of thing. So on my next visit I'll have him brought before me, fix him with a stern look and enquire if all is well. And be pretty forbidding if he starts to grumble!"

Dick Abel smiled. He said, "It's odd, they all look so sort of normal. Might be among our own officers, except these ones are rather more tidily dressed! It's hard to think of them being associated with, you know, the sort of ghastly things we're now learning about."

"I know. I know. Well, I'll be back in a day or two's time, Dick. What's the name of your senior German, by the way?"

Dick Abel glanced at the paper on his mill board and said, "Von Pletsch. Lieutenant-Colonel von Pletsch."

Adam nodded, thoughtful. "I'll see him next time."

"Right, sir."

Back at Battalion Headquarters, the May evening glowing and lovely, Harry Venables greeted Adam with a broad grin.

"Any news, Harry?"

"Lots of news. First of all Brigadier Ben, as we must learn to call him, takes over command on 28th of the month."

"Excellent!" One of Adam's colleague battalion commanders, considerably his senior in age and service, had been commanding the brigade temporarily, Ben Jameson's predecessor having already left them for higher things. Adam had resolved to wait until Brigadier Ben's arrival before broaching the matter of some local leave in Italy. None was being granted at the moment, although leave at home would soon start, but Adam thought that something could be worked and Ben, of all people, would be sympathetic. Adam felt it absolutely necessary to make contact again with Father Flynn. There might, there just might be news. Individuals were drifting to the surface, here and there, out of the dark waters of a destroyed Continent.

"What else?"

"Brigadier Frank's in Austria. Brigadier Frank Fosdike. He's in Schlemmert. Apparently he's in charge of some sort of high-powered cell, responsible to the Commander-in-Chief, dealing with inter-Allied liaison, something like that. He called in and we gave him a drink. He was in fine form!" Harry chuckled. He had been Frank Fosdike's Adjutant once, and while he was the most good-humoured and charitable of men he shared certain memories with Adam Hardrow which were by no means favourable. Adam smiled back.

"I'm sure he'll do it very well! If anybody can! Any other news?"

The Adjutant, Peter Jarrett, spoke. "Things going on pretty well as regards administration and delivery of stores, sir." Peter enumerated briefly, company by company, camp by camp. Then he said, "We're getting pretty stretched though, sir. You wanted D-Company clear for the next two days."

"I did. Bill Andrews and his chaps need it and I promised him that if its humanly possible. Well?"

"We've got rather a fatigue put on us, sir. It'll take a whole company. Train duty. Day after tomorrow."

"It sounds deadly. Why us?"

"I told Brigade it would be difficult, sir, played up how much we've been doing. Seems the others are all in the same boat. And this train duty is one of several."

"A whole company, you say?"

"Yes, sir. I've warned D. Major Andrews is rather cross."

"I expect so. What do they have to do."

"I've got the orders here, sir." said Peter Jarrett, "and I've to pass them on verbatim to the company detailed. Rather highly classified for what one would have thought was a pretty routine duty. There's to be a party, strength laid down, to accompany a train, entrainment point laid down, destination told to Movements, timings laid down. Then— "

"Peter," said Adam, "who or what is to be travelling in this train?"

"Refugees, sir. Those Yugoslav refugees, in Roger's camp."

"What, *all* of them?"

"The categories are laid down, sir. Some are to go to another entrainment point. But pretty well all, I think, yes, sir."

"And the horses?" Adam heard himself saying, mechanically, almost facetiously. He held out his hand for the order to which Peter Jarrett had referred. He read it and said, "what do they mean 'cordon duty'? A cordon found by the same company, but separate from the train party?"

"I think that's to make sure they entrain, sir."

"Peter," said Adam, staring at him and not at the written order, "Peter, where are they going?"

"Paragraph eleven, sir."

Adam looked at it. It said that the entraining Yugoslavs were to be told, on enquiry, that they were being moved, with their families, to internment camps in Italy pending further diplomatic negotiations. Another paragraph said that livestock would be impounded and slaughtered by custodian units. Adam thought of some of the horses he had seen. They might well be put to better use.

"It seems quite straightforward, Peter."

"Yes, sir. Brigade said there might be more requirements of the same kind throughout this month."

"Is the CO in the Mess?"

Bill Andrews's voice sounded, for him, extraordinarily rough and peremptory. It was ten o'clock in the evening and they had dined well in the Battalion Headquarters Mess. Harry Venables, something of a gourmet, had discovered the proprietress of a Gasthof which in happier times had obviously had a reputation for its cuisine, and had enrolled her as a kind of consultant and procurer of local supplies. There were regulations about dealing with the local population, particularly in the matter of trade or barter but Adam, wisely, turned a blind eye.

Adam recognised the Andrews voice. There was a sharpness to it wholly unlike the quiet, knowing tones which were Bill's norm and which still had power to irritate with their complacency, the same irritation which Adam remembered being occasionally aroused by outstanding young Lance Corporal Andrews before being sent for Officer Cadet Training, long, long years ago. He called out, "Are you after me, Bill?"

"Can I have a word, sir?"

"Of course. Can it be in here? Have a glass of wine. And sit down."

Bill declined the glass of wine and sat next to Adam in one of the ugly, cushioned chairs of the villa. Adam could see he was in a disturbed state.

"I don't know if the Mess is the right place to say this, sir— "

"Come on, Bill. Don't be haughty!" Adam smiled. It always took a bit of a conscious effort to be easy and agreeable with Bill but the effort was worthwhile. He had served the Westmorland Regiment loyally and well. He was family.

Bill said, keeping his voice low, "I'd be very grateful, sir, if my Company is never again taken for this duty. Train duty."

"It's certainly been a very long duty, Bill, if you've only just got back. I think Peter told me the whole thing would only last about six hours and the men be back in billets by five."

"That's not what I mean, sir."

"And, as you know, I'd meant the Company to have these two days off. Peter made the case to Brigade, I'm sure very ably, but they wouldn't budge— "

"That's not what I mean either, sir. The orders given to me were clear. I was to explain to the Yugoslavs, if they asked, that they were being transferred to internment camps in Italy. All of them, families, the lot."

"I know. I saw the order."

"It was a deliberate lie. I was instructed to lie to those poor people." Bill's voice was highstrung and his face was set. Adam had never seen him like this.

"A lie, Bill?"

"A thumping lie. My orders didn't explain where the trains were really going. It was only when we set off that the Movement Control chap accompanying our train told me. By then we were under way. All these trains have gone to the border, the Yugoslav border. And all these people were, and were by our orders, handed over to the Jugs. To the Tito people."

Adam stared at him. He said softly, "What happened, Bill?" Adam's face was now as grim as that of Bill Andrews himself.

Bill told him. His rather muffled, jerky sentences expressed as clearly as greater eloquence the hatred he felt at what he had to say.

"At the crossing place the train stopped. The people were tight-packed of course but there were plenty of heads out of windows.

"They saw, at once, the Jugs, the Partisans, Titoists, whatever you call them. They were all over the platform and then their boss spoke to a Movement Control man and they, the Jugs, began to climb aboard. All armed to the teeth of course. And the carriage doors were all locked, by order, before we left. I was told to get our men off, they were travelling in separate compartments. The Yugoslavs were locked in.

"Several people tried to smash their way out through windows. We saw one woman, pouring with blood, I think she'd cut herself whether on purpose or not I've no idea. Others tried to pull her back. Then, as the train moved off, there were several actually got out, jumped train. On to the lines. Including, I saw in the distance, two children. The Jugs shot them – straight away, machine gun laid down the line of the track.

"Our men knew what was happening, of course they knew what was happening. They could see it all. And they knew very well what was going to happen next."

"No doubt of that, I suppose?" Adam said, his voice rather shaky. He felt none himself.

"None whatsoever. We weren't the first train. There

were two very early this morning. Train party another Battalion, I'm not sure which. And when we'd formed up after leaving the train, pretty fed up, the men knew the score naturally – before we moved off to board transport, Sergeant Brailsford told me there was an Austrian wanted to speak to me, who spoke English. So I spoke to him."

"Yes?"

"He was rather a decent chap, educated. Wore one of these grey coats with green ribbon, you know. Sort of forestry official I should think. Anyway he was very respectful, took off his hat, asked if the British authorities knew what was happening to the Yugoslavs when they'd crossed the border.

"I said 'No, what do you mean?' And he said, still very respectful, 'Did you not hear the sound of shooting, sir?' And of course I had, we all had. They must have gone round the next corner, no more. Maybe five hundred yards. We'd all heard a rattle of fire, it went on and on and on. Like a range during a competition.

"This Austrian said, 'From the earlier trains several escaped and got back to Austria. One of them I have seen, they are Slovene people. They tell me that in the clearing by the line, I know it well, everybody was shot, everybody. Including the children. They tell me all the women were raped by crowds of Yugoslavs, Communist soldiers. Before shooting. And all the bodies were pushed into the quarry there. I know that well too.' That's what he said, sir. Quite a few of my chaps heard him, while he was speaking to me. I don't think they were surprised. We'd all guessed as much."

Adam stared straight ahead of him. What had Harry Venables said when they were discussing the Germans who connived at filling the trains to the death camps? "If they knew or even guessed, they're involved in the guilt."

"Thank you, Bill."

"I don't want that sort of job again, sir. And the Company—"

"Feel the same. Thank you, Bill. I'm sorry."

Bill Andrews always reckoned he knew Adam Hardrow pretty well, had known the CO from the Hardrow subaltern days. He said, "Well, I'm off to bed, sir." He knew that if anybody could strike a brave, stubborn, independent line Hardrow could.

"Goodnight, Bill."

"The acting Brigade Commander," said Peter Jarrett, speaking carefully, "won't be back until late this evening. Do you want—"

Adam's face was black. He said, "Who's there?"

"The Staff Captain, sir."

"Tell him, I've sent a personal and urgent letter to the Brigade Commander and to see he gets it without delay." But that, Adam thought may still be too much delay. Damn, damn, damn! It was the next morning. Adam had slept on Bill Andrew's appalling revelations. He had studied again the text of the orders which had been passed to D-Company. There could be no possible doubt that the instruction to lie "if asked" to the deported Yugoslavs, as well, obviously, as the orders for the handover itself, emanated from a high level. The phrasing was as if repeating an order received from above.

"If they knew or even guessed, they're involved in the guilt." Damn, damn, damn.

And what had been recently given maximum publicity, in the matter of War Crimes? The British Press had trumpeted that it would be no defence by a German officer or soldier, whatever his rank, that he had simply been obeying orders. Certainly not! If the order was to commit an illegal act, or could be seen as leading to a result unacceptable to the decent usages of civilised society or to the accepted laws and rules of warfare, then the recipient of the order would be guilty if he obeyed it. As guilty as he who gave it.

Damn, damn, damn!

Adam told Peter Jarrett to cancel the rest of his morning's programme.

"You're visiting the new POW camp B are taking over— "

"I'll try to get there tomorrow. Or the next day. I'm going to see Brigadier Frank Fosdike. Ring up that Headquarters or whatever his liaison cell is called and find out if he's in today." Five minutes later Peter said that Brigadier Fosdike would be back from a tour in the early afternoon and the staff officer who had answered the telephone had noted an appointment at 2.30 for the Commanding Officer of 2nd Westmorlands.

"How nice to see you, Adam! And what can I do for you?"

Adam told him the story of D-Company's experiences on the previous day. Frank Fosdike listened, nodded several times. sighed once or twice, then examined very carefully the points of his fingers. He had equipped his office, also in a requisitioned villa, with several very comfortable chairs and had placed Adam in one while he took the other. Two cups of coffee with plenty of cream and served in attractive china had come at a word from the Brigadier to the lance corporal who sat at a desk in the adjoining room.

"A distressing story, Adam."

Adam said nothing. The emphasis of "distressing" was wrong. Bother their distress! The incident had been disgraceful, and its authorisation vile and not to be born. "Distressing" indeed!

Brigadier Fosdike said that Adam couldn't possibly

begin to imagine how difficult certain negotiations had been. There had been claims to territory which the Allies, "acting with considerable firmness, I may say and showing, in my judgement, no little political courage", had refused to allow. In sorting things out tact and a bit of subtlety had been essential. There had been a serious risk of actual shooting between the British and their fellow-fighters against the Wehrmacht.

"If you mean the Jug Partisans," Adam said, finding his voice, "that wouldn't have bothered my chaps. Or me. We know them. We met them in Menzano, in Italy."

"I know. I know. Tricky people. But tricky people with a point of view, Adam. Politics and diplomacy aren't my trade or yours – although I'm having to learn fast, I regret to say, Ha Ha! But tricky people with a very definite point of view."

"The aspect of their point of view I'm concerned with, is that it's permissible to murder large numbers of unarmed men, women and children. After rape. And, I daresay, torture."

Frank Fosdike nodded. This headstrong, opinionated boy had hardly changed at all, he thought. He still supposed you could deal with complex issues by an over-simplified code of right and wrong, black and white, no shades of grey. Frank Fosdike changed the subject. How was the Battalion, the dear old Second Battalion?

Briefly, Adam told him. Then he said, "The point is, sir, that I shall be making an official report and an official complaint. Through Command channels, of course."

Oh dear, Frank Fosdike thought, through that insubordinate lecher Jameson, in fact. Another troublemaker. He said, "You must do what you think right, Adam. I much appreciate your coming to talk to me, very sensible if I may say so, and of course if you feel it right to make a special report you must do so. But from the way you've talked I have the impression it will be an – er – a somewhat *indignant* report. I don't think that's wise. The Powers That Be have got just as much moral sense as you, but they know what they're doing. They don't, I think I can say without indiscretion, like it much more than you, but duty is often unpleasant. You know that as well as I do."

"I don't think they have."

"Don't think who have what?"

"I don't think the Powers That Be have got just as much moral sense as I. If they had they wouldn't have instructed my company commander to lie to a lot of unfortunates in order to get them to go quietly to their own murder."

"I've explained that, Adam. It would have been absolutely unacceptable to have had those Yugoslavs running all over the place, trying to get away— "

"Why?"

"— trying to escape, to break through your cordon. You've told me you also had a cordon. Your men would have had to shoot."

"Why would that have been worse? Anyway I suspect my men wouldn't, in fact, have shot."

"That is not a very loyal or subordinate thought, Adam. I hope it's not characteristic of my old Regiment in these difficult times." Frank Fosdike stood up. On the whole the Hardrow family had brought him nothing but difficulty, despite his fancy for that very attractive Natasha, Adam's mother, a few years back. This tiresome and over-promoted young man had had his say and had better go. It was ludicrous that he was occupying the position held by Frank Fosdike himself only five years ago! Adam Hardrow was still an arrogant and ignorant subaltern at heart.

Adam stood up too. He said, "Then you can't help, sir? In this business? I thought maybe your duties now— "

"Good heavens!" Brigadier Fosdike said, with a great

show of commonsense briskness. "These things are settled at a *very* high level. I'm only a cog in the wheel. It was nice seeing you, Adam. I'll try to get over to call on the Battalion again one of these days. And I want to catch up on your family news."

Company Command had come unexpectedly to Will Barker but he was enjoying it and like his fellows he exhibited his prisoner-of-war camp to the Commanding Officer with a certain amount of pride. B-Company had taken it over only two days previously.

"Have you been briefed on this lot, sir? They're an extraordinary bunch."

"Tell me again, Will."

There was an enormous mass of figures camping in an area of perhaps two hundred acres. It might be a prisoner-of-war camp but it resembled some bizarre holiday outing. There were, as there had been with the Yugoslavs, a large number of horses, hundreds, perhaps thousands of horses. There were, obviously, whole families, women, children. Bivouacs were pitched in groups without attempt at regulation or alignment. Fires had been lit everywhere and cooking was in progress. No, thought Adam, hardly a prisoner-of-war camp as I remember them, all too well! A gipsy settlement, perhaps?

The majority of the male figures at which he now found himself gazing with Will Barker were in Wehrmacht uniform. Adam said, "I'm not clear—" He was unprepared for this. The Wehrmacht had surrendered and handed in their arms in disciplined cohorts. Even their bivouacs, when bivouacs had finally arrived, had almost erected themselves in regular geometric lines. There had certainly been no families – families, long separated, no doubt avid for news of loved ones, were in the bombed-out Reich if they were anywhere. But these . . .

Adam consulted the paper which Peter Jarrett had thrust into his hand, saying, "This will tell you all about B-Company's lot sir." Adam, to his shame, hadn't read it. Still fuming at the events of the previous day, still frustrated by the memory of the Fosdike interview, he had driven himself, fast and rather furious, to B-Company's prisoner-of-war camp. He was, by his own inattention, unbriefed.

"They're Russians, sir. All of them."

In North-West Europe it had not been uncommon to take Wehrmacht prisoners of Russian blood and everyone knew that many had been recruited, especially from the Ukraine, as the German armies had advanced in 1941. The Westmorland soldiers had learned, puzzled and incredulous, that considerable numbers of the inhabitants of the Soviet Union had welcomed the invaders as offering opposition to the hated Bolsheviks. How long this preference had continued nobody was sure. German atrocities against the civilian population of Russian had received considerable publicity.

"*All* Russians, Will?"

"Cossacks, sir, a lot of them. Or so they say. And some German officers in charge."

"Are all the officers German?"

"Far from it, sir. There are some *very* Russian officers! You can see a group of them over there!" As if aware that they were under scrutiny a group of men in fur caps, well-cut breeches and well-waisted tunics paused in their conversation and looked curiously in the direction of Will and Adam. They were about fifty yards away. One of them saluted.

Adam returned the salute, and turned again to Will. He had been thinking,

"Have we had any instructions about these, Will?"

"As far as I know, sir, they're Wehrmacht prisoners. I

suppose sooner or later they'll go to cages in England or Canada, won't they?"

"Perhaps. Perhaps." Adam tried to recall the terms of a signal he'd seen from Army Headquarters, copied to Battalion level. Something about boundaries and dates and Russians. He'd not read it carefully – it had not at the time affected 2nd Westmorlands.

Will nodded, "They've been disarmed, usual thing. And SS sorted separately, I imagine. That was done before I took over of course."

Adam started strolling towards the nearest group of prisoners, Will Barker trotting at his side. Will said that some of the Russians spoke good English. The process of separating officers from men and grouping them by ranks and categories was still in progress. Will said that the German officers, too, had some English speakers among them.

"I'm bound to say, they've been very helpful. The Jerry officers. They're obviously rather fond of their Russkies, Cossacks, whatever they are. And they certainly look after their horses."

"I can see that." It was like a stroll across Epsom Heath on Derby Day.

"There's more than one general among them."

"Then he," said Adam confidently, "will certainly be segregated and taken somewhere different. There are hundreds, if not thousands of generals in the bag, and I've been told there are separate generals' camps! A German, your general, is he?"

"They. There are several. No, not German. Russian."

They were approaching the small group which Will had indicated to Adam earlier. A figure, slender, erect, very smartly dressed, detached itself from the group and walked slowly towards the two Westmorland officers, as if with intent. Adam stood still and eyed him. When the

261

advancing Russian officer was four yards away he stopped and raised his hand to his elegant furred cap in a salute. Then he smiled.

"Lieutenant-Colonel Adam Hardrow, I see."

Will was halted, mouth slightly open. Adam paused a full seven seconds before he said, very quietly, "Great God! Uncle Alex!"

CHAPTER XII

Uncle Alex looked much as Adam remembered him from nearly six years ago – his mother's adored and celebrated Uncle Alex Kastron; Alexi Alexeivitch Kastron, once "the youngest Colonel in the Czar's Army", a cavalryman to the toes of his boots, neat, slender and now unmistakably weather-beaten. Uncle Alex, Parisian travel-agent after many vicissitudes, worldly-wise, entertaining, remembered by Adam as visiting London in September 1939 and as envying Adam his youth and his participation in a war. Uncle Alex with his rather mannered, charmingly inflected English, a language he was as much at home with as half a dozen others. Uncle Alex, lamented by Natasha in her letters as having "disappeared" from Paris at some time during the German occupation.

Uncle Alex, now a general in or at any rate fighting with the Wehrmacht. Uncle Alex, enemy prisoner-of-war.

Adam said again, rather mechanically, "Uncle Alex Kastron," and held out his hand. His mind was working, he supposed, but the situation was so unexpected and so astounding that he had no idea how to cope with it. Equally astounded, too astounded yet to be embarrassed, B-Company Commander, temporary Major Will Barker, stood a few paces behind him.

Uncle Alex did not appear in the least discomposed.

"It is good to see you alive, my dear Adam. And a lieutenant-colonel! A Battalion commander perhaps?"

"Yes. I – er – I'm sorry to see you here," Adam sounded and knew he sounded stilted. How on earth did one make conversation with an enemy General prisoner-of-war who happened also to be one's uncle? Perhaps fortunately, he didn't know Uncle Alex in the least well although the latter had always been a legendary figure in the Hardrow household.

Uncle Alex raised his eyebrows, shrugged his shoulders slightly and inclined his head. He said, "We are better off than some, one imagines. Naturally I am chiefly concerned as to what happens to my boys."

"To— "

"To my boys. To these brave boys—" his hand was waved towards the area of the enormous, scattered encampment and Adam remembered the delicacy of the Kastron wrist, delicacy and probably strength combined. He noted, admiring, the immaculate way in which Uncle Alex managed to be turned out, even in these unpromising surroundings. There was something not entirely unlike a shine on his immaculately cut field boots and his tunic showed his youthful-seeming figure to advantage. Uncle Alex, Adam knew, was all of fifty-eight or nine, a much younger brother of Adam's grandmother.

"Yes," Uncle Alex said, "that is naturally what troubles us most. What is to happen to my boys. And their families."

Adam supposed that kinship should be pushed into limbo. This man was an enemy and "his boys" were enemies, or had until very recently been enemies, shooting at Westmorlands or if not Westmorlands at other British troops. Or, at the very least, at their American or Russian Allies. He said, as correctly as he could, "All prisoners of war will be transferred to more permanent accommodation when arrangements have been made. I don't know where."

"No, I suppose not. You may be surprised, Adam, to find my boys here, fighting with the Germans and now British prisoners— "

Adam deliberately looked blank. Uncle Alex had always had an easy, friendly way of getting on terms with one and it hadn't diminished. He was continuing, for all the world as if he were discussing an interesting and transient political phenomenon, sitting in Natasha's London drawing room where last they'd met.

"— it is strange, of course, and it must seem strange to you. It's strange for me, too; after all I fought the Germans for four years— "

"I know."

"— and had many friends in your Army, in the old days." Uncle Alex sighed. He went on, "A lot of these boys suffered terribly from the Sovs, you know. The Bolsheviks. They don't care for the Germans, they're wholly different, but they reckoned their best hope of liberating their homes was to fight against the Sovs, the Reds, alongside. So when the Germans occupied the – the western republics, the Ukraine and so forth – it seemed a very natural thing for a lot of them to do. To join up."

"Join up" – conscious anglicism of which Uncle Alex was obviously aware. That quirk, too, was familiar.

Adam had heard this, although it was greeted with incredulity in the West. He remembered in France last year, however, a different sort of Russian prisoner – indeed Adam recalled a passage in an Intelligence summary which had set the Russian component of the Wehrmacht in the West at some extraordinary figure, one-quarter, even one-third – and although he felt, with unease, that he couldn't become involved in an extended conversation with Uncle Alex in these unnatural surroundings, he couldn't resist putting the point.

"Some of your soldiers, I imagine, were also once in the

Russian Army and then deserted to the Germans, or were taken prisoner by the Germans and changed sides?"

"Some," Uncle Alex said, wholly unabashed, "some, yes, are in that category. Their memories and motives, of course, are identical with those volunteers I mentioned. Only their circumstances differed. And Adam— "

"Yes?"

Uncle Alex smiled. He said gently, "I don't like to beg but I don't suppose you have such a thing as a cigarette?"

Adam shook his head and was starting to say, "I don't smoke," when, to his considerable surprise, Will Barker darted forward with an opened packet of twenty Players which he pushed towards Uncle Alex.

Uncle Alex took one with a slight bow and a charming smile, saying to Will, "Thank you. Thank you, sir. You are extremely kind."

Will muttered "Not at all." He looked and felt embarrassed. He thought there had been orders forbidding this sort of gesture, strict ones, but he couldn't exactly remember. And this old boy seemed some sort of relative of the CO! What a story!

Uncle Alex lit his cigarette, said "Ah-h-h!" with an expression of huge delight, raised his eyebrows to Will Barker as he inclined his head to him again with exaggerated courtesy and resumed to Adam.

"Then, of course, there are many, like myself, who have never been Soviet citizens. I had French nationality, as it happens, and there are many, of all ranks, who left Russia long ago, when the Bolsheviks finally won. I, as you know, was with Kolchak. When the Reds won I went to Paris after some time in Poland. But you know all that."

Adam knew some of it, it was Natasha legend. It was said, in fact, that Uncle Alex had himself been in the Ukraine, had just got away from the Kiev Soviet, but this was not the time and place for recollection of those ancient adventures. He nodded and said, "I hope you're in reasonable health."

"Thank you, not bad, not bad at all. We have all led a physically exhilarating life recently."

Adam gave a tiny smile. He said, "This is an extraordinary coincidence. I don't know what to say."

"I imagine not."

"I must be going now. I hope – I hope that things are being run as well as can be managed."

Uncle Alex's face was expressionless. He seemed to be considering Adam. He shot one look at Will Barker and then started speaking in a very soft voice so that Adam had to move a step or two nearer in order to hear.

"Adam, the Sovs would much like to get their hands on me, on us—" his gesture embraced the group of officers "—you can imagine that. And that would mean, of course, the GPU, torture and so forth before execution." His voice was matter of fact. Adam said nothing.

"I have told my brother officers that I know the British well. Politics have been very confusing in our era but I know the British well. I know we can expect a – a fair deal. I have reassured these fellows. Naturally."

Adam still said nothing. His face was set. He was watching Uncle Alex who was drawing on his cigarette and then fastidiously holding it between two fingers.

"I wanted to explain this, Adam. As you can imagine there is a great deal of concern everywhere."

Still, Adam thought, although my mother's favourite uncle you've been fighting for the Germans, and they've been beaten. He said again, "I must be going. I expect I shall visit this camp again."

"Good. Good. Our boys will give no trouble, you may be sure of that. And Paakmann, who is the senior German officer with our people is really a very decent fellow. He could have gone to a Wehrmacht camp but he wouldn't leave our boys. A good officer," said Uncle Alex, seeming to feel, accurately, that the phrase expressed exactly what he meant, to British ears.

"A good officer," he said again. "I shall hope to see you again – my dear Colonel!" He smiled, and Adam thought, with a stab of recollection, how charming his smile was. With another stab of recollection, too, he recalled how, long ago, his mother had sometimes said to him, "Darling Adam, when you smile you look like beloved Uncle Alex Kastron."

Adam held out his hand. That, at least, he could do. "Goodbye." A pause. "Uncle Alex."

"Goodbye, Adam. Give my love to my favourite niece when you write."

Adam had arranged, on the way back to Battalion Headquarters, another visit to Dick Abel's prisoner-of-war camp – by now, it appeared, wholly occupied by officers. He drove up and told Dick that he wanted to look round the company accommodation, tour the guard posts and had then better have the senior German officer brought before him.

Westmorland inspection complete, not without a certain amount of fault-finding which left Dick Abel more than a little sore, Adam found himself sitting at a barrack table in the small marquee which Dick had appropriated as company and Camp office. In front of the table an erect figure in Wehrmacht uniform. A smart salute. Dick Abel said, "This is Lieutenant-Colonel von Pletsch, sir. He speaks English."

Adam said in a stern voice, "I am Lieutenant-Colonel Adam Hardrow, Commanding Officer of the 2nd Battalion of the Westmorland Regiment. This camp is administered by A-company of my Battalion. Have you any complaints?"

Wolf von Pletsch said in excellent English and in a voice which was polite, correct but entirely firm, "Yes. I have."

Adam had not exactly been expecting this. After a brief pause he said, "What are they?"

Von Pletsch drew a piece of paper from his tunic pocket. He said, "With permission." He then began to enumerate from his notes. As he spoke Adam interrupted and nodded to Dick Abel.

"Make notes, Major Abel."

"Yes, sir."

Von Pletsch had composed his requests carefully. It was clear that he perfectly understood the realities of the situation, the provisions of international law and the limitations on what could be done. He spoke reasonably and very coherently. He also spoke concisely. Most of his requests concerned certain restrictions and orders which A-Company, acting on the instructions of authority much higher than Adam's, had imposed.

To most points Adam, after a word with Dick Abel, could respond with, "That seems reasonable," or "We'll look into that. I understand." To two of the von Pletsch points, however, Adam remembered enough of the already voluminous official instructions to shake his head.

"That will not be possible."

At one stage Wolf von Pletsch seemed disposed to question a refusal.

"If I may explain, sir. It does not seem reasonable—"

Adam kept voice and face firm. He cut in.

"Next point, Colonel von Pletsch. I am not prepared to discuss my decisions."

Von Pletsch bowed his head. Ultimately the interview ended. Adam had been considering his prisoner.

"I have one personal question for you, Colonel von Pletsch. Did you have a relation who served in some capacity in Spain, at some time during the war?"

"Yes. My brother."

"Ah! And what was he doing in Spain?"

A silence. Then Wolf von Pletsch's voice.

"Is this an interrogation, Colonel Hardrow?"

"No."

"Then I prefer that the conversation should end. If you please."

Adam nodded and stood up. He felt angry and snubbed. Snubbed! Somehow put in his place! And by a Jerry prisoner! For his part, Wolf von Pletsch marvelled at the coincidences of war. There might, of course, be more than one Adam Hardrow, Wolf had no idea if the name was common, but it was the name Anni Carlucci had confided to him, the name of the young Englishman who was responsible for her incarceration, perhaps by now for her death unless she'd survived in that remote village, with those nuns. As far as Wolf von Pletsch knew, the village wasn't in the area handed over by the Americans to the Red Army but he didn't know much and the ways of the Anglo-Americans seemed as conscienceless as they were inscrutable.

Anni's voice when she'd mentioned the Englishman Hardrow had held a tremor and Wolf had suspected some tender feeling there, something between them. He'd felt a touch of irritation and jealousy, natural to any man escorting an attractive woman and detecting a movement of her heart and senses in the direction of another – and a foreigner to boot. It might be, Wolf thought, that this Hardrow would like to know that he, Wolf, had recently seen Carlucci. Well, damned if he should! And what did he know about brother Heinrich? And what did it matter?

"Colonel Rufus would like to see you, sir. I've said that if possible you'd go over tomorrow morning." Lieutenant-Colonel Rufus Routledge, Commanding Officer of 7th Barsetshires and an officer of considerable seniority, was temporarily commanding the brigade, pending the arrival of Ben Jameson at the end of May.

"That's all right. Peter, do you remember there was a signal repeated to Battalions about categorising ex-Soviet prisoners?"

"Yes, sir. I'll look it up."

A little later Peter Jarrett showed Adam the signal in question. It said that the members of certain formations, including a Cossack Cavalry Corps, were to be treated as "Soviet Nationals", but that although "individual cases" were not, unless "particularly pressed" to be considered as such, certain persons, although of Russian blood, should not be regarded as of Soviet nationality. Such persons included those who had not been in the Soviet Union since 1930 or had not, before joining the Wehrmacht, been living within the 1938 boundaries of the Soviet Union. That means, Adam thought, their boundaries before they wolfed half Poland and the Baltic States! Well, at least that excludes Uncle Alex, on both counts, although I don't suppose it excludes many of his "boys". How perfectly bloody!

But understandable, I suppose, Adam thought, striving for fairness; if they were Soviet citizens, or in the Soviet Army, however much they hated it, there's probably no alternative to treating them as if they "belonged" to the Soviet Union now. And we can all guess what that implies.

"Thank you, Peter. Yes, that's the signal I meant."

Next morning Adam reported to Rufus Routledge. Rufus was a large, red-haired officer with red fluff on his cheekbones. He sometimes reminded Adam of a much more trustworthy edition of Oliver Macrae. In this case, however, the bonhomie was genuine. Rufus Routledge was a sound man, unaffected and sincere, although not exactly brilliant.

It was clear that Rufus Routledge was somewhat embarrassed.

"Adam, your report on the Yugoslavs— "

"Yes, Rufus."

"I've not sent it on to Division yet, but the General has heard you've sent something in. You know Brigadier Fosdike? Yes, of course you do, he's in your Regiment, used to command your Battalion."

"He did indeed."

"He's got some sort of special job overseeing inter-allied policy, that sort of thing. Access to the highest levels— "

"So I've gathered."

"— he, Brigadier Fosdike, is meant to pour oil on the machinery, identify points at which inter-allied agreement isn't working, you know. He's heard of your report. And he told our general."

"I told him about it. Fosdike."

"You told Brigadier Fosdike about it?"

"Yes. You were away and as people were being assassinated and, worse, I thought it possible Brigadier Frank might do something to stop it. I apologise if my seeing him has embarrassed you – I realise it wasn't exactly going through the usual channels but it seemed urgent." Adam was keeping his voice calm and unemphatic. Rufus Routledge stared at him. Adam was twelve years younger than he was.

"It's not embarrassed me, that's not the point. But he thinks you've got it all wrong and he's warned our General in that sense."

"Warned him that a troublesome report has been initiated within his command?"

"Exactly."

"Well," said Adam, "what do *you* think?"

"What do *I* think?"

"Yes. I'm under your command. What do *you* think? You've read my report. I assure you its true."

Peter Routledge frowned. These things were far outside his range of consideration, let alone opinion. They were political and complex and he hated even thinking about them. He cleared his throat, frowned again, fingered the pages of Adam's report which was lying on the table before him and then stood up, walked to the window, turned and looked hard at Adam. Then he returned to his table, sat down and said again to Adam, "You ask what *I* think."

"Yes," said Adam, "you've read it all. You know what's been going on. You know these wretched people were lied to by our orders, yours and mine. In effect, although I didn't know about it and you probably didn't either. And having been lied to they were packed into trains and sent to their deaths. Nasty deaths. After rape, in the case of the women. So I'm asking you, what do *you* think?"

"Bloody awful business, Adam."

"Quite so."

"High-up policy. Government. Negotiations about frontiers, minorities, all that sort of thing." Rufus was floundering. Adam nodded, patiently.

"Certainly. But because of that high-up policy, was it permissible to use soldiers, to use you and me and *our* soldiers – mine, anyway – to send people to their deaths?"

"I'm sure that wasn't what our government would have intended."

"Perhaps not. But it was perfectly easy to guess it was what would happen. Anyway it wasn't all done in an hour. It went on over quite a time. As I pointed out in my report."

"Adam," said Rufus Routledge, "what do you want me to do?"

"To send my report to Division. Saying in a covering letter what you think of it. You've said you regard it as a bloody awful business. All you and I can do is to say so."

"I can certainly do that. Certainly."

"And we can make clear that we'll have no part in anything of the kind again. You know what my officers have said to each other when discussing the Nazi death camps – and your officers too, I have no doubt. They've said, 'The Germans, ordinary Germans, ordinary German soldiers, must have known – or guessed – what was going on, look at the numbers involved in loading the convoys, and so forth. They're all guilty to some extent." That's what our chaps say. Well? What's so different?"

"I think it is," said Rufus Routledge, "a bit different. These – well, we aren't talking of death camps, Adam."

"It's always a a bit different, everything is. No, we're not talking of death camps. But we're talking of death. Murder."

There was a long silence. Then Colonel Routledge took a signal from under a blotter and said, "There's another fatigue come up, I'm afraid, not exactly the same but a bit – well, a bit similar. It's to do with the repatriation of Soviet nationals. Some of them are in one of your camps."

"They are. You mean in Klarsfeldt. A-Company."

"Yes. You see there's a firm agreement that the nationals of each of the Allies shall be returned to their nation of origin without delay. Russian POWs for instance. Or Russian slave workers. Back to the Soviet Union, or, to be exact, back to the Russian occupation forces. They've got plenty of our POWs, overrun by Red Army, same thing, back they come. All agreed by Churchill, Stalin, all that. *Quid pro quo.*"

"Quite."

"Can't really complain about that. Reasonable."

Adam said, "So now the Russians in Klarsfeldt are to be similarly dealt with, is that it?"

Rufus nodded. He said, in a low voice, "The ones in particular categories."

"I see."

"Some idea they'll resist."

"Rufus, the inhabitants of the Klarsfeldt camp, whatever their category, have been fighting with the Wehrmacht. They're not like liberated POWs. They're sworn enemies of the Soviet system. They'll have their throats cut, every one of them. They'll be treated as traitors."

"Well, you could say that's what they are."

"And their families are with them."

"I know. I know. But Adam this really is a top-level agreement, you know."

Adam did know. This was not unexpected. "When is this to happen?"

Rufus told him. He said that the authorities appreciated that there might be violent resistance. A major cordon operation would be put into effect. 2nd Westmorlands would have a part to play. Rufus looked miserable.

"Do you appreciate, Rufus, that a lot of the inhabitants of the Klarsfeldt camp are not Soviet nationals? They're part of one of these Cossack formations but they've spent their lives out of Russia – they're refugees from the Russian revolution in 1917 and they've been abroad ever since."

Like my uncle, Adam thought but didn't say. Rufus said that he realised there were different categories, he'd said so, some categories weren't affected, it was all appallingly complicated, it was distasteful, horrible even, he personally was thoroughly sorry for the poor bleeders who had to be returned, but there you were, that was high-level politics, we had to get our people back, obviously, and war was war.

There'd been a signal, too, saying that it was essential nobody in the affected categories got out of the net. The Russians were very urgent about that, and our side placed a lot of importance on it. Especially, they'd said, senior officers.

The bishop had a high opinion of Sister Gisela. For her part, she regarded him as too easy-going and unprepared to confront all and sundry in a good cause – generally speaking, the cause of the small Community of St Agatha. The bishop knew this and was undisturbed by it. He had the excellent quality, not universal among those in authority whether ecclesiastical or secular, of forming opinions of others unaffected by what he knew to be their opinions of him.

The bishop esteemed this Community. They were, for the most part, good, hard-working, devoted women and they laboured unselfishly for others. He fully understood the anxiety as well as the obstinacy in Sister Gisela's face now. It was perfectly true, as she had forcefully put to him, that certain districts of Austria were already occupied by the Soviet Army and certain other districts, by agreement between the Russians and the Anglo-Americans, were to be handed over to them for administration, "as the occupying Power". Sister Gisela asked the bishop if he and the authorities knew what that meant?

There were stories, and some she had heard bore the stamp of truth, terrible stories. Hospitals, convents, had been ransacked, the staff murdered, the patients bayonetted, thrown out of windows, the sisters . . .

"Yes. Yes, Sister Gisela. I have heard nothing, almost nothing but a recital of these horrors for some time now. I fear there is terrible truth in it. We live in a time of trial."

"Will that happen here?" asked Sister Gisela grimly. The fighting, she knew, had been over for nearly two weeks throughout Europe but the state of society was, if anything, even worse than before. If the Reds were to be allowed into this valley she needed to make a plan, and she needed to know how much time she had.

"No. No. I am assured there is no question of it. We shall be in an American zone of occupation. I am sure there will be correct behaviour."

Sister Gisela grunted. From what she had heard she was less confident. She asked about movement and communication and here the bishop was less encouraging. For some time, he feared, it would be hard to envisage anything like free movement, or expeditious postal services, or things of that kind.

"We must recognise, Sister Gisela, that this has been a battlefield until recently. Normal life has been so disrupted that it is inevitable time must elapse before it resumes. And the course of events will be dictated by the victors. We are in their hands."

Sister Gisela said that sooner or later, she supposed, people would be able to travel and get news. Nobody, she said, knew about their families, nobody knew who was alive or who was dead, and if alive what they had endured. The bishop nodded. He spoke of the United Nations relief agencies whose task would, he understood, include a good deal of the work involved in dealing with refugees.

"There are twelve million, Sister Gisela, twelve million who have streamed into Germany alone. From the East, to escape the, the— "

"To escape the Reds."

"Quite so. And they are, I understand, in a piteous condition. Truly piteous. There have been terrible things done."

"I don't suppose many people are finding it easy to pity Germans, Reverend Father. Or Germany."

The bishop made no direct response to this. He said, "Then there are the millions who were victims of the – the regime. The Reich. There are the unfortunates who were deported to work in Germany, who now have to be returned to their homes. There are the prisoners, of course, the prisoners of war, many of whose homelands are now occupied by – er, by forces they do not like. There are the inmates of these camps which the Reich Government established. Terrible places, what's now being disclosed is indeed terrible."

"And not very far from here, Reverend Father. There've been some of these inmates you're talking about roaming the countryside nearby, some of the sisters have seen them. Terrifying! Like skeletons, scraps of clothing hanging on them, not right in the head, obviously, and carrying all kinds of diseases, equally obviously."

"They are to be pitied, Sister Gisela. Their sufferings have, I am sure, been appalling."

"And inflicted in our name, Reverend Father."

"Austria—" the bishop began pacifically, but Sister Gisela cut in.

"— was a part of the Third Reich. And as far as this valley went, Reverend Father, an enthusiastic part until pretty recently."

"All of that is behind us now," the bishop murmured. He looked at his watch. Sister Gisela had presented him with a long list of queries and requests and he had other calls to make before returning to his office and seeing what could be done about some of them. He also had an important appointment with a General of the United States Army, with whom he hoped, at the least, to reach some arrangements about petrol. Sister Gisela, a paper in her hand, was showing no signs of finishing her business.

She was now talking about one of the women in her care, a refugee.

"We took her in, in the last days. She'd been in a concentration camp and had escaped. She was in very poor condition, physically, but she's a good deal better. Almost fit to travel. She wants to get to Italy, somehow. She doesn't know whether her small boy is alive. He was taken away when she was arrested by the Gestapo, or so she thinks. It's a typical case."

"Enquiries can be made," said the bishop mechanically.

Enquiries! There were million upon million enquiries being made, all over Europe. Helpless, destitute creatures, making small, pitiful squawks of enquiry as to whether anybody or anything from their previous lives still existed.

"Enquiries can be made. We have processed thousands such. One day, no doubt, the relief agencies— "

"This woman is an Italian citizen. She is the widow of an Italian and she has a home in Italy. No money here, of course, but no particular shortages at home, I think. Her name is Carlucci. Born Karlsheim. She's a Catholic. From what I gather of her story she was imprisoned largely because her family were involved in the plot to kill Adolf Hitler."

The bishop nodded. It was a curious feeling that one could now listen to such conversation without nervousness. The feeling was only three weeks old. And he was a bishop!

He said, "Karlsheim, you say?" Something moved in his mind. There had been whispers, he thought, of somebody of that name when treason had been muttered here and there last year. And had not one of his priests, a tireless parochial worker in the Danube valley, spoken the name in some connection very recently? Perhaps not. And probably irrelevance or coincidence.

The bishop rose to extend his ring for Sister Gisela's salutation.

"Sister Gisela, I have made a note of the name, Carlucci. Karlsheim. Rome is doing all it can and I shall attempt to discover something about the woman's child."

"She wants to travel there, that's what she wants."

"Naturally. That, I expect, will take time. We must be patient, patient. But I will notify the appropriate authorities of what you have said. When I can."

"It's rather an odd plan, sir," said Peter Jarrett who had been studying a written brigade order, "very detailed. Pretty large-scale. Quite like a battle. We hand over the Klarsfeldt camp to another battalion, Pembrokes."

Adam frowned. "Hand over administration, you mean? They relieve B-Company completely?"

"Yes, sir. The Pembrokes take over responsibility for the camp. Then there has to be an extensive categorisation, it's all laid down here, and certain categories are being sent to other camps later, in Bavaria as far as I can make out. The remainder, which Brigade estimate will be the big majority, are to be returned to the Russian authorities. At a laid-down hand-over point. The Pembrokes are to categorise and see to entrainment. The Barsets will act as train escorts. Our Battalion to find the cordon at Klarsfeldt and the Gunners are to form another cordon at the place where they get taken over. Where the, the— "

"Cossacks. Or some of them."

"Yes, sir. The place where they get taken over by the Russians."

Adam had passed a completely sleepless night, his first for ages. His conversation with Rufus Routledge played itself over and over in his mind like a cracked gramophone record. Could he have said more, said it more forcefully? Done more?

Peter Jarrett was continuing. The cordon was to consist of two companies at full strength, not less than 220 men. Adam looked irritated.

"Why can't they give the Battalion a task and let *us* decide how to carry it out and how many men are required? This sort of detail is idiotic interference."

Peter Jarrett had known this would be the CO's reaction. It wasn't going to be an easy morning.

"Its laid down, sir. And in our part of the orders it says, specifically: 'Two companies, 2 West R, at a strength of not less than 220 all ranks under overall command of the Battalion Second-in-Command'."

Adam's face was grim. "That is wholly intolerable."

"Yes, sir. I – I imagined you'd be a bit surprised. I had a word with the Brigade Major half an hour ago. He sounded embarrassed."

"Well he may be. I've never heard such impertinence in my life. You can tell him I, personally, shall be commanding that cordon. And that what my second-in-command does is my business, not his."

"Yes, sir. He explained that the order for Major Venables to do this duty came from Division."

"*Division*! Great God, what concern of theirs is— "

"Exactly, sir." Peter Jarrett very obviously knew a little more than he was saying and was extremely nervous. Adam controlled himself.

"What's all this about, Peter? You know something. Speak up."

"Well, sir, I think that report you wrote upset them. Or some of them. It was – well, I think it was thought to be pretty strongly worded."

"It was meant to be."

"I gather," Peter looked miserable, "I gather the powers-that-be know of it, of your report I mean, and thought, I sort of gather they thought, it would be, well, sort of more considerate to spare you the necessity to be too closely involved with this – er – this business."

"*Considerate!*" Adam looked so furious that Peter felt genuine alarm. He had, however, spoken the truth as he knew it and he stuck to his guns.

"Yes, sir. That's my impression."

A long silence while Adam stared at him.

"Thank you, Peter. I see."

After a moment Peter said, looking at the wall in front of him, "I think Brigadier Fosdike was at Division yesterday."

"I'm sure he was," Adam said. "I'm sure he was."

"We shall have to send a copy of our own order to Brigade, sir."

"You can detail B- and C-Companies for the cordon." Roger Bellew, too, had handed over responsibility for his charges to another battalion and Dick Abel would soon have resigned his to the Pembrokes. Poor devils.

"Yes, sir."

"And Major Venables will command. I shall be talking to him later this morning."

Peter looked relieved. Adam nodded.

"I, personally, shall be visiting the cordon, of course. When does the operation start?" And Peter told him that the cordon was to be in place at first light next Tuesday. It was Wednesday today. On the Friday the camp would be handed over to the Pembrokes and categorisation begin.

"Any troubles, Harry?"

Harry Venables said, "I'm glad we're doing cordon and not train duty or entrainment. My God I am."

"I'm sure you are."

"I went to liaise, have a word with the Pembrokes. I've never seen such a business. Perfectly horrible. Open trucks. And people sitting down all over the place squalling. They've got a pretty clear idea of what's up, that's obvious. Whatever they've been told."

"I expect so."

"The Pembrokes Company responsible for entraining have got pick helves. They're having to bash the poor buggers about in many cases, to get them on the trains! Its sickening! Women, the lot! And the yelling! The Pembroke Company Commanders are trying, with interpreters, to shout out that it's all right, they'll all be properly treated, it will be much better if they act quietly as instructed, that sort of thing. Some seem to believe it, some don't. Chaos!"

Harry Venables, generally these days debonair, looked wretched. He said, "And we've got orders to shoot, of course, if any break ranks and come this way. None has. From what one hears it might be more merciful if we did, in fact, shoot them."

"Or miss them."

"My sentiments exactly," Harry said, smiling for the first time, "or miss them!"

"I'm going to the Pembrokes to have a look myself, Harry."

"You won't like it."

"No. Did you discover what's being done about the ones who aren't Soviet nationals, the ones excluded from the order to return them? Dick thought there were at least a thousand of those. The ones who'd never lived in the USSR."

Rather surprisingly, Harry knew. He nodded and said, "Yes, there's a whole section of the camp for those. They're staying here for a while and of course the poor wretched buggers who are being knocked about and loaded on to the trains are trying to get to that part of camp. Naturally. And the Pembrokes have got a whole inner cordon to prevent it. They've got orders to shoot, too, just like us. And in several cases they've had to. Furthermore there've been a lot of suicides – both sexes. And some parents have killed their children then tried to kill themselves, imagine!" Harry said, forcefully. "It's all unutterably bloody. My chaps, Dick's boys, Roger's boys, are sick as hell with it. I only thank God they're not themselves involved in bashing these poor devils about, getting them into the trains. Or riding with them as escorts like the unfortunate Barsets."

Adam found James Evans, commanding officer of the Pembroke Battalion, standing by a small tent near the railway siding. He looked harassed. One train load had departed and it was now a question of keeping the lid somehow on the boiling kettle until empty trucks returned and further entrainment could take place. It wouldn't be easy. The nearest crowd of Cossacks with their families due for loading could be seen, surrounded by soldiers with rifles at the ready, about 200 yards away.

Lieutenant-Colonel Evans looked at Adam Hardrow without enthusiasm. He had never really liked him. "Hullo Adam. Cordon OK?"

"I suppose you could say so."

"Thought Harry Venables was to command it."

"He is. James, tell me, the Russians who aren't officially Soviet nationals, who aren't being sent back. They're in a separate part of the camp, I gather?"

James nodded and pointed. "We've got them right over against the wire, over there, a mile away. It was essential to put some distance between them and this lot. And to patrol it. We've had to shoot several already, trying to get from here to there."

"I suppose there are a good many? A good many staying, I mean, a good many over there?"

"Oh yes. I've no idea exactly how many, but a lot.

Sorting categories has taken ages, working day and night."

"I presume the officers were able to help a bit? There must, I imagine, be a good many officers? Over there?"

James Evans said, "There were."

"Were?"

"Were until yesterday. There was a special order, yesterday, very short notice. All officers were to be sent by truck to Bretten. The lot. They were to be told it was for a special conference about the future."

"To Bretten?" Adam stared at him. "To Bretten, James? But why?"

"Frankly, they're being handed over. To the Russkies."

"All categories?"

"All categories. No exceptions. We were given a list of names, particular ones the Russkies wanted, that sort of thing. We had to make sure all those particular ones were included, that they hadn't sort of melted into the landscape or anything like that, you know. Took quite a lot of doing. Then off they went, quite a convoy, quiet as anything."

"Utterly deceived."

James looked at him. Difficult bugger.

"You could say so. Anyway our orders were very clear."

"So there are now no officers here at all? They've all been handed over."

"That," said James Evans, "is what I said. And their German officers were handed over too. The lot."

Peter Jarrett spoke quietly,

"The Second-in-Command has reported, sir. The cordon's been stood down. About half-an-hour after you left. They'll all be back in billets before midnight."

"Yes."

"And we've got a visitor tomorrow, sir. Brigadier Frank

285

Fosdike. Apparently he's going round every battalion in the brigade, not just ours. I mean he's going round with the acting brigade commander in some sort of official capacity rather than visiting us socially, regimentally—" Peter's voice died away. "I imagine you'll be here, sir?" he added. "About ten, they said."

"Yes, Peter. I shall be here."

And next morning Brigadier Fosdike, a rather subdued Rufus Routledge beside him, was driven to the Battalion Headquarters villa. He climbed out of his smart staff car, and approached Adam with a smile which contained, it seemed, both anxiety and solicitude.

"Adam! Splendid to see the Battalion again!"

Rufus Routledge said, "You were asking about yesterday's operation, sir. The Westmorlands were on cordon duty."

"I know, I know. Most unpleasant. All very, very unpleasant, nobody's in any doubt about that. But I gather it all went off without incident, Adam?"

Adam said nothing to this. He looked at Rufus Routledge, acting brigade commander, and said, "What would Brigadier Fosdike like to do, sir?"

Frank Fosdike took the question. He smiled again, his rather melancholy smile, and said, "Really just a word, Adam, a short chat about how things are going, about all these rather tricky questions. Your Divisional Commander has agreed I should go around a bit, explain things, spread the word. And Rufus, here, is very kindly taking me round this brigade. I won't detain people long although it's always tempting to relax a bit when among old friends, waste their time and one's own, ha ha! But tell me, first, how are the family? How is that enchanting little sister of yours and her wild Highland husband? And how is your dear, dear mother? You must give her my especial good wishes when you write."

"My mother's quite well, sir, thank you," Adam said in his cool, steady voice, "quite well, as far as I know. I'll be writing to her later today and I'll certainly be mentioning you. I'll be telling her that you've just murdered her favourite uncle."

CHAPTER XIII

Harry Venables said, "There was a chap here from Army Headquarters, this morning. From Italy. He'd got a most peculiar-looking envelope for you. We asked him where he'd got it and he said that somebody from Army had been in Rome, and some priest had buttonholed him and asked if he could get a letter to a British officer, probably now in Austria. The padre said it was too important to trust to the mail service, something like that, and that mail is taking an indefinite time to travel from A to B. Which is true, of course."

Adam was only half-listening. It was 10th June. He had been out looking for a safe rifle-range site and had returned with a better appetite for lunch than he had had for some time. The beastly events of the previous weeks and the sense of outrage he felt were burned on to his mind and the scars would be there for ever; but twenty-six is a resilient age and, if one could temporarily drive out memories and quieten conscience, much in this part of Austria was good. The Battalion was in extraordinarily fine form, there were as yet no rumours of an impending move, Adam was enjoying Battalion command hugely, and now and then he was able to turn his mind from the fate of Anni and from the essential, the highest duty of finding her. For that, he had decided, the right moment would be when Ben Jameson arrived to command the brigade. Ben would understand, as nobody else could.

Ben would counsel, connive, assist. And in less than a week Ben would have taken over. Infuriatingly, it had been delayed.

And now here was a letter from Italy, a large, yellow envelope covered with a laborious, rather large hand and addressed to "Colonel Adam Hardrow, 2nd Battalion, The Westmorland Regiment". It could only be from Father Flynn. Forcing himself to wait a few minutes, to exchange news with Harry Venables about his morning's trip, to listen to Peter Jarrett's recital of various domestic dramas within the little Westmorlands' world, Adam finally and with a fine show of nonchalance opened the Flynn envelope. It was, he saw at once, a long letter. Father Flynn's discovery of a courier had been rapid and effective – the letter was dated only four days previously, 6th June.

Dear Colonel,

There've certainly been great happenings since I was enjoying that fine glass of whisky with you in Menzano, and the world's all over itself. I trust you're fine and that this reaches you in Austria. I met a nice lad who was going your way or so he said and seemed confident he'd get this into your hands.

It's possible we've found the lady, Anni Carlucci! It's quite a story. First of all there was a decent man, Berndt Wemmer, who was interned by the Germans and had met her during that time. Berndt Wemmer is a Viennese chap but he used to be a lecturer at Milan and he's got an old mother who lives there. He was let out of prison when the Nazis gave up four weeks ago and he managed to get to Milan, I've no notion how, and a friend of mine met him and got from him a list of the unfortunate folk who were with him, and sent the list to our people in Rome – we've lists and names and scraps of information coming from everywhere by one route or other, you can imagine.

There's an attempt to keep the record compiled and I'm in touch with it. And I saw Berndt Wemmer's list when they sent it from Milan, I used to know him, and there was Anni Carlucci's name on it!

But now's the snag. In his notes on his list Wemmer wrote that Anni Carlucci was taken away from them shortly before the end and transferred to the "main camp" – he and his group were, it seemed, in a separate part of one of these concentration camps. That was the last he saw of her, although he was sure that the whole camp was evacuated westward at about that time – it was very near the end of the war and the Reds were very near. So the trail ran out, but at least, I thought, she was in Austria, that was what Wemmer wrote although he'd no idea exactly where and of course he didn't know where the camp inmates were moved to but it had to be westward. In Austria, and recently.

It looked to me as if she'd been moved to one of the concentration camps in central Germany or central Austria. We know from all the stories we're getting that they were marching these poor creatures west and just packing them into other camps, constructed for many thousands less souls: and creating terrible conditions with the overcrowding and the lack of food and everything else. And to think all this was still happening less than a month ago! The Good Lord is the only one who knows how many died from all this, and we must not, I said to myself, presume that any one individual survived just because she was still sighted alive in April. She was a good young woman and I cared about her.

So I reckoned I'd write you a line, cautious, to say she must have been in Austria near the end, but may be living or may be dead. And then what happened yesterday? Bless me, another paper arrived. And this one's from a bishop, writing from near Innsbruck. And this bishop has heard of a lady called Carlucci, previously Karlsheim; and that's Anni for sure. And she's been looked after by some nuns, at a small place called Restenbrucke, Community of St Agatha. The bishop mentioned she'd been very ill, had a hard time, but she's better and she's alive. And it didn't sound as if she'd be moving yet awhile. He gave other names, of course, but this one he'd marked as having a child that had been brought up in Italy so it's certain. The bishop wrote his letter only a fortnight back, it's hot news for these days.

If you've decent means of getting messages or letters to Rome and can let me know I'll do what I can at this end. Maybe these international refugee organisations can help bring her home when she's healthy, or maybe you'd be able to see the authorities and get something better going yourself . . .

The letter ended with a flourish and what Adam supposed was a Cross and the signature "Brendan Flynn".

Adam had told Peter Jarrett that he planned an exercise for company commanders some time in the summer, if the Battalion remained in Austria. It would be a study of Alpine warfare, a map and sandwiches affair. Peter looked astonished.

"I see, sir. Of course they've – they've had quite a bit of mountain warfare. Last year."

"I know that. We'll never be in the Alps again, best take advantage of it."

"Yes, sir. You know we're – everybody – is confined to the Corps area unless with special leave?"

"Or except on duty. Quite right. This is duty. I'll be gone all day on a reconnaissance. I'll drive myself."

"You'll want the IO or— "

"No IO. No driver. If anybody wants me, say I'm on an exercise recce and I'll be back by dinner time." Adam, like many others, had managed to secure the uses of a comfortable civilian-type Mercedes saloon, "impounded" from the Wehrmacht. It would, they all knew, only be a short time before such delights were removed.

Harry Venables had walked in at that moment and heard a bit of the conversation. Harry, loyal and modest, nevertheless permitted himself a certain familiarity with the CO, a reflection of his previous seniority. He looked even more astonished than the Adjutant.

"An exercise, sir? TEWT, you mean?" A TEWT, a tactical exercise without troops, was by now a memory from other times, from training in England before they'd embarked for Sicily.

"Exactly, Harry. See a new bit of country."

"People will enjoy that. But why, if I may say so, sir, spoil their pleasure with a TEWT?"

"There's got to be an official purpose!" Adam smiled. "They'll like it. Anyway we may be too busy here. It may not come off."

"Or we may have moved."

"Or we may have moved." Adam had rather relished the subterfuge. Two days later, after a dawn start and with several jerricans of petrol in the boot of the Mercedes he was negotiating the mountain roads westward, a map spread on the seat beside him. Once again it was a glorious day, and Adam's heart was beating fast and happily. It had come, the day had come, he was sure of it! He had always had faith that he would find Anni, and now, surely, he had found her. She would need care, restoration, love and he would somehow see that the first two were provided while he poured over her the third. And he would, he was confident, persuade her quickly to share his own picture of the future.

He had made an outline plan. There was, in the same village as Battalion Headquarters, a liaison group of the United Nations organisation concerned with refugees – two Americans, one Dane who had spent the war in Canada, a French woman once married to a Czech (who was presumed dead but whom, she proclaimed very loudly to all who listened, she had anyway divorced at the beginning of the war) and a genial Irishman, a journalist by trade, who confided to Adam on a courtesy visit that newspapers were a tough trade in Dublin at the moment, while on this refugee business there was at least a whisky ration and the money was good. Adam had arranged to make life easier for this group in the small ways the military could provide and relations were cordial.

On the previous day Adam had talked to the group's senior, one of the Americans, by name Bill.

"Bill, I've got a problem. I've also got a bottle of Scotch." Scotch whisky seemed less available for the group than Bourbon and Bill, most unusually, preferred it. Courtesies were exchanged and Adam explained the problem. There was, there might be, a refugee, an Italian citizen whom he, Adam, knew well and of whose whereabouts he had heard. How should she be moved to Italy, where her home was, where her child was, from which she had been taken by the Gestapo a year ago? A released inmate of a concentration camp, one who had probably been seriously ill. What was the simplest way to send her home? Could Bill advise?

Bill sipped his scotch.

"Any complications? Ethnic Italian is she?"

"She was born a German. She's the widow of an Italian." Bill said that the office was handling refugees from all over. There weren't many Italians but there were some.

"She should register. Where is she now?"

"I'm not absolutely sure," Adam said, "but I think quite soon she may be here."

Bill eyed him. "Know her well from some place, do you?"

"You could say that."

"If you want to get her home as early as possible, the official way, get her to register if she hasn't already. The refugees office will handle it, kit her out, documentation, accommodation, travel papers— "

"Will it take long, Bill?"

"A few months, not more. Three, maybe. Depends."

"Its not far, Bill, not really far. To home. Just south of Rome."

"Not the point."

"No, I suppose not."

"Might be quicker if she were simply across the border in Italy. Make her way south via local relief organisations, even some public transport."

Adam thought of Father Flynn. "Or a friend with a vehicle if such a thing exists? So if we can get her across the border— "

"Yeah," said Bill. "Of course I haven't any resources for that." He looked at Adam speculatively. He liked Hardrow and liked the way he never seemed in the least concerned about the minutiae of official instructions. He'd get this lady over the frontier into Italy somehow, rules or no rules, of course he would. Hell, the British Army up here still answered to a high command down in Italy! Hardrow would fix it and no questions asked. If he actually wanted to send her, that was. Maybe he didn't! Bill said, carefully, that however such a person moved she would need certain essential documents and approved health checks and in that respect Bill's office could help. Adam thanked him.

So when Adam brought Anni triumphantly back to base, he reckoned he could manage the matter thereafter. It would be intolerable to let her go but he realised she would wish to see Guido above all things. And in the interval they would plan, he would tell her his ideas, talk about the future, plan, love, love and plan. She would be hesitant at first, of course she would, she would take time to get used to the idea of making life anew. But he would enthuse her, love her, carry her along. The Villa Avoria? Stonehead? Heaven knew! And meanwhile the world was still at war! But nobody thought the Japanese business would go on into 1947, peace must break out before too long. Europe at least was free of fighting although in turmoil.

Somehow, Adam knew, they would compose a future together. He glanced at the map beside him. The roads were narrow and twisting but he was making surprisingly good progress. There was a good deal of mist on the low ground but here and there a great mountain peak, still snow-covered, caught the sun and showed brilliant above cloud.

He thought of another facet of the plan. Of what he would say to "the authorities". His expedition to rescue Anni, with its bogus rationale, his "refugee" guest – all this would soon be common knowledge and there would be questions asked, eyebrows raised. Adam proposed to go to the highest authority appropriate and ask to talk. Probably it would be the Divisional Commander – Ben Jameson was still not due to arrive with the Brigade for another three or four days and Adam had not been able to wait. He would explain that by an extraordinary combination of circumstances his fiancée, who had been imprisoned by the Germans in a concentration camp, had turned up in Austria. He could imagine the sequel . . .

"Your *fiancée*, Hardrow?"

"Yes, sir. We hope to marry before too long now that the war is over and she has survived her awful experiences. The Colonel of my Regiment has given his approval, I'm glad to say."

"Really?"

There would be puzzlement, questions about the lady's nationality, a little of the story revealed. Adam chuckled. The Divisional Commander undoubtedly regarded him with mixed feelings, but that side was going to be all right.

Then Adam turned his mind towards the encounter with Anni. He was prepared for anything, he told himself. She had almost certainly been terribly ill. She would look wasted, fragile, different. She would be weak, where she had been self-confident, decisive and strong. She would find it difficult to make up her mind about anything – he could imagine. She might even – he dreaded this possibility but it had to be faced – have lost some of her memory, even her memory of Adam. That would be hard, very hard; but he would conquer it, memory would return and with it love. In those extraordinary, enchanted days when he had been sheltered by her in Italy, a refugee, threatened at every minute, she had shown love as he had never dreamed of it, passion as he could rarely have imagined, bravery and beauty melded. It had not been a passing fancy, a fleeting spasm of adventure and ecstacy. Adam had been special to her, as she to him, he knew it. It would all come back.

And he would have wonderful news for her – that Guido was alive and well and at the Villa Avoria! He would tell her that he, Adam, could see to everything, everything, the nightmare was over.

Might she be too ill to travel? Bedridden, even? It was

possible, of course, although the bishop, whoever he was, quoted by Father Flynn, had referred to her health being better, and some weeks had already passed.

But even if that were so – and it would be disappointing, a break in the dream – it would only spell a short delay. All, meanwhile, would be arranged. And then he would return to claim her.

Adam stopped the car and looked at the map again, impatient. There were now a considerable number of American Army vehicles on every road, large or small, the huge painted white stars prominent, but he was getting on well. It wouldn't be long now. Right at the next village, climb again for three miles, a small road going left where the larger road curved, and there, the map indicated, was the small place whose name he had. Restenbrucke. The Community of Saint Agatha.

Adam's heart was beating fast again. Twenty minutes. It could not be more than twenty minutes. And he had been thinking of this moment for more than a year and a half! The responsibilities of Battalion Command, the concerns of 2nd Battalion the Westmorland Regiment, featured nowhere in his mind at this moment. He was simply a young man in love and he started the car again.

Adam's German was competent albeit rusty, and he had no difficulty in explaining that he wanted to speak, please, to the person in charge. The Community of St Agatha was housed in a larger building than he had expected, a yellow-washed tall building with rows of high symmetrical windows, paint notable for its absence. St Agatha's had, inside, wide, high-ceilinged corridors, echoing gates which clanged to behind one, a pervasive smell of dust and what he fancied was medicament. Was the place a hospital? Not exactly, it seemed. Or a convent? Not exactly that either – there were several rather aged workmen shuffling about and through a window from the room into which he had been ushered without a word Adam could see an overgrown, sunlit garden and an old fellow sweeping leaves.

He waited five minutes, with mounting impatience. He had not given his name – the sister who had admitted him at the huge, heavy main door had simply eyed his uniform and bowed him in. The uniform of the victors, Adam caught himself accepting, not without complacency, opened all doors and no explanations were due. After the sixth minute, a dragging minute, the door of the room opened and an elderly woman came in. She asked if Adam understood German and on hearing that he did she explained that "The Superior", Sister Gisela, was away on Community business. She regretted.

"I have come," Adam said politely but firmly, "because I have been informed that a lady has been cared for here in whom I have an interest and for whom I have news. Her name is Frau Anni Carlucci. If she is here may I see her please?"

The nun, infuriatingly, said, "Please wait," and disappeared again. After only three minutes, this time, she returned.

"May I ask why you wish to see Anni Carlucci?"

"She is a friend of mine. And I have news for her, as I said."

"She has not been well. She is better now but still not very well."

Adam's heart lifted. "So I understand."

"You can speak to her. She is in our garden. There is someone with her."

Another nun, presumably; a person half-nun, half-nurse perhaps. Adam nodded and the nun opened a door for him and said, "They are somewhere down that path."

"Thank you." Adam gave her his special smile. He

found he could hardly breathe. He started walking down the path, slippery from mountain rain and with last autumn's leaves, unswept, contributing to the slipperiness. He walked fast.

The path turned a corner. And then, twenty yards ahead he saw them.

Anni! It must be Anni! He recognised the way she held her body although he couldn't yet clearly make out her face or see to what extent it had changed. Anni was facing back towards the St Agatha building, facing Adam. He took in, without understanding why, that she seemed shorter than he remembered.

Round Anni's shoulder, holding her tight, was a man's arm. Anni seemed somehow enfolded by the owner of the arm, almost as if the two bodies were joined. They stepped forward now towards him and again they seemed to move together as in some sort of grotesque three-legged race with limbs bound. Adam found that he, too, had taken several steps forward. When he was about ten paces from the couple he could see the man's face.

It was an appalling face – a face like something from an illustration to a work of horror-fiction, a face like a skull, skin yellow, eyes gleaming and mad, head absolutely bald. A grotesque. A grotesque on whom hung a shapeless woollen jacket, like the jacket of a pair of pyjamas. His legs were similarly attired.

They all looked at each other, stationary now, and silent.

At last Adam said, "Anni!" He heard his own voice. It sounded like a croak.

Anni, he could now see, looked many years older. Her face was lined and almost as palely yellow as her companion's. She was peering towards Adam as if she had difficulty in focusing.

"Anni!" He continued in English. His mind was completely blank.

"Anni, it's me. Adam. Adam Hardrow!"

Anni looked enormously puzzled. She said, "Adam Hardrow!"

The man with her said nothing. Inwardly Adam had named him the gargoyle, and felt towards him powerful aversion and measureless resentment. Anni was still peering, unsmiling. She hadn't moved.

"Adam Hardrow! Adam!" With the dropping of "Hardrow" a tiny something seemed to have been released and Adam said, "I discovered where you are. I've wanted, terribly, to find you."

She was still looking at him as if puzzled. She said, "But why are you here at all? In Austria?"

"With my Regiment, with the British Army, Anni."

"Ah!"

"Anni, I have news for you, wonderful news."

She nodded her head, still staring at him. Adam remembered that he had, in planning this scene, envisaged that at an early moment he would, somehow, catch her up in his arms. It now seemed wholly inconceivable. The gargoyle's arm was no longer round her shoulder but he was standing very close. The whole thing was hideous. When would reality return, intervene?

"Anni, Guido, little Guido is alive and well. He is at the Villa Avoria, at your home. He's perfectly all right."

"I know."

"*You know!*"

"Yes. A bishop heard, and told Sister Gisela. Somebody in Rome wrote to the bishop. I heard yesterday."

Adam said, "I'm glad. Its wonderful." His voice was mechanical. A tiny part of his mind fastened on to the extraordinary speed with which, in a Europe largely deprived of postal services, a Vatican correspondent had conveyed news to a bishop in Austria. He pushed away the spasm of irritation at being thus deprived of his role as bringer of joyous news. It didn't, surely, matter.

The gargoyle said something in German which Adam didn't catch. Anni responded equally inaudibly. Then the gargoyle spoke again. Adam felt wholly excluded. He also felt something not far from panic. He recognised that an edifice created by powerful imagination was collapsing all around him and that it was essential, somehow, to take control. Unsure what he was going to say, Adam spoke.

"Anni, I must— "

Anni interrupted. In English and almost formally she said, "I am sorry, I have not been well, I have not seen people, I have become forgetful."

To the gargoyle she said, "This is Captain Adam Hardrow. He is a British officer whom I was able to help when he was escaping from a prison camp in Italy."

With a wonderful, flickering smile which for two seconds made Adam almost feel that Anni had returned to him, it was so familiar, she said, "He saved my Guido, when a donkey bolted!"

Then, to Adam, "This is my brother, Kurt Karlsheim. He found me too. It is all very strange."

It was indeed very strange. Kurt Karlsheim spoke with difficulty. He spoke German at first and Anni supplied some detail, with Kurt shrugging shoulders and occasionally interjecting a sentence. Now and then Adam spoke a question, to help him. He was longing only to get Anni to herself. Kurt had been condemned in autumn 1944, in the aftermath of the attempt on the life of Adolf Hitler. He had been condemned in Berlin, condemned to death; but instead of immediately carrying out the sentence "the authorities" had kept him alive in first one, then another concentration camp, in particularly close confinement.

There seemed, Kurt said, no especial reason for moving him from one place to another, it seemed haphazard.

At intervals he was taken somewhere – not back to Berlin since the end of 1944 but to somewhere away from the camp itself for further "interrogation". Adam could at least in part imagine what that had meant although not until afterwards, when he considered Kurt's story, could he fully apprehend what the man had been through. Since March he had been in Austria, in the camp at Mauthausen. When the inmates of Mauthausen were released he had made his way to a priest's house and somehow heard that a Karlsheim was at Restenbrucke.

"Many died daily. But I, who had been judicially condemned to die, remained alive."

They were now strolling through the garden, the three of them, and Adam felt a very slight lessening of the sense of exclusion. Occasionally Anni, who was walking between the two men, turned her face towards Kurt as if in wonder. Once she turned towards Adam and touched his upper arm.

"You are very grand in your uniform! What are you, a captain still?"

"A lieutenant-colonel, astonishingly. A battalion commander."

"So grand, so grand! I thought battalion commanders were fat old men, no?"

"Not always. Or not now."

She was smiling, or trying to. Adam felt a prick of life, of hope. Seeking a connection which would unite them in a recollection, just them, he said, "I have seen Father Flynn, Father Brendan Flynn. It was he who got word to me about you. And about Guido."

"That Irishman!" She smiled again, gently, and said, "He certainly helped you, Adam." They were somehow

302

in a sort of communion again now, or so Adam dared to suppose.

Ignoring Karlsheim, he said, "He did indeed help me. He led me to you."

"And I helped you to get back to your Army."

"And have suffered for me as a result," Adam said, his voice tremulous, "I know that. Anni, I know that. You hid me and for that you've had this terrible, terrible time." He didn't know whether Kurt Karlsheim spoke English, but it was soon clear that he did, slowly but correctly.

The Karlsheim voice, deep and resonant, now chimed in, having followed these exchanges. "She suffered for both of us, Herr Hardrow."

Anni said, "Never mind all that."

"But it is true, Anni. As my sister you paid for whatever I did as well, perhaps, as for anything you did for Herr Hardrow here. We are fortunate, it is almost impossible to believe, to be still alive. Both of us."

Adam said, "We are all three fortunate to be alive," but to this neither returned a word.

Adam was driving home alone. Home to 2nd Westmorlands. His mind was recovering from a sort of numbness.

After a little, in the garden, he had said with embarrassment, "Anni, may I speak to you for a bit alone? There are certain things I wish to ask." It was difficult, he knew. Anni frowned slightly, but Karlsheim said something quickly to Anni and moved off towards the Community building.

"Shall we walk back a little, Anni? Back the way we've been?"

"If you like."

As they walked Anni started talking, a touch more animation in her voice, "Kurt has lived with death for nine months. Condemned to die, die painfully no doubt like many of his friends. He has not known, every morning, whether he would see the evening. And very often he has longed to die. They tortured him."

"I supposed so."

"They tortured him again and again. But he gave them nothing, he is sure of it. It is all he cares about. He knew they thought he had something, much more to give, it is why they kept him alive, didn't cut off his head right away. But he fooled them."

Adam nodded and she said, almost fiercely, "He fooled them! And he's alive. I escaped, you know. Like you did, once!"

A tiny sense of bond, of communion again?

"Yes, like I did, Anni. Anni, I've hoped to take you away."

He had then explained a little how it could be done, how he would care for her, smuggle her to Italy, set her on her road to Rome and home, to Guido.

"And then, Anni, soon— "

"Soon, what?"

Adam, haltingly, almost wretchedly, had told her that he had, for over a year and a half, lived mainly for this moment. He loved her, she knew that. He wanted above everything to make her his wife. They had been lovers – could she imagine that to him it had meant little, that his vows had been careless? Or her vows, for that matter, for she too had once declared love? Anni, he had said, Anni, Anni . . .

He had taken her into his arms then, but she was like a creature anaesthetised, she was inert and lifeless and so desperately thin that there was no sense of recollection or familiarity in his body at all. After a little, very, very gently, she had freed herself and pushed him away.

"Adam – I don't know anything. You must understand. I just don't know."

"You know you want to go home, see your Guido."

"Yes, and the refugees organization have already spoken with me. Here. They can arrange it in time."

"Anni, we can reduce that time."

Anni had sighed.

"That is very kind. But you see Kurt has just come, I am all confused. He and I were always so close. He needs me terribly. The sisters here are looking after him also. I couldn't begin a journey to Italy until Kurt's own life is healed a little. You can understand that. Guido, my dearest little Guido, I long for him but I know now that he is well. For these few weeks I must get stronger myself, and I must help Kurt to heal. You— "

"— can understand that," Adam had said, "of course I can." His plan had been collapsing as every second passed. Adam Hardrow, deliverer, saviour was fast becoming Adam Hardrow redundant.

He had said, "But in the future, Anni – because these things will get better, will pass. In the future – you and I – surely . . ."

His voice had died away and she had taken his hand and said, "Who knows, Adam? Who knows? Just for now Kurt and I have shared something and need each other. Need each other badly."

Stupidly, he said, "Need each other more than anything or anybody else, I suppose!"

And remarkably Anni's voice had been completely as he remembered it from the scented dusk of the Villa Avoria garden when he had bid her farewell in 1943, after making love for the last time. It was the same voice low, musical and entirely firm.

"Yes. Just for now. More than anything or anybody else."

He had bowed his head and turned it away from her. She had known that it was not she, the sick victim of the concentration camp, but he, the victorious and uniformed lieutenant-colonel, who was silently fighting against weeping.

"I am delighted to see you here, Ben," the General said, "and at least pretending to be fit."

Ben Jameson smiled. In the event his assumption of brigade command had been delayed and delayed again for the proceedings of a medical board. He had missed, to his irritation, a fortnight. It was already 16th June.

"My injury was stupid, painful and undignified, sir, but nobody could have called it serious. I was limping round extraordinarily quickly."

"Well, don't do more than you should."

"I never have, sir."

"You know the Brigade," the General said, "inside out. There've been a few changes, of course, in the aftermath of war and there will be more." He discussed them, mentioning the battalions of what from today was Ben Jameson's brigade.

"Of course your own Battalion you know almost too well."

"I called on them once when I was convalescent. They seem all right."

"They *are* all right. Young Adam—" the General looked at his knuckles and sighed.

"He can be a bit tricky, Ben. Splendid fellow, of course, grand fighting soldier and all that. He was your second-in-command— "

"He was my second-in-command, as you say, sir. He was also a platoon commander in my company once, five years ago. And, as it happened, he saved my life." The General nodded sympathetically.

"He's got strong views. He can upset people. He can be bloody rude, Ben. Bloody insubordinate, too." The

General referred, with delicacy, to a conversation he had recently had with Brigadier Frank Fosdike.

"I quietened him down and decided to say nothing about it until you arrived, Ben."

"Thank you, sir."

The General nodded again. He had an idea that Ben Jameson had a poor opinion of Fosdike. Internal Westmorland politics, family history, very potent! Then he told Ben about the Yugoslavs. And the Cossacks.

"None of us likes this business, and I don't blame Adam for feeling as he did. But he gives nobody else credit for feeling equally strongly, yet just keeping their mouths shut and getting on with it. He's an awkward devil. Still," the General added, "I like Adam."

"So do I, sir. Very much. He'll never be an easy subordinate, he's harsh with himself and everybody else, he sees issues as very black or very white, and he speaks his mind no matter to whom. But he stands up for his men, he's got what I think and have always found is an utterly sound sense of right and wrong, and he is capable of quick decision and action to match."

"A very fair summary, Ben."

"And he's got as much courage, both moral and physical, as any man I know."

"There's been a rumour," said the General, who didn't disagree with any of this, "that he's also got involved with a lady. Some sort of local. Italian or something."

Ben smiled. He said, "I've an idea I know something about that too, sir. And if it's as I think I can assure you it reflects nothing but credit on Adam, nothing at all."

"Glad to hear it. And good luck, Ben. You'll be visiting all your charges in the next few days, I expect."

"Yes, Sir. And 2nd Westmorlands last, in three days' time."

"Don't take me round the Battalion, Adam," Ben said genially, "not with any formality anyway. How are your camps?"

Adam told him. Ben nodded. "I'm going to have several camp days, getting my eye in, going from one to another. I'll see your companies then. For now, let's just have a talk."

They were sitting in the main sitting room of the villa, used by Adam as his office, and each was occupying a comfortable chair. Soldiering, both reflected, hasn't often been like this. And it's unlikely to be like this for much longer.

Ben Jameson started to speak. Very quietly, reflectively, his voice light and slightly ironic as ever, pausing now and again. He didn't suppose that this was the way to command with dynamism a brigade but it was what he wanted particularly to do just now. With Adam Hardrow.

"Adam, I know the Battalion's fine. But how are you?"

There was a brief silence.

"I'm fine too."

"Not true, Adam."

They looked at each other, and after another moment's silence Adam said, attempting a smile, "You know too much, sir."

Ben acknowledged this. Changing tack, he said, "Remember when you had supper with us, when you met Felicity for the first time as it happens, the day before we went to war? Remember?"

"I certainly remember."

"You couldn't wait to be with the Regiment in war again – in war again only twenty years after, treading your father's footsteps. Felicity and I smiled about your keenness, I remember that."

Adam could never prevent a small tremor of nerves when Felicity's name came up between them. He could still recall Felicity very clearly. Every square inch of her, as it happened. Ben was continuing.

"Well, now it's over, isn't it, and you feel deflated and unhappy. You've been creating a fuss about all these wretched creatures we're having to send to nasty deaths and worse, you're sick as hell that instead of the brave, free world we'd achieve after beating Hitler we've given most of Europe something as bad or worse. You feel it's been rather futile. Am I wrong?"

Adam said, "Not wrong. But overstating it perhaps."

Ben considered his finger tips.

"Adam, when you get a sort of global earthquake like this war a lot of the consequences are bound to be beastly. The passions let loose, the cruelties done on both or all sides, the sheer suffering and destruction – it couldn't have a quiet civilised ending. The zoo cages were blown open and the animals have been given the run of the streets. That, I'm afraid, is war. You were looking for a gentlemanly crusade, and what you got is what you've got. Furthermore there's been thirty years of it in Europe, one way and another. War, civil war, revolution, counter-revolution, tyranny, savagery, misery. That's the story of our time."

"I suppose so."

"It's not your fault, so don't behave as if it's on your personal conscience. All you and I can do is carry out the immediate tasks we're given as decently and humanely as we can. A simple principle, Adam. It's called duty, if you like." Adam thought this was amazing. He'd never heard old Ben so serious before. Or so pompous. Even the drawl was barely in evidence.

He said, "I still think certain sorts of so-called duty are wrong and certain orders should never be given."

"Agreed. And from me they won't be." Adam knew this was true. He watched as Ben Jameson pulled a cigarette from his silver case, and lit it. He continued, his eyes on his new and much loved brigade commander.

"I also get sick of our sanctimoniousness, of the way our politicians spout and our newspapers write as if our own conduct is invariably a model of principle, justice, humanity, while everyone else's is the reverse. Balls! Utter balls! Think of the callousness with which we've behaved here, right here, for instance!"

It was clear that Ben had heard of Adam's own indignant reactions to the brutal dispatch of Cossacks, of Yugoslavs. Ben said nothing and Adam talked on, voice quiet.

"I wonder how *we'd* have behaved under the sort of tests others, in other nations, have had to face!" He thought of Anni, of the skull-like face of Karlsheim. He thought of Stanislas Brink and wondered fleetingly whether he was alive, whether they would ever meet again. The "Bamberger Reiter" medallion, once pressed on Adam by the dying Paul Brink, still hung at his neck, in some curious way a perpetual reminder that mercy and decency have no especial linkage with nationality.

Ben flicked ash from his cigarette and looked at Adam. A quizzical look.

"You aren't, are you, suggesting it's all been wasted effort? A war not worth winning? The loss of a great many people you've minded about and cared for deeply – perhaps as deeply, you feel, as you ever will in life – not worth while? Is that how you feel?"

Adam thought of them. Of Ivan Perry, of Sergeant Pew, of Whisky Wainwright, of many, many others. How extraordinarily close they seemed at times. He thought, too, of the Ardennes, of Americans shivering on the ground before being shot by the SS like animals. So many pictures on the mind and many of them so confused.

He said, "No, one can't feel that. Of course it's been worthwhile. I often hardly know what I *do* feel – simply, I suppose, that, that— "

He sighed. Ben thought this had gone on long enough. He said, "Anyway, Adam, I know what you've been up to, I sympathise, but don't use your scruples like a club to beat us all with, if you don't mind. Now tell me about the lady. Any news?"

He listened as Adam, with difficulty, talked. Adam said softly, at the end of his brief, halting recital, "So I don't know. I just don't know. I felt more strongly than ever that she, Anni and her brother, all of them, have been living on a different plane from us. I felt the same when I used to talk to a rather marvellous German doctor, a friend of theirs actually, when I was in the bag. We, you and I, have experienced war, but war fought in company with our friends, certainly one sort of nastiness, all that. But *they've* lived through something that marks them inwardly, something infinitely worse. It sets them apart. And whether it means Anni and I will remain apart I've no idea."

Ben inhaled from his cigarette. With his rather languid manner reasserted again, with deliberate off-handedness, he said, "Probably."

"You think so?"

"Probably. You fell for her in pretty extraordinary circumstances. You were in an odd condition and so was she. You formed a picture which it was unlikely any woman could live up to. And, as you say, she's had experiences, beastly ones, which set her apart. Or so she must feel."

"So you don't, from what I've said, think— "

"That you've got a hope? I've no idea. But I think you should start living life afresh and without improbable dreams." They were both standing up now and Ben

Jameson knew that he was as fond of this stern-faced young man, a battalion commander but still impossibly young, as of anybody in the world. Almost.

"Start a new life, Adam."

"I suppose so."

Ben smiled. One couldn't leave Adam Hardrow alone with his seriousness.

"A little discreet promiscuity, what about that? It might be good for your health. It might even be good for your Battalion!"

"Is that an order, sir?"

Adam was grinning. A Sandhurst precept flashed into his mind – "Don't tell your subordinates to do things you wouldn't do yourself." Well, by that principle, Ben couldn't be faulted.

Ben laughed out loud. He said, "I know from the bitter experience of everyone senior to you how difficult it is to give an acceptable order to a man with a conscience like yours. Adam, Goodbye."